# ziggy,
# stardust
# & me

JAMES BRANDON

# ziggy, stardust & me

putnam

G. P. PUTNAM'S SONS

G. P. Putnam's Sons
an imprint of Penguin Random House LLC, New York

Copyright © 2019 by James Brandon, LLC.
Penguin supports copyright. Copyright fuels creativity, encourages diverse voices,
promotes free speech, and creates a vibrant culture. Thank you for buying an authorized
edition of this book and for complying with copyright laws by not reproducing, scanning,
or distributing any part of it in any form without permission. You are supporting writers
and allowing Penguin to continue to publish books for every reader.

G. P. Putnam's Sons is a registered trademark of Penguin Random House LLC.

Visit us online at penguinrandomhouse.com

Library of Congress Cataloging-in-Publication Data is available.

Printed in the United States of America.
ISBN 9780525517641

1  3  5  7  9  10  8  6  4  2

Design by Dave Kopka.
Text set in Adobe Caslon Pro.

*to my moonwalker magic-weavers*
*charlie, sylvie, and oliver blue*
*and to all the misfit mapmakers in the world,*
*this one's for you*

✳

## part one.

---

# BROKEN
# EVERYTHINGS.

*imagination is everything.*
*it is the preview of life's coming attractions.*

—ALBERT EINSTEIN

**1.**

—

*Saturday, May 19, 1973*

IT STARTS HERE: The day my world begins falling, we're sitting in Starla's bedroom watching *Soul Train*. On the surface, it's a typical Saturday morning—I mean, everything *appears* normal. Should've known better. I'm the master of that game . . .

After our usual pancake breakfast, we slink into our spots: Starla sits cross-legged on her ruby-red shag, gluing silver rhinestones to a pair of Levi's for some design contest she's entering. I bob up and down on her waterbed, flipping through the new *Interview* magazine she could hardly wait to give me.

We're quiet, lost in our own worlds, waiting for church to start on TV—well, our version of church anyway: *Soul Train*. It started last year after Starla snuck me downtown to my first-ever Ziggy Stardust concert, and let's just say, whoa: He blew my brains to smithereens. Maybe literally. He wore this skintight, leopard-print leotard and huge platform shoes so he towered over us, and his face was dusted in white powder and glittery makeup and his hair was fire-engine red, and whambamthankyouma'am I was *reborn*.

At one point, he shielded his eyes, scanned the audience, and sang "Starman" pointing directly at me. I swear his voice shattered my soul, and in that moment, the Holy Spirit boogied in me. Afterward, Starla said, *"Jesus works His miracles in mysterious ways. He reveals Himself in everything, if you're looking. Maybe Ziggy's your Messiah,"* and she wiped the tears from my eyes.

Since then, she's decided music's my religion. So every Saturday morning we hang out in her bedroom to watch *Soul Train*. (Finally, a church I can get behind.) And it's about to start in T-minus ten minutes . . .

The TV sits in the corner on a rolling cart. A commercial for kids' cereal crackles through.

Her window's propped open and a sticky breeze left over from the three-minute downpour wafts in. Typical St. Louis spring. The wind crinkles the collage of faces plastered on her walls, making them sing and laugh and chatter up a storm of politics. Cutouts of The Jackson 5 and Jesus and Coco Chanel and "Power to the People" signs, and every female hero of hers since the Birth of Man—from Joan of Arc to Joan Baez to Angela Davis to Twiggy. Oh, and framed pictures of her secret crush, Donny Osmond. Yes, really.

Roberta Flack drips honey on the record player. And Starla . . . sings. *"Killing me softlyyy . . ."* She's in her church's choir, but well-hmm, not exactly the voice of an angel. Bless her. Starla. My best friend of forever. People think we go together; I let them. It's safer that way . . .

And yes, Starla's her real name. Well, sort of real name. The name she was born with was DeeDee Lucinda Jackson, but she told me one night when she was five years old she had a dream, and in that dream Jesus came to her and said, *"You are from the stars and you came here to heal the world,"* so she made her mom and dad change her name to Starla. I think it's cosmically perfect, like her, and kind of fitting because her face is covered in a galaxy of freckles. And man, without her I would've been obliterated into Jonathan bits long ago.

*"Force fields come in many forms."* That's what Dr. Evelyn told me a few years ago after I told her Starla was like mine.

*"With his song . . . ooh . . . oohh . . . oohhh . . ."* she sings.

*Ohhohohohoh. Bless her, Father, she knows not what she does.* She is cute, though. Her hair's slicked down under a swirly orange headscarf. Tongue's curled to the corner of her tangerine-glossed lips. She looks like a sunset.

Back to *Interview* magazine. I flip through page after page of weird indecipherable conversations, some new Andy Warhol painting of Mao Tse-tung, far-out pictures of half-naked women colored in neon finger paints, and then

Oh.

Three bold words punch me in the face:

*"GAY IS GOOD!"*

Alongside a handful of hairy muscled men dancing together.

Oh.

Really.

What parallel universe are these furry dopes trippin' in? Not in this one. Not in Missouri. Not in this broken little town of Creve Coeur. Nope, these guys would go to jail here. Or get thrown in the loony bin. Or worse. Believe me, I know—

But boy, are they dancing. And kissing! And smiling so hard it torpedoes through the page, knocking me out cold, and

I sink into the picture . . .

*Music thumps. "Hey hey hey, Jonny Collins, glad you finally came out to play, play, play." His mustache tickles my cheek. "Sorry it took so long, my main squeeze," I say. "So many parties, so little time, you dig?" His arms engulf me. Sweat slides down his chest, gluing us together. His lips devour me, like we can't get enough, like there's never enough—*

"Hey! You hear me?" It's Starla.

I thrash the magazine closed; our world thunders back. "What?"

"You spaced out again."

"No."

"Yeah, you did. You okay?" Her eyes narrow, scanning me. They're this crazy green that look like two pieces of uranium glass under a black light.

"I'm fine."

"You hear what I said?"

"Nothing. No, I mean. What?" Happens a lot. The *space-out* thing. Aunt Luna once told me, *"Your imagination is your safe space, an escape pod to another dimension where you're free to be."* And she said mine's the wildest one she's ever seen. She's also a wackadoo hippie, so I don't know. But she's right, I guess, and it works, I guess, because I'm traveling through my imagination all the time. Where I'm most safe. Anything to escape this reality.

"Come down here. Next to me," Starla says, back to her glue gun. "I wanna talk to you."

"One sec." Because I can't move. Yeah. My hard-on is supernatural. Dammit. Also, it's sizzling. Like a downed electrical line. (Everlasting side effects from Dr. Evelyn's treatments. More on that soon.) But the two combined: definitely not good.

Starla doesn't notice, lost in her rhinestones. I roll the magazine up and stuff it in my back pocket. I'll stash it in my closet later so those guys are lost under my stack of *National Geographic*s for good. That's where they belong: tucked away. Where no one can find them.

I *carefully* adjust, wiggle off the bed, grab a pencil and some nearby paper, and start drawing to distract myself. *Did Starla know that article was in there? Is that why she was so hell-bent on giving it to me? No. She knows how I feel about that sick stuff.*

"Why do you like to draw my freckles?" she asks.

"What? Oh. Because they're amazing."

"I hate them. I feel like a spotted leper. *Ohhohooohooohooh* . . ." she sings.

"Are you kidding? They're your greatest feature. You're like a walking, breathing nighttime sky."

"You're incorrigible." She glues another rhinestone, which is now clearly part of a peace sign on the back left pocket.

I find a spot, trace a new constellation on her cheek. "See, I just found the Teeny-Weeny Dipper."

"Oh, Jonny Jonny Jonny . . ."

"Oh, Starla Starla Starla . . ."

"What am I going to do without you?"

"Huh?" I stop drawing.

She doesn't answer. Just drops the jeans and replaces the needle on the record. Roberta Flack drips again.

"Starla?"

She turns to the TV; *Soul Train*'s started.

"What do you mean, 'without you'?" I ask, grabbing her hand. It's sticky from the glue.

"I'm just . . . I don't know . . . I'm going to miss you, is all."

"I'm not going anywhere," I say.

"No," she says, turning to me. "I am."

*All the pictures on the wall gasp.* "What? Where?"

"For the summer. To D.C. Momma got some job teaching and Poppa wants me to, you know, learn more about the movement and all that jazz. I've been meaning to tell you, but—"

"Oh . . ." I don't know what else to say, so all I say is, "Oh . . ." again.

"I know."

"Really?"

"Yeah."

"Oh."

No. This cannot be happening. I haven't spent a summer without Starla since IT happened. I'm getting dizzy. The world tornadoes around us while we sit with our hands glued together in the middle. I close my eyes.

"You okay?" she asks, wiping my tears. Didn't even know I was crying.

"Of course," I say, mustering the fakest smile I can. I will not let her see. "I'm happy for you. Just gonna . . . miss you . . . you know . . ."

She lifts my chin. "Look, I know it's crazy, but I talked it over with my parents, and Momma says you could come with us if you want—wouldn't that just be everything?"

"Oh . . . yeah . . ."

"We're leaving the day after school gets out. That way, we're always together, and you'll be so sick of me by the end of summer you'll be *dying* to get back here." We laugh. Sort of. "Anyway, it would do you good to get out of this square little town, Jonny . . . see new things . . . meet new people . . . you know . . ."

"Mm-hmm . . ." I know she's still talking, but I can't hear. My brain's paralyzed. *She's right. I've never left the confines of Creve Coeur, but I've always dreamed of it: hitching a ride to California to be a rock-n-roll star. But I can't. Not now. Not until I'm forever fixed. How am I going to do this without her?*

". . . and we can camp out at the National Mall with all those Vietnam protesters. Maybe actually do something about that stupid, good-for-nothing war, you know? Come on, I don't want to do it alone. We'd have so much fun. Please say yes." She smiles: a tug-of-war smile. Because she knows.

"My dad would never let me, Starla. I'm only sixteen and—"

"You'll be seventeen in a few weeks! Poppa said he'd talk to him if you—"

"And I still have my treatments."

"Oh . . . right . . ." she whispers.

"You know I can't miss those." She shrugs. "I'm going to be fine, okay? Like you said, it's just a couple months. And anyway, you *have* to go so you can finally scream at Nixon like you've been wanting to. For both of us." I blot her tears. "Don't worry, okay?" I say this more to myself than her. I have one more set of treatments left, but I've never survived them without Starla around . . . I've never survived *anything* without Starla around . . .

"Yeah, okay," she says.

We sit in silence. It sounds like the world's crackling to pieces, falling down all around me, until I realize the record's ended and the needle's skipping.

"Come on," I say. "Let's go to church." I click the player off and turn the volume up on the TV.

We watch the *Soul Train* line.

Bobby Womack sings some funky version of "Fly Me to the Moon."

We hold hands the entire time.

I can't decide which one of us is afraid to let go.

That night, I'm in bed. Can't sleep. The full moon ripples through the cottonwood tree outside my window, casting little disco ball dots on my walls.

The flip clock on my nightstand says 3:13.

My body trembles. Like it's sinking in a bath filled with ice, but every nerve's afire. Radioactive. Had that dream again: Dr. Evelyn's whistling Bowie's "Life on Mars?" Smiling. Painted just like him, with that aquamarine eye shadow and thick pink slabs of chalk on her cheeks. I sit, propped up in a wooden chair. She straps me down. Wraps leather cuffs around my wrists. Buckles them. Tight. Then my thighs. Electric wires, coiled to a machine on the table in front of me, squirm out of each cuff.

She smiles, still whistling.

Cushioned headphones sink over my ears, muting the world. I see her lips move, but hear nothing. She walks out, taking the light with her. I'm sailing through space. Alone. Waiting. The slide projector finally buzzes on. Blinding me. Pictures begin whirling by, until—

An electric volt swims through the wires, singeing my thighs, my wrists, my heart. Round and round the projector goes. Frying my thoughts to oblivion—

That's when I wake up.

Except, I don't. Not really.

Dr. Evelyn says, *"Secrets feed the sickness,"* and I'm not supposed to keep them anymore to help me with mine, so . . . *DUN DUN DUNNNN* . . . First Secret: I am sick, those are my treatments, and this is how I'm being fixed.

So far, I think it's working. I really do. It better be. Or I'll end up like my uncle, in one of those padded rooms in the nuthouse, lost forever . . .

I grab the *Aladdin Sane* album from my desk—Ziggy's latest, the white one with a fire-red flash zapping his face. The *Mona Lisa* of rock. Iconic.

"You around?" I whisper.

*He lifts his eyes, smiles. "Hey, my little Starman," he says. "Look at you, you beautiful boy, my super-duper rock-n-roll alligator."*

"I'm scared," I say. "I can't do it, Zig. I can't do this alone . . ."

*"Hey now, hey now . . . You're going to be okay. You just gotta see beyond all this here, believe in who you really are out there in the stars. I do, baby."*

I nod, wipe the tears stinging my eyes.

*"Come on,"* he says. *"Let's boogie . . ."*

And for the first time in a long time,

I pray.

**2.**

---

*Monday, May 21, 1973*

MONDAY MORNING, I'M WAITING for Starla outside her house. Weird. She's usually the one waiting for me. The curtains are drawn, no Lincoln in the driveway. Huh. We've never missed a bike ride to school together. Did I miss something? Wait—did she mean she was leaving *the next day*?

No. She would have called and said goodbye and—no. Get it together, Collins, you're tired. Not enough sleep last night. Never enough sleeps any last nights. Breathe.

In.

Out.

*Ahhhhh.*

Okay. I love that smell after a morning rain shower in Creve Coeur: rusted earth swished with fresh laundry hanging on the line. Perfect thing to bottle up in a jar and open on a sticky summer day when you're sick of the smell of sweat. (And those dog days happen a lot in this part of St. Louis.) People think we live out in the country. Guess we do. Subdivisions have been creeping up for a while now, and with them, civilization, but mostly Creve Coeur's smack-dab in the middle of a patchwork quilt of farmland with a lake. And this means we live under a comforter of humidity for the summer. By the feel of it now, we're in for a brutal one. Grandma used to call it *the days and nights of molasses . . .*

Anyway, where's Starla? This is more than weird.

Still waiting.

My watch says 7:43. So, I don't know. I wait until I can wait no more, flop my satchel over my shoulder, jump on Stingraymobile and pedal off—who, by the way, is not *just* my bike; she's my velvet-black, candy-red-trimmed piece of fantastic. And I'm so lost in my crisscross thoughts of the mysterious disappearance of Starla, Bowie dreams and Dr. Evelyn nightmares, and Dad's nightly escapades (more on that later), I turn *left* at the corner instead of *right* and BOOM:

Scotty Danforth and the Asshole Ape Brigade.

No.

*"Navigate the negative."* That's what Dr. Evelyn says. I took it literally. I mapped out my own path to school, in school, and back home from school to avoid this very incident from ever occurring again. Nice to meet you, I'm Gaylileo. But hey, it worked, and otherwise it might happen every day. It started with Scotty and his half-wits a few years ago right after IT happened. (Oh, we *used* to be friends, but everything changed that day.) And one thing I know for sure: Once you're a target, you're always a target.

"Hey. Hey, Jon-Boy. What it is, what it is?" He puffs his shaggy black hair out of his eyes, not a single strand slipped out of place.

I say nothing, paralyzed prey. Also, still stunned they're here. I swear they just teleported from Planet of the Apes. I swear Scotty has this weird frigging ability, because why not, he's chiseled out of Michelangelo's leftover marble, so he might as well have superhuman speed as well.

"Awww, she looks so pretty today, don't she, boys?" He wraps his arm around my neck and rats my hair. A *total* bummer because I spent fourteen minutes this morning trying to get it perfectly swooped to cover the scar on my forehead.

I assume the Apes agree, but I only hear *"HOO OOO OOO"* and *"UH UH UH."*

He flings my satchel to the ground. Dammit. Hope nothing broke. "We missed you, Jon-Boy. Where you been hidin'?" His breath: a mixture of stale cigarettes and Juicy Fruit. "What's the matter? Can't speak? Lost your voice in Starla's pussycat last night?" He smooshes my face in his Rolling Stones tongue-lick shirt, which looks like it's about to swallow me whole.

The Apes go wild. I go limp. In my *National Geographic*s, when an animal plays dead, the predator usually gets bored and leaves.

Usually.

Instead: "So whatcha got for me today, Jon-Boy?" He wriggles his fingers through my jeans pocket and—*KAZOW*—pinches my balls so all the colors melt from the earth, puddling at my feet. *Don't scream. Don't scream. Don't show them fear.*

"What's this?" he asks, unfolding something he's grabbed.

My eyes hopscotch. *Focus, Collins. Breathe.* Okay, I see it now: a crumpled dollar bill. Dad forgot to leave me lunch money this morning, so I had to sneak in and grab it from a wad of cash sitting on his nightstand among an array of fine fatherly accoutrements: rolling papers, an empty Budweiser bottle—or two, or twenty-seven, I lost count—a glass of whiskey with a few cigarette butts floating in the muddied water. You know, the usual.

What I didn't see in the dark then, I see in the light now: a phone number scrawled across George Washington's face with the name "Heather" in fat cursive. And a heart. *"Call me."*

Oh no.

That means Dad met some chick last night, and that means this particular dollar bill is like getting the Golden Ticket to the Girly Factory, and if I don't get it back, Dad will kill me.

"Scotty, I need that—"

"It's *Scott*, you freakin' queer. We ain't in grade school anymore— What's this? A phone number?"

"Give it back. Please." Dammit, I hate my voice. Like a stupid titmouse.

"Awwww . . . po wittle Jon-Boy said pweeassse . . ."

The Apes grunt in approval.

"Who's Heather?" He flattens the dollar bill out, displaying it for all to see.

"*Ooooooooooo.*"

"Oh man, I bet Starla would love to hear about Heather. Don't you, boys?"

"Come on, quit playing around, Scott." I try grabbing the dollar, but he snatches it higher in the air. Yes, this is happening. And now I'm trapped in the middle of a smelly Ape huddle. If they don't kill me, their stink surely will.

*Think, Collins, think.* I'm shorter and skinnier and can slip through them in a single bound. Nope. They're clumped together like one big hairy wall.

Dr. Evelyn taught me some tricks when confronted with Barbaric Meatheads:

Rule 1—Compliment your enemy. "Hey, Scott, it's just a dollar, man. You've got plenty. You're the richest kid in the city." Which is true. He's the only kid we know who has a digital watch.

"Yeah, I know," he says. "But I want this one."

Doesn't work.

Fine. Rule 2—Close your eyes. Conjure lightning bolts from your hands. Blast them all to oblivion. Made that one up. Saw it on *Star Trek*.

"I'm gonna git me some Heather pusss-say," he says. He wads the bill in a little ball, starts playing hacky sack with the Apes.

Me: fumbling around, trying to grab it. Back and forth, back and forth. My hand barely brushes it each time. And then I trip. And smack into Scotty. And we lose our balance. And fall to the sidewalk with such a THUD the earth stops spinning on its axis.

The Apes go silent.

Me: splayed out on top of him.

Scotty: huffing and puffing, about to blow my ass down.

I have one second to:

*1) track a thick vein bulging from his forehead,*

*2) watch his hazel eyes flash to Hiroshima white, and*

*3) suck up another waft of fruity breath,*

before I grab my satchel, leap on Stingraymobile and zoom off, leaving Dad's almighty dollar scrunched in Scotty's palm.

**3.**

MY HEART PEDALS my chest, feet pedal Stingraymobile, speeding down the street. Or maybe it's the other way around. My satchel thumps my back, pounding my last breaths out.

Gasping an inhale.

Coughing an exhale.

Invasion of the Asthma Attacker.

Crystal thought: *I need PeterPaulandMary. Where'd I put it?* I fly around the corner. The football field's a few blocks ahead.

*"COME BACK HERE, QUEER—"*

*"HEY, JON-BOY! HERE WE COME—"*

My breath claws at my lungs.

*"DON'T ACT LIKE YOU CAN'T HEAR US! YOU CAN'T RUN FOREVER, COLLINS!"*

The stadium bathroom's only half a block away.

Fifty feet away . . . thirty-five . . . ten . . .

*"GOT YOU CORNERED!"*

I fling the door open, throw in Stingraymobile, and whambamthank-youma'amSLAM it shut, just before I see his grin glimmering in the sun.

Locked. He pounds on the door. The Apes join him, trying to

figure out this new metal square thing in their faces. I slump down.

"YOU CAN'T STAY IN THERE FOREVER, SISSYBOY."

"WE GOT YOU. COME OUT, COME OUT TO PLAY."

I reach into my satchel and dig through my books and smiley-face pencil case and the tape recorder I always carry with me—*not broken, whew!*—and finally find PeterPaulandMary, aka my inhaler, stashed at the bottom. Grab a few poofpoofpoofs—my steroid-filled elixir of fairy dust *ahhhhhhhhhh*—before settling down.

Bell rings.

"Shit, we're late," Scotty says.

"Catch ya on the flip, Jon-Boy," another Ape yells.

Fists beating chests slowly fade away.

Gone.

I inhale two more poofs. I'm back. A bit jangled, but back. I lean my head against the door and close my eyes. Damn. Missing first period. Anyway, it's biology and we're dissecting frogs *again*, and I've had enough dissecting for about seven lifetimes, thankyouverymuch, but still.

Another inhale: extra-piney, extra-bleachy. *Ahhh.*

Welcome to my other Home Sweet Home: the Stadium Bathroom.

Secret: This is where I eat lunch.

Oh, don't worry. I did my cafeteria time. Three years in the slammer. I somehow survived a new scene from *Lord of the Flies* every 12:06–12:46 p.m., until the day Chief Scotty stood in the center of the island and properly displayed my gym class jockstrap for all to see. He'd put ketchup on it and yelled, *"Let's all congratulate Jonathan Collins on becoming a woman today,"* then slingshotted it across the heavens so, of course, it landed perfectly on the pile of mashed potatoes on my tray. That was my cue to Exit Stage Left, never to be seen on Cafeteria Island again.

I tried eating with Starla a few times, but because she sits at a table full of girls, it felt like I was invading their Girlniverse. Tried joining a few other tables—the chess club geniuses and dramazoids were way too talkative, and the hippie stoners were way too . . . I don't even know—then one day, I found this spot. Been here ever since. Never been happier.

But I've never been in here this early. A different light sparkles through. Like entering a dream sequence . . .

Anyway. I have an hour. Should read our English assignment since I had no time last night. I pull out *Jonathan Livingston Seagull* from my satchel, along with my tape recorder and microphone to begin recording. *"Memorization helps spark memory."* That's what Dr. Evelyn says, so she asked me to record as many moments as I can during treatments to keep my mind sharp. Also, this is how Andy Warhol started *Interview* magazine, so I always pretend I'm famous and being interviewed by him.

Click.

*"Jonathan Livingston Seagull,"* I say into my mic. "A book about the meaning of everything." I flip through the pages and read one of my favorite passages:

> *We can start working with time if you wish . . . till you*
> *can fly the past and the future . . . and then you'll be ready*
> *to fly up and know the meaning of kindness and love.*

"Oh yes, I agree, Andy," I say to the toilets. "I think what he's saying is you only have right now to be kind. After that, it's gone; you've lost your chance . . . You're right, Andy, it is hard to do when you're being chased by Apes, but that's the test, I guess. Dr. Evelyn says, 'Tests teach the soul to grow,' so I guess that's what she means— Oh, and another thing: Love is timeless. So the only way to truly find love is to take a tin-can spaceship to another dimension and live there. With the other Star People. And Ziggy. Yup, makes perfect sense to—"

"Maybe he's trying to say somethin' else." Another voice echoes from a stall.

"Sh-boogie shit!"

"Sorry, man, didn't want to bother you," he says with a half laugh, half Hello, Cuckoo Collins.

I scramble up the door. "Sorry, I—" Perfect. I'm talking like an asshole into a stupid microphone and some guy's been going number two. "I didn't know anyone else was here. Jeez—"

"Yeah. Figured that." His feet drop down—*was he hovering?*—and man, his Chucks are thrashed.

"I should go," I say.

"Maybe he's tryin' to say something else," he says again.

"Who?"

"The author."

"Oh. Maybe, yeah—"

"You have to *believe* it in order to see it, right?"

"Huh?"

"You believe in time travel, man? Parallel universes? Stuff like that?"

"Oh, well, sure. Like *Star Trek* . . . ?"

"What?"

"That time when they teleport through an ion storm and return to parallel versions of themselves who are really mean and Spock"— *JESUS, WHY ARE YOU TALKING, SHUT UP, COLLINS*—"has this . . . goatee . . ."

"What?"

"Nothing."

"I mean, what's real and what's *really* real, man? Know what I mean?"

Okay, what is happening? This guy sounds wackier than me. Am I on some hidden-camera show? Are there *cameras* in here? That would be supremely messed up, considering we're in A BATHROOM. I try to laser-beam through his stall door to see him. Nothing.

"Not sure I do," I say.

"What?"

"Know what you mean. I should leave you—" Inching the bathroom door's lock to the right . . .

"Hey, I like what you were sayin' just now . . . in that tape recorder thing . . . kinda beautiful, actually . . ."

Oh . . .

"Yeah. I mean, imagine being able to just, you know, open that door in front of you and BOOM, you're in a parallel universe," he says. "Experiencing a whole different version of you. Far-out stuff, right?"

"Huh. Yeah . . ."

"That would be amazing to be able to change your life in a split second." He snaps his fingers. "And be a totally different person."

Yeah, actually that would be really frigging amazing.

"Who would you be?" he asks.

I don't move. I'm not sure why.

"I'd probably be the principal," he says.

"The principal? Of our school? Why?"

"To make all the rules. So people would finally listen and pay attention to me."

"Huh. Why think so small? Why not be president? Or why not be ruler of the universe, for that matter?"

He laughs. "Yeah, man, I like your way of thinking. What about you?"

I stare at his stall, waiting for some announcer to pop out. Nothing happens.

"Hello?" he asks.

"Oh, I don't know. A different version of me, I guess?"

"What would be different?"

"Everything."

"Oh."

Silence. The only sound: a *dripdripdrip* from the faucet.

"Deep stuff, man," he says finally.

This is weird, right? Talking to a total stranger who's in a bathroom stall? Talking to a total stranger at all? But I don't know. It's safer somehow having that barricade between us. Like I'm at confession. I want to say this, but that sounds stupid. I want to leave, but for some reason my Chucks are glued to this spot.

"You there?" he asks.

"Oh. Yeah. Uh. Have we met before?"

"No."

"Do you go here?"

"Kinda."

"Kinda?"

"It's my first day," he says.

"But—there's only three weeks left of school."

"I know."

"And you're starting today?"

"I guess."

"What year are you?"

"Junior."

"Oh. Same . . . You just move here?" I ask.

"Kinda . . ."

"Scared?"

"What?"

"Are you scared?" See, when people's voices trail off or they start using fewer words, it almost always signifies (a) fear, (b) hiding, or (c) both. I've had enough sessions with Dr. Evelyn to learn the tricks.

He laughs. "Scared? Me? Nah, man."

Lying.

I look down. A black smudge on the whites of my Chucks. Nope. Lick my finger and start rubbing. "Okay, well, listen," I say. "Piece of advice? Keep quiet and you'll be fine. Take it from me."

"I'm not really one to keep quiet, man."

"Suit yourself." *Out, out, damned spot.* I hate dirty anythings. "Anyway, I'll let you get back to . . . whatever it is you're doing." I stand, even though there's still a tiny visible speck.

"Did you think I was—"

"Good luck out there . . . I mean, if you need anything I can—I mean—"

"Thanks, man. Nah, I'm just . . . sittin' here," he says. "You know . . . waiting . . ."

Uh-huh.

"Okay, fine . . . hiding . . ."

I smile. "It's a good place for it."

"Yeah . . ."

I stare at his stall. His feet bounce so fast, he looks like he's trying to jackhammer down to the underworld. Oh, I know that feeling. "So I guess I'll see you in there, then . . . ?"

"Right on," he says.

I creak the door open.

"Hey, man?"

"Yeah?"

"Nice to meet ya," he says.

"Oh. Yeah." We laugh. Well, he laughs like a normal boy. I titter like a stupid termite. Okay, that's my cue. Catch you on the flip, *man*. I slam the door and peek my head around the corner.

All clear. No Apes. No hidden camera setup or weird parallel universe.

I don't think.

4.

NOPE. DEFINITELY DID NOT enter a parallel universe. Two hours later, we're back from commercial break resuming our normal hellacious schedule.

Third period. Health class. Which is essentially the second-to-last step to the entrance of Hades's gates. The last being PE. And because the classes basically bookend the day, it's a true miracle I ever make it out alive and escape back home unscathed.

The good news: The room's been in total darkness since class started. Makes it that much easier to disappear in the shadows and be forgotten amongst the Ape Troop.

The bad news: Today's special guest star is Officer Andrews from the Creve Coeur Police Department, hosting an exclusive screening of some archaic filmstrip from the fifties. It's like we're watching one of my family's old home movies:

*"What Jimmy didn't know was that Ralph was sick. A sickness that was not visible like smallpox. But no less dangerous or contagious. A sickness of the mind . . ."*

A mustached man with dark sunglasses smirks and skips on the screen. *"You see, Ralph was a homosexual. A person who demands an intimate relationship with members of their own sex. And Ralph is about to be arrested."*

Apes grunt and giggle and whisper strategic plans for their upcoming prom-date sexcapades. I sit in the middle, a driveling ferret that's played with every so often when they remember I'm there. Coach Peterson lounges in the corner reading *The Godfather*, oblivious as always.

*"Public restrooms can often be a hangout for the homosexual."* Two boys skip off the screen. *"Be careful who lurks in the shadows . . ."*

SPLAT. Some Ape nails me in the back of the head with a slimy spitball. It slithers down my neck. A few more grunts. I do not flinch; I do not turn around. Best to ignore. A few desk neighbors I sometimes play hangman with turn their backs on me, snickering.

I know why.

*"One never knows when the homosexual is about. He may appear normal and it may be too late to realize he is mentally ill. BOYS, BEWARE."*

The filmstrip *flipflipflips* in the background; the screen flashes a bright white, blinding us. Officer Andrews saunters to the front, eclipsing the room. It's possible they modeled the Incredible Hulk after him. "Folks, this is not a game," he booms. "These guys, they're dangerous. Pedophiles. Pathological. Sick. They'll do anything to get what they want. And when they want you, you don't have a prayer in hell."

A palpable silence in the room.

"Any questions?" I take it back: He looks like Mr. Potato Head. Like some kid forgot to put his lips on. All I see is a thick mustache in their place.

No one moves. Except I guess the Ape who nailed me in the head shoots his hand up.

"Yeah."

"Can you still get arrested?" he asks.

"Bet your ass, kid," he says. "You get caught, you're going to jail. Period."

"Like Jonathan's uncle?"

The Apes pound their chests and grunt so loud Coach Peterson actually glances up from his book. I slink farther in my seat, intensely enthralled by the ratted curlicues left behind in the spirals of my notebook.

"Hey hey hey . . ." Officer Andrews says. "Settle down . . . settle down . . ." I know he's looking at me. I know because he's the one who arrested my Uncle-Who-Cannot-Be-Named Collins ten years ago. And because it's a small town, the story is an everlasting scar on our family's name. Dad's still flipped out about it.

All I know is this: My aunt Marie and uncle Blank were picnicking on the beach at Creve Coeur Lake when my uncle walked into a public bathroom and, while standing at the sink, touched the shoulder of Hulk-man Andrews here. Next thing you know—*CH-CLINK*—he's being carted off. Aunt Marie thought he'd been kidnapped when he never returned, so she went to the police to report him missing and they told her why he was there. She was so humiliated, she took two razor blades to her wrist a week later, and these combined incidents threw my Uncle-Who-Cannot-Be-Named over the cuckoo's nest. All because of a single touch.

"Settle your asses down," he says. "Let it be a lesson to all you boys. Keep your eyes open, report any suspicious activity, and *beware*."

I hear nothing else; I don't even look at him. I'm one wrong move away from sharing a room with my Forgotten Uncle, so I keep my eyes down and play dead for the rest of class.

Officer Andrews eventually flips on another filmstrip, this one about how to properly put on condoms. *"You gotta put it on, before you put it in!"* This throws the Apes into a hormonal frenzy, but at least their attention's been diverted—

That's when I see it: His scuffed-to-hell Converse scoot across the floor and dart away. A folded piece of paper is left in their place. And scribbled on top:

*To my Toilet Time-Traveling Bud*

Oh man. The new kid's sitting behind me? When did he sneak in? Must've spaced out again. It's too dark in here to see anything anyway but *WHAT IS THIS PIECE OF PAPER*?! I slap my shoe on top of it and wait. I want to turn around, but I dare not move. Best to stay still, to stay forgotten . . .

Minutes later, the bell rings. Lights buzzzzz and flicker on. I slink further in my seat. As the Apes bumble away, I slowly pick up the paper and unfold it to read:

*FORGET EM. WHERE TO NEXT?*

When I look around to thank him, he's already gone.

## 5

AFTER LUNCH. FIFTH PERIOD. English Lit with Mr. Dulick. Honors. I say this not to be an asshole, but because (a) it's my only honors class and (b) it's my favorite class.

Anyway. I'm pretty sure I just created a tsunami in Vietnam with my empty-stomach gurgles. And why does it happen when it's most quiet in the classroom? A few girls giggle. I look around to see what idiot is causing a ruckus.

Quick rewind: Just before lunch, as I slinked through the halls to my private bathroom booth, Mr. Dulick noticed I didn't have a tray of food and asked me why. I told him about Scotty. Not to be a rat, but because I still had to get that dollar back: if not to save me, to save all of humanity from the Wrath of Dad. So when the final bell rang for class to start, Mr. Dulick sat on the edge of his desk, tugged at his flower-power polyester, and with his arms folded simply said, "Beam it back, Scotty." So cool.

Now we wait.

Scotty grunts, smooths his hair back with his fingers.

"Come on, man, life's too short for this kinda shit." Mr. Dulick, the teacher in our high school closest to our age, is also the only teacher who allows us to cuss in class. With one rule: It has to accentuate a passionate belief.

Scotty huffs for all the class to hear as he empties out the pockets of his red-and-white letterman jacket. And each thing is like a countdown on New Year's Eve:

*5) A condom*
*4) A pack of Juicy Fruit chewing gum*
*3) A rumpled pack of Camel cigarettes*
*2) A Blues Note Tavern matchbook*
*1) My wadded-up dollar bill!*

I almost cry. I swear a chorus of angels starts singing from the clouds Dulick painted on the ceiling. Scotty slaps the dollar in my palm, and through gritted teeth whispers, "Faggot," before turning back to face the front. Whatever. I can just make out the scrawled heart overlaying Washington's ascot as I stuff it back in my pocket.

GURRRRRGLE. Dammit. The noise is so loud I make sure I haven't split my desk table in half before looking around again. This would be the moment I'd see Starla give me a reassuring smile to put my mind at ease. But she's still MIA. Sick maybe? Abducted by aliens? The mind boggles.

We stare at Mr. Dulick; he stares at the ceiling. His face is extra-dewy, with thick sideburns glistening on his cheeks, and his eyes—normally bright blue—are full of red squiggles. Secret: He smokes a lot of grass.

Aaron Worthington, my desk neighbor, who's sometimes called Aaron Worthlesston because his father gambled all their money away and now they live by the lake, elbows me. He puts his fingers up to his mouth and sucks in real deep like he's smoking and choking on a joint, then laughs.

Jane-Anne Halstead giggles next to him. They call her Firecrotch either because (a) her hair is a crazy bright red, or (b) because she got caught having sex under the stadium bleachers one day and for weeks she couldn't stop scratching herself.

I ignore them both and stare at Mr. Dulick. He swishes some brown curls behind his ears, then looks out the window. The trees outside sway, brushing the sky with little pink flowers that pirouette from their branches. The last signs of spring.

Nobody moves.

Everyone stares at him, then at each other, then back to him.

Mr. Dulick wipes his eyes. Is he crying?

*"To fly as fast as thought, to anywhere that is, you must begin by knowing that you have already arrived,"* he writes with orange chalk.

"Five years," he shouts. Jane-Anne jumps. "That's all, man. Five frigging years." We stare unblinking, frozen in time and space, wondering, waiting . . .

"The planet. Mother Earth, man, you know? Us. We're all dying. Our resources. They're just running out." He ambles around the desk. "The pollution, the people, it's all too much. And there aren't enough resources to help. Five years, man. That's it. That's what they say is left of us. Nineteen seventy-eight's our last year on Earth . . ."

Jane-Anne starts crying. And a few other whimpers echo through the otherwise still and silent room. I don't blink. Afraid if I do, I'll miss something.

Mr. Dulick presses his hands against his head, squeezing them tight, then lifts them away with his fingers spread wide and—"POOF. All gone. Everything. The A-bomb, man, it had nothing on this. Sneaking up on us this whole damn time . . ." He shakes his head and looks out the window again.

The whimpers in the classroom grow louder. He doesn't hear, stuck in his mind someplace else. It's Lacey Tarrington, in the first row, who raises her hand, and after not being seen or called on by him, clears her throat to speak for us all, "Mr. Dulick, sir . . . you're scaring me."

He snaps back. "Oh, I'm sorry, I didn't mean to—Oh man." His hands forage through his thick curls. Two huge pit stains look like a Rorschach test under his arms: I'm thinking bat wings.

"Listen, I've been reading this book," he says. "This world. It's become overpopulated. We've hit our limit. We can't keep up. But listen—" He flies behind his desk. "This," he says, pointing to the quote. "This is how we will survive. This is how you can make a difference. Now. To change all that. This."

He's smiling again, gazing into our eyes. Eyes still shell-shocked from whatever just happened. Dulick's known for Shakespearean-quality dramatics, but this is over the top even for him.

"You guys," he says. "You guys are all so beautiful, man. You know that, right? You are the future. You are the ones who can change all this. You."

I don't believe him. And as he scans each face, inching ever closer to mine, I dart my head down, whistling "The Girl from Ipanema" in my head.

Then: The classroom door creaks open, and a gigantic needle scratches across the planet's vinyl. Because as Mr. Dulick leans against the blackboard, I see the scuffed-to-hell Chucks saunter in.

"Heyheyhey," Dulick says. "You made it!"

Time stops.

He stands in the doorway in bright blue jeans and a white tank that both cling a little too tight. And his long black hair and amber skin radiate against the sun streaming through the open blinds.

Oh . . . man.

He hands over a pink slip of paper, his eyes locked on Mr. Dulick.

Dulick scans the note, then grabs the new boy in a tight embrace. "Welcome, man, welcome. I'm so happy you're finally here. We're lucky to have you, Webster."

He mumbles something into Dulick's chest, arms dangling at his sides.

Dulick pulls away. "What's that, my man?"

"Web. That's it. That's my name."

"Me Lone Ranger," Scotty says. Idiot.

Everyone laughs, of course. Almost everyone.

"That's enough," says Dulick. "Webster, why don't you—"

"Web," he says, not backing down. This kid's tough.

"Web. Sorry. Why don't you take a seat. We'll try to catch you up."

He shuffles to the back of the room, and as he passes me I lift a small *Hey, it's totally far-out that we met in the bathroom* smile, but I don't think he notices. Instead, he slumps into the chair a few down from Starla's empty seat.

Mr. Dulick claps his hands. "Let's get to it, shall we? *Jonathan Livingston Seagull.*"

I half listen, tracing my fingers along the seagull's feathers on the book's cover, and as I trace, I ever-so-maybe-not-at-all casually inch my head around to get a better look at him.

He has no books, no satchel, no pencils, nothing. He just sits. Staring at the desktop. A castaway on his own Desk Island. Something about him looks sad, lost even. But also, it's strange: He shimmers. Like a transporter or—

His eyes flit up, smacking mine. I quickly look away.

My stomach rumbles again, but I ignore it. My wrists start stinging: another one of Dr. Evelyn's enduring side effects. I ignore that, too.

His neighbor, Samantha Jordan, the Quintessential Queen of

Everything, has pushed her books and macramé purse as far away from him as she can. If Starla were around, she'd shove all her stuff over in its place. If I had any nerve at all, I'd walk over and do the same.

But I don't.

Instead I stare, and soon my eyes glaze over and—

*I fly over Desk Island, soaring through the fake painted clouds.*

*The new boy is far ahead of me. He's been doing this a long time, you can tell, a master flier: loop-de-loos and somersaults and skyward bolts at break-neck speed. He looks back to make sure I'm okay. "Look at you!" he yells. "Heard you were a rock-n-roll star, man, but didn't know you could fly, too! You're doing beautifully!" "Oh yeahyeahyeah," I yell back. "I come from the stars, so it's easy-peasy for little ol' measy. Follow me, I'll show you where I'm—"*

"Earth to Mr. Collins. You there?" We're back in the classroom. "Jonathan?" And Dulick's yelling my name. The new boy stares back, a slight smile curved on one side. I flip around, wipe the sweat from my forehead. "Hey, man, you ever going to answer me or are you just waiting for the bell to ring?"

"Sorry, what?"

"Jonathan . . . Jonathan Livingston . . . ?"

"Are you talking about me or the book?"

Titters all around. Cheeks flush. *I turn myself into a seagull and flap madly through the room, poking eyes out with my beak like everyone's Tippi Frigging Hedren from that scary* Birds *movie, before busting through the window and disappearing in the clouds forever.*

"Both," Dulick says. "I'm asking you, Jonathan Collins, to talk to me about the paragraph in *Jonathan Livingston Seagull*. You know, the book we've been reading the past few weeks?"

I don't move. More titters. GUURRRGGGLLLE. Dammit. I look around. Aaron snickers and points at me.

"Soooo . . ." Dulick's sitting on the edge of his desk, book in hand opened to some page I do not know, radiating a smile. Okay, he's a good guy.

"How 'bout this," he says. "Why don't you come up here and read it for us. Refresh our memory."

He's an evil villain.

I've made it the entire school year without once having to stand up in front of the class, and now with only three weeks left to go my worst nightmare's coming true.

"Hellooooo . . . lost in spaaaaccceeee . . ." Aaron raps his knuckles on the table and chuckles. He has a piece of spinach stuck in his teeth, but I don't tell him. Asshole. Some friend. I mean, I guess we aren't *friend* friends, but at least we've never broken the unspoken "protect your classroom neighbor" rule.

I scrape my chair against the linoleum. My brain screams *RUN*; my feet drag me toward Dulick; the result is some weird twitchy thing I can't seem to control. I somehow make it to the front of the room without high-kicking someone in the face. I'm definitely short-circuiting.

Mr. Dulick hands me his book—I forgot to bring mine up with me—and whispers, "You got this, man."

I clear my throat. In my head my voice is Winston Churchill orating to a crowd of thousands. Instead it comes out like Goldie Hawn on *Laugh-In*:

"*You can go to any place and to any time that you wish to go . . . I've gone everywhere and everywhen I can think of . . . The gulls who scorn perfection for the sake of travel go nowhere, slowly. Those who put aside travel for the sake of perfection go anywhere, instantly . . .*'"

Mr. Dulick's crying again. I'm not sure the rest of the class notices, though. Being so close, I can feel the heat from his face. Secret: His breath does in fact smell like grass.

"Should I go on?" I ask.

The second he opens his mouth I'm ready to dart back to my seat. Instead he says, "What do you think it means, man?"

"Oh. Uh. I don't know." I don't even know what I just read. Too focused on not puking all over Lacey Tarrington. Or creating a sinkhole in the classroom from my stomach rumbles.

"Sure you do. Think about it," he says. "Read it again if you have to."

"I guess . . . I don't know . . . I guess it means when you put a limit on something, you're trapped. But if you think bigger, you're free." I keep my eyes on the book. Mr. Dulick doesn't move, so I'm sure it makes no sense. The giggles in class confirm it. "I mean, I don't know . . . I'm probably wrong. Right?"

"No, my man. You are very right." I lift my eyes. "Very good, Jonathan. With a name like a seagull, you're going to fly freakin' far."

"Can I sit down now?"

"Yes, you may sit down."

Without looking at anyone, and carefully stepping over Scotty's canary-yellow Pumas that he'd stuck out in the aisle, I walk back to my desk and sit quietly for the rest of class, not moving an inch.

Just before the bell rings, Mr. Dulick decides he hasn't tortured us enough for the final few weeks of junior year and throws the guillotine blade down on all our necks.

"Okay," he says. "Here's what's going to happen these last few weeks. Partner up with someone you've never partnered up with before. Talk about the rest of the book like we did today. Really think about its meaning—every word, the symbols, the metaphors. And then, together, you'll share a five-minute presentation of what it means to you."

Oh no. An echo chamber of moans and groans and *"Come on!"*s and *"Oh man!"*s fills the room as my brain instantly starts fizzling. Here's why:

1) Presentation. *Let's get one thing clear: This is not your run-of-the-mill-read-from-a-three-page-book-report-and-call-it-a-day presentation. No, Mr. Dulick's presentations mean one thing and one thing only: Broadway-caliber performance. If your presentation isn't worthy of a Tony Award by the end, you might as well drown yourself in the Missouri River. And it counts for fifty percent of your final grade. In other words: Big. Frigging. Deal.*

2) Partnering up. *I mean, I wasn't even the last person to be picked on a team for dodgeball in PE. They'd forget I was standing there altogether.*

3) Talking. *To anyone except Starla. Tried it once in a kingdom far, far away. Decidedly not good at it.*

"Hey now. Hey now. This is going to be good for you," Dulick says. "We have to learn to work together, friends, if we have any chance of saving the planet. Now, hurry. Partner up before the bell rings."

Okay, I highly doubt the inevitable destruction of the planet will be thwarted by a three-minute Bob Fosse tap dance to some story about a seagull, but our fates are signed, sealed, and delivered.

Everyone scrambles for a partner.

Everyone, that is, except me and the shimmering, lonely boy on Desk Island.

Perfect.

**6.**

___

RIDING STINGRAYMOBILE HOME. Letting the wind carry my thoughts away. Trying to, anyway. My wrists and thighs are aflame. Stupid effing side effects. *How am I going to work with him? I can barely stand in front of the class on my own without hurling myself out the window, but with HIM? Oh man. He seems nice, though. He gave me a note in health class, for Ziggy's sake! We can be friends. Yeah. That's what normal people do. But that smile: It's slightly crooked and dints two dimples on his cheeks. And his hair, the way it glistens like a Black Sea on his shoulders. Or his eyes, the way they spark*—ZAP! A shock zips up my leg. *Ow. No. Stop. You know better, Collins. You're so close now and no*—*I'll talk to Ziggy when I get home. He'll know what to do . . .*

God. I pedal onward, following the sounds in the wind to deflect. Whatever it takes. *Navigate the negative.* So. I've heard each city has its own white noise soundtrack. In New York, it's horns beeping. In Los Angeles, palm fronds slapping the sky. In St. Louis, it's the rattling of cicadas. They're just starting to emerge and their song can usually lull your thoughts to a deep sleep. Usually. It starts working some . . .

But as I round the corner, I'm jolted back: Dad's golden Cadillac glints in the driveway. Oh no. Why is he home? He's usually at the

Blues Note by now. Damn, my plan's foiled: Sneak up to his room, throw the stupid dollar back on his nightstand, run.

Instead, as Stingraymobile wobbles up the driveway, my heart wobbles up my throat. I throw them both down on our porch, and creep open the screen door. Only it hasn't been greased since 1927, so it screeches through every room in the house.

I peek my head around the corner. Dad's still asleep on the couch. I think. A rerun of *Leave It to Beaver* plays on the TV. Okay. I can just sneak past, dash up the stairs, replace the Bill of Dreams on his nightstand, and no one's the wiser. The theme from *Batman* starts playing in my head.

I hit the second stair when:

"Hey." He speaks. I freeze.

"Hey, Dad." I inch around. "Why are you home?"

"Where is it?" He doesn't move, doesn't even open his eyes. I'm not convinced he's actually talking. It could be my brain has created invisible words flying from his mouth. Wouldn't be the first time.

"Where's what?" I whisper just in case it's the latter.

"Don't play this game with me." Nope. It's him. "I ain't got time for this crap. Where is it?"

"Sorry. I needed lunch money and—" On the plastic table next to the couch: an empty glass of whiskey, two empty bottles of Bud, and his Playboy ashtray, so piled with cigarette butts I can barely see one of the girl's boobs. Three drinks in. Still safe.

"Where is it?" He flings his eyes open. I scrape through my pocket and iron the dollar out best I can before handing it to him.

"What happened to it?"

"Sorry. It's not my fault I—"

"I'm still *home*. Because you stole my money." Okay, *technically* this is not true. When Grandma died, she left all her money to me. I just can't touch it for another five years, when I guess the world's going to end anyway. Figures. Until then, he can use the funds at his disposal to *keep us both comfortable.* And since he was laid off two years ago, he doesn't look too hard for work. *"Goddamned Vietnam War! There ain't never any construction jobs in this city no more,"* he says. Every day. Not true. Still, not the time to bring up this minor detail.

Instead: "I know. Sorry."

"She's been waitin' for me to call. You know that? And I couldn't. I had to sit here. All day. Waiting for your thievin' ass to git home."

"Yessir."

"So help me, if she don't pick up—"

He springs from the couch. I squinch. He's never hit me, but still, one can't be too prepared. Instead, he pushes past, tripping over the two steps that lead to the phone in the kitchen. "Goddamn shag," he mutters, falling against the wall. He picks up the receiver, each number ticktickticking like a jackhammer as he dials.

*Please pick up, please pick up, please pick up.* I see three things:

1) *Jesus on a wooden cross, speckled with gold dust, hanging above our TV. It was Mom's. Yeah, was. When I was born and she pushed me out of the dark, I sucked up all the light in the world and she was gone. Aunt Luna said it was divinely orchestrated, but she also thinks St. Louis is the astrological center of the universe, so I don't know . . . And even though Dad and I don't go to church anymore, we refuse to take it down.*

2) *A framed needlepoint hanging next to the cross:* HOME IS WHERE THE HART IS *in orange squiggly letters. Grandma's. Well, Dad made it for her when he was little because Grandma used to say it every day like someone would say "Good morning." (She loved it*

*more than "Heaven itself" because he worked for months*
*on it and misspelled* heart.*) We leave it up even though*
*we both think it's a stupid cliché. No offense, Grandma.*

3) *Beaver's dad holding the crying Beav on TV. The volume's*
*turned down, so I can't hear what they're saying, but I*
*imagine it's something like, "There, there, my sweet son.*
*You could do anything and I would still love you more*
*than my bottle of whiskey." Or some such jive.*

"Hey. Heather? . . . Hey, hey, it's Robert. . . . From the Blues Note last night? . . . The one who bought you tequila shots? . . . We made out in the bathroom, and . . . Yeah, hey, that's me."

Man. This girl sounds like the prized Blue Ribbon Whore at the St. Louis County Fair. At least she's home.

Dad puts his hand over the receiver. "Pour me a drink, willya, son?" he says.

I duck under the bar and grab a fresh glass: two ice cubes from the tiny freezer, Jack Daniel's halfway, splash of soda, squeeze of lime. Glance in the mirrored wall behind me, brush my hair down to cover my scar, run back with the drink.

He's crouched on the floor now, twirling the telephone cord like a thirteen-year-old girl. He used to be movie-star beautiful—I've seen old pictures—tanned and muscled with sandy hair and a smile that broke girls' hearts. Now he's a melted-down version of that: a Robert Redford waxwork dummy that got thrown to the curb.

"Mm-hmm. . . . Yeah, baby," he says. "I'll meet ya there tonight."

Gross.

When he shoos me away, I dart up to my room. Safe again. *BAT-MAAANNN.* Muffled schoolgirl gabs waft through the cigarette smoke drifting up the stairs. Something like, "Can't wait. . . . Be there or be square. . . . I'll bring the coke, you bring the grass." Romeo and Juliet, eat your heart out.

Anyway, he's happy. That's what matters. I close my door, grab *Aladdin Sane* off my desk, and duck into my closet.

Secret: Behind my color-coordinated clothesline is a small door that opens to a tiny room. No one knows about my secret closet. Not even Starla. I think everyone needs a secret place in the world, a place you can count on to keep your dreams safe . . .

I have no idea why it exists, but because our house was built in the twenties, I've always imagined it was a hideout for some gangster named Bubs McGee or a little boy hiding from war criminals. And now it's my own hideaway from Adolf Dad and every other radioactive particle in the outside world.

Look, Dad wasn't always this way. I mean, he was never one of those super-happy-hippie kids singing on the hillside in that Coca-Cola commercial, but he also wasn't the town drunk. No, I broke something in him after my fateful day at the lake in 1969 when IT happened and everything changed. That's one of the reasons I still work so hard to fix it. It's my fault he is who he is now . . . and I don't know if either one of us will ever be right again . . .

When I flip on the light,

*Mom's portrait turns to me, smiles.*

*"Hey, Beetlebug."*

"Hey, Mom."

*"Good day today?" she asks.*

"Weird day today."

*"What happened?"*

"Later. Now I gotta disappear."

*"Sure thing, sweetpea." She sits back, floofing her hair in her handheld compact.*

39

I turn on my record player, put the cushioned headphones on, and drown my life away to the greatest album in the history of ever: *The Rise and Fall of Ziggy Stardust and the Spiders from Mars*. I've played it every day since the concert last year. The whole damn thing is positively genius, but the beginning gets me every time: a slow, steady drum, *ch-chch-ch, ch-chch-ch*, a *sttrrrrummmm* of guitar, and then, his voice . . .

Oh man . . . his voice . . .

At the concert, when that *struummm* happened, red lights faded up onstage and I finally saw the audience in all its glory: mini alien-Ziggys flocking the orchestra pit. Screaming. Glimmering. Crying. One of them, with Bowie's same fire-orange hair, bumped into me. He blew glitter in my face, said I was "shiny enough to make a wish on," and kissed my cheek. Ziggy sang. My heart stopped. And the rest, as they say, is history . . .

I clutch *Aladdin Sane* in my hands, and before I can even ask:

*Ziggy's eyes lift and twinkle. "Don't you worry, little Starman, I'm here. Ch-ch-ch-change is comin', baby. You gotta turn and face the strange. It's the only way to survive."*

"I'm not ready."

*"We never are. Remember: Friends are your greatest force fields, my superstar space invader."*

"You're right . . ." I say. "It's the only way . . ."

*"Wanna boogie?"*

"Let's." So we pray.

The hundreds of Ziggy eyes I've cut from magazines splatter my closet walls. *They blink and sing along with us.* I reach into my satchel, unfold the crumpled note—the one he gave me in health class—and pin it up next to Mom's portrait. To keep us safe.

"Yeah . . ." I whisper. "Where to next, Web?"

7.

*SLAM. SCREEEECH.* HOURS LATER, Dad's Cadillac whizzes away. I throw my headphones off and crawl out of the closet. The sun's disappeared, leaving behind a burnt glow. I peek through my curtains: Starla's window flickers like a strobe light. She's alive! Probably watching the news. I dash downstairs.

With fourteen minutes before *The Sonny & Cher Comedy Hour*, I only have time to throw one of Dad's fried-chicken TV dinners in the oven and call her. Not ideal, but it'll have to do. I grab some Ritz crackers and peanut butter while I wait.

"Hey, baby love. What's crackin'!" "Killing Me Softly" blasts through the receiver. Of course.

"Whatcha doin'?"

She turns down her player. "Working on my Levi's."

"Cool. You're definitely going to win their contest."

"We'll see . . . You okay? You sound funny."

I smear a cracker, stuff it in my mouth. "Where were you today?"

"Downtown. The women's march. You forgot again? You sure you're okay, Jonny?"

"I'm fine. That's right." Still don't remember. "How was it?"

"Totally far-out. Throngs of women's libbers gathered around the Arch screaming for equal rights. It was beautiful. Some even carried wire hangers, yelling, 'Never again!'"

"Why?"

"*Roe v. Wade.* I mean it *finally* passed in January, but do you know how many women had to die at home before abortions became legal?"

"No, I—"

"Oh! There was this one woman being carried in a wooden coffin, pretending like she was dead . . . It was fantastic!"

"Wow."

"And some were only in their bras. You would've *loved* it."

I chuckle. "Yeah . . ."

"I felt so alive, Jonny. To be part of it all. Such a great time to be a woman. To be free from the shackles of The Man. It's crazy out there, you know . . ."

"Yeah . . ." I never know how to respond to this. So I smear and stuff another Ritz in my mouth. "Well, I'm seriously bummed you weren't in English today."

"Why, what happened?"

"We had to partner up for a presentation."

"Oh crap."

"Yeah."

"Who'd you get? Aaron the Squarin'?"

"Nope. This new kid."

"New kid?"

"Yeah, he just started today. He's American Indian—"

"Really?"

"Yeah . . ." I rub my fingers on the gold-flecked wallpaper, tracing a pattern that strangely looks like his crooked smile.

"Far-out. Was he at Wounded Knee?"

"No, he was walking fine, he—"

"Jonathan!"

"What?"

"I'm talking about the place in South Dakota? That site on the reservation where hundreds of American Indians were slaughtered over a hundred years ago? That's one of the reasons they took it over."

"Oh. I don't know."

"Wounded Knee's only the greatest occupation of our *time*. I almost went there with Poppa to help them—you don't remember me talking about this?"

"No. What is it?"

"You gotta pay more attention, Jonny. This is important." She clicks off Roberta. Man, this really must be serious. "Here's the skinny: The American Indian Movement seized the site back in February for seventy-one days. Barricaded themselves in to bring attention to, like, *generations* of injustices they've had to suffer through. Then Nixon's cronies showed up and tried to force them out, surrounding the perimeter so no one else could get in. There was gunfire and fighting every night. A few Native people died. It was tragic. The whole country was watching . . . You never flip on the news?"

"I mean . . . No. Why were they there?"

"Ow!"

"What happened?"

"Stupid sewing needle—trying to stitch my name on the hip and—anyway, it's like what *we're* trying to do, you know, fight for who we are. But they did it to the most supreme degree, Jonny. After they occupied the site, Native peoples from all over the country started showing up in solidarity—it was beautiful. That's why Poppa almost took us there, but Momma thought it was too dangerous."

"Well, yeah, I mean if there was gunfire and fighting—"

"Can you blame them, baby? They're sick and tired of being ignored, having everything they own stolen out from under them, you know? So they stood together to take their voice and lands back, and fight for what's been promised them for, like, *hundreds of years*: to finally be free from the white man's rule. *Whambamthankyou-power-to-the-people-SHAZAM.*"

"Whoa."

"Yeah. Totally inspired."

"Did they win?"

"Depends what you mean by win. They negotiated something, but if history tells us anything, they'll be swept right back under the rug. They brought more attention to who they are as a people, though, and in my eyes, that's a huge win."

"Maybe Web was there. He said he just moved here. Not sure from where . . ."

"We should ask him. That would be so fantastic—"

"Yeah—"

"Who else was missing from class today?"

"Can't remember."

"Maybe I can join you guys. You know, we can make it a threesome—"

"Starla!"

"Is he cute?"

"No—I mean I don't know—anyway, that's a good idea." I grab the TV dinner out of the oven even though it's still cold. "NOT the threesome thing, the working together thing. That'd make everything easier. Let's ask Dulick tomorrow, okay? Look, I gotta—"

"Go. I know. Sonny and Cher. To be continued." She smacks a kiss and hangs up, and I set up the TV tray just as Cher flashes on the screen singing "The Long and Winding Road."

Hours later, I squint my eyes open. The empty remnants of a foil-covered TV dinner sit on the table. Cher's voice still jingles in my head— No. The phone's ringing. What time is it?

I fumble into the kitchen, pick up the phone. "Hello?"

"Jonathan? You okay, son?"

"Who is this?"

"Chester. From the Blues Note Tavern. You okay?"

"Oh. Right. Hi. Yeah. I'm fine. Why?"

"It's two in the morning. You comin'? Should I call someone?"

"No, no. Sorry. I'll be right there."

"See you in a bit, kiddo."

I hang up the phone, slip on my Chucks, and walk the thirty-seven blocks into town to pick up Dad.

## 8.

*Tuesday, May 22, 1973*

THE NEXT MORNING: "Come on, baby, we're gonna be late," Starla yells, parked on her gold Schwinn Stingray outside her front gate. (Normally a boys' bike, but she defies any gender stereotype every chance she can get.) She looks like a Sears catalog ad, poised in her bell-bottom jeans and halter top she made from a Josie and the Pussycats T-shirt.

I pedal faster. Her fluorescent pink lips: two flares guiding me in the morning fog.

"Long night again?" she asks.

"Guess so, yeah." I grab a few poofs from PeterPaulandMary, tracing another one of her freckle constellations in my head.

"Asshole," she says, looking toward my house.

"Whatever. Let's go."

We ride in silence as we always do. The only sound: Starla's newly woven hair beads tinkling through the morning breeze.

Minutes later, we turn the corner. The football field looms in the distance.

"Hey, you ever think about going to prom?" she asks. Her head tilts back.

"No. Why?"

"It's coming up. Just curious. Lindsey called last night after we talked."

"Oh yeah?"

"Yeah, she's looking for a few girls to go with. Thought it could be fun. Oh, and she's my English partner, I guess—"

"Oh no. Really?"

"Don't worry, you're gonna be fine. I'm sure he's— Wait, is that him?"

It is. Sitting in the shade of an oak tree by the parking lot, smoking a cigarette. Alone.

"Oh, honey, he's not just cute. He's a damn fox. Come on, I wanna meet him."

"No, we should just—"

"Come on . . ."

Oh man. We park our bikes; she pulls me forward.

"Hey, I'm Starla."

"Hey," he says, still looking at the dirt. He's wearing the same thing as yesterday, but his hair is parted in two braids.

"Hey, Web."

He looks up and lifts that dimpled smile. "Oh, hey, man."

"I . . . uh . . . like your red bandanna . . ." I say. "It's funky."

"Thanks, man."

We don't move. I look at Starla, Starla looks at Web, and Web looks back down at . . . the anthill.

"So . . . I guess—"

"You're Native American, right?" Starla asks.

He nods and squints up. "The Oglala Lakota Nation, yeah."

"Right on . . . Were you at Wounded Knee?"

He nods again. "You know about that?"

"You kiddin'? We watched it every night on TV. My old man

almost drove us there to help you out. What's happening to your people—it's a travesty, brother."

They stare at each other.

For a long time.

He stands, brushing dirt off the back of his jeans. Takes another drag of his cigarette. "You black or somethin'?" he asks her.

"Yeah," she says. "Dad is. Momma's white."

"Cool."

Her eyelashes, thickly coated with mascara, *batbatbat*, closing and opening like a Venus flytrap. Why is she looking at him like that? Maybe he likes her. My body tightens. What the hell am I feeling? Never felt this before.

"Is that where you're from?" I ask. "Wounded Knee?"

He turns to me. Seriously, his eyes are like two tiny Milky Ways that spin you to another dimension and—

"Nearby," he says.

"Ah. Cool," I say.

"Ever been?" he asks.

"No . . ."

"It's beautiful . . . Big, open plains. Rolling hills and ridges. Sunsets are otherworldly, man."

"Really? I love watching sunsets . . ."

"Me too . . ."

"Well, the bell's about to ring," Starla says, "so I'll catch you boys on the flip. See you inside, Jonny-boo." She winks at me, squeezes my shoulder, and walks away.

Oh.

Uh.

I try to follow her up the stairs. Nope. Seems my legs have a mind of their own these days. They're stuck to this spot. Web kicks a few pebbles under his feet. He stubs his cigarette out. I should say something. What else do people say to each other to make friends? Can't be that hard. *Boy, weather sure is strange, isn't it? Going to be a long summer.* No. My palms are sweating, shaking, even. God. My pockets! I shove them in my pockets.

"You only talk when there's a bathroom stall around?" he finally asks, laughing.

"Oh. Ha-ha. Sorry. Yes—NO, I mean—" God, Collins, so not good at this making friends thing. So not good.

"I had a dream about you last night," he says.

"You . . . what?"

"I know. Crazy, right? I was thinking about what you said in front of class yesterday. About that quote in the book."

"Oh." *What did I say?!* "It's a book, you know—a *cool* book, I mean. The seagull one. You're right— Oh! That reminds me—" I reach into my satchel and push the book in his face; he flinches back.

"What?"

"Sorry. Didn't mean to—you don't have a copy, so I thought you could have mine. Since we're going to be partners and all, for the presentation, I mean—"

"Cool, man. Thanks."

"Sure . . . sure . . ."

He flips through the pages, smiling. His braids dangle on his shoulders. His golden skin . . . still glistens. His thick lips are so red it looks like— He's staring at me.

This time, I don't look away.

He closes the book. "It really is beautiful, isn't it . . ."

"Yeah . . . it really is . . ." My wrists twinge.

The first bell rings, making us both jump.

"So . . ." I say.

"Guess I'll see you in there," he says.

"Yeah, see you . . ."

I run inside. My legs actually move, but my brain definitely does not, and oh man, I take it back. His eyes aren't two Milky Ways; they're black hole vortices and apparently they spaghetti my brain.

Oh man, oh man, oh man, this is not good. Not good at all.

## 9.

"WHAT IS YOUR DEFINITION of love?"

This guy. If the earth isn't going to kill us in five years, Mr. Dulick surely will before then. He reads each word as he writes on the blackboard, another quote from *Jonathan Livingston Seagull*:

> *His sorrow was not solitude, it was that other gulls*
> *refused to believe the glory of flight that awaited them;*
> *they refused to open their eyes and see.*

"Man, that's some gorgeous poetry right there," he says, lost in the chalk swirls.

Please don't cry again.

He claps his hands, snapping everyone back to attention. Scotty, asleep on his arm, pops up.

"Love," Mr. Dulick says. "What does it look like to you?"

Suzanna Levine raises her hand high in the air.

"Miss Levine, yes!"

"My brother," she says. "When I visit my brother."

Mr. Dulick walks down the aisle, placing his hand over his heart. He stops in front of her. Her bugged-out eyes blink through her glasses.

"Oh my, yes," he says. "Yes. Your brother, Suzanna. Yes. A few different kinds of love right there, sister. Tell us more." He looks up, still holding his heart, and now her hand. Can't tell if he's crying yet. From this angle, it's hard to see through his thick sideburn bushes.

"Well . . . he . . . loved our country," she says. "Like a service. He loved to serve . . ." She twists the silver dog tags hanging around her neck.

"Yes, yes, that's right, sister, he did . . . and . . . what else . . ." His eyes swoop around the classroom. It's like watching an evangelical baptism, I swear.

"And . . . and . . . when we visit him . . . at his grave . . . I love him . . . I miss . . . him . . ." And there she goes. Floating down her river of tears. Starla rubs her back. She does not support the Vietnam War. None of us do. And Suzanna is one of the many reasons why. Last year she was all hippie smiles and sunshine. Then her brother was killed somewhere in Vietnam, and her smile began to fade into blackness. Sometimes she'll start crying for no reason, and rumor has it she sleepwalks through her house at night looking for her dead brother.

Mr. Dulick closes his eyes, takes a deep breath.

I quickly glance over at Web, who sits with his hands folded in his lap. He stares ahead motionless. Either he's praying or contemplating world domination. Can't really tell.

"Who else?" Mr. Dulick says, gliding around the room.

Scotty shoots his hand up.

"Mr. Danforth?"

"*Playboy*," he says. Cretin. I swear he speaks only in two-syllable increments.

The Apes grunt and girls squeal, but Mr. Dulick doesn't skip a beat.

"Ah yes, a very different kind of love. Tell us more, my man." He props himself against his desk and folds his arms. His polyester shirt bulges a bit in the middle so you can see tufts of chest hair peeking through.

"Uh . . . I guess . . . you know, man . . . come on . . ."

"You brought it up. And a good answer at that. Why does that mean love to you?"

"I mean . . . you know . . . the women, man." He acts like he's holding two big boobies in front of his chest. "There's so much to love." He high-fives an Ape sitting next to him. Some girls giggle nearby.

"Okay, Mr. Danforth, I'll interpret: sexual love. An important aspect of human development. Stimulation is good, but sexual love is deeper, more sensual . . . connected . . ."

Two more seconds and I'm out the door like the Flash. I hate this crap.

"What is it about sexual love that makes it deeper?" Dulick asks.

Scotty looks confused. Like Poppa Ape's taken his toy away and he doesn't know what to do anymore. Firecrotch raises her hand.

"Yes?"

"Like when a boy looks deep in your eyes as he moves in to kiss you, and he slides his hand underneath your bra, and you know you're the only one in the world at that moment?" Jesus. She asks the question innocently, but come on. Even Scotty whips around to see if this chick's for real.

"Yes, Miss Halstead," Dulick says without skipping a beat. "A true sexual love knows no boundaries. It is limitless beyond the stars. Into the heavens. Where time disappears and everything falls away . . ." He throws his head back to look up at the ceiling.

And he's crying.

Here we go again. We stare back, lost, wondering and waiting, when:

"That's it!" he yells. Everyone jumps. "Get together with your

53

partners and talk about this quote." He runs behind his desk, slapping his hand on the blackboard. "What is the one love that's bigger than any love we've talked about today?" He throws his arms in the air and croons like a preacher. "And this weekend I want you to take your partner to the one place that makes you *feel that love* to use in your presentation!" Oh no. "Oh yes, this is going to be *good*, kids, so so good."

"*Come on, Dulick, it's prom this weekend!*" sings the room in almost perfect harmony.

"Even better. Lots of opportunities outside of school, then. And don't think for a second you can skip out on this one—you'll tell us all about it on Monday."

"*Come. On!*" I almost join in on the chorus this time.

"Chop-chop, beautiful people, only a few minutes left of class."

Chairs scrape the floor as everyone mills about, grumbling. Starla's already rapping with Lindsey: They both love Jesus, so that's a no-brainer.

Web doesn't move, so I plop down in Samantha's seat. It's still warm and makes me gooey-gross inside. Warm chairs. I don't know, like I'm sitting on someone's leftover germs. Anyway.

"Hey," I say.

"Hey." He flips through the seagull book. Sweat beads on his forehead. Up close he looks tired. Too tired for someone his age. Too tired, like me . . .

"Do you use Irish Spring soap?" I ask.

"Yeah, why?"

"Oh . . ." No. I've had all day to think about what I would say to him next, and that was not it. "I mean, I meant to thank you for the note in health class yesterday, I thought it was far-out!" *Huzzah!*

He lifts a smile. "Glad you got it."

"Yeah—"

"They're assholes," he says, still flipping.

"I know."

"All of 'em."

"Yeah."

"Fuckin' cops."

"What?"

"White cops. They're all goons."

Oh. Something's shifted. Not sure what. His cheeks flush as red as his bandanna. His Chucks bounce to holy hell. I don't know what to do with this, so I say the first thing that pops into my head: "Navigate the negative!"

Definitely did not mean to say that out loud.

"Huh?"

"I mean—" *God.* I want to slap myself. Don't. Instead, I look down and shuffle my shoes on the linoleum, hoping I can dig a hole to fall into. "My, uh, doc told me that once, so I . . . kinda look at it as being a mapmaker, you know, never mind." Oh man. I can't believe I just told him that.

"What do you mean?" His Chucks stop bouncing, so . . . I keep going! Have no idea why. Like someone pulled a string on my back. I can't control my mouth.

"If something negative pops up in my life, I look at it as a chance to, you know, discover a new direction to take, or find a different feeling to think about so I don't let it win—kinda like a game. It's stupid, never mind. Never told anyone that before, heh-heh . . ." My shoes seriously can't dig fast enough.

"Neat," he says.

"Huh?" I glance up.

"It's a neat trick. I dig it."

"Oh. Okay. Cool . . ." God, those eyes. Fierce but soft. Like his voice. They definitely scramble my mind, which is not a good thing, all things considered. I look down, drum my fingers on the desk. "So, anyway, I guess we should talk about love or whatever."

He starts jiggling his Chucks again.

"I mean, it's a crazy assignment, but Dulick said we—"

"Not really good at it, man," he says.

"What?"

"Talking around other people."

"Oh, well, it's okay. Me—"

"Or love."

"—neither."

Oh.

"We could start off easy," I say. "Like, what's your favorite album?"

"*Dark Side of the Moon.*"

"Sweet. Pink Floyd totally gets it. Ever hear *Meddle*?"

"No."

"Some don't like it. I do."

"Is that your favorite?"

"Oh no. Mine's Ziggy Stardust anything."

"Cool, man, Ziggy's far-out."

"You know Ziggy?"

"*This is ground control to Major Tom . . .*" he sings softly.

"*You've really made the graaaddee . . .*" I whisper. We laugh quietly. "Yeah, I definitely feel like some space oddity who's landed here on Earth and—" I stop myself. Damn. Said that out loud, too.

"I feel ya, man," he says.

"You do?"

"All the time . . ." He leans on his elbow, drawing figure eights on the book cover with his finger. "But my dad used to say, 'The things that make you different are your superpowers,' so . . . anyway . . ."

"Huh . . ." *Wish I could believe it . . .*

"Yeah. And I never told anyone that before, so now we're even." Two dimples poke in his cheeks, but he still looks down at the book.

"Okay, we're even," I say.

"So, hey, man." He sits up suddenly. "I don't really have a place of *love* to show you for the presentation or whatever. Here, I mean."

"Yeah, I don't either."

"Where should we go, then?"

"Oh, uh, I don't know. There aren't many places around here. We definitely can't meet at my house."

"We can't meet at mine either," he says.

"Oh." *Didn't expect that answer. Makes me instantly curious why.*

"Wanna just meet at the lake?" he asks.

"No!"

"Okay . . ." He flips through his book.

"I mean—" *Damn.* "I don't know . . . let me think." *But I can't. Like, at all.* "I mean . . ." *Oh man oh man oh man.* "I guess that's the only place—"

"Saturday?"

"Uh, I guess, yeah. Oh, but not in the morning, I'm with Starla. Later in the day?"

"Okay," he says.

"Okay," I say.

My chest is hammering. I'm surprised he can't hear it. Maybe he can. His bouncing feet match its rhythm. And I know for sure he's casting a spell on me with those eyes: I'm getting dizzy and sweaty and twitchy and—

"Ow!" My wrists zing. *No. Dammit.*

"What's wrong?"

"Nothing." *Stupid treatments. I knew it. I can't do this. I can't think of him like that. How's this ever going to work?* I throw my hands in my lap. Rub them together. Look at the clock above the blackboard. I think it's broken: stuck in a tick-tick-click on the same second over and over again.

"You're kinda weird, man."

"Yeah. Guess that's what my old man pays the lady for, heh-heh."

"I dig it," he says. "Not like the others."

"What others?"

"The other white boys," he says, gesturing to Scotty and the Apes at the front of the classroom, currently huddled like cavemen around some giggling girls. Almost forgot anyone else was in the room.

"Nope. Not like them," I say. "I am definitely different than them."

"Different, huh? Maybe that's your superpower . . ."

"Yeah . . . maybe . . ." *Do not look at him. Do not get caught in those hypnotizing eyes. Stay focused on the broken clock above the blackboard so I don't feel any more stinging—*

"Your hair's so blond, man. Almost white."

"Hmm? Oh, yeah—"

"Cool scar," he says.

"Huh?"

"The scar. On your forehead. Pretty far-out. How'd you get it?" He starts to push my hair aside.

"Don't!" I brush my swoop back down to cover it.

"Sorry, man."

"It's okay. I just—" I take a breath. "So, anyway, about love . . ."

"Yeah . . ."

Bell rings.

Praise Ziggy.


After school on our bike ride home, Starla tells me she and Lindsey are going to church on Sunday. "I like Web," she says.

"Yeah . . ."

"What are you guys going to do?"

"Oh, just meeting at the lake, I guess." I try to say this as casually as *"Man, how about them Cardinals?"* Doesn't work.

"What? The *lake*? You don't even like the lake, Jonny."

"Yeah I do."

"You sure? You haven't been back since—"

"Yes. I'm sure." I shoot lasers into her eyes.

"Okay. Okay . . . I just thought you never wanted to go back there."

"Well . . . I am."

"*Well* . . . I think it's good for you," she says as we pull up to her house. "Hey, you have a session tomorrow, don't you?"

"Uh-huh."

"Maybe you should talk to her about it, she—"

"I will." I start to ride off but she grabs my handlebars to stop me.

"She's there to help you, Jonny."

"I know, I know."

"Good." She kisses my cheek before skipping her Schwinn up her driveway. "See you tomorrow?"

"Of course."

Okay, screw Dulick's five-year apocalyptic prophecy or Starla's impending departure. She's right. This damn Presentation-for-Your-Life is definitely going to kill me before then.

## 10.

THE NEXT AFTERNOON, it's Wednesdays with Dr. Evelyn, and I'm a cold corpse on her long leather couch. Can't move because the squeaks sound like ten million cicadas screeching in my eardrums. So instead I stay frozen, strapped down without the restraints. Been lying here almost four years now.

Patchouli smoke slinks from the lighted stick on the bookshelf. I see two new things:

> *1) A snow globe with a tiny plastic Arch and riverboats, sitting on the bookshelf*
>
> *2) A macramé plant holder hanging in the window in front of me, empty*

"Where's your plant?" I ask.

Dr. Evelyn sits behind me, scribbling notes in her notebook like a Spirograph gone mad. "Oh, yes," she says. "I must get one. A client made that for me for my birthday. Isn't it beautiful?" Her voice: a hypnotic pendulum.

"When was your birthday?"

"Last week. The big four-oh," she says and laughs.

"Wow. A milestone year. Something big's supposed to happen in a milestone year."

"Oh yeah?"

"Yeah. Get ready."

Her bangles clang together. "Bracing myself," she says. "You too, by the way."

"Me too what?"

"Have a birthday coming up. A milestone one at that."

"Oh. Yeah. Guess so."

"Guess so? It's the big one-seven. Pretty milestoney in my eyes," she says. "In a few weeks, isn't it?"

"Yeah."

"Any plans?"

"Got a few up my sleeve." Lying. Seriously, plans? Party for one, in my closet? Usually it's dinner with Starla and her parents, but she'll be gone. Man. Just the thought stabs my stomach. "It's a pretty plant holder," I say, changing the subject.

"Thank you. What kind of flower should I get?"

"What kind do you like?"

"So many."

The macramé net sways. *I leap up from the leather couch, squeeze my head through the yarn, and twisttwisttwist it around my neck like a noose. Fare thee well, cruel, cruel world. It's been swell, but time for me to go back to the stars . . .*

"Maybe some kind of vine," I say. "They grow like crazy and are easy to take care of. We have one in our living room. Makes me feel like I'm in *The Jungle Book* sometimes."

"Oh yeah? Good idea. *The Jungle Book*'s fun."

"Yeah. I'm definitely like Mowgli dropped off in Man-Village—" Oh no. I try reeling the words back in, but I'm too late.

Scribble scribble—*Aha! I knew he was crazy!*—scribble. Dammit. Usually I'm on lockdown for the question-and-answer portion of this stupid game show.

Secret: I've been doing this so long I know all the rules. Answer each question with the right amount of *"Everything's grrrreat!"* sprinkled with a few dashes of *"I've still got this issue. Wah!"* Sound too grrrreat, she'll see right through you.

Usually that's what happens. Today, everything's upside down. I could barely focus on tying my damn shoelaces this morning, and in English, my brain was so scrambled when I sat with Web all I could gibber about was Pink Floyd and how I thought Roger Waters was the Socrates of music. God. Web kept laughing, so he for sure thinks I'm a Looney Tune. Anyway. *Concentrate, Collins. Don't let her in.* I stare out the window. Little tributaries of rain wriggle down the glass.

"You sure you're feeling okay, Jonathan? You look a little paler than usual."

"Just tired."

"Have you been feeling this way for a while?"

*Uh, yeah.* "Not really, no." Which winding labyrinth to take her on this go-round? "Just the past couple days. Nerves, I guess. We have to give a presentation in front of the class. You know I hate that kinda stuff." Hook, line—

"Yes, I see."

And sinkered.

Scribblescribblescribble. "It's good for you, I think. Don't you? Helps you push through your fears."

"Yeah," I say.

"We must face our fears if we're to face our fate."

I mime these words along with her. I swear I've heard them 10,728 times since I first walked into this office. "Yeah," I say.

"Do you have to do it alone?"

"No I'm with Web and—"

"Web?"

Dammit, foiled again. "Yeah. He's this new kid at school. Doesn't talk much." *A cue I should be taking right about now.*

"Is he nice?"

"Huh? Yeah. He's nice. I don't know. He looks a little sad, I guess. We're meeting this weekend at the—" *SHUT UP, COLLINS.* My nerves twist with Dr. Evelyn's scribblescribblescribblescribblescribble.

"At the what?" she asks.

*Think, think, think.* "The roller rink!" Damn, should've thought of that before. A perfect spot actually. We could play *Pong* at the arcade and skate. Or Kmart! Kmart's like Switzerland; nothing bad ever happens at Kmart.

"The roller rink?"

"Yeah. With some friends. Just trying to make him feel welcome and such."

"I see," she says, after I swear she's torn circles in her page. "That's nice of you. And good for you, too, I think. Stepping out of your comfort zone."

"Yeah." I swallow. "Facing my fear to face my fate!"

She laughs, but still scribbles.

"Guess that's what that means, huh?" I say, trying to change the subject again. "The things that scare you the most are the things that bring you closer to who you're meant to be." Or whatever . . .

She stops writing. "I like that, Jonathan."

Raindrops slither faster down the window. The world outside's now under a blanket of gray, like the filmstrip in health class. Skipping every so often, too.

"Does your father know about him?" she asks.

"What? No. Why?"

"Just curious. He's always wanted you to make new friends."

"Yeah. Guess I'll tell him." Lie. Duh. Time to travel down a different path. And fast. "Do you think the earth is dying?"

"What?"

"Mr. Dulick said he read it somewhere. Something like we only have five years left. You hear about that?" Sweat drips down my cheeks. I think it's sweat. Can't tell, can't move.

"No," she says. "Do you think it's dying? That we only have five years left?"

"I don't know. It would figure, though. Since that's when I'd be free."

"What do you mean?"

"Five years. I'll be twenty-one. I can finally go to California."

"Yes, that's right, when—"

"When I get the money Grandma left me."

"And you can—"

"See the beaches and palm trees and swim in the ocean and make music in Laurel Canyon with Mama Cass and Joni Mitchell and be a rock-n-roll star and finally *be* somebody."

"Yes. But why can't you—"

"I bet everything shimmers like a disco ball there." I close my eyes to the colorless world outside. "A snow globe city. Like your collection. Only with glitter."

"Is that what you picture?"

"Yeah. So I guess if the world ends, then—"

"How do you find that freedom now?" She finishes a thought I didn't even know I had.

We sit in silence.

No scribbles. No squeaks.

"I don't know," I say, opening my eyes. "I don't know if that's possible."

"I think it is," she says. "And I think you're close to finding it out, too."

"Really? Why?"

"Because of the progress you've been making." I can tell she's smiling by the way her voice lilts.

"Oh. Of course," I say. "Right."

Bangles jangle. She stands. As she walks by, honeysuckle and jasmine drift with her. I quickly wipe my face and smile. She sits on the other end of the couch, lifting my legs so my feet tangle in the drapes of her long flower-patched dress.

Dr. Evelyn is definitely a psychedelic version of Catwoman: huge blue-tinted glasses shielding her eyes, hair pulled up in a ponytail stretching her smile, and her skin's extra-kissed from the sun, like a piece tore off and landed smack on her cheeks.

"You haven't had any more of those feelings, have you?"

"Oh . . . no. Definitely not. I'm fixed."

"How's your memory?" she asks. "You're practicing the tricks I taught you?"

"Yeah. I've been using my tape recorder."

"Excellent. And it's working?"

"Guess so. Course I wouldn't know if I didn't remember it."

She laughs. This time I get to see the Cumberland Gap between her two front teeth.

"No, I think it's working. I really do," I say.

"Good . . . because we won't be seeing each other for a couple of weeks, you know."

"Oh, right. You're going to some psychiatry conference?"

"In Hawaii, yes. So the next time I see you, we'll be doing your final

treatments. And I just want to make sure that . . . you still want them."
She stares, the Spirograph scribbling in her eyes now.

*Don't let her in, don't let her in.* "I do . . . want them. Why wouldn't I want—"

"Because . . . I've been thinking . . . there may be other ways . . . to help, I mean."

"Other ways? But these are our last ones. Why stop now?"

"I don't know. I just . . . want to make sure you're ready for them again, Jonathan. They take so much out of you, and—"

"I'm definitely ready. Besides, Dad would never let me stop them now and—"

"But it's still what *you* want?"

"Yes. It is."

She studies me. Hard. She opens her mouth to say something, then stops. After a few long minutes of this, she says, "Okay, I think you're ready, too."

I can't see it in her face, but I can hear it in her voice: She's lying.

Huh.

I don't say anything else.

I'm afraid to.

Afraid she'll know I'm lying, too.

## 11.

---

I TAKE THE LONG way home after the session. Stingraymobile pedals forward, even though I'm sure she's about to grow wings and shoot me to the heavens because of this crazy wind. Raindrops *taptaptaptaptap* my plastic raincoat. My thoughts cyclone through me: *Why was Dr. Evelyn lying to me? What did she mean by "other ways"? To fix me? Whatever they are, they can't be good. Could she see through me? Dammit, I should've never mentioned Web. And why did I agree to meet him at the LAKE? I know! When I see him tomorrow, I'll suggest the roller rink! Yeah. He's probably super smooth on skates, too. Just glides along the rink like Archangel Gabriel or something, beaming just as bright. God. What's the number to the nearest asylum?*

As I round the corner to my house, the wind howls: *"Turn around now, Jonathan! Save yourself . . ."* Nope. It's Led Zeppelin. For real. Dad's singing down the block for all of Creve Coeur to hear, apparently. Jesus.

I pop around to see if any of the old pickle neighbors are peeking their heads through the curtains, phone receivers to their ears, cops on the other end. Not yet. But damn, it's going to be one of those nights.

Dad Zeppelin has torn holes through the screen door. I carry Stingraymobile onto the porch and walk in to see:

1) *Our orange velvet couch covered in strings of Christmas lights*
2) *Dad in his Jockeys hanging said Christmas lights, dancing on the bar. Uh.*

Music thumpthumpthumps the mirror, Dad humphumphumps his reflection in the mirror. No. It smells like skunk, which means one of two things, and I know for certain there's no live skunk waddling through the house.

"HEY, DAD!"

He throws himself against the mirror. "You scared the hell outta me, man!"

"Sorry!"

"*Staaiirrrwayyyy* . . . Hey, help me . . . *tooooo heeaavveeennnn* . . . with these lights." His cigarette bounces up and down between his lips, each word springing off it like a diving board.

Okay, light mood. I'll take it. I drop my satchel on the couch, turn down the music before it ruptures my eardrums, and duck under the bar to help him. Draped in all the lights, he kinda looks like a dancing diorama of the solar system.

"How was your session today, son?"

"Good."

"How many more treatments you got?"

"One more set."

"Then you're fixed for good."

"Yeah, for good . . ."

"Proud of you, bud. Knew you could do it. You're DY-NO-*WHOA-OA-OA*—*" He boogies his butt and topples over a few bottles before I cradle the rest in my arms. "Damn, son. Good thing you—" He starts coughing. I snatch his cigarette before it hits the shag and stub it out on some girl's boobs in his Playboy ashtray.

*BATMAANNNNN.*

His cough, meanwhile, turns to the Penguin's retch or something gross—

"You okay, Dad?" I pat his back.

"Yeah . . . yeah . . . I'm fine. Grab me a Bud, willya?" I do. He guzzles it and settles down on the sun-yellow recliner: heaving, wiping his brow.

"You sure you're okay?"

"Finish it for me." He waves to the lights, takes a few more glugs. "Goddamn, son. You look just like your momma sometimes. Them eyes . . . your white hair . . ." Oh boy, here we go. "Hey. I ever tell you 'bout the time your mom and I was on that Tilt-A-Thingy at the senior carnival?" Only 1,726 times. Who's counting? I actually love this story. I love picturing them before me. "And, man, you shoulda seen it, her hair got so tangled up in mine, we were stuck together, you know, like—"

"Taffy?"

"Yeahyeahyeah, and . . . they had to . . ." He starts laughing, which instantly turns into another cough-typhoon.

"Cut your hair out so you looked like the Two Stooges?" I say.

"Man . . ." He pounds his chest. "Whoa . . ."

"You okay?"

"Yeah." His eyes glaze over, staring through me at the bar. "She was somethin' else . . ." He's there now, lost in their laughter, still spinning on the Tilt-A-Thingy. "Man, I miss her."

"Yeah . . ." Guess we're all stuck whirling in our heads sometimes. "So, what's the occasion for the lights? Memorial Day?" I ask, grabbing another strand off the couch.

"Huh? Oh. Heather. She's coming over. Thought I'd spice things up a bit—MAN, I LOVE THIS SONG!" And he's up again, turning the knob to a thousand decibels. This time using the coffee table as his dance floor, kicking magazines off with each move.

"WHEN?" I yell.

"*Drank all my . . .* What? *. . . wiiiinne . . .* Soon . . . I don't know . . ."

"Maybe you should get dressed?"

"What?"

"CLOTHES?" I pull at my shirt.

"Why bother?" He winks and gyrates, and I swallow some barf.

I lift the strand. "Where do you want these?"

"Dance with me—" He claps his hands and pulls me toward him.

"Oh. No, I'll—"

"Put those down and dance with me, son."

"No, no, I should just—"

"Come on, man. Loosen the hell up." He grabs the lights, slinging them over his shoulders. "You're always so damned serious. Dance. It's good for you." He flaps his arms. I think he's doing the Funky Chicken but I can't be sure. His thin blond hair's spiked up; his furry body jiggles; his mouth hangs open. With the lights wrapped around him he looks like he's being electrocuted. "Why aren't you dancin'?" He flings my arms to the sky. "That's it, son. Helps clear your mind. You gotta let go, man. Let go of all that crap in there . . ." *THWACK.* He slaps my forehead and closes his eyes and travels to a fake galaxy far, far away.

Well, I like when he's happy, and I've learned a few moves from *Soul Train*, so I bounce my knees and shimmy back and forth and close my eyes and—

*Together we walk the* Soul Train *line . . .*

"*Name's Cheetah. Uh-huh. I'm the new cat in town. Here to show you a few boss boogies to take your prom date to the starverse of make-believe. Can you dig?"*

"Hey yo, daddio," Charlene squeals. "You the finest man I ever did see. Where'd you learn those moves, babay?" I become a man possessed: *sh-boogying—uh uh uh—on the dance floor, circle forming around me, clapping, screaming, ding-donging,*

*Ding-donging,*

Ding-dong,

DING-DONG.

Oh no. The cops. Record skips. Dad's at the door. I dart to the stereo, twist the knob down, and dash up the stairs just before he opens it.

They are not cops. No, they are . . . not exactly sure what. I see a pair of wet rats standing on their hind legs dressed up like a girl and boy. She's in a red-and-gold Dairy Queen uniform, skinnier than me, with a big bowl of hair dripping down her tiny head and too much makeup smeared on her pinched face.

Her friend squirms behind her in a stained T-shirt and faded Cardinals mesh cap: a thicker boy-version of her, with a creepy, lopsided smirk like the Joker's. Must be high or something.

"Hey hey hey, Heather," Dad says. "Welcome, baby!"

"Robert-Bobert, you're in your underwear!" And, boy, if that's not the funniest thing she's ever seen in her life, I'd hate to be around for whatever is. Oh man, that laugh. I think my ears are bleeding.

"Who's this?" Dad asks, shaking her friend's paw.

"My brother. Hal. Remember him? It's okay he came, right?"

"Oh, right on! Yeahyeahyeah. Hey, man. Sorry, I would've at least put on some pants." Dad laughs.

"Nice to meet ya." Hal walks in. More like slithers. Yup, definitely high. He sees me and waves. I wave back and bolt.

*Have fun, kids! Don't do anything I wouldn't do!*

I slam my door, dig through my satchel, grab the first library-borrowed book I find—Carl Sagan's *The Cosmic Connection*—and crawl into my closet. I switch the light on. Say hello to Mom and Friends. With my headphones secure, I flip on Ziggy, wrap myself in one of Grandma's crocheted afghans, and disappear . . . sort of.

Because all the while, I try to navigate the thought-storm that's been ripping me to shreds this entire time: Dr. Evelyn's lying, Starla's leaving, and Web's, well, Web's everything.

## 12.

*Saturday, May 26, 1973*

IT'S FINALLY SATURDAY and I'm on the beach at Creve Coeur Lake, now convinced I have entered some bizarro parallel universe, and waiting for a unicorn or maybe a merman with wings to come charging out of the water.

Never thought I'd see this place again.

My nerves are so jangled I'm walking around like a creature from *Night of the Living Dead*. Feel like one, too.

Web wasn't at school the past two days. Maybe he's sick. Or went back home. Or officially decided that yes indeed I am a Looney Tune and he needs to stay as far away from me as possible. Still, I don't know how to get ahold of him, so I came here to wait. In case he does show up.

I see:

1) *A few boats floating in the water and silhouettes of men*
   *with thinly arched fishing poles*
2) *A cliff in the distance with a trickling waterfall*
3) *A trailer park village on the other side of the lake covered*
   *with strewn-about toys and trash, and*
4) *Behind me, a row of shanties on stilts made out of*

*papier-mâché that I'm pretty sure will be blown to bits if I sneeze. They look condemned. I think they are.*

I park Stingraymobile against a big rock protruding from the sand, sling my satchel over my shoulder, and plop down. The lake breezes through me: a mixture of crisp air and fish stink. I close my eyes, feel the sun ignite my nerves, and let each ray detonate a new thought. *I shouldn't be here.* KAZAM. *I can't trust myself yet.* SHBLAM. *I'm still sick.* CRRRACK. I know. *I'll spend the next three months in my closet and have Dad slide me a tray of bread and water under the door every day until Starla gets back.* KAPOW. God.

Even church this morning was weird. Starla was quiet the entire time, working on the finishing touches of her Prom Suit. (*"It's not a* dress,*" she said. "I refuse to bow to the pressures of the patriarchy any longer."*) (Turns out this is also why she's going to prom tonight with Lindsey and that group of girls.)

Seriously, what am I going to do when she goes away—

A shadow moves across the sun; I squint my eyes open.

"God, Web, you look like one of Sagan's effing starfolk," I say. OUT LOUD. AGAIN. What is happening to me? Used to be: thought, ponder, thought, silence. Now it's: thought—*KABLOOEY* out of my mouth.

He does, though. In that book I'm reading, Carl Sagan says we're all starfolk and we'll one day colonize black holes. I think he must've met Web when he got the idea. He stands above me, a perfect halo around his head, shirtless and glimmering like every pore in his body is hatching a firefly, his hair sticking to his skin. Also? Who knew there was such a thing as a twenty-four-pack set of abs. Jesus.

All this time, by the way, sharp stabs keep pricking my veins. *Effing Evelyn side effects. I knew I shouldn't have come back here.*

He's still standing. Not moving, not saying anything. Then FINALLY: "What were you doing?"

"Huh?"

"Just now. You were mumbling and making *Batman* sounds."

Wait. I was. "Oh, uh . . ." Can't even think my way out of this one. No one's ever seen me do that.

"It's cool. I get stuck in my head a lot, too," he says.

"Yeah?"

"My dad showed me a trick once. Kinda like that mapmaker one you taught me. Wanna hear it?"

"Sure."

"So each thought is like an invisible string, right? Grab one like this—" He acts like he's pulling a long string from his forehead. "Then blow it in the wind and watch it float away. Keep doing that till your mind's clear. Works every time." He laughs, then hikes up his jeans, and plops down next to me.

He smells like a boy who's been playing outside all day.

I haven't moved. I think I've turned to stone, I can't be sure.

I'm thinking I'd really like to be one of his thoughtstrings and be blown far, far away, when he says, "So this is better, right?"

"What?"

"You know, not sitting in a classroom. Or on a toilet."

I laugh. "Yeah. Guess it is." I'm staring forward, but I know he's looking at me: My wrists and thighs are afire. *This is never going to work. We can never be friends.* "So, where have you been? You weren't in school and—"

"Didn't feel good."

"Oh. Well, I'm glad you're okay now . . ."

"Yeah. I was beginning to wonder if you were ever going to show," he says.

"I was beginning to wonder if I made our whole conversation up."

"Happens to me all the time."

"Really?"

"Yeah, man. But that's half the fun of life, right? Trying to figure out what's real and what isn't. You cold or somethin'?"

"Huh?"

"Your wrists. You keep rubbing them together."

"I do?" Dammit. Caught again. "No, it's just—"

"Here. Let me warm you up." His hands wrap around mine. A volt sweeps through me.

"OW!" Like a frigging live wire, this one. I pull my hands away, tuck them under my knees.

"Sorry, man. You okay? I thought you were cold. I didn't mean—"

"I'm fine. It just—it happens sometimes. Never mind."

"Oh—"

"So is this your place or something?" I ask, grasping any thought-string I can.

"My place?"

"The assignment."

"No. Not really."

I laugh. "Then why are we here?"

"Don't know. First place I could think of, I guess."

"Ah. Okay."

He looks down, feet burrowing in the sand. He's lying, but I don't pry, mostly because I don't want to be pried. So I face the water and: whoa. The sun, now a blazing fireball sitting on the edge of the lake, silk-screens the clouds like a Warhol.

"Wow," I say.

"What?"

"That." I don't blink. Because this is the painting I want to live in forever. *I'm lost, surfing the light waves in my mind, caught in the swells, when:*

"Hey, you hear me?"

"Huh?" He's standing now, hand stretched inches from mine.

"Come on, let's go."

"Where are we going?"

"Just come on, jeez!" And somehow he's wrestled my hands free and pulled me up in one fell swoop. This time his hand doesn't electrocute me. It melds into mine. And we're sprinting across the beach, until we stop at the base of the cliff.

"Looks like she's crying again," he says.

But before I can say "Who?" he's thrown himself against the rock, his hands suctioning upupup the side.

"What the hell are you doing?"

"Come on, man! There's a better view up here."

"Up there? Are you crazy?" Panic's rising in my voice, stomach's rising in my mouth.

He looks down. Already he's somehow six feet above me splayed against the rock, his eyes brimming with wildfire. "Yeah, I am," he says. "And so are you. Come on." And—*thwoop thwoop thwoop*—he continues to climb.

"Wait. Stop. It's so steep. What if we don't make it what if we fall what if we die what if we—"

"What if aliens come down and take us away in their ship," he yells.

What? No. A logical answer in other situations, maybe, but not this one.

"Seriously STOP."

"Seriously TRUST ME." He looks back down.

I think I've turned into stone again. Scratch that, I *know* I have. I can't move.

His eyes sink into mine. "Trust me," he says again.

Okay, there is no explaining the next series of events except to say that perhaps aliens did come down and beam me up, because in the next second: slick rock against my palm, steel-toed Chucks locked in a crevice, satchel flopping on my back, I'm climbing. Seriously, climbing. Even though my brain decided to stay behind.

"Yeah, man, that's it, good. Keep going. You can do it—"

He's still talking but I can't hear. Because how in Ziggy's name did I end up on the side of a freaking cliff at *Creve Coeur Freaking Lake*? I don't know. Keep charging forward. Eyes lasered in on the soles of his bare feet, palms licked with sweat and slime so I cannot tell where my hands end and the rock begins. I cannot tell what I am right now.

Yes I can.

I am part of the Fantastic Four. I am the Thing! *Rock bursts through my skin. Lungs expand with so many extra gulps of air I choke on the freedom. As I clamber up I feel more invincible, more unstoppable, the Combatant Rock Climber of—*

My foot slips from under me.

"Sh-boogie shit!" I scream, just in time to see Web hurl himself up. My skin skids across the rock. Hands claw. Legs scramble. "HELP!"

Web peeks over, eyes grow so wide they consume me. "Hold on, man, I got you!" He extends his arm to latch onto mine. "You're not that far. Don't look down, just look into my eyes."

I do. And KER-THWOOP, he swings me over the edge.

Web: flying backward.

Me: clawing forward, nails digging into moss and dirt. I flip onto my back.

And burst into tears.

"Oh, hey, man, you okay?" Web crawls over to me.

"I don't—mean to—sorry, I don't cry—I never cry, I'm sorry I'm sorry I'm sorry . . ." I say through my sobs. I can't stop it. *What is happening to me?*

"S'okay, man, just let it out. I get it. I get it . . ." It sounds like a lullaby, which makes me cry even harder for some reason. He doesn't make a move toward me. I am glad for this: He somehow knows to leave me alone.

I turn onto my stomach, bury my face in the dirt.

Carl Sagan says black holes may be "apertures to an elsewhen." Plunging down one, we'd reemerge in another epoch of time. So I grab a black crayon in my mind and furiously squiggle a black hole, to disappear into another epoch of time.

**13.**

———

IT'S POSSIBLE I DID disappear. I can't be certain. I lie on my stomach for another one thousand nine hundred and seventy-three years until I stop crying.

Here's the thing: The last time I *really* cried was when IT happened. That was four years ago. Dr. Evelyn has always warned me about this moment: *"You can't hold it in forever,"* she'd say. *"Eventually the dam's gotta burst."*

I'm not sure why NOW of all frigging times my brain decides it's time for the dam to burst, but it's done. And the only reason I stop and flip back over is because I've inhaled so much dirt there's a severe dust storm tornadoing through my lungs.

I reach into my satchel, pull out PeterPaulandMary—poofpoof . . . poof poof—two extra for good measure—wipe my face, and sit up.

Web sits cross-legged, staring into what's now become a Van Gogh swirl of setting-sun oranges and pinks and reds and yellows.

I do not know what to say. I do not know what to feel. It's a megastorm of embarrassment and relief that won't stop billowing through me. And at any second I might start crying again. "I'm . . . sorry—"

"Don't," he says.

"Don't?"

"Don't say sorry again, man."

"Oh, I just didn't—"

"No. You just did. You felt It."

"What?"

"The Great Mystery. Happens when you face your fears. You were cracked open, man. It's a beautiful thing."

*Oh. Well, I got a million more fears where that came from,* I think. And I swear he's flipped some switch in my brain to hear my thoughts because the next second he's laughing.

"What?" I ask.

"Your face. It's streaked in mud."

"Oh. Oh God—" I start scrubbing it off.

"Don't do that," he says, holding my hands. "It's kinda cool . . ."

"Oh . . . I . . ."

He stares, tracing my face like I do with Starla. "Wow . . ." he whispers.

"What?"

"Your eyes, I've never noticed them before, they're—"

"Oh. Yeah," I say, jerking my hands back. I plop them in my lap. "Different colors, I know. It's supposed to be hereditary, but no one else in my family has it, and it's weird because my mom and dad have blue eyes, so I've always wondered where the brown one came from and always hated it because *of course* it's just one more thing for the Apes to make fun of."

"Whoa," he says.

Seriously, just whoa. "David Bowie has them, too."

"Far-out."

"Yeah."

His eyes meld with mine and—*I do not notice the stinging sensation zipping through my veins . . . I do NOT . . .* "You're right," I say, my voice quaking. "The view's way better up here."

"Yeah . . . isn't it?" He looks away and I sink into my skin again.

Boy, is it. The view, I mean. Like sitting in the middle of a kaleidoscope.

"Broken heart," he says.

"What?"

"The lake. It's the shape of a broken heart."

"Really?" I sit up on my knees to see.

"Yeah. Some American Indian chick jumped over this cliff because of some white man—of course—breaking her heart."

"For real?"

"It caused the split in the lake."

"Where?" I'm looking, but can't see.

"There." I follow his point, still can't see.

"Where?"

He holds my arm, points it at this barely visible crack in the middle, a darker shade of blue that curves to the edge of infinity.

"There," he whispers in my ear.

"Oh . . . I . . . see it . . . wow."

"They say this waterfall only appears when she's crying, her ghost jumping off the cliff over and over in this kind of never-ending anguish."

His voice prickles my skin. "Seriously?"

"Seriously."

"How do you know this?"

"We American Indians love your legends." He falls back on the grass, laughing.

"It's kind of perfect," I say, lost in the water's ripples.

"What?"

"That we live on a broken heart lake."

"Yeah? Why'sat?"

"Kind of like everything else. Broken heart in a broken city on a broken earth with tons of broken people . . ."

"True . . ."

"Bowie says everything's broken today. What we thought we knew isn't true anymore, and the future isn't as clear as it once was. If we need truths, we can make them up ourselves . . ."

"Deep stuff, man."

We watch the sky turn to a purple-pink.

After a long silence he says, "You shouldn't hide, you know."

"What?"

He looks at me, hair caught in the wind, sweeping the sky, becoming the night. "All those things you've said—"

"When?"

"Just now. And in the bathroom that morning we met. And in class, what you said about the book. I like the way you see things, man. You shouldn't hide it from everyone—"

"How do I see things . . . exactly?"

"I don't know. You're sweet, I guess . . . Compassionate . . ."

"Huh . . ." Whoa. Is that something guys say to each other? And does this mean *You're a stupid nitwit* sweet or *You're the most supreme angel I've ever met in my entire life* sweet? I do not know!

"So, what about love?" he asks.

"What?"

"Our assignment."

"Oh, right. I don't."

"You don't love?"

"Nope."

"Why?"

In the distance, the paper-doll fishermen pull their boats up to shore, and farther down the beach people gather bits of wood into a pile. "You know Carl Sagan?"

"The one you keep bringing up, you mean?" He laughs. "Yeah, I know him."

"Okay. I've been reading his new book and he says the planet Venus is like this big sulfurous star. Broiling temperatures, volcanic lava rivers, noxious gases, all that. Basically, Venus is hell. And, basically, that's exactly what I think of love. Love is hell." As if on cue, the pile of wood in the distance starts to sparkle.

"Wow," he says. "Really?"

"Yeah."

"That's so not true, man."

"Yup. It is. Trust me. Your turn."

"My turn?"

"Yeah. Where'd you move from?"

"Oh, we're playing this game now?"

"Guess so . . ."

"South Dakota. Pine Ridge Reservation. I'm a member of the Oglala Lakota Nation. That's my true home. You know it?"

I shake my head. "I mean, Starla told me some stuff . . . but what's Lakota mean?" He lifts that crooked, dimpled smile again. "What?"

"No one's ever asked me that before."

"Oh . . ." I shrug. "So tell me."

"It means 'friends and allies.'"

"Cool." *That sounds about right . . .*

"There's seven bands of Lakota peoples—like subtribes—and I'm Oglala."

"And what's that mean?"

"You wanna know more?" I nod. The twilight splashes against him, making his skin glow. Carl Sagan starfolk, I swear. "Well . . . it means 'to scatter their own' . . . and, well, you know all those old pictures you see in your history books of Natives in headdresses riding horses and fighting the cavalry, or hunting buffalo on the Plains or whatever? That's usually a depiction of Lakota peoples back in the day—but, hey, man, don't go asking me to do some crazy war-whooping, magical Indian crap for you—"

"Got it."

"We're a strong people," he says, facing the last spatters of sunset. "Made even stronger after living under years of white people's oppression, and we value family above everything—" He stops suddenly.

I wait for him to continue, but he never does. "So you live here now . . . with your family?"

"For now, yeah. But not my *whole* family. That's huge. Just my grandfather and uncle. This guy's letting us stay at his place while we're here . . ." His face is curtained by his hair, so I can't be sure, but . . . is he crying?

"So . . . then . . . why are you here?"

"Sorry, Bowie boy," he says, wheeling back, wiping his cheeks. "Your turn. How'd you get that scar?"

"What? No," I say, swooping my hair back down to cover it. "Too soon."

"Too soon for what?"

"You can't start off easier, like what's my favorite color or some-thing?"

"What's the point, man? Life's too short for trivialities."

"Come on. I like white—"

"Nope, not what I asked—"

"Because it's like a blank slate and—"

"Cool, but about that freaky-ass scar? It's like you're Flash Gordon or—"

"Ziggy Stardust."

"Yeah, man, Ziggy." He reaches toward me.

"Please don't," I say. "I really don't like it—"

"Does it hurt?"

"No. I just hate it and—"

"Come on, then, tell me, it can't be that bad."

"Web. Drop it, really."

"It's your turn, man—"

"God, FINE. I tried to carve a Ziggy flash with my dad's razor, but it hurt so bad I stopped, and now it looks like a fucked-up question mark like I'm the fucking Riddler or something end of story I win."

The sky melts into a dark-purple watercolor. I look down. More shadows dance around the fire below us.

"Whoa," he says quietly.

"Can't believe I just— No one knows I did that. Not even Starla." I feel the tears brimming in my eyes again; I quickly brush them away. God. What is it with this guy? It's like I'm talking into a mirror or something. Or to Ziggy. Or in my imagination . . . But, no, he's really here—

"I won't tell anyone," he says. "I promise."

And, damn, it's like my scar knows we're talking about it: It starts searing through my skin, singeing my brain. "Thanks," I say, not rubbing it, not giving it the satisfaction it seeks.

"It's strange," he says.

"What is?"

"Being here with you. I don't know. I don't really have anyone to talk to, I guess, anyone who'll really listen to me . . . never really thought of that before."

I look up. "Me neither."

"It's kinda nice."

"Yeah . . . it kinda is . . ."

A spark rips through my wrists, burning my thighs. I jump. Fuck.

"You okay?" he asks.

"I just . . . We should get back," I say, standing. "Before it gets too dark. I'd like to at least *see* myself fall to my death on these rocks."

"Yeah, I'm scared of what you might ask me next anyway."

We look at each other, and we laugh.

He pops up, charging in the opposite direction.

"Where you going?" I ask.

"The path over here to take us down."

"Meaning a path that could've taken us *up*?"

"Yeah, man, duh," he says. "But what would've been the fun in that? Come on."

*Is this guy for real?* There's no time to think.

"Hey, by the way, the Riddler's my favorite," he yells, disappearing in the darkness.

"Really?" Cool.

I run to catch up and disappear, too.

## 1-4.

THIS PATH ENDS UP being a perfectly manicured trail that winds like an easy-breezy creek down the hillside. For real.

Still, he holds my hand and leads. The glistening on his back fades in the shadows with the *swishswishswish* of his hair. His smell: peppery sweat and sunshine. His hand: padlocked to mine. I am safe. Especially because I know my life is in no danger from some Rock Descent to My Death.

We reach the bottom in minutes.

"Seriously. That existed earlier," I say when we reach the clearing.

He laughs. "You'll thank me for it one day."

"Doubtful."

"Come on," he says. "I'll take you to your bike."

By now, the beginnings of night are peeking through, like a deep purple blanket that Starla glued some rhinestones to. And booming through the breeze: Wolfman Jack and the Rolling Stones?

"What the hell." Web stops. I fumble into him. The lit sticks from earlier are now a blazing bonfire. A blazing bonfire dotted with dancingdrinkingdrugging Apes and their dates, glowing in their prom night finery. And parked behind them with doors wide open and speakers blaring: Scotty's cherry-red Trans Am. Oh no.

"Let's go around." I grab his hand. He won't budge.

"They're not supposed to be on this side," he says.

"What?" But there's no time to answer. The King Ape grunts. Scotty. "Seriously, let's go."

"No way, man," he says, barreling toward them.

"What? NO." I jump in front of him. "Where are you going? Just leave them."

"What the hell they gonna do to me, man?" he says, fixated on the beasts in tuxedos.

"Trust me. You don't want to find out."

"I'm not scared of them."

"Fine. But I am. Web, look at me. WEB." He does. "It's not worth it. Let's go."

"You shouldn't do that," he says, his eyes pulsating. "You shouldn't let them treat you like that."

"Who the hell cares? They'll get what's coming to them someday. They always do. That's what Dr. Evelyn says, and I—"

"Man, seriously, your doctor don't know shit. No offense? But white people never get what's coming to them. Not ever. Get outta my way."

He pushes past me, an avenger hell-bent on a mission to what, I don't know.

"Well, la-diddy-da. Look who came to join us." Yup, it's Scotty, and yup, he's drunk. "Where's your dresses, girls?"

"What the hell you say, man?" Web yells back.

Oh no.

"Whoa. This kid's got mouth. Might need to get some Dial soap and wash that Indian dirt out."

Apes laugh and make those stupid war-whooping sounds. Original. The girls squeal nervously, trying to pull the Apes back into their arms.

"Come say that to my face, you ugly white boy. I can kick your ass to the moon and back."

JESUS, THIS GUY.

I grab Web's arm. "What's the matter with you? Let's go."

"You should listen to your girlfriend, you little redskin." Scotty guzzles the rest of his beer, throws the bottle in the fire, beats his chest, and belches. "Or maybe you should come over and say that to MY face." He slicks his hair back, then whips off his powder-blue tuxedo jacket in a tangled mess and throws it to the ground.

"STOP it! Both of you!" Samantha yells, flowing over in a powder-blue chiffon something. She's maybe had one too many bottles of everything at this point. "Come on, Scott, no fightin', remember . . . we still have to go to prom . . . it's our special night . . ." She's mauling his chest like a weird cat in heat.

Scotty continues to grunt. "You wanna piece of this, Indian princess? Huh? Huh?" The Apes *hoo-hoo-hoo*. Their dates paw their faces to bring them back to their bra hooks or whatever.

Web's eyes seethe with the fire. No one moves. Then the unthinkable happens: He starts laughing. I'm talking maniac-on-the-loose laughing. A few girls fumble into their Apes' arms, thrown off balance.

"You stupid. Cowardly. Goon," Web says. "You wouldn't know what hit ya if you even tried to get near me."

My heart's hurtling so hard against my chest I swear it's causing seismic waves in the lake. I don't know this person. This is not the person I just shared one of my deepest, darkest secrets with. This person is some dark shadow version of him. And he scares the crap out of me.

Apparently he scares the crap out of everyone else too: Every Ape's mouth hangs open, stuck in his wrath. It's Scotty who eventually snaps us all out of our trance. "What . . . hell . . . call me?" So stunned and shaking, he forgets words.

"You heard me, white boy."

"Web. Stop." It's all I can think to say.

"You . . . how . . . dare you . . ." Scotty's vibrating. His black hair smolders. His face flashes the color of the bonfire. His eyes are a whirling mass of . . . fear? Could it be? I've never seen this look in Scotty's eyes before. It's entrancing. "Come here, pussy. Let me at him." He pushes past a Stunned Ape, but the Wicked Witch of the Midwest grabs his arm.

"NOT TONIGHT." Samantha whips him back. (I know she's not that strong.) "There'll be NO fightin' tonight." She hiccups.

She looks at the other girls, giving them a telepathic all-knowing nod they each seem to understand. They pull their Apes away from the circle, back to the lake, back to their beers, back to their bra hooks.

Only Scotty and Samantha remain.

"You're lucky she's here," Scotty says. "Or I'd—"

"You'd what?" Possessed Web says, not backing down.

"Stop it. Just take him and GO," Samantha says to me. Like I'm his keeper now or something? "GO!" she says again through another hiccup.

I grab his arm. "Come on, Web."

He relaxes, somewhat. Enough for me to move him at least.

As we walk past, she starts cackling, "*I'll get you, my pretty. And that little toothpick creature, too.*" Or it's possible she says, "See you at school." I can't be sure. I can't be sure of anything right now.

When we leave the light of the bonfire, I turn to Web. "Hey. Look at me." He does, still heaving. "Just . . . navigate the negative, remember?" It's a stupid thing to say, but it's all I can think. He's looking in my eyes and—

It works. I think. He's there with me. Just us again, like we were on the cliff. I could be making this up, but . . . I can feel it. Like we're linked together in thought. Like it's a mind-meld. He nods. Does he feel it, too? . . .

Scotty breaks our spell. "You think this is over, girls? Well . . . you can't always get what you want!" And he starts singing the Stones, and the Apes grunt, and the girls dance, and all is right with their world again. For now.

I pull Web farther away to safety. "You okay?" He stares at the ground, maybe drawing his own black hole to disappear into.

"Sorry. I didn't mean to—I gotta go," he says.

"Oh, okay, me—"

And he's gone, melting into the shadows.

I don't wait around for him to come back charging toward the Apes or to give me a high-five goodbye or whatever it is guys do together. I jump on Stingraymobile and pedal for my life away from that Bonfire of Hell and all its evil ways.

I let the breeze whip my thoughtstrings to the stars, pulling them out one by one from my cluttered head. I'm thinking: *What the hell just happened? I can't believe I just shared the secret about my scar. Was Scotty really scared of Web? Was Web crying? Is he okay? Where does he live? Should I try to find him? Who IS this guy?*

As I turn the corner to my street, all my thoughts have floated away. All clear. Huh. Pulling the strings from your head actually works. Cool.

Good thing, too, because as I get closer to my driveway, a whole new set of thoughts comes thwomping through my brain when I see:

*1) A neon-purple black light glowing through the living room window*

2) *Dad and Heather's silhouettes swaying in the purple window*
3) *Dad and Heather's silhouettes actually doing more than swaying. Jesus.*

I open the screen door. Jimi Hendrix rasps. A thick cloud of skunk-weed creates a blinding fog for an easy escape up the stairs. I dart past. A flash of Dad and Heather, buck naked, painting each other with Day-Glo paints that make them look like two bleeding aliens. Don't know. Don't care.

Whambamthankyouma'amSLAM door shut. I jump on my bed. Grab my black marker. Hide under the covers. Draw a black hole. And disappear for good this time to an elsewhen. Where my body isn't being ravaged with this burning pain.

Where we're safe.

And instead of taking the escape pod in my imagination to another galaxy, I go someplace new:

Where Web and I are lying under the stars, still talking about broken everythings.

# 15.

---

*Friday, June 1, 1973*

IT'S BEEN A WEEK. Dad's living his alternate reality *"Leave It to Beaver at Creve Coeur Lake"* life with Heather. Guess she lives in that trailer park. Makes sense. Anyway, he's been gone all week, not back until tomorrow night, and for me this equals *actual sleep.* Good thing, too. Finals week. Aced them all. But that damn Presentation-for-Your-Life still looms in the shadows. Starla's been so supernaturally obsessed with hers we've barely talked. She's basically spent every free second with Lindsey plotting the most *"Outta sight show you've ever seen, baby!"*

So, this is all to say: It's Friday night and Web's coming over to work on our presentation.

Oh man. The thought alone makes my stomach somersault.

I lie in bed waiting, lost in my Day-Glo poster of Neil Armstrong's first footprint on the moon. The purples and pinks are extra-illuminated with the beginnings of twilight painting the sky outside, seeping through my open window. There's no moon out tonight. Kind of perfect actually. A smell of rust in the air. A storm is coming.

The flip-clock on my nightstand clicks over.

7:11. Ch-click. 7:12. Ch-click. 7:13.

He's late. We didn't talk much this week, because of finals and all, which makes me wonder if the whole secret-sharing-on-the-cliff thing actually happened.

7:15. Ch-click. 7:16.

Maybe he's lost. I don't know. I have no idea where he lives, so I drew the map from school for him to follow.

Ch-click. 7:18.

I've never had to give directions to my house before. I've never had anyone over before. God. What was I thinking? Stupidstupidstupid idea. Where's my marker? Hurry up, scratch a black hole in the shag, disappear to another epoch of time.

Ch-click. 7:20. Doesn't work.

Pink Floyd wavers through the floor from the record player in the living room. *The Dark Side of the Moon* album. Patchouli incense perfumes the air. It's the only kind I could find behind the bar. I stashed the boobie-covered ashtray there, too—and Dad's assorted other girlie paraphernalia—and plugged in the still-hanging Christmas lights.

Ch-click. 7:23.

It's no big deal, Collins. You're just friends. That is all. Dr. Evelyn says, *"Good friends are good force fields,"* and that's exactly what he is. Yeah. Maybe I should call Starla to see if she wants to come over and—

Doorbell rings.

He's here.


"Hey."

"Hey."

We stare through the screen door.

Web, in his usual uniform: white ribbed tank, bright blue jeans, and beat-to-hell Chucks, but draped with a shiny black windbreaker like a magic cloak. On it, a white pin, with the silhouette of an American Indian morphing into a peace sign and the letters AIM stamped in red. Web, emptying a bag of sour-cherry candies in his mouth, his lips the color of the red sea. Web, a piece of sun caught in a cage. Web—

"Hey, man, can I come in?"

"Oh. Right. Sorry. Yeah. Sorry—" I rub my wrists together.

He walks past, smells like burnt toast and honey. "Whoa, this is your house?" He saunters down to the living room like he's perusing an art museum.

"Yeah, I guess." I'm still standing at the screen door. Dumbstruck, possibly, that he's actually here. I check the neighbors'. No old pickles peeking through curtains, no lights on at Starla's, no lights on any-where, actually. I'm thinking he sucked up every light he walked past. He's the frigging Star of Bethlehem in my living room. It's blinding.

"So I guess you're rich or something?" he says, brushing his bare feet through the shag. (He flicked off his Chucks the second he walked in.)

"Not really. I don't know." I pick his shoes up and line them by the door. "It's all stupid anyway."

He laughs. "Says the white guy with all the money."

"Oh . . . that's not what I—"

"We're used to it. White people take everything from us—"

"Oh, sorry, I mean—"

"It's all good, man. 'What goes around, comes around . . .'" He lifts a bottle of Jack Daniel's behind the bar, fiddles with the Christmas lights. "We may not have a lot of money, but we're richer in spirit than any white guy I've ever met—no offense."

A burst of thunder cracks through the clouds, followed by a pattering of rain. I jump, grab my chest. *Jesus. Relax, Collins.*

"Who's this?" Web turns to the painting above the fireplace. Some neon paint splotches left over from Dad and Heather's lovefest the other night stain her dress. Effing alien lovers.

"That's Grandma," I say. The painting was finished days before she died seven years ago. She sits, holding a red rose to her lips, looking into her vanity mirror in her favorite dress—the blue-gray one dotted with yellow peonies. Her white-blond hair, the same color as mine, perfectly scooped, coiffed, and sprayed.

"She's beautiful," he says.

"Yeah. She is." *She turns her head and winks.*

"She looks like you," he says, peeking over his shoulder. His eyes sparkle, and then: He dimple-dimple smiles.

"Want something to drink? A Coke, Tab, Bud?" I ask, darting to the kitchen.

"Water's cool," he says, swaying to the music. "Pink Floyd, man. Right on. Such a good song. *MONEYYY . . .*"

I run back. He's still singing, but on his knees now, flipping through the records. I sit by him on the steps.

"Intense collection," he says.

"Music's my church!" Yup, said that out loud. Forgot about the whole can't-control-thoughts-escaping-my-mouth-when-he's-around thing.

"Really?"

I mumble something that's supposed to sound like *"Yeah, whatever,"* but instead it comes out, *"Shubbuddudba,"* so I shove the glass of water in his hands, close my eyes, and start swaying to the music like him.

"Far-out. Never thought of it like that, but yeah, I can dig it—OH, NO WAY!" My eyes spring open. "This is my A-bomb heaven right here, man!" He's holding *Tapestry* by Carole King.

"Really?"

"Oh yeah . . . *a tumb-a-lin' down* . . ." He sings this while shaking his chest back and forth. He flips his hair back and curls his tongue.

I laugh. "You know you look like Cher, right?"

"Uh-huh. BAZOW!" He busts out a Sonny and Cher album. Damn. Thought I hid that one. "So, does that make you my Sonny?"

"Oh. Uhh . . ."

"Just kiddin', man. I dig these guys. Little folksy for me, but you know—OH, NO WAY." And he's gone again. It's fun to watch. More than a kid ogling candy in a window. He's in the frigging chocolate factory *swimming in the cocoa stream and bouncing on gumdrop flowers and licking whipped cream mushrooms—*

"Hey, I got some grass," he says, snapping me back.

"Oh. Okay." Secret: Never tried it before.

"We don't have to, though, whatever you want."

"No, no, it's groovy . . . man." God, seriously, when I try to sound cool I sound like Jiminy Cricket.

"So, okay . . . got a light?" He holds the joint up.

"Oh yeah, sorry, yeah." I duck under the bar.

"Hey, you sure you want to do this? Really, it's no big deal."

"Yeahyeahyeah."

"Ever smoked?"

"What? Oh, uh, yeah, uh-huh, lotsa times." God. We have eighteen thousand lighters and now I can't find one. "Here you go," I say, like a rabid puppy.

"Oh." SweetBabyZiggy, it's the silver one shaped like a penis and the flame sparks out of the hole. Yes, really. "Wow. Okay, then."

"Flibbityboops." Actually comes out of my mouth.

"What?"

"Nothing. Never mind. I—"

He lights the joint. "Don't make me laugh." His voice sounds strained. He's inhaling so deep, he sucks up all the oxygen in the room. God, does it hurt? Are his lungs exploding? "I put some tobacco in it. Better that way." Probably why it smells a thousand times better than the usual skunk spray. But seriously, how is he still breathing? Is he dying? I'm suddenly regretting not paying attention to the CPR lecture in health class. I just kept looking at that dummy's mouth and seeing the Ancient City of Germs—

"Here," he says, handing me the joint.

Okay, yes, alright, my turn.

I don't move.

He smiles. "So gently suck on it like you would a straw getting the last drops of a yummy milkshake."

He actually says this. Okay, alright, yes, I can do this. I inhale. *Oh, holy whoa, oh, no, oh—*

"Good, man, now take another quick, deep inhale like this, but don't cough."

I do. And SH-BOOGIE-BLAMMO it chars my lungs. *WHAT THE HELL WERE YOU THINKING, COLLINS? Stupid stupid stupid. Don't cough, don't cough, don't cough. Why don't you cough? Coughing's good. Coughing's good when HOLY HOT CHARCOALS ARE DRIBBLING DOWN YOUR THROAT and—*

"You can let it out now," Web says.

I do. Along with a Cyclone Cough that spins us to the Land of Oz, and I think my lungs are on fire and HELP—

*"Herestopletmehelpyou."* He tries to pat my back but I'm running around the room looking for a bucket of ocean to swallow.

"JONATHAN. STOP. HERE."

He hands me his glass of water. I gurgle, cough, spit . . . all over his face.

"Oh . . . Whoa," he says.

That image—of Web flicking water from his eyes and brushing away hairs stuck to his cheeks—makes me laugh so hard it sweeps me away to another dimension, and I'm going,

going,

gone.

*Dots of starlights on either side of me blast into hyperdrive and we're sailing, sailing, sailing through a Carl Sagan wormhole.* To boldly go where no man has gone before!

*Redorangeyellowgreenbluepurple redorangeyellowgreenbluepurple light waves splash against my flailing body. The blue-green star planet now just a teeny dot I see every 360 degrees. Flying so fast. In an ocean of nothing. In a black sea of everything. I have no spacesuit. No helmet. No breath. Nothing. Choking, gasping—*

"HEY." Web slaps my back. "Hey, man, look at me." He grabs my face. My head feels like it's going to flop right off or float away like a big red balloon. His eyes: two whirling galaxies. His skin: glittery dust. I make a wish and blow on him to see if he floats away.

"HEY." He slaps my face.

"OW. What'd you do that for?"

"Look in my eyes."

"I AM."

"No. Stay with me. You're breathing funny. You okay?"

Wait. I am? Oh crap, I am. The trapped breath: gnashing at my lungs, steeling to get out.

"What do I do?" Web yells.

"PeterPaulandMary," I wheeze out.

"What? What are you talking about? The record? JONATHAN. Stay here. Look in my eyes. I'm right here. Right here for you."

"Behind bar," I say. "Inhaler."

He darts up and flashes back in two seconds, I swear.

"Here," he says.

"Jesus." Poofpoofpoofpoofpoof: My superhero elixir springs my lungs back to life, and *ahhhhhhhhhhhhhhhhh*, I fall back on the shag.

We sit in silence for a few minutes.

"Man," he says. "You scared the shit outta me. You okay?"

"Yeah. Thanks . . ."

"Peter Paul and Mary? What the hell, dude?"

I shrug. "Inhaler's so boring. Like, ''Ello. I'm an inhaler. I help you inhale.'" I say this with a British accent. I have no idea why.

He laughs. "Right on."

"Also, I named it after Grandma's favorite group. After she died, I got asthma. This way, she's still living in me."

He stops laughing. "That's beautiful, man."

Our eyes meet.

"I think I should sit up now," I say.

He pulls me up, and, whoa, okay, I am most definitely, without a doubt, one thousand percent, stoned out of my gourd. I'm guessing that's what this is anyway. We're back in my living room but everything's moving in hyper-color overdrive.

"Wuh-owww," I say.

"Yeah, wow . . ."

"Damn, this really is a good song."

"Oh man, yeah. 'Brain Damage' is so bitchin'. Pink Floyd gets it."

"Yeah, they totally get it. Oh! I have an idea." I drag over two yellow beanbag chairs that were stuffed in the corner. We plop down, squish ourselves in, and look up at the ceiling. "That's better, right?"

"Yeah, man. *So* much better."

We sway to the music, our hands doing some synchronized-swimming-through-the-stars thing. *"I'll see you on the DARK SIDE . . . OF THE MOON . . ."* we belt to the heavens at the same time—surprising each other—and burst out laughing.

"It's fun seeing you like this," he says.

"Like what?"

"I don't know. At school, you're so . . . quiet."

"Oh. And you're not all ''Ello, me name's Web and I live on Desk Island, where no one can talk to me and I won't talk to anyone.''" Seriously what is happening with this British thing?

"You are so weird."

"*Different*, you mean?"

"Yeah, man . . . different."

"Best part about me," I say, from out of nowhere. Who is this guy? I like this guy. I feel like I'm carbonating. Like I just downed three bottles of Fizzy Lifting Drink.

"That it is, Jonathan. That it is . . ."

My hands still soar through the air. "Not as weird as you, though."

"You think I'm weird?"

"Well, not weird, exactly . . . Mysterious."

"Mysterious, huh?"

"Yeah."

"You like mysterious?"

I smile.

"Anyway. It's totally different for me," he says.

"How?"

"Because, man, I don't fit in here."

"And what, you think I do?"

"Well, yeah. For one, you're white."

"Uh. What about Starla and, like, I don't know, all the other black kids at our school? That means nothing."

"It means *everything*." The word flings from his mouth; I drop my hands. "You can't know what it's like . . ." he whispers.

"Sorry . . . I didn't mean . . ."

The record ends. Needle clicks back to starting position. Player clicks off. We lie in silence.

"And if you tell me to navigate the negative, I'm going to tickle you to death."

So I do. Just to see if he means it.

He does.

"WEB! Stop! Oh my God! Stop!"

"I warned you!" He straddles my waist. A spark zips through me.

"OW. STOP. Seriously, stop! I can't breathe."

"Oh. For real?" Starman looks down on me. Christmas lights twinkle all around him. Black hair flows like a stormy sea.

"I mean, no. Not like that. I mean— We need music." I spring up, flipflipflipping through the records, like someone pressed Fast-Forward on my tape recorder. Trying to find the perfect song right now. "Ugh. Where is she?"

"Who?"

"Roberta."

"Who's Roberta?"

"Roberta Flack." He shrugs. "You don't know Roberta Frigging *Flack*?!" He shakes his head. "She is the Supreme Soul Goddess of the Universe, The Mother of All That IS. Her voice drips honey and slathers you with kisses and you just roll around in its sticky sweetness for the rest of your life forever glued to her heartbeat, because DAMN, that girl will take you on a rocket ship to your dreams and never return."

He stares at me. "Whoa."

"Yeah. Whoa is right," I say, flipping through the albums again.

"So I guess you like her?"

"What?" *Where's her album?* I hear Web laughing behind me, which makes me start laughing, and the album covers soon join in. *Diana Ross might be right for this moment, or Carole King could be good, too, OH OH, Aretha Franklin? No but yes but no—*

Oh. Dusty Springfield's *The Look of Love*. She'll do. I start the record. Then plop back on the beanbag of sunshine. Oh yeah, she'll do just fine. I close my eyes. I know he's looking at me because I can smell his sour-cherry-candied breath.

"Our friendship doesn't depend on things like space and time," he says eventually.

"What?"

"The quote Mr. Dulick gave us from the seagull book. For our presentation?"

"Oh. Right. Forgot about that."

"*If our friendship depends on things like space and time,*" he says again, "*then when we finally overcome space and time, we've destroyed our own brotherhood! But overcome space, and all we have left is Here. Overcome time, and all we have left is Now.*"

I look over. "That's the quote he gave us? You memorized it already?"

"It's deep stuff, man. Beautiful."

He tucks some hair behind his ears and has a grin stretched across his face. He looks like a cartoon. I start giggling.

"What?" he says.

"I don't know. Guess we should work on the presentation or something—"

"Yeah . . . guess so."

"It's hard to concentrate . . ." I say.

"Sure is . . ."

"Your eyes are so—I don't know—they do something weird to me . . ."

"Yeah? Yours do something weird to me, too, Jonathan . . ."

"I know. The Apes make fun of them all the time—"

"That's not what I meant."

"God. I just thought of something," I say, sitting up.

"What?"

"The Apes. And Scotty. He's been sick. We haven't seen him since that night at the lake and— Oh man, they're going to have a field day with us up there, they're going to think we're so gay or something and—" I stop myself. Damn. Said that out loud, too. I study him, waiting for a reaction: a nervous tic, flinch, anything.

Nothing. He just stares back.

"Why?" he finally asks.

"Because . . . I don't know—"

He lifts that dimpled smile. "Who cares what they think?"

I close my eyes. Dusty Springfield purrs in the background and I just now notice my wrists and thighs are burning. Screaming. Oh man. "I . . . feel like I'm on a rocket ship to the moon . . ." I whisper, pulling whatever thoughtstring I can find. Because I do.

"Me too. *There's a starman waiting in the—*"

"Holy sh-boogie YES!" I jump up.

"What? What happened?"

"Of course. That's it."

"What? What's it?"

"Come on. I want to show you something." I duck under the bar, grab the two black lights, and start to lead him up the stairs. "Wait. Grab those." I point to the beanbag chairs.

He does, plunks them on his head. I giggle.

"What?" he says.

"You look like a snow cone," I say.

"What?"

"Never mind. Come on!"

The snow cone follows me to my bedroom.

# 16.

"OH CRAP, THE RAIN!" I bound over to my desk. Dammit, left my window open. The windowsill's soaked. My curtains hang like homemade pasta noodles. The cassette tapes on my desk . . . dry. Whew.

The white glow of the streetlamp buzzes on and streams through as makeshift moonlight. (I leave the lights off on purpose.) I've started to pull the window down, when he stops me.

"Wait!"

"What?"

"Why you closing that?"

"Because it's raining?"

"So? Don't you ever run outside when it storms?"

"Uh, no."

"Oh man, you're so missin' out. I do it all the time. Helps clear away the clutter in my head. You gotta *feel the rain, man*," he says like a spaced-out hippie, laughing.

"I just don't want my tapes to get wet."

"So move them." I do.

"Come here." He sits on my desk, pats the spot next to him. "Now lean out a little—don't worry, I gotcha." And he does, his arms wrapped around my waist. I ignore the electric current zipping through me because:

Whoa.

The wind's whirling through the cottonwood tree, a vibrating mass of leaves like it's the Earth's tambourine. We're so close to the tree my body's shaking with it. *Ohmanohmanohman, it DOES feel good.* The cool rain streaks the sky, pinging the roof, dousing my wrists and forehead and thoughts. I close my eyes. "*Whambamthankyouma'am-* SHA-ZAM!" It rips out of my mouth. I can't help it. I don't care.

"Yeah, man, right on. See? You feel it, right?"

"OHmanohmanohmanohmanohmanohman."

"Yeahyeahyeah."

He's laughing. I'm orgasming. Wait, am I? I pop my eyes open and look down. No tent. Whew.

"Too bad the moon's not out," he says.

"The moon. That's right. That's why I brought you up here." I bounce off the desk.

"What are you doing?"

"You. Wait there. No, come down here on the floor next to me."

"Uh—"

I grab the black lights, and start feeling the wall for the outlet. There. Plugged in. "Okay, you ready for this? Well, come on!"

He leapfrogs down next to me. "What are we looking at?"

"You want to go to the moon with me?"

"Yeah." He's dimple-dimple smiling. I can feel it in the dark.

"Look ahead. Ready?"

"Uh-huh."

I flip on the black lights.

Whoa.

It's *way* better than I imagined.

The poster hanging on my wall springs to life. *And in one fell Carl Sagan swoop, we're teleported to the surface of the uranium glass moon. Web's laughing, I think. Can't hear him. Space swallows any noise. We kick up a moondust storm with our bare feet. It's soft and tickles the toes and strangely smells like coconut suntan lotion. We stop at Neil's footprint, a perfect neon-orange oval with perfectly carved ridges.*

Not one of them broken.

"Holy whoa," he says.

"I know."

"'2TM 4VR A.L.' Who's A.L.?" he asks, reading the inscription on the bottom of the poster.

"My aunt Luna . . ."

And like that, just saying her name, I'm transported back to the one misty morning in our living room . . . And the sounds of the moon landing start beaming through the TV:

*Beep . . . beep . . . whooosssssshhhh . . .*

*Beep . . . beep . . . whoooosssssshhhh . . .*

The lunar module enters the left side of the screen. We scream. I'd made a spacesuit for the occasion out of two black garbage bags, crinkly dryer hoses for arms and legs, and a fishbowl covered in aluminum foil.

Aunt Luna had donned her favorite fluorescent green floor-length dress. She'd covered her face and arms in Day-Glo green makeup, and made a headband with pipe cleaners and cotton balls she'd colored with green marker that boingboingboinged in all directions. Her inspiration: *My Favorite Martian.*

Dad had molded these pointy ears out of Silly Putty and dressed up like Spock. But it was so hot that day they kept melting, so he ended up looking like Dumbo.

Which made us laugh and laugh and laugh.

We eat MoonPies and moon pizzas and moon milkshakes made with Oreos, glued to the TV with the rest of the world.

*Beep . . . beep . . . whooosssssshhhh . . .*

The lunar module going down . . . down . . . down . . . a poof of moondust . . . Aunt Luna Martian wraps us with her tentacled arms, crushes my spacesuit against her. Spock Dad beams on the other side. We're one big ball of alien love.

Then: *"The* Eagle *has landed."*

We wail to the heavens and I'm sure I see Neil Armstrong look around to see where it came from. He bounces down, step by step, floating, airless, free.

*Beep . . . beep . . . whoooosssssshhhh.*

*Beep . . . beep . . . He's on the moon!*

We scream again. I'm trying to see. My breath fogs up the glass. Aunt Luna is a glowing swirl of green, her face now streaked with white from the tears washing away the paint. Spock Dad smiles so big it fills the room.

*"That's one small step for man . . . one giant leap for mankind."*

Aunt Luna lifts me in the air. I'm crying, but I don't know why. She turns my fishbowl to face her and slaps it with a big green gooey kiss. We're spinningspinningspinning in a plastic crinkle tornado. All I see is the radioactive love beaming from her eyes. And Spock Dad's smile whooshing by like we've entered warp speed.

*"To the moon, Jonathan, to the moon! We just went to the moon!"* That's all she kept saying over and over, and I saw her spinning, and Neil Armstrong bouncing, and Dad still smiling through one gooey green kiss, and it was the first and only time I understood the meaning of love.

"Whoa, really?" asks Web.

I snap back. God. Didn't even realize I was talking out loud. "Oh. Yeah . . ."

"What happened to her?" he asks.

"Don't know. She disappeared the next morning . . . Sent this poster to me from Woodstock a few weeks later. Haven't heard from her since."

"Damn, man."

"Yeah."

We're lost, drifting in space.

"You ever lose someone close to you like that?" I ask softly.

He's quiet for a long time, then: "Yeah."

"Who?"

He does not answer.

"Web?"

Silence.

Still.

Nothing.

Then: "Jonathan?"

"Yeah?"

He slowly inches his fingers over my palm.

My breath stops.

"Okay?" he asks.

*No. I can't do this. I shouldn't do this . . .* "Okay," I whisper.

A zing. His fingers tickle mine. Carefully. Tenderly. We clasp our hands. My heart vibrates. A stab of electricity shoots down my spine. He tightens his grip. I don't move. I don't breathe. I don't know.

Then gently,

delicately,

I squeeze our hands together.

The world falls silent.

A tear trickles down my cheek.

And another.

I don't want to let go . . .

But it hurts. I can't do it.

"I think . . . some music would be good right about now," I quiver out.

"Oh, okay," he says.

"I'll be right back."

I disappear into my closet. My heart's afire. Everything in me burns. I wipe my eyes. Ziggy eyes sparkle all around me.

*Mom turns her head, smiles and says, "You're okay, Beetlebug."*

Yes. I am okay.

I sweep up the album and record player, and dry my eyes again to be sure. When I step back into my room, Web's sitting on a beanbag chair holding my tape recorder.

"Hey," he says.

"Hey." I drag the record player across my room.

"So where'd you just come from?"

"My closet. There's this little room in there that—" I freeze. Oh. Man.

"Cool. Can I see?"

"No! I mean—sorry—no one knows about it—I mean—one day . . . maybe . . . ?"

"It's good, man. Your secret's safe with me . . ."

We look at each other and smile.

"So, this is cool," he says. "Ever use it?" He clicks the buttons on my tape recorder, twists the microphone.

"All the time." There's only one album to play right now, so I slide it out of its sleeve and place it on the turntable. Lift the needle, slide it over: white-noise static, steady *ch-ch-ch-ch* drums, *strrrrrummmmm* of guitar . . . *ahhh*. Ziggy. Never fails.

"Excellent song," he says. "Damn, you're right about his voice. It's like from another planet."

"That's Ziggy's story actually," I say, drumming the air with my fingers.

"Really?"

"Mm-hmm. He came down from the stars to save all the lost people of the world, until they took so much from him they ravaged his soul and he became bits of stardust forever floating through the sky."

"Far-out."

"Yeah, He is definitely my Messiah—" *Dammit. There I go again.*

"Right on, man. So, you wanna record something now?" he asks.

"What?"

"On your tape recorder."

"Really?"

"It'd be fun."

"Well . . . I guess. If you want. Grab a tape from the desk." I slink over next to him. We lie on our stomachs, propping ourselves up with our elbows, facing each other. I push Play/Record:

"Test. One, two, three. Hello out there. This is Jonathan Collins reporting to you live from the moon. I'm here with—what's your name, sir?"

"Web."

"You have to talk into the mic."

"Oh. WEB."

"Whoa, not that close."

"Sorry. Web Astronaut."

"Better. Okay. Mr. Astronaut, what brings you to the moon today?"

"I came here to find something."

"Okay, what did you—"

"And to get away from all the people on Earth."

"Why do you want to do that, Mr. Astronaut? Why are you laughing?"

"This is weird."

"You wanted to do it."

"Okay. Okay."

"So, Mr. Astronaut. Why did you want to get away from all the people?"

"Because, man, everyone down there's all FUCKED UP—"

"Web. Language. And not so close to the mic, it gets distorted."

"Sorry. But it's true."

"Why do you say that?"

"Because those people? They got it all wrong. They think they're doing good with their fighting and ignorance and discrimination and all that. But really, they're killing the earth with it."

"Yeah."

"So that's why I'm here. On the moon. It's safe and quiet here, Mr. Collins."

"It really is."

"No one to bother us, no one to hurt us. Just us."

"Just us . . ."

"On the moon."

"On the moon . . . together . . . where nothing's broken—"

"And we float to the stars like your Ziggy—"

"And overcome time and space to get here, like Pink Floyd does in *Dark Side of the Moon*—"

"So all we have left is Now."

"Hey, like the quote for our presentation!" I yell.

"Yeah! We can do it on the moon!"

"With music!"

"Yeah!"

"By gum, I think maybe we just figured out our assignment, Mr. Astronaut!"

"Good. Now that that's done and we're still on the moon, you have to answer me this deep and personal question about your childhood, Mr. Collins."

"Oh, wait, I thought I was the reporter—"

"What's your favorite Popsicle flavor?"

"HA!"

"Not so close to the mic—"

"Right. Easy. Bomb Pop. You?"

"Oh, for sure it is the Push-up Pop. Orange all the way."

"Good one . . ."

"Yeah . . ."

We're silent for some time, still facing each other.

"I like being on the moon with you, Mr. Astronaut," I whisper.

"We can come here anytime we want, Jonathan."

"We can stay here forever."

"I'd really like that," he says softly.

"You would?"

"Yeah . . . I would . . ."

". . . Me too . . ."

He takes my hand, traces some lines on my palms. It stings, but I ignore it. "And maybe one day we won't have to come all the way up here to be safe, you know? Maybe one day we can stay . . . down here . . . you know?"

"Maybe . . . one day . . ."

"Yeah . . ."

"Yeah . . ."

"So . . . Web Astronaut . . . did you find what you were looking for?"

"Yeah, Jonathan. I think I did."

That was recorded hours ago. Now here I am again. Alone. Lying on my bed, staring at the Day-Glo moon poster, without the Glo, flipping his jacket-pin around in my hand. (It fell off when he bounced down the stairs to leave.) I think I'll put it in my closet next to his note. To keep him safe. For now.

I rewind and play the tape over and over again,

listening to his voice,

listening to my voice,

listening to us . . . together . . . in our imagined world that's more real than anything I've ever felt before—

*How can a feeling be so bad if it makes me feel so good?*

I don't know . . .

I close my eyes, still feeling the softness of his palm wrapped in mine.

# 17.

---

THE NEXT MORNING, church is canceled.

Starla's *"too overwhelmed with the presentation and end-of-school-year stuff and just everything else going on. Please don't hate me, okay?"*

*"I could never,"* I said.

Anyway, I'm way too distracted by last night, so I jump on Stingraymobile—the second-best thing to do in Creve Coeur on a Saturday morning—and let the wind funnel through my thought-strings. I whiz through the neighborhoods, zigzag through boys playing baseball in the street, the fresh-cut grass stinging my nose. I disappear in the sun's rays so no one sees me.

I pedal and pedal and pedal, navigating my never-ending thoughts about being with Web on the moon. *Yes, it was real. Yes, it happened. And yes, this is a terrible-no-good thing. You know better, Collins. We can only be friends. Just friends. Friends hold hands. That's normal. Look at Starla. You hold hers all the time and it's fine—but—the way he held yours was so different. Careful. Fragile, even. I don't— No. You cannot. You must not—*

Stingraymobile stops. I'm back at the lake.

Laughter radiates across the waters. I make a visor with my hands.

Dad at the trailer park. A round little boy squeals at his feet, bounces up and down. Dad kisses the top of his head, then lifts him on his shoulders and runs in circles through clothes hanging on the line, galloping like a horse. Heather watches, laughing.

I pedal down the beach, stopping at the crying cliff, and squint up, trying to see through to the clearing. He's not there.

I ride back down the shore, stuffing crushed cans and bottles and trash in my satchel. I remember Starla taking me downtown to the first Earth Day protest a few years ago, screaming under the Arch, *"If you aren't part of the solution, you're part of the pollution."* Man, am I going to miss her . . .

Back and forth I pedal.

Sand and pebbles and thoughtstrings kick up all around me, nicking my legs, biting my thighs.

Back and forth.

I'm waiting for him to appear out of nowhere like last time, so we can talk about American Indian princesses and Carl Sagan starfolk and broken secrets—

And then it happens. I see him. I almost call his name, but stop myself, and quickly hide behind a rock. He's bounding down the steps of one of those shanties on stilts, the ones that loomed behind us when we first met on the beach.

"I'll be right back!" he calls out to someone or no one, I'm not sure. His hair whooshes behind him like a sea of raven feathers and he's flying, flying, flying to the forest of oak trees, disappearing in its thick, canopied shadows. Gone.

Oh.

*This* is where he lives.

I should go. I need to go. Before he comes back, before he sees me.

I jump on Stingraymobile and try to pedal, but only get a few feet. She won't budge. I'm stuck. My heart tries to break free from its connecting valves.

I look down. Of course. It's THE spot. How could I not recognize it from last time we were here? Where the Prom Night Bonfire from Hell once blazed, now only a dry puddle of blackened ash and scattered gray sticks and broken glass remains. My only proof I did not make it up.

The spot.

Where IT happened.

Four years ago. The Hateful Summer of '69. The summer of my first kiss. Right here. A moment that's supposed to be branded forever in time, a moment I'm supposed to forget. Right here.

The moon had only been stamped with Neil Armstrong's footprint for a month. We looked up and talked about that and whispered to each other, and our arms crisscrossed behind our backs, our hands in each other's pockets. And we turned, leaned in, our lips smashing together, sparking every nerve in my body to life for the first time. And then we—

My eyes spring open.

A rustle in the trees behind the shanty.

"Who's there?" I yell. No one answers. "Web?" Another rustle, then a figure disappearing in the shadows of the forest. I look down.

A tent in my shorts. Oh no. Was Web watching me? Did he see? Oh man. Reason #3,279 I hate wearing shorts: They're too tight, too small, and hide NOTHING. I adjust my boner, pack it away for the day. Forever.

I hop back on Stingraymobile. Sort of. I wiggle myself on the seat until I can pedal away, shoving the memory back into a black hole. Trust me, it's better that way. For me, for him, for the universe . . .

Can barely hold the handlebars, my wrists crackle.

Can barely see, my eyes fill with water.

Can barely pedal, my legs are two electric live wires.

I ride up our driveway, wobble inside.

I pull the Ziggy album off my desk, hide under the covers.

"You there?" I ask. He's so blurred from my tears he looks like he's a fading mirage. "Zig? You there? I need you. I need to talk to you."

But for some reason, he never answers.

## 18.

*Wednesday, June 6, 1973*

I CAN'T FOCUS ON anything right now.

It's the last two hours of junior year and the Presentation-for-Your-Life has finally arrived.

We're sitting in Dulick's classroom—excuse me, the *BROADWAY STAGE*. God. A white sheet-curtain drapes down from the ceiling in front of us with "LOVE IS FREE" spray-painted at the top.

We've only seen each other at school since that night in my bedroom. And we've only practiced our presentation twice. And except for the times he had to keep reminding me the Apes weren't going to beat us to a bloody pulp for our idea, we've barely spoken.

It did make me wonder if everything that happened that night actually happened. Good thing it's tape-recorded, because there's no doubt about it: It was real.

He's back on Desk Island, staring down at his feet, jiggling his legs so fast I swear he's trying to paddle to Hanoi. Yeah, I feel ya, brother.

I recite the lines Dulick gave us from the seagull book over and over again in my head, while watching snippets of other presentations:

1. Firecrotch and Adam Worthlesston covered the "stage" in plastic, handed raincoats to the front-rowers, and played a rousing rendition of

the last scene from *Romeo and Juliet*. Typical. Boring. (And not without irony: Her parents refuse to let them go together because he's *poor and lives at the lake.*) So they reenvisioned it as the final scene from *The God-father*, killing everyone in their families instead, splattered red paint and all. And at the end they screamed, *"Your hate will never kill our love!"* Lacey cried because she didn't put her raincoat on and looked like a "bloody maxi" (the other girls' words, not mine).

"B!" screamed Dulick from the back of the room. "An interesting, albeit morbid vision on the power of requited love."

2. Starla and Lindsey dressed as two nuns and reenacted the crucifix-ion of Christ, crying real tears at His feet. And I mean *real* tears. I don't know how she did it, how she made herself weep like that, but manohman she had everyone bawling with her. Even Scotty. Then, when Jesus came off the cross in the Resurrection—which was actually a life-size card-board cutout of Donny Osmond swathed in a bedsheet—they threw off their black habits to reveal sparkly gold minidresses underneath, and ran around the room making everyone clap along like we were in their gospel choir. Very *Jesus Christ Superstar.*

"A," Dulick sobbed. "Music *is* the food of love! Play ON!"

3. Scotty, who usually doesn't take anything seriously, except for talking about sex and beating up toothpick creatures, surprised me the most. He walked out dressed as a FULL-ON WOMAN. I'm talking big boobies made from water balloons, I'm guessing, blond Marilyn wig, skintight sheer white minidress that left NOTHING to the imagination, and smeared makeup that Samantha probably did for him. He ran behind the sheet after singing some warped version of "Happy Birthday, Mr. President."

Then Ape Cory came out dressed as President Nixon, mask and all, waving his hands in flopping peace symbols saying, *"I never did it!*

*I never did it!"* He joined Scotty behind the sheet and they acted like they were MAKING OUT, holding a sign at the end that said, LOVE CAN BE CLOAKED IN LIES.

Yes, everyone laughed. And yes, Dulick gave them a "B for taking a risk and making a social commentary at the same time!"

Then: "Jonathan and Web. You're up, daddios!"

He yells it even though I'm sitting right next to him, and like Pavlov's dog, the second I hear my name I almost immediately poop my pants. But as calmly as possible I say, "I need five minutes, please. May I be excused to the restroom?"

He says, "Of course, my man, take all the time you need."

Web shoots me a look and I reassure him with a quick nod to set up the room and take his place.

I bolt to the bathroom and stare in the mirror. Hard. David Bowie once said the reason he became a rock-n-roll star was because, *"If you just amass the courage that is necessary, you can completely reinvent yourself. You can be your own hero."*

So I summon the almighty forces of every superhero ever created and I ask them, for just five minutes of my existence, to help me be someone else.

And five minutes later, that's exactly what happens.

I peek my head through the small window in the class—*STAGE*—door.

Blinds have all been closed. Check. Starla sits in the back with the record player ready. Check. Two black lights are plugged in. Check. Web sits on Dulick's desk staring at the linoleum, kicking the front of it with his bare feet every few seconds. Check. His face and body are streaked with Day-Glo paint, barely visible in the regular fluorescents—but I can tell they're there—and he's shirtless. Some girls are *whisperblushgiggling* to each other. Ready to kill or pounce, I'm not sure.

Everyone else: my *National Geographic* closet pages sprung to life. Animals dangling on their desk chairs, grunting, laughing, mating. And me: a space invader, looking at a petri dish labeled SUBSPECIES: HORMONAL TEENAGER.

Deep breath. Close my eyes. Open the door. Across the room the needle skips, and everyone goes silent. I open my eyes and witness the literal manifestation of jaws dropping.

Web's wearing a thin black mask. *His idea, because he wanted to be as anonymous as possible and hide his soul from the classroom.* He looks at me. And smiles. "Just us, remember? To the moon," he whispers.

I flip off the lights and lift my arms, extending the long white silk of Starla's kimono, and glide across the room. Underneath, I'm wearing our tiny white gym shorts and Starla's white lace-up boots that lift all the way to my knee, and nothing else.

I'd studied his picture so many times I had it memorized by heart, so when I threw the makeup on it was like I had been doing it my whole life: extra-bright white powder splashed all over my face, a sea of shimmery pink streaked across each cheek, and a huge golden glittery moon in the middle of my forehead.

I am Ziggy Stardust.

I take my place behind the desk.

Web takes his in front. "You look amazing," he says.

"So do you." I give a slight nod to Starla, ignoring the Ape growls in the front row, and SweetBabyZiggy here we go.

White-static noise. Needle hits the place on the record: "Time" by Pink Floyd from *The Dark Side of the Moon* album.

A low rumble lifts from the player's speakers.

*Ticktock, ticktock, ticktock, ding-dong ding-dong, cuckoo cuckoo*: a thousand clocks crescendo to a loud *BRRRRINNNNGGGG, BRRRIINNNGGG, BRRRIIIINNNGGG.*

Plug in black lights. KAPOW. Web's Day-Glo paints spring to life. Two neon-red streaks fall from his eyes like a stream of tears. On his chest: a fluorescent blue earth pulsates with his breaths.

A collective gasp from the audience.

WAY better than I imagined.

*Cl-clock, cl-clock, cl-clock, cl-clock*, a drum of heartbeats pulses through the rings on the record.

*STRRRRRUUMMMMMM* of the bass guitar.

"I AM TIME," he yells, with a little extra force. He lifts his arm and moves it inch by inch like the second hand on a clock. "I am The Man. The only one here in control. I make your thoughts. I give you power." He claps his hands above his head and freezes.

*Cl-clock, cl-clock, cl-clock, cl-clock*, another *STRRUUUMMMMMM*.

I slowly rise behind him. "I am space," I say. It squeaks out of my mouth like a goddamn gerbil. I close my eyes, remember who I've become, begin again. "I AM SPACE," I yell. *Yes, yes, oh yes I am.* I stand on the desk and lift my arms. "I am chaos. I am your true voice. I am different. I am here to make you feel."

"Like a queer," Scotty says. The Apes grunt.

*STRRRUUUUMMM. Da Da DUUUMMMMMM.*

Web flinches, and for a second I'm sure he's about to run over and punch them in the gut. Instead, he turns to face me. "Space," he says, quivering. "You cannot be with me. You cannot be here. Only one of us can live. And it can only be me. You must leave now!"

"Time," I say, looking down on him. "I will not leave. There is nowhere for me to go. Without me, you would not even exist."

Web leaps on the desk. "No!" he screams. A few girls jump. "You are not allowed to be here!"

*Da Da DUMMMMMMMMMM.*

"I have no choice!" I yell back.

SMACK: He fake-slaps me across the face and I tumble off the desk, planting myself on the floor in a Spider-Man crouch. I hear a few chairs scrape against the linoleum, the audience rising to see.

*Da Da DUMMMMMMMM cl-clock, cl-clock, cl-clock, cl-clock,* the music swells.

He lifts his arms. "Go. Now. You will never survive this Time!"

I spring up. "I will not go! If you don't accept me, one day *you* will die!" I swipe my hands across his chest and smear the blue earth all over him so it looks like a splattered mess of heart—

A shock sweeps through me. For a moment, I jump out of my fake skin back into my real skin. NO. *Not now, not now, not now.* I close my eyes and take a breath before opening them again, looking into his. Set phasers to stun.

"I will not leave!" I yell again, stepping back into Ziggy. "You must embrace me if we are both to live. Embrace me for who I AM!" I jump back on the desk and unsnap my kimono in one sweeping RRRRRIIIIPPPPPP, flinging it above us so it sails down to the floor. Underneath, my chest is covered in the same gold glittery moondust as my forehead.

A few more gasps erupt from the audience.

"I don't know how," he says.

I grab his fists. "We must *see* each other for who we really are. Beyond this form. It is the only way."

*Cl-clock, cl-clock, cl-clock, cl-clock* fades away.

A silence fills the room.

Then: "You're right," he says just over a whisper. "Overcome space, and all we have left is Here."

"And overcome time, and all we have left is Now," I say.

"And the Here and Now is where Love lives," we say together.

We look in each other's eyes as if we're the only two people in the classroom, the only two people in the universe.

Then, softly, he says, "I see you."

"I see you . . ."

And for a few seconds, we are still. I hear nothing, see no one else.

Except Web and me, breathing . . .

Our arms twine together. We slowly pull ourselves into a yin-yang hug, standing on the desk of Mr. Dulick's classroom full of broken people, in broken little Creve Coeur, which sits in the middle of a broken country, which floats on a broken planet, which spins in the middle of a solar system that exists in a galaxy among a bazillion others beyond space and time . . .

Breathe in.

Breathe out.

Breathe in.

Breathe out.

His chest slides against mine, his sweat melting the incessant stings from my treatments, like the raindrops did the other night. His heart pounds so hard and fast I cannot tell which one is actually mine.

I slink back into my skin. Unwind myself from him and fold my arms tightly to my chest. For a second, I'm convinced I actually did stop time: Everyone's expression is frozen.

Then: "Faggots." Scotty breaks the silence with his subspecies asshole fuckface voice.

A few Apes snicker.

I feel Web tighten up next to me. Jesus, not now. The dynamite's lit; his fuse sparks. I grab his arm as Dulick springs up from the back of the room, clapping. He runs down the aisle. Starla looks at me with this half-moonbeam-of-love, half-I'm-not-sure-what look on her face, like when she told me she was leaving for the summer.

"That was . . . I don't know . . ." Dulick says. "I can't find the words . . . It was—"

"Queer-tastic?" Scotty says. Apes grunt. Web's fuse burns down to nothing. My stomach clenches.

"Just . . . beyond, man. Far-out. Outta sight. Fucking beyond."

Well, *this* silences the Apes. Dulick NEVER uses the f-word even though he allows it in class. His face is wet, streaming with tears.

Secret: He does not—I repeat, he does NOT—smell like grass.

"A-plus-plus, man." An extra frigging plus? "This here," he says, turning to the classroom, wrapping an arm around each of our shoulders. "This is how the earth will survive beyond another five years. This."

He's radiating heat like he just swallowed the sun, and beaming at us with the same force. "Thank you," he says, grabbing us in this awkward threesome bear hug thing. "Thank you."

Scotty makes kiss-smack sounds and soft war-whooping calls, and my face is so close to Web's I not only see it, I feel it: Thousands of firecrackers explode in his body.

Oh no.


There's no time to celebrate the victory of Extra Plus Presentation.

The minute the bell rings, Web darts out of the room and disappears. I run to the bathroom to scrub my makeup off and do my quick-change.

Only one class remains of our junior year: the final step to the Gates of Hades, PE.

*Squeak sq-squeak sq-squeak*: fifty tennis shoes jumping and skipping against the waxed wood floor. Dodgeball. Perfect. It smells like the armpits of Satan in here. Seriously, do Apes shower? Are they allowed to bathe? Do they just lick themselves clean? I ask these and a thousand other questions during the *National Geographic* special I'm currently producing in my head: "Killing Collins, the Lame Llama in the Corner."

Coach Peterson throws me in the middle of some wild grunting troop the minute I walk in. I have no idea what I'm doing except to know one rule: Don't let the ball hit you. I must say, it's the one activity I've gotten really good at over the years. Strangely, though, I barely have to move at all today. It's almost like they're purposely avoiding me.

And stranger still, Web never shows. Smart move. Bummed I didn't think to do the same thing: Dash out of school and thrive on the high of Victorious Extra Plus! But, come on, he could've thought of me, too. If nothing else, a *"Bye, have a good summer!"* would've been nice . . .

*Maybe he's conjuring some crazy bonfire in the boiler room and he'll burst through the waxed floor, splintering wood pieces in all directions, slaughtering everyone in sight (except me!) with his fire-breathing pet dragon we named Ziggy Floyd. I'll jump on its back and wrap my arms around Web's waist as we soar into the sunset and—*

Coach Peterson blows his whistle and screams, "COLLINS. Hit the showers!" I look up, the Lone Llama all alone. Dammit. Spaced out again.

When the locker room's metal door creaks open, it is eerily quiet. Like walking-through-a-haunted-house-and-waiting-for-the-next-thing-to-jump-out-at-you quiet. Rows of lockers, empty. Showers, empty. Bathroom stalls, empty. Man, how long did I space out for?

I weave through the locker maze, cupping my hand over my nose, because it smells like the Apes wiped their feces all over the lockers. That, and Ape sweat. Never a good combination. Even the bleachy pine doesn't stand a chance.

For a moment, I breathe a sigh of relief and realize, *This is it. I made it. Junior year complete. Presentation done. Alone at last! Praise Ziggy, I'm alone at last!*

Then I round the corner. And my thoughts are quickly obliterated along with every cell in my body. Scotty and the Asshole Ape Brigade. Clumped together in a huddle of muscle stink, smiles spread across their faces like one big cackling demon.

"Thought you could get off that easy, Collins?" Scotty says. "Told ya at the bonfire we'd be back."

My first thought:

My second thought: *Run.*

I turn around only to smash into an Incredible Redneck, a towering mass of Apeness that makes King Kong paltry in comparison. He even smells like rotten bananas, I swear. His teeth are just as yellow and spotted. He pushes me back.

"Hoo, hoo, hoo! Ah, ah, ah!" The Apes have their toy back. *Think, Collins. Think.* The one superhero gift of being skinny? I'm fast, squirmy, and can slip in and out of the teeniest cracks in the blink of an eye.

I dip down and try to slide between some Ape's legs. His calves clamp against my ribs in a vise grip bear trap. I fling out a noise that sounds like a compressed accordion. The Apes love it.

"Hoo, hoo, hoo! AHAHAH!"

"Where's your girlfriend?" Scotty barks.

PATOOWIE. Some Ape lands a spit wad in my eye. Like acid pouring through my skull. I'm blinded for a few seconds and try to wipe it clean of burn, and when I open my mouth to scream:

PATOOWIE. Another spit wad splashes against my tongue, slides down my throat. I gag. Tastes like rotted tobacco that's been chewed all day and burns holes in my esophagus, I swear.

"Goddamn, he's like a squirmy squirrel," a four-hundred-pound buffoon says. He lifts me up. This only makes the Apes grunt louder.

My mind is paralyzed. I can't think of a single superhero move or escape plan, so I play dead, freezing every nerve in my body, careful not to show an ounce of tremble as I stand in the middle.

"Where's your fucking girlfriend?" Scotty yells, inching closer to me.

"Leave him alone," I squeak out.

"I didn't hear you, FAGGOT." He's inches from my face now.

I try talking to him telepathically, knowing what I really want to say could never be heard by the others: *"We were friends once, remember? We hung out every day. We rode bikes to imaginary worlds. Remember?"*

I swear he hears me: A flash of sadness cyclones through his eyes. His shaggy bangs feather up when he puffs some air. "What'd you say, queer?"

"Leave him alone," I whisper. "Do whatever you want to me. Just leave him out of it."

A smile sweeps across his cheeks. "Well now, boys, ain't that sweet? Wittle Jonathan says we can do whatever we want to him."

"HOOHOOHOO! AHAHAH!"

"What d'ya say, boys? What d'ya think we should do?" His eyes creep all over my face, like he's slowly burning his initials in me with an electric cattle prod.

He's so close his muscles push against my ribs. His body: a rippling mass of ripe sweat. "I've had about all I can take of you and Tonto," he says so only I can hear. He slaps his hand on my cheek. "What the hell you thinking, hanging out with him, huh? Don't you know better?"

I push the tears back in my face.

"Answer me!"

"No," I say.

"No what?"

"No. I don't know any better."

He laughs and steps back to join the rest of the Apes, and the last bit of color drains from the world when he looks down.

I follow his gaze to see it: the unmistakable, undeniable Boner of Baskerville.

No.

A thousand thoughtstrings cyclone out of me, not one of them making sense.

"Holy shit, he really is a fag," one of the Apes screams.

"NO I'M NOT!" The words blast out with such force, Scotty falls back. I turn to run, then:

"LEAVE HIM ALONE."

Everyone stops.

I look up to see him: Web. And from my vantage, he's suddenly twenty feet tall, standing on a bench.

"What the hell—" Scotty says.

"Leave. Him. Alone," he says again.

"Web, just go," I say.

"Listen to your girlfriend, Chief Sissy Spirit," Scotty says, standing.

"I don't want to hurt you. Just let him go." His body vibrates, fists clenched at his sides. I swear he's holding fireballs.

"Are you for real, man?" Scotty asks.

"You heard me."

"Check out Injun Queer. Protecting his girlfriend."

The Apes grunt and holler.

"Let him go, you white piece of shit."

"Get that faggot squaw!" Scotty yells.

The Apes lunge for Web. His arms swing back. His hands shoot forward. KAPOW. A blast to Scotty's jaw.

Scotty falls, grabbing his cheek, blood spurting from the side of his mouth. He screams.

The others jump. Web leaps higher. His arms lash left and right, clocking any Ape who even dares get near him. They fall and fumble back up, stunned but with even more fierce determination to kill.

An Ape grabs Web's hair. His eyes bulge, and he screams with such ferocity, I have to slap my hands over my ears. The Ape similarly stumbles and—BOOM!—is kicked in the nuts.

Scotty struggles up, but before he can even take a few steps, POWPOWBLAM! Web left-right-left slugs him, knocking him out.

A mountain of moans.

Web: heaving, bleeding from the nose and mouth.

Me: scrambling over the Ape pile to grab his hand.

"Come on, let's go," I say.

He doesn't move.

"Hey . . . HEY . . . Look at me." He does, and wobbles his head as if seeing everything for the first time. "Hang on to me. Let's go!"

We fly, zigzagging through the locker room.

When I push open the doors, the sun blinds us. Somehow life continues as if nothing's happened. We morph into one body and become the Flash, running with breakneck speed to the fields. So fast, the grass under our feet barely bends. I don't stop until I know we are safe and out of sight.

The minute I do, I'm suddenly lost in a field of kryptonite: powerless, weak, fading. Like ten Incredible Rednecks are stomping my lungs. I fall to the ground, grabbing my chest. Crystal thought: *I need PeterPaulandMary*. A wildfire rages within. I try to focus. It's stuck in my satchel, stuck in my locker. Won't make it home.

"Where is it?" he says.

"Sa—tchel—"

And he's gone.

My legs, my hands, my face goes numb. Everything becomes a yellowed, burning blur. Every inhale grips my lungs tighter, until I'm
going,
going—
"HEY." Web. "HEY. OPEN YOUR EYES."

I do. His are still pulsating. The left one: half-closed, swollen, and splotched purple.

He pulls me up, holds my head, puts PeterPaulandMary in my hands. "Here." Jesus. How did he get back so fast? Did I pass out?

A few thousand poofs.

I let myself swim in his eyes, let his voice bring me back. I want to wipe the blood from his lips, but my arms are lead.

The sky, the clouds, the fields slowly hopscotch into focus.

Short, quick breaths still dagger my lungs.

But it's a breath.

I am breathing.

"Okay," he says. "Okay . . . okay . . . okay . . . you're okay."

I'm not sure if he's saying this to me, or himself.

"You're okay, right?" he asks.

I nod.

"Okay . . . good . . . good . . ." He springs up; I freeze. "It's no one. It's nothing. You're safe here. I doubt they'll ever come after you again, okay?"

I can only nod; my chest still burns.

He spits out the blood that's pooled in his mouth. "I gotta go. Okay? You okay?"

I nod again. He sprints off, disappearing in the fields.

I sit, lost in a sea of waving grass.

I throw myself down.

Clouds shape-shift, taking me on a caravel ride in the winds. Far, far away. I wave my arms in half circles to make a grass angel.

Rivers of tears fall and form little puddles,

in the flattened wings.

## 19.

MY BRAIN HURTS.

I'm lying in Starla's bed trying to decipher Einstein's *Relativity*—the next book in my line of library-borrowed books. Might as well be trying to decipher ancient alien hieroglyphs. Or girls. Or boys for that matter. God.

Starla's packing. Sort of. More like frantically buzzing around her room, throwing this shirt in and that skirt out and this dress in and shaking all about. I'm just as nervous. It's our last day together for three months . . .

Oh, and those ten thousand thoughtstrings that tornadoed out of me in the locker room two days ago—*How did Web know to find me? Is he hurt? Is he safe? Did he feel that moment in the presentation, too? That moment when he looked in my eyes and no one else in the universe existed, and we maybe actually did travel to the moon? And, oh yeah, that one time THE APES SAW ME WITH A TENT AND NEARLY KILLED ME*—and on and on and on. Been trying to stuff them down a wormhole in my mind ever since. Nothing's worked. They're all still tangled in my head.

Been hiding in my room since the Battle of the Apes, only to emerge in the thick of night to pick up Dad from the Blues Note. And waiting to see daylight once I was sure the streets were safe. Today, it happened. They left for some kind of retreat in the jungle or something. Baseball camp, I think. That's what Starla said. Don't know, don't care, they're gone. Even Scotty, who knows nothing about baseball and probably lugs his bat around like a caveman's club yelling, "Ooga booga." Asshole.

Anyway. Two months of Ape-free living. Until it all cycles back again. *"The present is the greatest present."* Another one of Dr. E's annoying quotes. But she's right, I guess, and it works, I guess, because right now is the first time since that day in the locker room my stomach hasn't felt like it's birthing a machete. Sort of. I also can't stop thinking about my final treatments starting in a few days . . .

Or maybe it's because I'm finally with Starla. I don't know. What with her rabid packing, and the frankincense burning in every corner because she's *gotta protect herself from the evildoers on her travels*, I'm so dizzy and nauseous, I have to clap my book shut, grab the Lite-Brite from her closet, and start ker-plinching tiny pegs into the board to try and distract myself.

"I don't know, Momma doesn't want me to bring so much, but I'm not wearing just *anything*. I mean, I know we're only doing a few marches, but come on, aren't you supposed to make a statement every time you're out? This one or the red one?"

She holds up two cotton miniskirts with her added embellishments of beads and rhinestones. Nearly identical. I have no clue.

"Both," I say. Always a safe answer. *Ker-plinch, ker-plinch.*

"There now, see? You get it. You totally get it. Yeah, exactly. Both. They're each different. Have their own value and look and feel and, yeahbabyyeah, both. Settled. Both it is." Good Lord. She stuffs them in a duffel bag that keeps bobbing up and down on her waterbed. "Now for the accessories." And she's off again, rummaging through an empty closet.

*Ker-plinch ker-plinch, ker-plinch.*

"Oh, I *have* to take my sewing machine, of course, because my jeans are going to win that Levi's contest, baby, you better believe, but there's still *so much* work to do." She runs from one corner of the room to the other, grabs a few sewing supplies, and—"*OW!*"—steps on a few plastic pegs before returning to her closet. *"Killing me softtlllyyy . . . hm hm hmmm hmmm . . ."*

"Hey, are you going to take your record player?" I ask.

"Hmm? What? This one or this one?" Two macramé belts.

"Both."

"Right. Both. Now, what?"

"Your record player? You taking it?" *Ker-plinch, ker-plinch.*

"No. Why?"

"I'd love to borrow this record while you're away." She sits on her waterbed, draped in a thousand belts. "And her *First Take* album. So, you know, I can have you close all the time."

"Oh, Jonny, of course you can." Today she's painted black lines underneath her eyes to "look like Cleopatra," and her hair's poofed out from a swirly hot pink headband. This, combined with her swirly hot pink dress, makes her look like a pop-art painting. Or a stick of cotton candy.

I look back at the glowing pegs. "Also, can you believe Web's never heard Roberta Flack? I mean who hasn't heard Roberta Flack? Silly boy . . ." *Ker-plinch, ker-plinch.* I grate my wrists and rummage through the box. There aren't enough greens for what I want to create, so I grab a few extra reds and purples and—

When I look back up, she's sitting cross-legged on the shag in front of me.

"Done packing?" I push the Lite-Brite aside and sit up, relieved. Our knees touch. She holds my hands and twines our fingers.

"I really like Web," she says.

"Oh. Me too . . ."

"I'm glad you've been hanging out with him."

"Yeah . . . he's . . . you know . . . a good guy . . ."

"And I'm especially glad he was there for you the other day. I don't know what I would've—" A few black streams suddenly wriggle down her face.

"Starla . . ."

"I'm sorry I haven't been there for you—"

"It's okay—"

"These past few weeks have been so—"

"You don't have to—"

"I've been so consumed with school and leaving, and I was so happy seeing you working with Web, you know . . . I mean, he seems like a really sweet guy. And that presentation you did was just . . . outta sight, you know? So beautiful . . ."

"Oh . . . thanks . . ." *Did she see that moment between us, too? Did I not hide it like I thought I did? Did anyone else see? Maybe that's why Scotty went ballistic. Maybe it was real. I should tell her everything now. Before she leaves. Maybe she'd know what to do, how to fix this mess I'm in.*

"I just want you to be happy, Jonny. And you seem different now . . . happier, I mean—" She wipes a tear from my cheek I didn't even know was there. "Are you?"

*Am I? Is that what this is?* I shrug.

"And, you know . . . you can always tell me anything. Anything at all . . . You know that, right?"

*I knew it. She can telepathically hear me. Can't you, Starla? Well, here's the truth: Web is the dreamiest dreamboat I've ever met, a whambamthank-youma'am sucker punch to my heart. And when he held my hand, I thought I'd burst into stardust right there. And when he looks in my eyes, I feel . . . safe. How can that be? How can a feeling that's so wrong feel so right, Starla? Huh? Help me, please.*

Instead, Roberta Flack sings in the background, filling the silence with my answer.

"Anyway," Starla says, "since I'm not going to be here, I want you to watch your back this summer. Okay? There's a lot of assholes out there."

"I know."

"Promise me you won't hide away in your room all summer and you'll hang with some *friends*."

"Ha. Okay."

"Promise me you'll spend more time with Web."

*Oh. She did hear me. You heard me, didn't you, Starla? Right. We're just friends—which is about the greatest thing that's happened to me since you came into my life—and when you're gone, he can fill your shoes—not that your platforms could ever be filled, baby. You know what I mean. Yeah, that's it, isn't it? It's the only way . . . Just. Friends.*

I nod.

"Good," she says, clapping our palms together. "Look, I get it, it's not easy . . ."

"What?"

"All of it. Life. You know?" She leans in closer so I can smell the butterscotch on her breath. "It's wild out there, Jonny. Everyone's fighting for something these days. No one's safe. Like, there's no more rules anymore, you know? We're all out there on our own. But . . . with the Lord's help you'll make it. You hear me?"

"Oh. Okay."

"Let His love be all that matters and you'll—"

"Starla, I—"

"I'm only trying to help."

"I know." I place my hands on her cheeks, feel her tears against my palms. I want to osmose her freckles into my hands so I can always hold a piece of her.

"I have something for you," she says. "Close your eyes."

"What? You don't have to—"

"Close them." I do.

I feel a cold lump land in my palms. My eyes open. The cross she made when Mrs. Oliver took us to the Saint Louis Art Museum. She'd given us each a red ball of clay to "mold into an abstract definition of hope." Starla, of course, shaped it into this cross and even carved a crooked little body on it. I threw mine out.

"I can't take this, it's your favorite," I say.

"I want you to have it. Hold it when you feel lost or scared and He will be there. *I* will be there. Just think of it as Ziggy on the Cross," she says.

"Ziggy on the Cross?"

"Yeah."

We laugh. Kind of.

"Okay, then, Ziggy on the Cross. Thank you." I grab an envelope from my satchel. "And this is for you . . ."

"What is it?"

"Postcards. Already stamped and addressed. So you can take me with you and send me a piece of your adventure from time to time."

"Oh, I will, baby." She folds her arms around me. "You'll be with me everywhere I go . . ."

"And now you have to promise me something," I say, pulling back.

"Anything."

"Forget about me."

"What? I could never—"

"I'm going to be fine, Starla. And I'll only be fine if I know you're having the most fantastic time out there in the big, bad wild for both of us. Okay?"

She wipes her eyes, streaking her face. "I promise."

"Good."

"You're perfect, Jonathan Collins. Just the way you are. You hear me?" She pulls me in tighter.

*I wish I could believe you, Starla . . .*

She whispers, "To be continued."

And for some reason I think: *This will be the last time we will ever hold each other again.*

## 20.

*Saturday, June 9, 1973*

MY EYES BURST OPEN. Saturday's sun blazes through my curtains. And my flip-clock says 1:08. Whoa. I've never slept this—I'm late for church!

I bound out of bed, then I realize: Wait. Church is canceled for the summer. I peek through my curtains to see Starla's driveway, empty.

She's gone.

I slip into the clothes I'd picked out last night, and before Dad wakes, I leave him a note taped to the fridge:

*AT LIBRARY ALL DAY. BE HOME LATER.*

Then I jump on Stingraymobile and head back to the lake.

Zaps be damned! I can push through it, because we're *just* friends. Nothing more.

Promise to Starla: kept.

A comforter of clouds hides the sun, but the afternoon air is already thick and steamy. Surefire sign of a stick-to-your-skin St. Louis summer to come. It's happening already. Kids wiggle in front of Mr. Farley's ice-cream truck, parked at the edge of the water, while their parents wait in air-conditioned cars. It's the kind of day you don't dare go outside.

Yet, here I am.

Shouldn't have worn my black T-shirt, I guess, the one with the triangle and rainbow prism shooting out of it: *The Dark Side of the Moon* album cover. But I had to. Also in my haste I forgot to put on deodorant. This never used to be a problem until recently. Now I smell like a burning landfill. Damn.

I casually turn to his house. It sits high in the air, a shanty held up by wooden stilts. And the stairs barely have any paint left on them: Little flecks keep peeling off, floating down to the sand with the breeze.

Web doesn't think I know where he lives, so I'm hoping he'll see me and come charging out again . . .

Nothing happens.

So I sit, staring at the ice-cream truck.

And I wait.

Hours whirl by: The line of kids springs forward, the clouds glide like dandelion seeds, and the bright-orange sun fades behind the trailers.

Still nothing— Wait. Maybe he's gone. Maybe when he said he had to leave, he meant *leave* leave, as in back-to-his-rez leave. I didn't even think about—

*Twing-aling twing-aling twing-aling.*

Mr. Farley rings the ice-cream truck's bell, signifying the end of the unofficial first day of summer.

I have two choices:

1) *Turn around, get back on Stingraymobile, ride home, watch reruns of* Batman *and* Star Trek, *and no one's the wiser*
2) *Get two ice creams as planned, walk up the stairs, and see if he's home*

Really, is there a choice here?

# 21.

I WALK TOWARD his house.

Okay, what's the big deal? I just came to surprise him with a Push-up Pop thank-you gift for, you know, saving my life and all *because we're friends*, and then I'll say something like *"Hey, maybe we should hang out sometime this summer,"* and he'll say, *"Cool, man,"* and then I'll jump on Stingraymobile and ride home. Done.

I reach the bottom of his stairs and look up. Suddenly I have vertigo. Suddenly they look like they're swaying and tilting and growing to fourteen thousand steps instead of the fourteen I counted a thousand times. Suddenly I want to run.

I don't.

First step-creak. *Maybe this isn't such a good idea. You should go back home now, Collins.* Second, third, fourth step-creaks.

*Wait a minute: You did not think this through. You aren't supposed to know where he lives, remember? And anyway, he's probably not even here. And also anyway, he probably doesn't even want to see you anymore. School's over, presentation's complete, he's killed five Apes, WHAT MORE DO YOU WANT?*

Eighth, ninth, tenth step-creaks. *WHY DO YOU KEEP CLIMBING?*

It's like my brain is yelling in one version of me, my legs are wobbling up in another version of me, and meanwhile, little creamy orange driblets keep tapping my thumb like a water torture thing. JESUS.

Thirteenth, fourteenth.

I think I might be dead. I read somewhere that soon after you die you poop and pee yourself. I swear to Ziggy if I so much as look down and see such business I'm dropping these goddamned Popsicles and running.

I look down. Okay, no. Just a puddle of orange from the Push-up Pop that basically no longer exists and basically makes this whole thank-you gift about as worthwhile as a puddle of pee and poop.

This is stupid. Stupidstupidstupid. I'm leaving. Anyway, it's dark now and I should get back before—

The door flies open.

A whoosh of heat flashes through me like somehow I just opened the doors to the sun. I can't even swallow.

And it is not Web standing in front of me. No. It's an ancient version of Web. His dad, maybe? Grandpa? His long white-and-black hair is straggled like a wet mop, and he's wearing nothing but frayed denim shorts. I think he might be melting. I could be imagining this.

I close my eyes tight. Open them again. Nope, he's still there.

I blink. And blink. And blink.

"This is fun. I could do this all day," the old man says. Whoa. His voice like nothing I've ever heard before. It's like the Jolly Green Giant, but it's deeper, like the thump of your own heartbeat.

I blink again.

"I would say for sure I'm winning, since you keep blinking," he says, "but maybe your rules for a staring contest are different?" He laughs.

For a second, I am put to ease. "Sorry. So sorry." I look down. "Does Web live here?"

"Jonathan?" Web emerges from the darkness. He's wearing nothing but loose boxers.

I swallow the lake.

"What are you doing here?" he asks. It's part surprise, part accusation.

"Sorry. I didn't mean to . . . I just came by to give you this." I thrust the Push-up Pop toward him like an idiot. It's now an orange glob of goo in a paper wrapper on a stick. "And say thank you."

"Oh," he says.

Stupidstupidstupid idea.

"I should go. Sorry again. Catch you later." That's what I wish came out of my mouth. Instead: "Shabbadebops." *Sweet Ziggy, what is wrong with me.* I turn to hurtle down the stairs or crash through the broken railings.

"I figured you must be the white boy," the old man says.

*The* white boy? I've been talked about before?

"Yeah," Web says. "Sometimes he speaks in tongues. Jonathan, this is my grandfather, Dennis Standing Bear."

"You cause a lot of trouble," his grandfather says.

"I know, I know," I say. "I should—"

"He'll be right out." And he slams the door.

"Oh. Okay," I say to the door.

I hear muffled words in a language I don't understand. Maybe they're arguing. Maybe Web doesn't want to see me anymore. Maybe he's in trouble for paralyzing five high school boys and he's going to prison and they know it's my fault. I'm the frigging *troublemaker.*

Okay, decidedly now a bad idea. I did what I wanted to do, I said my thank-you, I'm going. Down the steps, back to my home, back to my room, back to my closet, back to my records, back to my—

"Hey."

I flip around. Bright blue jeans, white ribbed tank clutching his chest and abs, shining black hair, and his twinkling eyes: like the sky decided to rest in them for the night.

"Hey," I say, shoving the Push-up Pop at him. God.

"Thanks. Nice shirt."

"Thanks." Cool, he noticed. "Are you okay? I mean, from the other day."

"Yeah, man."

"Cool." I rub my fingers against the grainy wood; paint flecks stick to my skin. "Your eye looks better," I say. It does. Somehow in the span of three days it went from purple mess to yellow nebula. Of course it looks cosmically cool.

"They ever come back for you?" he asks.

"No. They left."

"Left?"

"Yeah, they're gone for the summer. Did you get in trouble?"

"Yes and no," he says. "Let's go."

He sweeps past and smells like a funnel cake. "Hey, how'd you know I'm staying here?" he asks, unfolding the wrapper.

"Oh. Uh—" I look down, slowly unwrap what's left of my Bomb Pop, which I now realize has streaked my arms in red, white, and blue stripes. Perfect. Anyway, I can't lie. Not now. "I came back here. Last week. I saw you."

He slurps his ice cream down like a tequila shot. "I know," he says. "I saw you, too." He laughs and bolts off.

He *did* see me, AND MY TENT. I knew it. Ohmanohmanohman. I can't. I just. There's no. What the. My brain is fizzling.

"Why didn't you—say something—"

"Come on," he yells. "Let's go to our spot."

## 22.

WHEN I REACH THE summit of the crying cliff, I grab a few poofs of PeterPaulandMary and glide over to Web.

Because his eyes have built-in night vision or something, he's clearly been settled here for seven years waiting for me. Sprawled out on the mossy patch, arms folded behind his head, he's lost somewhere in the sky. The three-quarter moon shines a perfect white glow on "our spot."

I flop down next to him, follow his gaze, and KAPOW.

Whoa.

Above us, someone's plugged in the Lite-Brite, I swear. I'm tingling. More than that, I *am* the Lite-Brite. And all the plastic pegs inside me zing to life.

I can't help it. I start giggling. "Whoa."

"I know, man," he says, turning to me. "Whoa."

We lie side by side. The only other sound I hear: our synchronistic breathing.

"Don't you wish we could go up there?" I ask after a while. "And look back down on all this and laugh?"

"We can in our mind."

"Like the moon," I say.

"Like the moon . . ."

I tuck my hands under my head, smiling. "You know, Carl Sagan says we're all made of star stuff. Everything is made of it. When stars die they fall into our atmosphere and turn into these chemical compounds that become things. Sometimes they become people."

"Far-out."

"I know. I hope one day we'll all see each other without these stupid labels and instead see each other for who we really are. Starfolk."

"Yeah," he says. "One day . . ."

"Yeah . . ."

We're staring. We're swimming. We're lost.

"Your turn," I say.

"My turn what?" he asks.

"It's your turn. Last time we were up here, I was the one to answer a question. Now it's your turn."

"Oh, so this is a continuous game that, what, goes on for our lifetimes?"

"Maybe."

"Okay, then. Fire away."

I nestle my cheek in the earth, facing him. "Why do you get so angry?"

"Oh."

"I mean seriously? Sometimes I'm just waiting for your skin to turn green and your muscles to rip through your clothes and you're going to start eating people like they're little gummy bears."

He laughs. "Yeah. It's a problem."

"So?"

His face hides nothing. You can see the wheels cranking, the mind gears spinning. Either he's about to punch me in my face or—

"You really wanna know?"

"Yeah."

"It's kind of a long story . . ."

"Okay."

His chest grows into a balloon, like he's taking a deep breath for both of us. "Once upon a time—"

"Wait. For real?"

"What?"

"Once upon a time?"

"Yeah, man. What, are there rules on how to tell a story now?"

We laugh.

"Okay, then, go," I say.

"Once upon a time," he starts again, slowly. "There was a little boy. And this little boy loved his father very much." His eyes glaze over, disappear in the night. "After his mother died, the father taught this little boy everything he knew. They had dreams. To drive across the country and eat a different slice of pie from every diner they could find. To be the first American Indians in space. Together, the father and son were indestructible. They were invincible." The stars explode in his eyes. His voice drifts away.

"Then one night, driving in the middle of pitch-black nothing, two red and blue flashes appear in the sky. Carole King sings on the radio. A white cop beams a light through the window. The little boy's father is dragged out of the car." He yells, punching the wind with his words. "Crunching. Beating. Screaming. 'Shut the fuck up, Injun, go back to your land!' 'This *is* my land!' 'Don't you talk back to us!'" Pools of sweat drip from his forehead. "More screaming. Crunching. Beating. The little boy crawls in the back seat, curls up, cries. The cops drive away. A huge dust cloud blows all around the father and son. The little boy opens the back door. He looks down. His father lies in a river of blood. His eyes, dilated. The little boy's superhero was dead."

It wasn't sweat dripping from his face.

I want to reach out, but I'm paralyzed.

"From that day on, the little boy vowed to avenge his father's death. To make the white man pay. And one day—" He wipes his face with his shirt and looks at me. Starburst heat radiates from his body, slapping my face. I don't move. I don't blink. I honestly don't know what to do.

"I win," he says, and chuckles.

The world skips back to life: Crickets chirp, soft curly moss sticks to our cheeks, the waterfall cascades below us.

"She's crying," I whisper.

"Yeah . . ."

Something's happening. My heart starts fluttering; my stomach starts tingling. Before I can figure out why, he leans in,

and kisses me.

Oh.

His soft lips cushion mine.

Whoa.

He closes his eyes. I close mine, and slowly open my mouth. He tastes so— He feels so— Our tongues begin to tangle and—

A static charge rips us apart. I push him off, sit upright. "No! What are you doing?"

He shoots up with me. "Sorry, man. I thought you wanted to—"

"No no no no no—" I rub my lips. They're sizzling. "You shouldn't have— Oh man, oh no—I have to go—" I try scrambling up. My body won't move. It's plastered to the spot. My chest feels like a thousand butterflies flapping their wings, trying to escape. I start pounding it with my fist to squash them dead. "I just—why did you—I don't know, I—" A tear leaps from my eye. I swipe it away.

"I thought you liked boys. I mean, I thought, you know, me."

"I do—I mean—NO, Web. We can't—out here—we can't—you know the trouble we'd get into—it's *sick*—we could go to *jail*. I can't—WE can't—I *can't* like boys. It's wrong. I'm NOT allowed to like—NO—" Tears spill. I close my eyes so tight my muscles start to ache. I wish. I wish with all my might we were up in the stars looking down on us, laughing.

When I open them, we're still here.

The three of us.

Me and the American Indian princess: crying forever tears.

And Web: His face twists, but his eyes, oh man, his eyes still glow like a perfect starfolk . . .

And all I can do is.

All I can do is.

All I can do is grab his long black hair and pull him in so tight I become him.

Our lips collide. Like two crashing meteors who've been waiting our whole lives for the impact.

And he smells so sweet, like boy sweat and soapy springs.

And his soft long hair, like delicate feathers, caresses my cheeks.

And when I think, *This is what it's supposed to feel like,* it dissolves in his mouth and he whispers back to me, *"Yes."*

Bolts of lightning strike my nerves like a wild electrical storm. I flinch, but stay connected to him. Locked. This may be the only time. The only time I can ever feel this again.

And I want it to last forever . . .

A cackling laugh slams us back to Earth. "What the hell you guys doin'?" some girl yells.

I panic and push Web off. "Get off me, you queer!" explodes out of me. "You . . . you fairy. Get off me!" I yell this so loud, it causes another rip in the lake.

Girl: *"Jonathan?"*

Web: "Jonathan?"

Me: "Just GO!"

I can't look at him. I'm about to jump off the cliff, join the American Indian princess, when I hear: "Hey, hoochie-coochie momma! Jesus, this waterfall's slick." Dad? He's climbing up the cliff. NO.

"What are you—" It's Heather. "Were you and that boy—"

"Is this little squaw botherin' you?" A glowing demon in a red hat squirms next to her. Her brother, Hal.

"What?" I say, wheezing. "No. I just. He just—"

"Here I come, baby! Ready or not!" Dad. Closer.

I push Web. "GO!"

He looks at me, stunned, broken. It rips me in half. "Don't," he whispers. "Don't be like them—"

"Just GO! Please."

He stumbles up, runs, disappearing in the trees.

I swipe my eyes, try to grab my breath, my heart. Trees uproot, rocks crumble, stars die, the moon falls, falls, falls with the American Indian princess.

"That's right. Run back to yer own land," Hal yells.

"Don't tell Dad I was here," I say to them. "Please." Heather twitches her nose. Hal smirks. "PLEASE."

"I can't promise nothin'," she says.

"Jesus, this waterfall's crazy," Dad yells. "How'd you climb up there so fast?" He's near the top.

I run. Slide and roll down the other side of the hill. Fumble through the sand. Jump on Stingraymobile.

The world blurs around me in a watercolor of sick and shame. The Lite-Brite in the sky's unplugged. Clouds cover the moon. Was it even on? Were there ever any stars? Probably not. Probably imagined them. Like I imagine everything else.

I throw Stingraymobile on my porch. Run upstairs. Slam closet door. Wail to Ziggy on the Cross. I punch the walls and slap my face and want to beat myself to a bloody pulp.

I hate what I am.

I hate what I did.

The same thing that happened to me at the lake.

At the spot. When IT happened.

When Scotty gave me my first kiss.

# 23.

---

*Sunday, June 10, 1973*

I HAVEN'T MOVED.

I haven't eaten.

I haven't stopped crying.

I've withered and wilted to a puddle of nothing.

More than I deserve to be.

I'm holding Ziggy on the Cross. Squeezing it so hard. Praying to be someone else. It doesn't work.

I slap my headphones on, turn the player to max volume, try to nuke my thoughts. Doesn't work.

The Ziggy eyes in my closet don't blink.

Mom doesn't smile.

I can't even stand to hear my own voice.

I am sick.

I am broken.

I can't wait for tomorrow.

I will fix this. Once and for all.

There's no other way.

The cross in my hand breaks in half.

## 24.

*Monday, June 11, 1973*

NOTHING'S COMFORTABLE. I HAVE to sit on this stupid Oriental rug thing that may as well be a splintered board, because if I hear the squeak of that leather couch one more time I'll dial up Nurse Ratched myself. I'm this close as it is.

It's so hot in Dr. E's office, the paint's dripping off the walls. Crying. The room is crying for me. Because I have no tears left inside me. My T-shirt's pricking my skin like it's sewn together with thorns. I try to wrestle it off me, fling it out the window. I try to wrestle my skin off, zip into a new one. Nothing works. Nothing.

Except one thing: the treatments. That's the only reason I came out of my room, the only reason I'm here. If it doesn't work now, nothing will.

Crouched on the floor, head between my knees, I rub my wrists together like they're two pieces of kindling, like I'm going to start a fire and burn myself away.

That's the hope, anyway.

I jump up when she walks in.

"How are we today, Jonathan?" She's all sunshine and lollipops and I rip it to shreds with one daggered look. "What happened?" She throws her blue glasses on the desk and her eyes grow, filled with the skin-crawling care of every mother on the planet. Don't deserve it. Not now.

I start pacing behind the leather couch. I can't look at her. "It happened again," I say. God, my voice sounds like a termite.

"What?"

"You know what," I say, still pacing.

"I need you to tell me."

"No."

"Jonathan. I need you to tell me if we're to move forward today. Sit down and—"

"NO."

*Maybe if I pace fast enough and hard enough, it will rub the wood to nothing and it will break in pieces and I'll fall to the center of—* No. Not now. Not playing this stupid imagination game. You're here. You have to deal with this. It's the only way— Crap. I think she's talking. She is.

"—and maybe you're not. There are other ways, so maybe this isn't—"

"What?" I stop, look at her. Her hair's twisted back, stretching her face, which makes her look even more worried than she probably is. She's wearing some long dress that I'm pretty sure was made from my grandma's polyester pants cut up and patched together. "What did you say?"

"I said we could discuss other ways, other options to—"

"NO. Absolutely a thousand percent no way. It has to be this way. It has to be. I have to fix this. I have to get rid of this for good. Please."

We stare. I dare not blink, flinch, budge. I cannot let her see fear or she won't let me do the treatments.

Her eyes wrinkle up. She wipes them with her sleeve. Is she crying?

"Sit down," she says. I do.

"Close your eyes, take some breaths, please." I do.

"Now. Tell me again. What happened?"

When I open my eyes, she's sitting at her desk, hands folded in front of her, focused. Her eyes and voice back to *analytical doctor*, far away from *overprotective mom*. Thank Ziggy.

I can't believe what I'm about to say. But it has to be said if this is going to happen. "I kissed him."

She nods and calmly says, "Kissed whom?"

"Web."

She nods again. "And how does that make you feel?"

*How does that make me feel? Like I was living in the middle of Fourth of July fireworks. Like I was exploding with so much joy there would have never been a Vietnam War because my joy would have caused world peace.*

"It's wrong and I'm sick." That's what I say. Because anything else and I'll be carted off right here, right now.

She looks at me. "Do you believe that's true?"

"Yes."

"I've known you a long time, Jonathan. You're one of the brightest people I know. And you've made some wonderful progress over the past four years." She swoops in front of her desk and sits on the floor in front of me.

I still don't blink. I'm not even sure I'm breathing anymore. Maybe I'm dead and this office is purgatory. God, that's the most sense I've made of anything lately.

She holds my hands. "I know we planned to do your final treatments today. And I thought maybe it was the right thing because of everything you've been telling me, but—"

"But? But what? And why are you talking past tense?"

"But I don't know, Jonathan. I'm not sure it's right now."

"Yes it is. It has to be right. This is the only way. I hurt him. Web.

You should've seen the look on his face when—GOD—I'm so fucking tired—sorry—of hurting *someones* because of this, this . . . sickness. I did to Web what Scotty did to me and—"

"What?"

"Right after his Ape friend caught us kissing, Scotty punched me to the ground, called me names, made my life a living hell. Then Dad found out, and he was about to throw me in jail or the nuthouse or—I don't know what—but instead he found you and you fixed me. Because I am sick, Dr. Evelyn. I need to be fixed again. Please. I don't want to be this person anymore. I don't want to— Are you going to tell Dad?"

Her eyes are wide. Tears slide down my face, but my eyes stay locked on hers. Because I will not back down.

"Only if you want me to tell him."

"No. I most definitely do not want you to tell him. He'll flip, and then who knows what and— No. It was a mistake, Dr. Evelyn. A mistake that can be fixed again. I know it can. Please."

She stares. And stares. And stares. Then she shakes her head and looks out the window. "There may be other ways . . . I don't know . . . I've been researching . . ."

"No. There is no other way. DR. EVELYN?" She snaps back. "Please."

This time I see it. A lonely tear springs from her eye. I follow its slow stream down her cheek.

"I need you to be one hundred percent certain this is what you want," she says.

"I've never been more sure of anything in my life." For once, the truth.

Neither one of us moves.

Then she wipes her tear away and says, "Let's go."

# 25.

WE WALK DOWN the hall. It's only a few doors down, but I suddenly feel like she's donning a black-hooded robe and dragging a shiny blade behind her that scrrraaaaappppes against the linoleum.

I hold on to my wrists.

We don't speak.

She opens the door, flips on the fluorescents. The lights give the fresh coat of piss-yellow paint an extra gloss. There's the smell of disinfectant spray and rubbing alcohol: extra-pungent, extra-clean. Almost too clean. I'm pretty sure this is the room Rosemary just had her baby in.

A mirrored wall behind the wooden table and chair reflects back someone I don't recognize. I jump when I see myself: paler than usual, eyes hollowed, stained with red and circled with blackness. God. At least I remembered to put on deodorant.

"Okay," she says, pulling a screen down over the mirror and plugging in the slide projector. "Do you remember everything here?"

"I think so, yeah."

I sit in the chair, familiarize myself with the setup:

*4. A huge box, like an amped-up record player, dotted with knobs and numbers and scientific words I don't understand.*

*3. Four electric wires with leather-buckled cuffs, connected to*
*the box, each neatly wound in front like little rosaries.*

*2. Extra-padded headphones, so thick and cushioned an*
*A-bomb could go off and I wouldn't know.*

*1. A red panic button of relief, also connected to the box. Push*
*it, the slide on the projector changes and the pain stops.*

"You know not to turn any of the knobs, right?" She fidgets with some wires. "We've put them at the exact levels they're supposed to be."

I nod. She stops and looks at me. She smells like dead flowers.

"Jonathan, you're sure you want to do this? We can—"

"I'm sure," I say.

". . . Okay . . ."

She buckles a cuff around each wrist. "Too tight?" I shake my head. She hands the other two to me. I buckle them around my thighs.

"Lean forward now, press your face into the finder," she says, adjusting it to fit my head. A viewfinder extends from the box, not unlike the red handheld View-Master my grandma gave me for Christmas one year. But without the Hanna-Barbera slides.

"This," she says, handing me the button. I sit back in the chair. "This is your key, remember? Press it anytime. Anytime at all. If it's too much, we'll move on. That simple. Don't push yourself too hard, okay? This is for you, not for me."

My heart's vibrating, readying itself for the attack.

"Last thing," she says. "Remember, it's best to keep your mouth shut. Staying quiet keeps your thoughts focused and steady for the fullest impact. I'm right there in the next room if you need me."

She smiles, but like a doctor who just told you you have cancer, and places the headphones over my head.

The Infinite Silence of Space.

*Whoosh whoosh whoosh.*

I lean forward, suction my forehead to the finder, one step closer to the black hole. The fluorescents flip off. Darkness. My heart throbs in my ears.

*Whoosh whoosh whoosh.*

I close my eyes. And I pray to my broken Ziggy on the Cross. Four words:

Please. Forever. Fix. Me.

A distant hum pierces the silence. A slide projector clicks on, filling the screen in front of me with a blinding white light. My eyes squint and adjust.

*Okay, okay, okay, you can do this, Jonathan Collins. You can forever fix yourself.*

Ch-click. The projector's carousel turns, revealing the first slide in my viewfinder:

A picture of a beautiful, tanned blonde in a polka-dot bikini fills the screen. She's lying on her back in front of a painted tropical beach backdrop, looking up at me as if to say, *"Oh, you naughty, naughty boy."* Her bikini strap's undone, so the minute she sits up she'll be topless.

I feel sorry for her. Her eyes look sad and lonely and desperate. Probably made two dollars posing for this. Probably wants to be a famous actress or something. I wonder if she knew what she was posing for. I wonder if she knew she was posing for someone like me, looking back at her, all strapped in like some crazy electrified pervert. I wonder if she would have posed if she knew—

Ch-click. The carousel turns.

The bikini-clad blonde is replaced with a different slide: a tight-trunk-wearing Mayor of Mansville. Jesus. His perfectly rippled muscles crash against the rocks he's posing on, bulging extra-big between the legs. His feathered hair and mustache match the blond patch on his pecs. I swallow. He looks like Scotty, except older and—

A volt sweeps through my thighs, shocks my penis. FuckingFUCK. Another volt pierces my wrists, shoots up my arms, electrifies every nerve along its path, blasts them to smithereens.

I scream.

*Keep your mouth shut, keep your mouth shut, keep your mouth shut. Keep your thoughts focused to fix this once and for all.*

Legs convulse and twitch.

Arms spasm and sting.

Fingers tremble over the red button.

*Don't push it, Jonathan. Not yet. You need to keep going. You need to forget. You need to fry this part of you, obliterate it into a bazillion bits so it can never be pieced together again.*

My nerves strangle inside me.

*SweetZiggyontheCross, it hurts.* You deserve this. Take it. Don't back down now. It's your last chance. Your only hope.

The image flashes in front of me, in and out of focus, shaking in a fit of spasms with me. Skipping around like a TV channel that's out of sync.

*Keep going, keep going, keep going.*

I push the button.

Ch-click.

Another girl appears on the screen. This one's wearing a sheer pink negligee cuffed with feathers, combing her long black hair in the mirror. You can just see a small tuft of hair poking through down there.

Her image blurs. Tears must be streaming down my cheeks. I can't feel them. I can't feel my face. Everything goes numb. I push forward. Determined to fix this once and for all.

Round and round the carousel goes.

Round and round the pictures flash: A boy appears, I am pulverized; a girl appears, I am not. That's the trick; that's how I know it's working. The relief I feel seeing the girl is the relief I'm supposed to feel in the real world. That's how I know I'm normal, how I'm forever fixed.

Each slide clicks forward, clicking me back into the Me I'm supposed to be.

Round

and

round

and

round.

Until there's nothing left of me but the stillness of space.

The fluorescents flicker on, singeing the air.

Dr. Evelyn lifts the headphones.

She half smiles and wipes my face clean of sweat, tears, and shame with a damp cloth.

"How are you, Jonathan?" she asks.

I try to open my mouth to speak, but nothing comes out. I just nod. My eyes feel wild, like they're bulging out of my head. I can see through things: frenetic dust bits bouncing in every direction. Colors pulse. My entire body: aflame. *I am the phoenix rising from the ashes*, I think. Even though I feel like anything but.

"You did it," she says, unbuckling the cuffs from my wrists and thighs. "Made it through the entire carousel of slides." She's not smiling anymore.

I nod again. It hurts to nod. It hurts to move.

She hands me a glass of water. My brain thinks I grabbed it. I see it in my hands. But it's not. Instead it falls, splashes all over me. Dammit, looks like I pissed myself. Or maybe I did without knowing.

"It's okay, it's okay," she says. Her eyes look desperate, examining me like a specimen under a microscope. "Let me help you." She pours another glass, lifts it to my mouth. I sip some, but most of it gurgles out and down my chest. God.

I turn away, throw up in the plastic bucket next to me. Throw up what? There's nothing left of me to throw up. The little bit of water, I guess. She wipes my face clean.

"It's okay," she says again. "It's all part of it, remember? You're okay." She lifts my wrist, feels my pulse. Which is probably equal to that of a rabbit clutched in the jaws of a coyote. "Why don't we go lie down in my office for a minute, okay?"

She pulls me up. My brain thinks I'm standing. I see myself standing. So why am I on the floor? I can't feel my legs. They're wobbly pieces of goo.

"It's okay, I gotcha," she says.

I'm a drooping dandelion, flopping down the hall in her arms. With no seeds left. Wishless.

She lays me on the couch. I don't even hear the squeaks.

I have no idea how much time has passed, but when I open my eyes Dr. Evelyn's looking at me and the sunlight has shifted to the other side of the room.

"How are you?"

"Okay," I say. "Better." My brain forms thoughts and words again. I smile and sit up. Rub my head, my face, my arms, my legs, make sure all the pieces are still there.

She sits on the floor next to me. "So, you did it. The final treatment."

"The final one."

My scar sears my brain, but I don't let her see. Stupid scar. That's why I put a razor to my forehead a few years ago: to give myself the Ziggy Bolt. Since I'm branded an electrified freak for the rest of my life, I thought I could become Ziggy and help all the lost children of the world.

Yeah, right.

"We'll give it some time to settle in before we assess—"

"I definitely think it worked," I say. "I am fixed."

She nods and starts talking some psychobabble hooey I don't understand, so I close my eyes to get lost in the place I feel most safe: a distant galaxy far away from here—

But instead, I see his face.

Still.

Even after all that.

Web's smiling face, tickling me on the moon. His lonely face lost on Desk Island. His broken face splashed in tears. Before he ran.

And for the first time since that day it happened at the lake, I think,

*Maybe I can never be fixed.*

＊

# part two.

## TIME
## STITCHERS.

*i saw your spiders weaving threads*
*to bandage up the day.*
*and more,*
*those webs were filled with words*
*that tumbled meaning into wind.*

—JAMES WELCH

## 26.

*Monday, June 25, 1973*

"YOU BELIEVE THIS CRAP? This guy says Nixon knew all along, that he was in on it."

It's Monday night. Dad's pissed because the Watergate thing keeps preempting *All in the Family*. Fine by me. I hate that stupid show. We're watching this together with the rest of the world because:

1) *it's on every flipping channel, and because*
2) *he wants to help me "stay out of my goddamned crazy head," because*
3) *it's been two weeks since my last electroshock space adventure!*

You know what I realized during this last round of treatments? It's like how Wally West became the Flash or Bruce Wayne became Batman or David Bowie became Ziggy Stardust: They first had to be transformed to stimulate their superpowers.

Yeah.

Anyway. At the end of our final follow-up session today, I gave the most Dulick-worthy presentation of my life:

                    DR. EVELYN
How do you feel?


                         ME
                    (smiling)
I feel great. Alive. Awake again.
Supercharged.


                    DR. EVELYN
Feeling any side effects? Stinging
sensations? Memory loss?


                         ME
Sometimes. But that's a good thing,
right? Means it's working?


                    DR. EVELYN
Mmm . . . I suppose . . . Any questions
on your mind?


                         ME
                    (still smiling)
Just one.


                    DR. EVELYN
Shoot.


                         ME
Were you always this pretty?


                    DR. EVELYN
                    (laughing)
What?


                         ME
I feel like the treatments zapped
some new hyper-color vision in me.

**DR. EVELYN**
(still laughing)
You seem happier, Jonathan.


**ME**
I am happier. It's like I had to go
way down to come way up.


**DR. EVELYN**
(hook, line, and sinkered)
Makes sense.


**ME**
Oh, one more question, I guess.


**DR. EVELYN**
Mm-hmm?


**ME**
Will you tell Dad I kissed Web?


**DR. EVELYN**
(not laughing)
Not if you don't want me to.


**ME**
I do not. It was a mistake. A mistake
that I have forever fixed.


**DR. EVELYN**
(that Spirograph-scribbling-in-
her-eyes look again)
Well, I have some ideas for you
both . . . to help sustain this feeling. But when I call your dad to tell
him my assessment, I won't tell him
that. My lips are sealed. (She hands
me a cupcake.)

                              ME
            What's this for?


                          DR. EVELYN
            Your birthday last week. I didn't
            want to distract you from the treat-
            ments . . . your dad said it'd be best
            if I waited.


                              ME
            Oh yeah . . . thanks . . . thank you.


                          DR. EVELYN
            He'll be . . . very proud of you,
            Jonathan, and the work you've done.
            I'm sure of it.


                              ME
               (stillstillstillstill smiling)
            Oh, I'm so sure, too. I'm so so sure.


(Me exiting Purgatory, still smiling from cheek
to cheek. Smiling so hard my cheeks actually hurt.
Smiling past Debbie, the receptionist. Smiling
until the elevators close. Smiling until I see
myself reflected in the steel. Smiling until the
crying waterfall bursts through me in ten thousand
tears . . .)


Church bells clang me back to the living room. No, Dad's ice cubes
are rattling against his glass. And he's yelling at me, or the TV. One
can never be sure where he's looking when he's one . . . two . . . three
drinks in. It's the TV.

Is that guy's face actually skipping, or is it the stupid side effects?
No, it's skipping. Dad arrggghhs, flips up the recliner, slaps the side.

"Can't trust no one no more. Not even the damned president. And all this new terrorism crap, people hijacking planes? What in the hell's the world comin' to? Git me another drink, willya, son."

I grab his glass, duck under the bar, pour the usual. The guy on TV rattles on:

*"I told the president about the fact there was no money to pay these individuals to meet their demands. He asked me how much it would cost. I told him that it might be as high as a million dollars or more. He told me that was no problem."*

"Voted for that crook, goddammit," Dad yells to the air. I wait until he stops thrashing in his chair before handing him the glass. He looks like an elephant seal. And smells like one, too. Like he just flopped out of the stinky lake and left himself baking onshore for a few days. He's decided to only live in his Dennis the Menace boxers as of late: Father's Day gift from Heather's little boy, I guess. Whatever. I gave him the best present any dad could ever ask for: a Shiny, Brand-Spanking-New, All-Cured Son!

I curl back on the couch.

A cigarette dangles from his lips. "When I voted for that guy a second time, I said ain't no other way he could've won that much without lying and cheatin'." He's flickflickflicking the penis lighter, but only sparks shoot out. I hide my face under Grandma's afghan so he doesn't see me laugh. *When I peek up, she's laughing so hard her painting vibrates. She winks at me.* "Ain't no one can get ahead in this world without some lying and cheatin', GODDAMMIT!"

"Here, let me." I crawl to the other side of the couch, grab his cigarette and lighter, and start flicking it myself. Now he sees what I saw and a laugh comes roaring out, which quickly turns into a heaving cough.

"You okay, Dad?"

He nods and shoos me away.

A couple more penis flicks and I hand the lit cigarette back to him. *Grandma looks down, worried.*

"Where'd you learn to do that?" he asks after a few more chest thumps.

"What?"

"Light a cigarette."

"Oh, I don't know. Watching you, I guess." I turn back to the TV.

"Well, don't."

"What?"

"Don't you start up with this smokin' crap," he says. "You hear me? What with your lungs and . . . everything else . . . you fixed yourself, son. I'm proud of ya. No sense in muckin' it all up by makin' yourself sick again." He flicks his hand in my general direction. "Just don't be an asshole."

"Okay," I say.

We stare at the TV.

*"I began by telling the president that there was a cancer growing on the presidency and if the cancer was not removed the president himself would be killed by—"*

Then it happens. His image appears again, skipping and scraping through the guy testifying. Web. Torn and broken. A face I'd previously only seen in the mirror. Now projected back to me, because of me.

And still he's smiling. Glimmering like a starfolk.

Of course I've thought about every possible way to go back. To sneak away, hide, and wait. To apologize, or have him spit in my face.

But I can't.

I can't wonder what he's doing right now.

And right now.

And right now.

I can't taste his cherry-candy lips, feel his heart pounding in my mouth.

I can't.

And I can't turn off the light switch he's flipped on inside me, no matter how hard I try. And I have tried. Tried so hard.

But I can't.

I know I'm not supposed to feel this way and I hate myself for it, but . . . I can't stop thinking about him—

A jolt zings my thighs. I wince, but try not to flinch. I have to learn to live with this, because . . .

Secret: I know now I can never be fixed.


Ice cubes clinking again. Dad's looking at me.

"Huh?" I ask.

"Pour me another drink."

He blinks. And rattles the ice in his empty glass.

## 27.

---

*Thursday, June 28, 1973*

A FEW DAYS LATER, my first postcard from Starla arrives! It's the one I gave her of the Arch at sunset. On the front I'd written a note:

*FIND YOUR WAY HOME.*

I run upstairs to my closet.

A Polaroid's stapled to the back. She's standing in front of a rectangular pool of water that seems to shine to infinity; a teeny-pointed pillar looms in the background. Her hand's outstretched in a peace sign and her hair's poofed out like a cumulonimbus.

On the bottom, she's scrawled:

> *Where MLK once stood, I now stand.*
> *Fight the Power. Fighting for You.*
>
> *Starla xx*

*JONNY-BOOOOOO!!!!*
*Great God A'Mighty we're finally here!* ☺ *First*
*stop: Washington Monument. (Picture attached!) The*
*biggest protests landed right here! All for one reason:*

*E-QUAL-I-TY! I swear you feel the ghosts of history here. So many people put their lives on the line for something greater than themselves, you know? It's chilling. But now, HERE I AM. For us. I carry you with me everywhere. I hope you're out having fun with Web. YOU PROMISED! Remember: If you feel lost, hold on to that cross! He (meaning ZIGGY of course! ☺ ) can fix anything that's broken!!*

*To be continued,*
*Starla xxx*

I hold the Polaroid for hours, osmose every little color, line, and freckle into my brain. She's only been gone a couple of weeks, but it feels like a couple of years. And without being able to talk to her, or see her, or feel her hands in mine, she already feels like a ghost of my history.

I wipe my face with my sleeve and grab the pieces of cross. Haven't touched it since it broke in my hand that night the stars fell from the sky and Web ran away from me. Maybe she's right. Maybe by fixing the cross, He'll fix me.

I blaze downstairs to get the superglue from the junk drawer. The *Batman* theme hums in my head. As I reach the last step, I hear Dad on the phone.

". . . Yes, Doctor—Evelyn, I mean, sorry, ma'am—yes, I'm doing everything you told me to do. . . . Yes, I just want to help him, too. . . ."

Oh, it's The Talk: The Seal-of-Approval, Gold-Star-Student, Twirl-from-the-Mountaintops-because-the-Hills-Are-Alive-with-Your-Cured-Son Talk. Or she saw right through my Oscar-worthy performance back on Monday.

I slump against the wall out of sight.

"Oh, yes, ma'am, I think he's much better. . . . Yes, he seems very happy. . . ."

Okay, so far, so good.

"Yes. . . . I see. . . . Well, that's good news. . . . Oh, yes, that's right, he used to love cooking. Hasn't done that in so long. . . . Yes, I'll get him cooking again, don't worry. . . . We should have you over sometime. . . ." He laughs. "Yes, he's a great kid, a really great kid. . . ."

Okay, this is getting weird. I'm waiting for Rod Serling to open our front door and introduce the next episode of *The Twilight Zone*.

"Well, I think so. . . . Heather? Oh, she's a good influence, sure. Kind, outgoing, hardworking, always asking about him, of course. . . . Why?"

Hey, Rod, you're late for your cue.

"Oh, a job. . . . I hadn't thought of that. . . . Perhaps she can get him one at the Dairy Queen—that's not a bad idea. . . . Well, thank you so much, Doctor. . . . Evelyn, I mean. I'll definitely . . . What's that? Oh, more ideas! Wow, you sure are full of them, aren't—. . . I see. . . . I thought you said he was . . . I see. . . ."

Oh boy. Something's changed. I can feel it pulsing through the walls: *Bruce Banner holding back the Hulk. He's up and pacing now, smashing holes in the floor, trying with all his might not to turn green, not to rip through his clothes.*

"I suppose if you think . . . I'm not sure where we'd . . . Oh . . . I suppose the lake could be an easy enough option for us, but . . ." Did he just say the lake? He just said the lake. Oh no. "Right, yes, okay then, Doctor, if you say so. . . . Oh, thank you, and you as well, ma'am. Nice talking to you, too."

He punches the phone through three walls. It smacks against

my head, and knocks me unconscious. Basically. Okay, I'm still piecing the one-sided puzzle together, but one thing's clear: It's not good.

He's slamming pots and pans and drawers and screaming an encyclopedia of obscenities. As he stomps by, I bound down the stairs like I just popped out of my room. "Hey, Dad, how's it going?"

He's dressed in his favorite white cotton shorts, which end high above the knee, and his favorite *"If this van's a rockin' don't come a knockin'"* T-shirt, which bulges at his stomach and is already stained with sweat marks. And it's barely noon.

"Well, look who waltzes down before lunch today." No, no, I did not say this to him. He says this to me. Yes, really.

I laugh. "Yeah."

"That was your *doctor*," he says.

"Oh yeah?"

*"Oh yeah."* He charges to the bar. "She seems to think you've still got work to do!"

Fuck. The hallway sizzles and skips out of focus; my body turns radioactive: an instant Pavlovian response. She saw through it. "Oh?"

He scratches through his thinning hair like his scalp's on fire and looks at me. And oh, I swear to you if looks could kill—no, if looks could chew your heart out and spit it in the toilet, then flush it down so it ends up rotting in a sewer.

"You know how I feel about this crap, Jonathan."

"I know."

"You wanna end up like your good-for-nothin' uncle?"

"No! I'm—"

"You wanna drag this family in the dirt, is that it?"

"No."

"Jesus Christ," he says. And shakes his head. He turns to walk out the door. "I can't think about this shit right now. I'm going to the Blues Note. Pick me up later." And he's gone.

I can't move. My hands clench so tight they're bleeding.

I stare at the door. And I chuck the two pieces of cross at the wall so they can never be fixed again.

# 28.

---

I JOLT UP, SCREAMING.

Am I drowning?

No. Just sweat. An ocean of sweat, but still.

The only light flickering in the room is from someone testifying on TV.

The clock on the stove says 9:37 p.m.

Okay, I can't watch this Watergate crap. I'm sick of staring at my ceiling and talking to myself into my stupid tape recorder. Mom's asleep. Grandma's bored. Starla's gone. I'm going to the Blues Note. I know it's early, but it's been a while since I hung out there. Scotty won't be playing pool because he's still at Caveman Camp. Be good to see Chester again and, hey, maybe Alma's there and we can play darts and catch up and I have to get out of this goddamn house.

Anyway, they say fresh air is good to clear the head. Whoever "they" is. I want in. I want to be a "they" who decides these things, because frankly, I'm sick of playing by other people's rules.

When I step outside, it's like someone's thrown Dr. Evelyn's ugly quilt dress over my head. Suffocating. I'm not even sure one can call it air anymore. I grab a few poofs of PeterPaulandMary and walk a few blocks and my Pink Floyd shirt instantly sticks to me so I can't tell where it ends and my skin begins.

Welcome to Grandma's "*nights of molasses.*"

It is eerily silent. Motionless. Like walking through a still life. Bikes strewn over lawns. No breeze to snap half-open screen doors shut. Feels like I'm the only person alive right now. Fine by me. My thoughtstrings are company enough: *What did Dr. Evelyn say to Dad? Did she tell him I'd been faking it all along? That I need a thousand more treatments? Or to be sent to the loony bin or prison or Vietnam, even though the war's over— Wait. Did she tell him I kissed Web? No. His reaction would've been far worse. Nuclear. But, damn, I should've never told her about that night on the cliff . . . at our spot . . . Maybe she knows I can never be fixed . . . And what about the lake? Why is it always about the stupid frigging lake? There's something there. Something at the lake . . .*

The faint rattles of trees slowly fade in. A few others join in a small crescendo. More cicadas are hatching.

Lightning bugs glitter the sky. Used to love catching them as a kid. Running around my backyard with Grandma, feeling them flutter against my palms, glowing like little alien heartbeats, and stuffing them in a jar with a lid I'd poked holes in.

Used to love it. So much simpler then. I wonder if I'll be saying that ten years from now . . .

When I round the corner to town, the buzz of neon glows in the distance. Main Street, USA. Everything's closed up for the night. Even the moon. Hiding somewhere behind the clouds. Perfect.

BL_ES NOT_ flashes in shimmering yellow fluorescent. Appropriate. Especially considering I'm about to walk through the doors of Dad's church.

# 29.

CAROLE KING CROONS ON the jukebox. "Will You Love Me Tomorrow." Yes, really. From Web's second-favorite album of course. SweetBabyZiggy. NO ESCAPE.

Dad's slumped over himself on the corner barstool, smoldering. A cigarette dangles from his lips. He's gesturing to Chester, who looks more interested in whatever's on his rag than what Dad has to say. They both look up at the TV to watch the Watergate thing.

Some guy's playing pool with Alma, this one biker chick I befriended who basically lives at the bar with Dad. Can't see who's with her. The lamp that hangs over the table is the only source of light at the back of the bar.

"Hey, Chester," I say.

"Heya, kid," he grumbles. Not because he's mean, but because he's a hundred and eleven years old. Give or take. "How's it goin' these days?"

"Okay."

"You're early," says Dad in the corner.

"I was bored. Take your time."

"Man . . . ohman . . . Chesler . . . He sure looks like his momma . . . you know that?"

Chester ignores him. "You feelin' alright, kiddo? Your dad says he's not feelin' too hot." Chester's a cross between the Godfather and Clarence—that angel still trying to get his wings—always in a perfectly pressed white button-down and black pants. Sometimes you have to look really hard through the furrowed relief map of wrinkles all over his face to see even a hint of a smile, but still, he's one gooey mess of goodness. If he likes you.

"Yeah, I'm fine. Make it a double," I say, slapping the bar with my hand.

"Comin' right up." He starts to make my Shirley Temple.

I wave to Alma, who's already setting up the dartboard for us to play. Good. She doesn't talk much either.

"So, what do I owe ya, my main man?" a voice calls from the other end of the bar. When I turn to see who it is, my heart splashes down the counter and lands right in front of the guy who was playing pool.

My first thought: Web.

My second thought: No. It's not. I'm imagining again. But man, this guy sure looks like Web, so I'm not too far off my rocker. Yet. Same long black hair, same white T-shirt, but definitely older and thicker. And he's staring at me. Smiling.

"Can't get you another?" Chester asks him.

"Thanks. Two's my limit. Closing out for the night," Web Doppelganger says.

"You got it," Chester says.

I smile back. I think. I'm hoping my face contorted to a smile and someone picked my jaw off the floor.

"Cool shirt," he says.

I try to say, *"Thanks,* The Dark Side of the Moon's *one of my personal favorites."* Instead, I say nothing. I can't speak. My mouth is wired shut. God.

"I have the same one. Such a boss album," he says.

SAY SOMETHING. Nope. Instead, I nod like a rabid chipmunk. He laughs. Chester walks back with his check.

"Thanks again," he says to Chester, laying a few bucks on the bar.

"Anytime. You're welcome here anytime, friend."

The guy looks back at me, nods, knocks the bar with his knuckles twice, and walks out the back door.

I need to sit down. I'm being haunted now. This is decidedly not good. Not good at all.

Chester slides the Shirley Temple down the bar. "You sure you're okay, kid? You look like you seen a ghost."

Before I can reply, or find out who that was, Dad's voice pummels through. "GOTDAMNED CROOK. I voted fer him, Chesler, thought he was a goodun! Ended that damn Vietnam War a few months ago, ya'know, and—Chesler! Did you vote fer him?"

Chester shakes his head. Dad slumps in his stool for the rest of the night while I play darts with Alma in silence. (I beat her 9–4.) Sometimes words are so overrated.

When Chester's closing up, he waves me over to help him uproot Dad. Man. This is the most drunk I've seen him in a long time. No doubt because of me. Because of what Dr. Evelyn told him earlier. I try to fling his arm over my shoulder, but it's so heavy it knocks me down. Alma runs over to help. They drag him to the Caddy through the back door and slump him in the passenger seat.

"You're a helluva kid," Chester says as I roll down the passenger window.

He's standing under the bug zapper, the only light in the parking lot. Every few seconds a sizzle pierces the stillness.

"You know, I could . . . I mean if you . . ." He scratches the back of his head with his towel. "Look, what I'm trying to say is, I got this brother. He's a cop here in town. One of the good ones. One you can really trust . . ."

We're looking at each other.

"He can help you, is all I'm sayin'. You don't need to do this alone, kid. He can help your dad find—"

"Don't worry, Chester. I got it."

"Yeah." He looks down. "Just, you know, if you ever change your mind . . . if you ever need anything at all . . ."

"Thanks."

"Okay." He folds his arms over his chest. The towel dangles in front like a surrender flag. "See you tomorrow, then?"

"Yeah, see you tomorrow."

My life.

**30.**

THREE RULES FOR DRIVING Dad home:

*1) No talking*
*2) No music*
*3) Drive slow*

Usually he sleeps, and I'm a lonely astronaut navigating the fields of space: discovering new stars, protecting the Earth from alien attacks, you know. Anything to escape here.

Can't do that tonight, though. Tonight, he's belching and burrowing in the velour like an angry warthog. Have to lift my shirt over my nose to cover his rotten liquor puke stench because there's no frigging breeze: It smells rusty and stretches like taffy, a percolating thunderstorm.

I hum "Moonage Daydream" and drum my fingers on the wheel and try to breathe, but—

"Are you happy?" It speaks. More like alien hieroglyph drunk-talk, but over the years I've learned to translate.

I glance over. He's curled up in a fetal position against the door, looking out the window, unmoving. I'm sure I imagined it. Or he's talking to some ghost of his own history. I keep humming and drumming.

"HEY. Are you HAPPY?" Nope, it's him, wobbling and snorting in my general direction.

"Uh . . ."

"Cuz, you know, Jesus Christ, son—" He laughs. Crazy-killer-clown-in-the-car laughter. "I don't know what to do anymore. I don't know how—" He starts crying. Not crying, sobbing. God, he's drunker than I thought.

"I'm happy," I say. "I'm happy."

"Good," he says. "Goodgoodgoodgoodgood. Cuz, you know, as long as YOU'RE happy. As long as YOU'RE happy . . ." He's back to crazy-killer-clown laughing. What's going on here? What exactly is he talking about?

"Are you happy?" I ask. The worst possible question, but it's all my brain can think.

"Happy," he says. "Ha . . . paaayyyy . . . Happy happy hap hap happyyyyy . . ." He grips his hair like he's about to pull the last few strands out. "I tried to stop them. I said, 'No, can't we do something? We have to save them both . . . we have to . . .'" He's flailing his arms, lost in the blackness. Not again. Not now. He's teleported back to that hospital room, back to the day I was born.

"And I thought long and hard. Long and hard, you hear me? And no one. NO ONE should have to make a decision like that. Ever." He's staring out the window. My stomach's twisting tighter with each word. "But I did. I had to. And I chose you. Because you're my son. Because that's what she would've wanted. She never would've forgiven me if she'd woken up and realized—"

He thrusts his head out the window. I swerve to the right, reaching for him. He pushes me away, punches the air between us. "NoNONO. You listen to me!" I clench the steering wheel and keep driving.

"I prayed and prayed and prayed, you hear me? I was right there when it happened. I'll never forget—all that blood. I kept mopping her forehead with a cloth. Didn't know what else to do. And there you were, screaming and kicking. She sees you and smiles, and they rush you away, and then . . . she was gone. And I sat there alone, thinking, '*I just killed my best friend.*' I killed . . . my best friend . . . I killed my—"

He looks out the window, crying again.

My hands clutch the wheel so tight I may rip it from the dash. Thunder tears through the clouds. Rain rips down. Wipers skip across the windshield but barely clear the glass.

"I don't know . . ." he says. "I just don't . . . know . . ." And he's gone again. Passed out.

I pull into our driveway and run inside, slamming my bedroom door. I fling open my window, lean out as far as I can—bolts of lightning crackle; thunder rockets; rain pelts the trees—*Ohmanohman it feels SO GOOD.* I am drenched.

I close my eyes, picture Web and me on the window's ledge, screaming into the sky as we hold each other and the wind whips around us. *"You gotta feel the rain, man!" he screams. We laugh. "Yeahyeahyeah!"*

And then it stops. Just like that. Poof. The blinding rain turns to a soft drizzle, then to silence.

I look around. Everything cries. Except me.

Dad sleeps, curled up in the front seat of the car. I want to scream out the window, "*I know you chose me over Mom! That's one of the reasons I've tried so hard to fix it. I don't want your choice to be for nothing!*"

Instead, I close my window.

The storm has passed.

My heart, though, still feels the thunder.

## 31.

*Friday, June 29, 1973*

THE NEXT MORNING, I peek through the curtains. Everything's extra-sparkly from the rain. Except Dad, who's still asleep in the car. I grab the *Aladdin Sane* album from my desk and lie back on my bed.

"Hey, Zig, you around?"

He doesn't move.

"Zig? You there? I know I haven't seen you in a while, but—"

*Ziggy lifts his eyes, smiles. "Hey, little Starman, you're hunky-dory in my heart just as you are."*

"Uh-huh . . . Where have you been?"

*"Here. There. Everywhere. Didn't think you needed me anymore . . ."*

"I need you now more than ever."

*"You're not alone, Jonathan. I'm always dancing in your heart. You know that, right?"*

"I guess."

*"Oh, come on, beautiful boy, let's boogie," he says.*

And for the rest of the morning, we pray. I still don't cry. I can't. Maybe the treatments dried up all my tears.

A few hours later I'm downstairs. Coffee's finished percolating. I pour a cup and sit at the kitchen table. Dad's still sleeping in the passenger seat. (I wrapped him in one of Grandma's afghans, but he barely stirred.)

Anyway. Trying to read more of Einstein's *Relativity*. Thinking maybe the electric shocks stimulated some new brain cells, ignited some new synapses to make me a genius. No such luck. It takes me ten minutes to read one sentence, I swear. But I power on, determined to understand. Anything to help me get out of here.

I'm stuck on this sentence about a flying raven traveling the velocity of yabbadabbadoo when—

The screen door creaks open: A zombie from *Night of the Living Dead* stumbles in. His T-shirt's flung over his shoulder and his big, furry belly is just as pale.

"Coffee?" I ask. He nods, wipes his face. Like he's trying to erase his life.

I look up. *Grandma stands with her hands on her hips in the painting.* Oh man, is she pissed. She hates when he drinks. When Dad built the bar in our living room she called it *The Devil's Den.*

He clears his throat, mumbles something.

"What?" I say, matching Grandma's impatiently tapping heels.

He clears his throat again, stares into his mug. "I miss her all the time, you know. The only woman I ever loved." He's holding the mug like he's holding her hands again. "She knew something was different. She'd tell me all the time—" He looks at me. "You were different. You were special. You were going to change lives."

Oh. Not what I expected.

We sit in silence.

"She said she loved you more than anything," he says. "Said she always would no matter what. Asked me to promise her to do the same." He looks back down to the mug, her hands. "I don't know what else to do, son. Your doctor says . . . I've done all I can to help—"

I snap out of the spell he's somehow put me under. I knew it. Dr. Evelyn. That's why he's losing his mind: their conversation yesterday. *Grandma leans in, straining to hear.* "What do you mean?"

He's shaking his head, but he's not saying anything. This could mean a thousand things. I suddenly feel like we're at the cliff-hanger of a *Batman* episode: *Is Jonathan's father sending him to prison? Is he going to say he isn't his real father? What's going to happen to Jonathan Collins? Tune in next week. Same Bat-time. Same Bat—*

"We're going to the lake."

"What?"

"For a week."

"What!" Oh no. Nope. No way. Uh-uh. I'm off to the races. "I don't need to go. You go. You *should* go. Get some fresh air, get away, you've been cooped up here with me for a couple weeks, you need some time alone with Heather or whatever, but I'm good, I'll be fine, I can take care of myself, I can—" I'm spinning. I can't catch my breath. There aren't enough words to fill the room.

He stands. "I don't have a choice. Neither do you. Doctor's orders! Guess we need some 'father-son bonding time.'"

"Why?"

"You're not fixed."

Each word impales my heart. "How does that even help?"

"How the hell should I know? She did some *fancy* research. Guess it's all my fault now—" He starts to pour more coffee.

"What? That's not—"

"Said something about you not having a momma, and me being *too distant* from you, and BAM, you are who you are. Now that's some shit right there." He puts the percolator back on the counter. "So we gotta go someplace for you to step deeper into your *masculine energy*—she actually said that, your *masculine energy*—and some other hippie-dippie New Age crap I don't know . . ."

"What—but I don't—why the lake?"

"It's the only place I could think of!"

"I don't want to go." I can't go. I won't go.

He laughs. "Think I do? It's not up for debate. I ain't gonna be the one to blame for your mess. Not after all this time. And I already talked to Heather."

"What? You did? When? What did she say?" I know I'm sounding more and more frantic. I can hear it. But it's like being stoned to death with each new thing he says.

"She don't know why we're going. She just thinks you want to spend time with her. Got it? We're going to the lake. We're going to have a good time. Because if we don't, and this damn *bonding thing* don't work?" He shakes his head again. "Well, I don't know what. Just pack your bags. We're leaving in a few hours."

"What? Today? Now? We're going now?"

"You got big plans or something? Yeah, now. You gotta get out of that crazy head of yours all cooped up in that crazy room. Get up there and pack your bags."

He fails to realize my *crazy room* is the only place I actually feel sane in this world.

This is what Dr. Evelyn meant by helping me?

Some help.

I'd rather do a thousand more treatments.

# 32.

A FEW HOURS LATER, my bags are packed and I'm waiting in my closet. I'm a jittery mess. Maybe had one too many PeterPaulandMary poofs since the conversation with Dad. I click on my tape recorder to record this moment, should it be my last:

"Good afternoon. This is Jonathan Collins coming to you live from my closet. Today is Friday, June 29, 1973. It is 3:27. Dr. Evelyn says I am not fixed—which is a news flash to no one—and I'm being sentenced to death by means of Creve Coeur Lake. Should I not return, please give all my albums to Starla." I click it off. Then click it back on. "Oh, and please tell Web I am sorry." Click.

God. I should've run off with Starla while I had the chance.

It's quiet in my closet. Like everyone's just as shocked as me. Ziggy's eyes don't blink and sing. The *National Geographic* pages don't sway. Even Mom's portrait is silent. It's the only picture left of her in existence: an 8x10 painting from her senior year. Saved it from the Massacre of 1966. (A few days after Grandma died, Dad got so drunk he decided to burn everything of Mom's. No explanation. He just screamed *"No more, no more, no more . . ."* while he torched everything in the fireplace. I grabbed this portrait when he wasn't looking.)

"Listen. I need your help," I say, holding her in my hand. "I know it's only a week, but still, I need you to protect me and hide me. From everyone, but especially Web. If he's even there. If he's even there. He could be gone; he's probably gone; I hope he's gone—no I don't. If I could just see him once I would— No— *Aggghhh* I don't know! I just need to get through this, I NEED to, okay? To make Dad and Dr. Evelyn think I'm forever fixed so they'll leave me alone for good. Please."

*"You'll be fine, Beetlebug." Mom winks, lifts a smile.*

"There you are! How can you be so sure?"

*"A mother always know these things . . ." Her voice a cross between a melodic angel and a cooing dove. And she looks like she gave Marilyn Monroe a run for her money. "So, off to the lake, are you? To spend some quality time with Dad?"*

"If that's what you want to call it."

*"He wasn't always this way, you know. I would've never fallen in love with him if he was."*

"Why did you fall in love with him?"

*"Are you kidding?" She leans in and whispers, as if other girls around her might hear, "He was dreamier than Dean and Brando and Clift combined. Everybody loved him. And I was the lucky girl who got him."* *She winks and sits back.*

"What happened to him?"

*"Life. As it does."*

"You mean me."

*"You, yes, and a thousand other pieces, sweetheart. He was breaking apart long before you came into the picture."*

"Why?"

*"I don't know, honey. I guess some people just don't want to play the game."* *She lifts a compact, starts applying lipstick, each stroke careful and precise.*

"What game?"

*"You know better than anyone. Life's hard sometimes." She looks at me*

*from behind the mirror, puckers her lips.* "I see it as one big game. You take gambles, you take risks, sometimes you're sent back a few spaces, sometimes you move far ahead of the pack, but always, always, you get to choose to play. Every moment is one big choice to play. And once you choose to play, at the end of the day, you always win."

*She pop pop pops her lips together, kisses the mirror, clicks her compact shut, smiles. My mom.*

"You really believe that?" I ask.

*"You know what Al said the other day? 'The universe is always conspiring for your greatest good. It's up to you to see it that way.' Had to write that one down."*

"Who's Al?"

*"Albert. Sorry. Einstein. He's such a card, he—"*

"Wait. You talk to Albert Einstein?!"

*"Oh, sweetheart, we play poker every Saturday. Man's a genius, it's true, plays a mean violin. But let me tell you—" She leans in again, whispers, "Can't play a lick of poker to save him."*

We laugh.

"I got his book from the library!" I say. "Have no idea what it says!"

*"Oh, he is a hard one to follow, but he'll be thrilled. I'll let him know." She floofs her hair, adjusts her sweater, sits back.*

"I wish you were really here right now. Not in my stupid imagination . . ."

*"Oh, me too, Beetlebug."*

"I'm sorry."

*"For what?"*

"Everything."

*"Oh, honey, don't let's waste your time on all that. Now, tell me, what's all this talk about wanting to hide from Web? Love that name, by the way."*

"You know why I can't see him."

"*But he's so dreamy. What's there to hide from?*"

"I don't know . . . everything . . ."

"*Come on now, tell me. We promised. No secrets.*"

"I can't let them know that I'm . . . I mean, I can't let them see—I know I can't be fixed because I can't stop thinking about him . . . like *that*, I mean . . . and I don't *want* to stop thinking about him, you know? And I'm afraid if I see him, well . . . I can push through the pain, all the shocks and everything—I mean they hurt but . . . God, I thought I'd at least convinced Dr. Evelyn—"

"JONATHAN, TRAIN'S LEAVIN'! CHOO CHOO! LET'S GO."

I turn to the door. "It's Dad. I have to go."

"*Just play the game, sweetpea, and you'll be fine. I'll see you when you get back!*"

I kiss her cheek and hang her back on the wall.

"JONATHAN, WHERE THE HELL ARE YOU?"

"Coming!" I grab a few albums and my three force fields for added protection:

*1) The* Aladdin Sane *album*

*2) The Polaroid of Starla and me on our bikes*

*3) My Ziggy on the Cross pieces. Just in case. Arsenal complete.*

I'm leaving Mom here.

To keep my dreams safe while I'm away.

## 33.

"JESUS. YOU WORKIN' for the CIA now?" he yells from the car, toweling his face with his terrycloth shirt. "Why you gotta bring all that other crap for?"

"Because if I don't bring my record player and my albums and my tape recorder and microphone, I will drown myself in the lake before you can say *scrumpdillyicious* and haunt you for the rest of your lonely no-good miserable life. That's why."

That's what I wanted to say. Instead: "Because." That's all I say. I have a strategy: Talk as little as possible, do as little as possible, and thou shalt be saved. Off to a smashing start.

For the record, even though every other nerve in my body is fried, my sense of smell is still working: Dad's Brut knocks me unconscious the minute I open the car door. Probably trying to cover up the smell of the grass he just smoked.

"Hurry up, son. It's hot." He slides his gold aviators on. I throw my two bags in the back seat and creak the passenger door closed with a heavy slam—

And we're off! Seriously. My head smacks against the headrest. I swear he thinks he's Evel Frigging Knievel. I squeeze my stomach so I don't hurl all over the seats.

In between belting out lyrics to Aerosmith's "Dream On," Dad's giving me the skinny on the week ahead:

Dad: "*Maybe tomorrow*—Heather's letting us stay in her brother's trailer. He'll stay in hers. And she's gonna stay in her friend Bernadette's place with her boy—*the good Lord'll take you away* . . .*"

Me: "OKAY."

Dad, swerving the car while lighting a cigarette: "Wait'll you meet Harry—*Dream on, dream on, shabbalabbadingdongdoo*—you'll love him. That's her son. I think he's three or something . . ."

Me, grabbing the wheel, deciding whether or not to swerve into the fields and bring a fiery end to it all: "CAN'T WAIT."

When we pull into their gravel driveway, I purposely avoid peering across the lake to Web's house, but SWEETBABYZIGGY, I'm mustering every superpower I've ever learned trying not to look.

*I got this.*

*I got this.*

Heather stands in between two trailers, wearing her DQ uniform and a bucket of makeup, holding a round hairless Tribble—excuse me, that must be Harry. She waves and whispers something in his ear. Probably: "*We're gonna take all their money and get out of this hellhole. Smile!*" Because in that next second he does and flaps wildly in her arms.

Dad honks and waves back.

I clutch the Ziggy cross pieces in my pocket and pray I get out of this alive.

## 34.

I THINK I'M ACTUALLY breathing water, not air. Stagnant water in a landfill. No wonder the rats build their nests here. Where's PeterPaulandMary? Poofpoof.

Harry wriggles out of Heather's arms, squealing, *"Wee wee wee all the way home,"* or maybe it was, "Wanna pway cowboy with Hahwee?" He bounds over to Dad, who starts chasing him around the trailers. Within seconds, Dad's bent over coughing, trying to catch his breath. Harry jumps up and down *pew-pew-pewing* him with a fake gun, then runs down the path to shoot at some guys playing horseshoes.

"How you been?" It's Heather. I jump. She's scratched her way over without me seeing. That's the thing about rats: They're fast.

"Fine." I grab my satchel and luggage from the back seat.

"Haven't heard from ya in a while. Ever since that night on the—"

"Which trailer's ours?"

She's rail thin with huge, feathered hair frizzed on her head and teeny features on her face, currently highlighted with streaks of powder-blue eyeshadow and bright pink blush. Like some kindergartner mistook her face for a Barbie styling head.

She cracks a smile, twitches her nose. "I got your balls in my hands," she says. Or it could be, "That one." She points to the trailer on the left and leads the way. And I definitely do not look behind her across the lake, EVEN THOUGH I SEE MOVEMENT.

*I got this, I got this, I got—*

Dad pops up from behind the trailer, scaring us both. He sweeps Heather into his arms and she giggles. "Not now, not now, I gotta get to work!"

"It won't take that long," he says, throwing her over his shoulders.

"Make yourself at home, Jonathan!" she yells before being sucked into the trailer next door.

*Thanks so much for the kind hospitality! Will there be continental breakfast served or . . . ?* Never mind. Okay, twenty minutes in, only 8,620 to go. I did the calculation before we left. Never going to make it. I walk inside.

The good things:

1) *The trailer itself is pretty decent: a silver metallic Airstream, like I've always imagined driving to California. One day.*

2) *. . .*

3) *. . .*

Okay, the bad things: everything else. But just to name a few:

1) *The air on this side of the lake smells like rotten fish guts and I'm regretting not bringing Dad's gas mask from the garage*

2) *Everything in the trailer is covered in this thin layer*

*of—I don't know what—it's not dirt or dust, more like*
*grit-grime-getmeouttahere*

*3) The interior's wallpapered in Corvettes and Bud girls and*
*the ceiling's covered in* Playboy *centerfolds and their*
*HOLYMOTHEROFGODS. How am I supposed to*
*sleep at night with those things winking at me?*

Moving on.

First things first: set up my record player. I plunk it on the fold-down table in the "dining area" and line up my three force fields in perfect four-inch spaces, then look across the water into Web's—

Movement. I think. YES, something definitely moved over there.

Oh man.

I can't help myself. A pair of binoculars hangs by the door. I grab them and peer through. There's a line of . . . twenty-seven kids jiggling their legs, waiting for Mr. Farley to give them an ice cream. Sweep to my right. Nothing. Everything looks empty, boarded up. No fires or flares signaling me to come rescue him, or Web holding a sign that says, COME BACK TO ME, JONATHAN! Nothing. No doubt, I imagined him. Okay, snapoutofit, Collins, you're becoming a crazy Manson Family Stalker.

Yup. Put the binoculars back, snap the curtains shut, and PULL YOURSELF TOGETHER. I flip on my Ziggy album, skipping directly to "Suffragette City." Perfect song to distract myself and drown out my noisy neighbors.

Next order of business: not unpacking until I clean. I grab a towel, the cleanest one I can find, and start wiping everything down. Dad comes barreling in, breathless.

"Turn that crap off," he says. "We're gettin' a bunch of stuff for the barbecue. What do you want?" He wobbles over to one of two twin beds and wipes his man-sweat all over the sheets. Marking his territory, I guess. Noted. My bed is on the left.

"Granola," I say. The only thing I can think of right now. My brain's still trying to compute thoughts into words.

"Granola?"

"Yeah. It's supposed to be good for you."

He dries his face. "What else?"

"I don't know, maybe—"

A pockmarked demon with a Cardinals hat appears in the doorway. Nope. It's Hal. Forgot about him. Did he tell Dad he saw me that night? Oh man.

"You remember Hal," Dad says. "Heather's brother—"

I extend my hand. "Nice to meet you." *Stay calm, stay cool, you got this, Collins.* He does not take my hand to shake it. Instead, he grins. A scar on his left cheek stretches to his ear.

"You guys met," Dad says.

"We did?"

"At the house a few weeks back?"

"Right! We did! Yeahyeahyeah, sorry, silly me, I forgot." *Whoa. Reel it in, Collins.*

"All good, my man," he says. "I forget things all the time." He winks.

My hand's still extended like an idiot. He finally grabs it. Ick. It's cold and supremely slimy. I try to pull mine away, but it's stuck. Even though we aren't shaking anymore.

"You comfortable?" he asks.

"Huh?"

"In here. Place okay?"

"Oh. Yeah. Fine. Thanks."

"Good. Good."

It's possible he's slowly sucking up my soul, I can't be sure. I finally wriggle my hand free and try to casually wipe it on my shorts.

"We'll be back," Dad says.

"See ya later, Jonathan," Hal says, lifting a smirk. Holy heebie-effing-jeebies. This guy's definitely been at the lake too long. I watch them drive off. Hal looks back.

8,577 minutes to go.

## 35.

LATER, LONG AFTER the sun has been smothered by a quilt of stars and the mist from the lake has risen like a creeping fog and more newly hatched cicadas have joined in the eventide symphony, we're sitting around a fire with Hal and the three men they based the movie *Deliverance* on. Gee. Zus.

I'll call them BillyBob, Porky Joe, and Five-Teeth Terry for all the obvious reasons, I think. Mostly because I don't remember their names, but also because they're the type of guys you want to try and forget anyway.

*"Nothing but trouble and then more trouble,"* Grandma used to say. *"You stay away from those Lakers. They bite off squirrel heads and use their bodies to beat you senseless."*

I used to question Grandma's authority on the subject, dismissing it as part of her flair for dramatic storytelling. Now, no question about it, it's possible that legend was based on these three hillbillies.

After endless rounds of beers, joints, and snarls that have been circling me for seeming hours, we sit in silence. The only sounds: the soft crunch of a plastic pail rolling in and out with the tide, and bits of barbecue from the makeshift rotisserie dripping on the burning wood.

"What the hell you come out here fo'?" BillyBob says suddenly. I jump, and I think a little pee squeezes out of me. BillyBob's the clear leader. He's the long-bearded one in bib overalls who's quite possibly eight feet tall and has a right eye that twitches every few minutes. And besides the eye-twitch thing he doesn't move, his hands permanently folded on his lap.

Dad throws his arm around my shoulder. His thirty-hundredth bottle of beer sloshes all over me. I do not wipe it off; I do not move. "We come here for some father-son time. Boy's growin' up. Becomin' a man."

"You be careful with that pecker, boy," Five-Teeth Terry says. "Don't you go fishin' in no ponds yet."

A boom of laughter. And they're off:

"Or if you do, make sure to put on your fishin' vest." Porky Joe.

"Yeah, but don't forget to take out the hooks and bait first." Five-Teeth Terry.

"Unless she like that kinda thing." Joe.

"And if she do, lemme know!" Terry.

This is really happening. Who needs Johnny Carson. Dad's keeled over in a fit of laughcoughs with everyone else. Except Hal. Who just sits and smiles across from me like some slimy snake from SuckYour-Soulsville.

I stare into the fire and bob my shoulders up and down so it looks like I'm laughing with them.

"Ain't you hot, boy?" BillyBob asks me after the laughter winds down.

"No, I'm fine, thank you." Did I mention everyone else in the circle is shirtless? It's true. Perhaps some tribal man thing.

"He's so skinny we could use him as a spit for the next barbecue," Terry says. This coming from a man who looks like he's made out of five twigs tied together. Still, he scares the crap out of me. My bowels clench.

"Gotta git some meat on them bones, boy," BillyBob says. "He's right. You're skinnier than a got-damned girl. Here." He cracks open another bottle of Bud and hands it to me.

"No, thank you," I say as Dad whispers in my ear, "Take the beer." I do. Now I'm an art piece on display. They're staring, waiting for me to drink, I guess. Part of the initiation? Or sacrifice? Gross. It tastes like warm piss. "Mmmm," I say, wiping my mouth like I've seen Alma do at the bar.

They laugh.

"You boys could borrow my fishin' boat," Porky Joe says. He's picking bits of meat out of his teeth with an unusually large knife. "She's my baby, but don't never really use her no more."

"Yeah, cuz you'd sink it the minute you sat down," BillyBob says. Terry howls so hard at this he spits his beer out, dousing some flames.

Joe wobbles up, pulls the knife on him. "What's so funny? You so damned skinny I could slice you in two with my eyes closed."

"Now, now . . . relax . . ." BillyBob says. "Sit yer ass down, Joe. We got guests." He shifts in his lawn chair, looking at us. "Heat does some crazy things to yer head . . ."

"Heh, yeah. We'd like that," Dad says. "To borrow your boat, I mean."

Joe settles back, picking his teeth again. He has no neck. He looks like an angry Weeble. "Anytime."

"We'd like that, wouldn't we, son?"

"Yeah."

"How old are ya, boy?" BillyBob asks.

"Seventeen." I sound like a mosquito.

"Wassat?"

I clear my throat, lower my voice, try to be manly. "Seventeen." Now I sound like a burping hippo. I take another swig of piss.

"You ain't one of them hippies, are you, boy?" Terry asks.

"Nosir."

"'Nosir.' Boy's got manners, he does," BillyBob says. "Good boy."

"Yeah, I raised him good," Dad says.

"You stay away from them hippies, boy. All that love and peace and bullshit. Some sicko queers is what they are."

I stare hard into the fire; Dad's grip tightens around my neck.

"Nothin' but sissy faggots is what they are," Joe bursts in. "They don't know what it's like to live with nothin'. They act like that's a *good* thing. Try gettin' your supper outta the lake, then we'll talk!" He's yelling at the fire like it's suddenly Public Hippie No. 1. "Goddamned government's tryin' to kick us outta here, but we're stayin' till they arrest us, ain't we, Terry."

"Yep. This here's *our* land—"

"And it's the best place on earth—"

"'At's right! Redneck power!" Terry throws his bottle in the fire.

"And quit protestin' a war you know nothin' about," Joe explodes. "These men comin' back are heroes. And you screamin' all over them, shovin' your flowers in their faces and all that *bullshit*." He's slashing the air with his knife like he's stabbing all the hippies of the world. Is he psycho?

"Hey hey hey now," BillyBob says. "What'd I tell ya, boys? Calm yourselves down. These here gentlemen are our guests. We gotta be cordial and all. We don't know their politics and such." He turns to us and smiles. Not a cordial one. One that's on the edge of slicing our throats.

"What? No, man," Dad says. His voice has changed, quivers almost. "We're with ya, man. We get it. Don't we, son?" I nod.

"Oh, because, you know," BillyBob continues, "you got that big ol' house of yers out there. And this big ol' golden *Cad-il-lac* and I'm thinkin', 'Hey, this guy's got some money. Shit. He prolly got lots of money. Maybe they think they're different than us, you know. Maybe they even think they're better'n us.'"

"Yeah." "Mmm-hmm." "'At's right." The others agree. Pitchforks may have been raised; I can't be sure. I'm not looking.

Dad tries to laugh, but it sounds like he's mating with a squirrel instead. "Oh, no, my man. Better than you? Not at all. We don't think that, do we, son?"

I shake my head.

Everyone's silent. My heart quickens. I know we're being watched. I know at any moment we may be smothered in hickory sauce and skewered over the fire. This is it: the scene that was cut from *Deliverance*. I close my eyes, try to picture the grounds so I can navigate my ass out of there in two seconds. Can't think of a clean getaway, so I land on the drowning option.

It's Hal who finally breaks the silence. "Well, lookee there, the dirty Indians are back."

I spring my head up. Everyone's turned in their lawn chairs. Except me. I can't move. Afraid of what I'd do. Like leap in the lake and swim madly toward him, even though I can't swim.

"Why's that family lettin' them stay at their place?" Five-Teeth Terry says.

"Get them off our land!" Porky Joe.

"Thought you got rid of them dirtbags, Hal!" Terry.

"Oh, Hal beat the crap outta one of 'em, alright," BillyBob says, quieting them.

"Yup," Hal says, eyeing me. "Some Indian was puttin' the moves on Joe's girl. You shoulda seen him after I kicked his ass. Boy couldn't breathe after I was done with him. All covered in blood. Gave a whole new meaning to *redskin*."

They laugh.

"You shoulda done more," Porky Joe says, still glaring across the water. "They been here over a month now. 'At's a month too long. When you gittin' rid of them for good?"

"Oh, don't worry," BillyBob says. "We got somethin' special planned to take care of 'em once and for all. Then they'll know their place. Ain't that right, Hal? Whoo boy, they ain't see nothin' yet."

They laugh again.

*What the hell does that mean? Is Web safe? Am I safe? What if these psycho hillbillies think I'm one of them? What if I'm becoming one of them just by sitting here? Is that what Web meant on the cliff when he said, "Don't be one of them"?* I try to burn all my thoughts in the flames, but they sizzle back to life and leap through the scar on my forehead. Multiplying.

And the way they talk about Web and his family. Like they're nothing. No. Like they're dirt. Dirt they can stomp on just because they can. I don't know. It makes something bubble inside me. Boil.

So lost in my head, I don't hear the final crackles of fire die down. I don't even hear the hillbillies leave. Or Dad crawl into the trailer. I don't move until the last flame becomes a glowing ember in the sand and I look up to realize I'm alone. And still alive somehow.

I sneak inside to grab the binoculars, then run back outside and peer through them.

Oh. Man. He *is* there. My heart: a skip-skip-skipping stone across the lake. Web sits cross-legged on his balcony—in his underwear!

I swallow. Feel a tingling in my tummy and between my legs and KA-ZAP. Ow. *Breathe through it, breathe through it*—he's shirtless and sparkling and every one of his muscles ripples like the water. Like he *is* the water.

And I want to drown in him.

SH-CRACK. OW. Like I'm buckled up to the electric wires again. Anyway, if there were a panic button in my hands I wouldn't push it. No way. I don't ever want to change this View-Master slide.

He's looking up at the stars. I wish I were up there now. Then he'd be looking at me. Ohmanohmanohman.

*I got this I got this—OW!*

*I most definitely, absolutely, without a shadow of a doubt, one thousand percent*

*don't got this.*

## 36.

THE NEXT MORNING, I have officially decided drowning is NOT how I want to go.

After Porky Joe gave Dad his aluminum boat, two fishing poles and a tackle box—and apparently a few beers and Godknowswhatelse—we're spinning in circles in the middle of the lake while Dad sings the theme from *Gilligan's Island* doing some weird striptease jig. No.

Welcome to father-son bonding, day two.

I've tried peeking over at Web's house numerous times—to wave and let him know I'm here, or watch him flip me the bird, or I don't know what—but we're spinning so fast it's a true miracle we haven't tipped over.

*"Three-houurrrr touuuuurrr . . ."* He whips off his fishing hat and waves jazz hands. This just got weirder. "Hey, relax, son, Jesus Christ . . ." He tries lifting my arms to the sky, but they're superglued to my chest, so his attempts are futile. "Just like your momma. She hated the water, too—hey, I ever tell you 'bout that time your momma and I spent the day at the Lake of the Ozarks eatin' all them hot dogs, and we was in her daddy's boat, and she got SO SICK—"

That's how she got the nickname Anne Frankfurter. Not the time, Dad. I'm about to hurl.

"Oh MAN, that was some fun-nay shit . . . little gross, but funny.

Man . . . oh man . . ." He's in a good mood at least. But for the record: If we capsize, I will use Dad as a flotation device. *Navigate the negative.*

After he paddles us around and we disappear behind the trailers, he throws the oar at me and cracks open a bottle of beer. "See how I did it?"

"Yeah."

"Good. Billy's right, you got arms like a girl. You need to build up them muscles. I'm here to help you, son. Now, pay attention."

"Okay."

"Lesson one," he declares to his classroom of no one. "Appearances are everything. You gotta look like a man so people think you're a man and leave you alone." *Guzzle, guzzle belch.* "Lesson two." SPLASH. He throws the empty beer bottle in the lake. I sweep it up with the oar and throw it back in the boat. "When people think you're a man, you start *thinking* like a man—where's my damn cigarettes?—and when you start thinking like a man, the world's at your fingertips. Got it?" He fumbles with the lighter, lights a crumpled Camel he found in the tackle box, spittooies out a few flecks of tobacco. "Got it?"

"Got it." Whatever. No clue. Just please stop talking and please don't let there be thirty lessons or I'm jumping. Also, paddling's for the birds: It's been five minutes, my arms are blazing, and I think I'm dying.

"Oh. Oh, I know." He takes a long, wheezy drag and points his cigarette at me. "Your girl's gone for the summer. We need to find you one while we're here. Can't believe I didn't think of that before. You ain't never had a good piece a cherry pie till you had one from around here."

Yes, he said that. Yes, he believes that. As Starla would say, *"Sometimes I have no idea how you are a spawn of that man, baby, no idea."* Yeah, me neither, baby.

"Yup, that's exactly what we'll do. I'll ask Heather. Yessir, that's the ticket right there. We'll fix you for good, boy, if it's the last thing I do. You'll see. You will see."

Oh.

Oh, I do see now.

Satisfied with his lessons, he lies back and guzzles the rest of his beer in bliss. I keep silent. Less chance of him remembering the conversation in the first place, because the heat has made him extra-drunk, extra-fast, and within minutes he's passed out.

At last.

The sun weighs the sky down.

I fan my chest with my shirt, close my eyes, and float. We bob up and down. Water slaps the aluminum sides; the faint breeze brushes my hair. Feels like we're the only two people on the planet right now, floating in the middle of nothingness.

*"This is nice," I would say.*

*"Yes, it is," Dad would say.*

*"Being here with you," I'd say.*

*"The Dynamic Duo," he'd say.*

*"Yeah."*

*"Yeah."*

*"So much to explore."*

*"So much adventure."*

*"Together," we'd say.*

*"You're a good kid. Just the way you are."*

*"Thanks, Dad. I love you."*

*"I love you, too, bud."*

Dad snoregurgles me out of my dreamstate.

I look at him, wipe my face. "I'm sorry you chose me," I say. "And not Mom."

I float alone.

Take my shirt off, let the sun burn through me, burn me away.

Close my eyes and float.

## 37.

"DAMN, BOY, YOU LOOK like a lobster. Put your shirt back on."
Dad's swatting me with his fishing hat.

Oh, he's right. I sit up and inch into my T-shirt, now sewn-together
pieces of sandpaper scratching my raw skin.

"What time is it?" I ask, still trying to find my brain in my body.
The sun somehow flew across the sky, kissing the edge of the earth.

"How should I know? I ain't no Roman philosopher." Okay, no
idea what that means, but whatever. Dad's already thrown his shirt
back on. I think he must have dunked it in the lake first because it's
stuck to his skin like a piece of plastic wrap. Not a bad idea actually.
Who cares if there's toxic waste in the water, at least it'll cool the sting
and the fact it feels like I'm CURRENTLY BEING BARBECUED
BY THE THREE HILLBILLIES.

Oh man.

Before I can tear mine off, though, he's thrown me the oar. "Hurry
up and paddle back. Heather's treatin' us at DQ. Don't wanna be late
for supper." Sure don't. Guess the fishing trip's been canceled. Fine by
me. He cracks open another beer and we float back in silence, save for
the sweet melody of coughs and guzzlebelches . . .

As we near the shore, I see it: A barely visible stream of smoke drifts skyward from behind Web's house! Close my eyes, count to five, open them again. It's still there. Which means it's true: I did see him last night and I can—

"Hey, watch it, boy!" Dad grabs the oar from me, pushes against a rock we were seconds from smashing into.

"Sorry!"

"Pay attention, dammit."

"Sorry."

"Jesus."

"Sorry."

The tin-can trailers are only yards away now. Focus. *You got this, Collins, you got this, you got this—*

The second we reach land, I bound off the boat and nearly fall to my knees, kissing every rock onshore. But I don't. It would ruin my plan.

"Get changed," Dad says once we're inside the trailer. "We're leavin' soon."

I take a breath, exhale a Dulick-presentation sigh. "I don't feel well. I'm going to stay here and sleep. Too much sun." Please let this work.

He doesn't move.

Neither do I.

Then: "Your loss," he says.

I almost grab him and hug him and start dancing his freaky *Gilligan's Island* jig. Don't. Would be a dead giveaway. But my heart's like a zeal of zebras racing from a lioness. I crouch on the bed, holding my knees against my chest to hide it.

Another hour passes before he leaves. I wait for him to drive away before peeking out the trailer's window. And then I wait eleven minutes more, just in case it's a sneak attack and he returns. He doesn't.

Okay, I don't have long. Superhuman Speed: Activate.

I slink into my Pink Floyd T-shirt and black shorts, pull up my tube socks to cover the sunburn, fling my satchel over my shoulder— OW, HOLY FIREBALLS, BATMAN—grab my records, and peek outside.

Nothing. No one's around. Go.

This is it.

This may be my only chance to see him.

# 38.

THE CICADAS BEGIN THEIR ceremonial rattle through the wind. Quietly at first, calling to each other, then they slowly crescendo until the wind itself is trembling through me.

Each step closer to him I feel more like Holden Caulfield. Like a goddamned phony. Like I'm crossing an invisible line of betrayal to a place I don't belong—

Wait. What am I going to do? Apologize to him? For what? For being the Supreme Asshole of All Time? He wouldn't hear it. And I wouldn't blame him. This is crazy. Stupid. Sick. That's the word. Sick. I should go back.

I look at his house. My brain says, *"What the hell do you think you're doing, Collins?"* My heart says, *"GO, MAN, GO."*

I go.

The cicadas grow silent, and with them the wind. Dead. Like they know.

It's still and black. There's no moon out tonight. Perfect.

I round the corner. Mumbles and murmurs and a soft boom of laughter, like distant thunder: his grandfather. A soft orange glow illuminates the blackness behind their house. SweetZiggy, my hands are shaking. I shove them in my pockets.

Boards still cover the windows, and now the front door, too. A light flickers inside, one you can't see from across the lake. A few steps are splintered and missing. Soiled wrappers and broken bottles litter the front. Asshole polluters of the world.

I tiptoe like a loon, stopping each time I reach one of the wooden stilts holding up the house. Count to three, move forward. I wore all black so I'd blend in. Instead, I look like some wacky robber from the movies. Okay, this is decidedly the worst idea ever spawned by man. What am I doing over here? This is serious lock-me-up-and-get-the-death-penalty stalker crap.

Still, I peek through the bushes.

Three people sit around a small firepit dug in the sand. His grandfather's face glows like a piece of fossilized amber. His hair disappears in the night. I only know it's there because the ends look like blackbirds fluttering on his shoulders. He wears denim shorts and a REO Speedwagon T-shirt, the one with the blue angel wings. Cool.

"The look on his face," he says. He throws his hands up and makes this face where his eyes bulge out real big and says, *"Aoooggga!"*

Everyone laughs.

I can only see the backs of the other two. They wear black windbreakers like Web's. But neither one of them is Web. Maybe he's inside, but I can't go in. This is stupid. I have to get out of here before anyone notices, before they call the cops. I'm going.

I smack right into his bare chest.

"Hey."

"JESUS!" I slap my hands over my mouth.

A supernova explodes in my heart. Is it possible to be frozen while everything inside you feels like it's melting to goo? Just curious.

"Ouch," he says.

"Huh?"

"Your face. You look like a can of Coke."

"Oh. Right. Yeah. Too much sun today—out there in the—stupid sun, heh-heh . . ." My wrists ignite. I squeeze them, trying to smother the sting. I know I can't think this, but—*Oh man. His eyes. How could I have forgotten those deep brown eyes. Like two Hershey's Kisses I want to lick and slowly melt in my mouth. And his skin. I swear it glimmers. Probably tastes just as sweet as it looks, like golden honey, and*—ZAP. NO. STOP. You are here for one reason and one reason only: to apologize. Form the words, get them out, and get out before it's too late.

"Did you just eat sour-cherry candies again?" I ask.

"Yeah, why?"

"Oh."

"So, you stalkin' me, man?"

"What? No! Sorry! I mean, I just came over to tell you that I'm sorry. Here—" I shove the records in his chest. "I mean . . ." God, this is harder than I thought. "I wanted to give you these . . . as a sorry-gift? . . . I guess . . . I don't know, I just thought you'd like them . . . maybe . . ."

He holds the albums, staring at me. He's a few inches taller than me and my cheek would nestle perfectly into his chest— No.

"Also . . . yes, okay," I say. "I did want to see if you were alright and all that, and it appears you are, which is a really great thing and, yeah, okay, fine, I might be stalking you. A little." Help me.

He doesn't say anything. Okay, time to go.

"Anyway, Web. I really am sorry. You deserve better. A better friend. You don't even have to forgive me. I wouldn't blame you if you didn't . . ."

I watch his Adam's apple bob up and down as he swallows. Maybe it's a sign of affection. I swallow back. He does nothing. Maybe not. Right, okay. You said it. Now go. "I'll see you around—"

"Carole King's *Tapestry*?" He flips through the records. "One of my favorites . . ."

"Oh. Yeah. I remember you said that, so—"

"And the infamous Roberta Flack, huh?"

"Yeah . . . I mean . . . you haven't really lived until you've heard her. It's—"

"*Aladdin Sane?*" He looks at me.

"You have it already?"

"No, man. It's just . . . isn't it your favorite?"

"Well, I mean . . . he's the grooviest, *obviously*, and he really helps me when I'm—I mean I thought he could help you now . . . maybe . . ." *Ziggy lifts his eyes and winks.* "I want you to have it."

We don't move.

For a long time.

"I was really mad at you that night," he says finally, clutching the albums to his chest.

"I know . . ."

"Still kinda am."

"Right . . ."

"But . . . I don't know . . ." A slight curve starts to inch up his right cheek, when—

"OW." A hand grips my shoulder from behind.

"Sorry there, big guy." I've heard that voice before. I whip around. It's the Web Doppelganger!

"Oh, heyheyhey!" he says. "How you doin', my main man? Damn, lookit you, you're like the Human Torch!" He smiles a bright crescent moon, then does some weird hand-jive thing with my hands I guess I'm supposed to know, and grabs me in a bear hug. Me: Raggedy Andy in his arms.

"You two know each other?" Web asks.

"Know each other? Heck yeah! Two days ago, was it?" He pulls me back.

"That's right. Hello again," I say.

"Yeah, yeah. Great place that is. Great man, that Chester. Only place in town we can really go where it's safe." He's still smiling. So bright it's almost blinding. He wears a bone choker tied around his neck, and his eyes seem to have each caught an ember from the fire and ignited.

"This is my uncle Russell," Web says. "Uncle Russell, this is . . . Jonathan."

"Oh, you're Jonathan? So glad to finally meet you, my man. Officially." He grabs my hand again. This time, I have sense enough to shake.

"You too. I love Smokey Bear."

"What?" he says.

"Your shirt."

"Right, right." He laughs and it's like a roaring waterfall, cooling and relaxing. "Only you can prevent forest fires," he says, putting on Smokey's bear voice.

"Yeah . . ."

"Why don't you come over and join us?"

He starts to pull me toward the fire; I panic. "Figglyfops!" flies out of my mouth. God.

"What?"

Web chuckles. "He talks in tongues sometimes."

"Oh, thought I was missin' out on some jive you kids are usin'. A man needs to know these things to keep up. Come on." He leads me to the circle.

Oh no. I look behind me to see if there's any movement at the trailers. None that I can see from here, but if they return and I'm not there—

"I'm glad you came back," Web whispers in my ear.

I'm staying put. For now.

The second we approach, his grandfather stops talking to the woman who sits across from him on a wooden stump. They stare, stuck in mid-laugh. Like I caught them telling a joke and took a Polaroid.

"Uh. Hello," I say. And lift my hand, spreading my fingers like a stupid Vulcan. I seriously do this. And now I'm frozen. I can't put my hand down. Someone please say something.

"Look what the cat dragged in!" Uncle Russell says. "It's Jonathan! Sit." He plops me down on a log between him and Web's grandfather.

Web sits on the ground next to the woman, fixated on *Aladdin Sane*.

"That's my wife, Sunny," Uncle Russell says.

"Hello," I say.

"Heard a lot about you," she says.

"Oh?" *That can't be good.* Her face is soft and warm. Her hair's twisted in two loose braids and she's wearing a rainbow-colored vest, stitched in such a way that it looks like the bird is about to fly right off her chest. She laughs. I dart my eyes back to hers. Oh man. Does she think I was looking at her breasts? Oh God.

"So, the troublemaker returns," his grandfather says, reclining back in his lawn chair.

"Oh . . . Yeah . . ." I brush some pebbles together in a little mound.

"Lookin' the part, too," he says, chuckling. "A little devilish, if you ask me."

"Oh, heh-heh . . . I was on the—it was so hot today and . . . never mind . . ."

"He's teasing," Sunny says.

"Yeah, he's the Lakota jokester," Uncle Russell says. "Always pulling pranks when you least expect it. Better watch your back." He punches my arm playfully. I rub it, smiling. Thinking it might be permanently bruised now. Damn, that hurt.

"Wanna hear a joke now?" his grandfather asks.

"Here we go," Sunny says.

"Knock knock."

"Oh, uh, who's there?" I say.

"Cash."

"Cash who?"

"No, thanks, I prefer peanuts."

Web shakes his head.

"Oh, I get it. Good one," I say.

"Please don't encourage him," Sunny says.

"Knock knock—"

"Who's there?" I ask.

"A broken pencil."

"A broken pencil who?"

"Never mind," he says. "It's pointless." He laughs so hard at this he nearly falls out of his lawn chair.

"Oh man," I say.

"See? What'd I tell ya?" Uncle Russell says. "Back on the rez, people flee when they see him coming toward them. Slam their windows shut, bolt their doors." He winks.

"Yeah, just wait'll we get home to Pine Ridge," his grandfather says. "Been over a month now. I have a whole notebook full of 'em."

"*If* we get home . . ." Web mumbles. The circle goes quiet. I watch Web's smile slowly melt in the fire. Sunny rubs his back. He looks like he's crying . . . Hard to tell out here, but—

"Hey!" Grandfather booms, thumping his lawn chair down in the gravel. I jump. Web lifts his head. He *is* crying. What's going on? "We're gettin' back home. You hear me? No news is good news. Don't you get lost in that crazy maze in your mind—you know better. What was it you said? 'Navigate something something . . .'"

"The negative," he says softly. Our eyes meet.

"Right. You said it helped. So do it. Everything happens for a reason, you hear me, Web? You know I don't think what happened is right, but it's done. We're together now. That's what matters. Those white goons are gonna get what's coming to them, trust me. Sometimes these things take time, you hear?"

Sunny kisses the top of his head, strokes his hair. "You can't blame yourself, hon . . ."

"You know what your dad used to say to me growing up?" Uncle Russell says. "'White men are lost little boys, scared of what they don't understand.' And if it scares the hell out of 'em, they gotta get rid of it . . ."

"Including us," Sunny says.

"Ain't that the truth," his grandfather says.

Everyone stares off in different directions, silent. *What are they talking about? Why is Web crying? Why is he afraid he won't get home? He said something on the cliff that night about a white cop—I should say something. But what? If Starla were here she'd know what to do. She'd flip if she were sitting here, actually. What was it she talked about that day I first met Web? About going somewhere to help them. That must be what they're—*

"Wounded Knee!" I blurt out. Crap.

They look at me.

"I mean . . . isn't that . . . why you were at Wounded Knee?" I run my fingers through my hair, scratch the back of my head.

His grandfather lifts a smile. "That's exactly why the movement came to the Knee. You heard about that, then?"

"I mean . . . my friend Starla . . . she told me something about . . ." I shift on the log. Web looks up at me, lifting his crooked, dimpled smile. "But . . . What happened? Why were you there?"

His grandfather eyes me. "We were fightin' for our voice to be heard again," he says.

"That. And all the corruption we're dealin' with," Uncle Russell says. "And the racism. And our poor living conditions. I could go on—"

"I just wish they hadn't destroyed so much land," Sunny says. She holds Web's head against her chest. "All those people fighting. So many homes were ruined . . ."

"But seeing our peoples show up in support, coming together like that from all over Turtle Island—"

Uncle Russell leans into me. "That's what we call North America." He winks.

"That never happens."

"Those goons weren't getting through that wall of Red Power!" Uncle Russell says.

"No, sir . . ."

Web wipes his eyes, lost in the fire.

"Starla said it was dangerous," I say, sitting up. "That people even . . . got killed . . ."

"We lost a couple men when they started shooting—" Uncle Russell says, shaking his head. "We all knew what we were gettin' into, but, man—bullets whizzed all around us—like we were in Vietnam. They blocked us in. Wouldn't even let people bring us food or water. Cut off our electricity. Tried to force us off our land *again.*" He squeezes my shoulder. "But you know something, son? We stood our ground. For *seventy-one days.* We didn't back down."

"Yeah, we finally put a face to who we are, let the world see all the promises and treaties those white men have broken all these years . . ." his grandfather says, looking up at the sky. "That's what we showed 'em when all those cameras and news people came . . . Man, it was somethin' else. You shoulda been there, Jonathan."

Everyone's silent again.

Until Uncle Russell chuckles. "I still keep picturing all those white people seeing us on TV like that!"

"Oh, you know they kept hitting their sets, thinking the color was off!" his grandfather says, slapping his lawn chair.

"Probably haven't seen so many Natives together since *The Lone Ranger*!" Sunny says.

They laugh.

Web stands, brushes off his jeans. "Come on, Jonathan."

"Oh. Okay. Where?"

"Just come on," he says, walking toward the house.

I stand. "Uh. Thanks for . . . having me here," I say to the others. "I'm glad, you know, you're okay." God. What a stupid thing to say.

Uncle Russell smiles, pats my back. "Nice seeing you again, kiddo."

"You too—I mean, nice seeing you again, too. All of you . . ." I do not do a Vulcan goodbye again, thank God. I wave. And as soon as I leave the circle, I hear them whispering in a language I don't understand.

# 39.

WEB CLIMBS THE BACK steps.

"You okay?" I ask him.

"Yeah, why?"

"I mean . . . you were just . . . What happened back there? What was he talking about not going home and—"

"It's a long story . . . You comin' in or what, man?" He holds the screen door open.

"*Inside*? No way, Web, I can't. I have to get back over there before—"

"Over there? Over where?"

Dammit. I really didn't want him to know. I promised myself I wouldn't say anything. Mostly because I don't want to be thought of in the same galaxy-breath as them, but—

"We're staying there. Dad and me. With his girlfriend."

"Oh."

"For a few more days."

"Really?"

"Yeah."

"Oh."

We turn to the trailers. I left the light on, so now it looks like two eyes are staring back at us, taunting us. Still, no one's back.

"They're all assholes," I say.

"Yeah."

He doesn't move. It's possible he's trying to create a windstorm with his mind to blow the trailers to kingdom come. Or now he's *really* pissed at me. Either way, can't blame him.

"Anyway, I should go—"

"What? No. Come on." He bounces down the stairs and grabs my hand to pull me up.

"I can't. I should really get back before Dad knows—"

"I got something for your sunburn."

"Oh?"

"It'll just take a few minutes."

"Well . . . I mean . . ." My brain says, *Go. Now. Before it's too late.* My heart says, *Too late.* "Okay. Thanks. But then I need to go."

His grandfather and the others stop talking as we ascend the stairs. I swear someone even turned the volume knob down on the cicadas and crickets and birds and the entire universe.

"Are you sure this is okay?" I ask him.

"Yeah, why?"

"They're all staring."

"Oh. They're curious is all . . ."

"Curious? About what?"

"Come on."

We walk inside. Whoa. Holy Heatwave, Batman. My body instantly starts sweating. I'm getting dizzy. I sit at a wooden table in the center of the room. Web disappears, rummaging through some drawers.

I see three other rooms and they're only a few feet apart and they're each curtained in a faded tie-dyed tapestry. There's a tiny fridge in the corner next to the fireplace. And next to it, a wooden crate stuffed with canned goods and generic foods like a box of Rice

Crunchies and bags of "Cherry-Flavored Powdered Drink Mix."

Underneath me: a vibrant star-shaped rug in yellows and reds and blacks and blues. Woven so perfectly it thumps in and out like a heartbeat when you look at it. I close my eyes. Breathe.

"Your house is neat," I say.

"It's not my house."

"Oh. Right. Whose is it?"

"A friend of the family's."

"Hey, it's like a hundred and fifty degrees in here," I say. "Why don't you open some windows?"

"Can't." He disappears into another room.

"Why not?"

He doesn't answer. He's making so much noise he may be constructing a new wing on the house, banging drawers open and closed.

A small bookshelf stacked with old books sits against the wall, propped up with cinder blocks and a record player. An herb smolders in a bowl. Patchouli maybe? Aunt Luna used to burn that all the time. Hers smelled like the forest floor, but this one's more minty.

He runs back in heaving and sweating, carrying scissors and a spiky plant.

"You okay?"

"Yeah. Just trying to hurry."

"Oh." Right. Because I. Need. To. Get. Back.

"Why can't you open a window?" I ask.

"Hiding."

"From what?"

"Not what. Who."

"Who, then?"

"Those assholes across the lake, man."

"Seriously?"

"Yeah. Take your shirt off."

"WHAT?"

"So I can put this on." He puts the plant on the table and cuts some leaves. A little clear goo oozes out.

"What is it?"

"Aloe. It'll help. Trust me."

"You learn that from your grandfather?"

"Yeah. And from the ancient Greeks and Romans and Egyptians and Chinese and—"

"Okay, I get it."

"So . . . ?"

"Right." Besides the presentation, which doesn't count because it was dark and I was covered in gold glitter, I've never let anyone see me without a shirt. I mean, I barely let *myself* see me without a shirt. I close my eyes, slowly inch it over my head.

"Ouch," he says.

"I know. I look like a piece of red construction paper."

"No. Looks like it hurts."

"Yeah . . ."

He dabs the aloe on my forehead. A cold, slimy prickle from his fingers starts to tingle through my scar. "OW."

"Sorry, man. It may hurt at first, but it'll help, I promise." He whispers this. Oh boy. I keep my eyes closed.

His fingers start to sizzle. Could be a side effect from the treatments. But could be his fingers. Because, oh man, the way he's touching my skin . . .

And now his hands . . .

Oh God, his hands.

I forgot how soft they were. Like dryer sheets. They massage my chest.

"Feel okay?" he says to my cheek. His breath tickles my neck.

I can't answer.

He keeps massaging. A shock rips through his hands, like paddles on a defibrillator charging my heart. *Breathe through it, breathe through it, breathe through it—*

His hands move to my legs. Sweet. Ziggy. No. Like the electric cuffs are wrapped around my thighs. Scorching. *Breathe, breathe, breathe through it . . .* I can't . . . do it . . . it hurts—I open my eyes.

He's inches from me, his hands glued to my legs . . .

I breathe in.

He breathes out.

He inches closer.

I'm so hard right now you could launch rockets off of it and I wouldn't feel it. But I know he can. It's pressed against him. And it burns so bad, a tear falls from my eye before I can stop it.

He wipes it away. "You okay?"

I nod.

We sink into each other's eyes, like that moment in the presentation, the only two people in the universe . . . Being apart from him these past two weeks, I almost forgot what it felt like. Almost . . .

"I'm glad you came back," he whispers.

"Me . . . too . . ."

"You shouldn't have said those things that night," he says. "You really hurt me."

"I know, Web. I'm—"

"I didn't think that was possible. That you could hurt me. That *anyone* could. Not like that . . ."

"I'm sorry. I was scared. And when I get scared, I get all crazy inside. That's not an excuse, but—"

"You shouldn't let them do that to you."

"What?"

"If you didn't hide, maybe you wouldn't feel so crazy inside . . ."

"I wish it were that easy . . ."

"Yeah . . . I know . . . me too . . ." He wipes another tear off my cheek, sits back on his knees. His hair's parted in the middle and floats down his chest. "It's funny, I . . ."

"What?"

He looks down. "I don't know, man . . . Being here . . . with you . . . I'm usually so lost in my head, but when I'm with you . . ." He picks at the frayed hole in his jeans. "My thoughts just kinda float away, and things . . . make sense again—even now. It's hard to explain . . ."

I lift his chin. The second my fingers touch his skin, a volt zips through me. My breath shudders, but I do not flinch.

"I missed this," he whispers.

"I . . . missed this, too, Web . . ."

"I wish . . . we could just . . . I don't know . . ."

"I know . . . me too . . ." His lips are so close I can smell the sour-cherry candies and I want to taste them in my own mouth, feel his breath in mine, but . . .

I can't.

"I have to get back," I say to the woven heartbeat rug. Easier that way.

"Oh . . ."

"I mean, I want to stay, but it's not safe for me to be here—" I carefully slink back into my shirt and start walking toward the door. I feel tears brimming my eyes, but I will not let any more escape.

"Hey . . . Bowie boy." He stands, holding himself like I wish he could be holding me. "Maybe you should come back tomorrow . . ."

I don't move.

"We can hide from those assholes together . . ." he says.

"I . . . can't, Web."

"Yeah . . ." He tucks some hair behind his ear, shuffles his feet on the wood floor. "You remember that recording we did in your room?"

"Of course."

"We can always go there, you know? To the moon. It's safe at least . . ."

"Yeah . . . yeah it is . . ."

"I'll see you there, then?"

"Yeah . . . okay . . . I'll see you there . . ."

He lifts his dimpled smile. "I'll just . . . wait on the balcony first. To make sure you get across okay . . ."

I nod and walk out the door, just before the tears start rolling down my cheeks.

So Einstein says, "The universe is always conspiring for your greatest good," huh? If that were true, we wouldn't be living here. Not in this broken time, not in this broken city, not on this broken planet with my broken Ziggy cross pieces. No. We'd be on our caravel ride through the stars. Together.

When I finally reach the trailers, I turn back to wave.

But he's already gone.

## 40.

THE NEXT MORNING, I'm burning up. I lift my head from the pillow. Oh. It's like the sunburn's burning me alive. I must have a fever . . . or something. What happened to me last night? What was in that aloe goo? Every nerve in my body is a solar flare and the world's wavy, like entering a dream sequence on TV. No doubt, *instant karma* for seeing him last night, as Aunt Luna would say.

I. Don't. Care.

"Hey. Son. You alright? You don't look too good," Dad says, shaking me. It comes out real slow. Like someone pressed Play halfway down on my tape recorder.

"I think I have a fever," I try to say, but the words melt on my tongue.

"Get some rest," he says. "I'll get you a cold towel."

I flop back down, close my eyes, and swim far away,

back to my dreams . . .

*I'm standing in the middle of the lake again. Alone.*

*"Web? Where are you? Help me! I'm stuck!"*

*Ziggy on the Cross rises from the water. Waterfalls rush on either side of him. He unhinges his wrists and jives to the music. "Come on, Starman, remember what's in the middle of space and time? You gotta let yourself go.*

*You gotta go back to him."* Then he inhales and bursts into a million red shimmering stars—

A muffled voice in a distant galaxy calls my name: *"Jonathan."*

I try to answer.

*"Jonathan."*

Someone's shaking me.

"Jonathan!"

I jolt up. It's Dad.

"Am I dreaming?"

"No."

"What time is it?"

"Five or somethin'. You've been sleepin' all day. You okay, son?"

"I guess?" I lean my head against the trailer wall, slap my palm on my forehead. I'm sweating and trembling and a wildebeest is scratching to get out of my lungs, but I'm back. I think. And my fever's cracked. I think. I grab a few PeterPaulandMary poofs, towel my face with my T-shirt. Doesn't do any good; it's soaked.

Dad cracks open a bottle of Bud, hands me a glass of water. "You look like hell. Drink this."

The door's open, and a quicksand of air swelters through. Hal and Heather stand together, arm in arm, plotting my tragic demise.

"We're goin' a few trailers down for a barbecue," says Dad. "Some cat's just got back from Vietnam. Comin'?" He sloshes beer down his chest, swipes it with the back of his hand. "You hear me?"

"Yeah," I say. "I'm going to stay. I need to rest."

"You remember why we came here, right?"

"Yeah . . ."

"Uh-huh. Fine. I'm givin' you this day, son, but tomorrow? You do what I say. Got it?" He slams the trailer door.

I slink out of bed, stumble over to the kitchen sink, and slop my head under the faucet to let the water cleanse me like a rain shower.

Okay, I'm back.

Sort of.

I dig through my satchel to find the book Ziggy talked about in my dream—*Jonathan Livingston Seagull*. And I read the quote aloud. To Web.

> *"Overcome space, and all we have left is Here. Overcome time, and all we have left is Now. And in the middle of Here and Now, don't you think we might see each other once or twice?"*

I look through the binoculars.

"Yeah," I whisper. "I think we just might. Once or twice . . ."

**-H.**

———

*Monday, July 2, 1973*

THE NEXT DAY, DAD wakes up with the same fever I had. Or something like it. He's beet red, covered in sweat, and can't stop coughing. At one point he wobbled to the bathroom to pee and told me to "Stay put!" Then he fell back asleep, swimming away in his own fever dreams.

Fine by me.

I spend the morning alone whispering into my tape recorder:

"This is Jonathan Collins coming to you live from Creve Coeur Lake. This just in: A Literal Watergate. Reports have been flooding in that one step on the Broken Heart Lake will singe your soul and destroy your mind and leave you running back and forth across the waters like a starved madman. No survivors have been reported. Stay away. Far away."

I seriously might be losing my mind. All I can think about is how to get myself back across the lake, but every scenario ends in destruction. And the impossibility of seeing him again is worse than being strapped down to the Electric Box of Shame. I swear it's ripping me apart inside . . .

I grab my chest, twist my T-shirt . . .

Lift the binoculars from the wall and peer through.

Still. Nothing.

Hours later, Dad wakes me. He has his usual props: bottle in one hand, cigarette in the other. He's hunched over himself, huffing, his thin hair splotched against his forehead. "Come on, get ready, we're going over to the barbecue." He looks pale and gray. Like someone forgot to paint him in a paint-by-numbers.

"There's another barbecue? Didn't you just—"

"Yeah, there's another one. The guy's a goddamn war hero. We should be celebratin' him every day."

"You sure you're okay, Dad? We could just—"

"I'm fine." He grabs a towel from the sink and wipes his face. "Come on. Get movin'. Heather's already over there. Don't wanna be late." Sure don't. Damn, no getting out of this one. I need to put up a few thousand force fields. My powers have severely diminished since being here.

I throw on the Pink Floyd shirt for added protection, but apparently Dad's fever dreams have also made him a fashion columnist for *Field & Stream*, because he makes me change. Over and over again. Jesus, what's the big deal? Nothing I choose is right. After three costume changes—

> 1) *favorite turquoise polo and white tennis shorts ("You're too*
>    *rich-looking.")*
> 2) *Cardinals T-shirt and matching red cotton shorts ("You*
>    *look like a Popsicle.")*
> 3) *yellow tank top with cutoff denims ("You look like a god-*
>    *damned girl." UGH.)*

—we settle on my Eagles album T-shirt because it has an eagle on it, and we're back to the white tennis shorts.

SweetBabyZiggy, didn't know we were going to a Trailer Park Cotillion Ball. Dad goes shirtless with a ratty pair of denim shorts he's worn for the past three days to present me. He hands me a six-pack to take as a gift for the guy back from Vietnam, and off we go. Me: clutching my Ziggy on the Cross pieces, safely stashed in my shorts pocket. Can't be too prepared.

The sky is a brighter purple tonight, like someone left the black light on. It makes the water glow extra-blue and the trailers gleam extra-bright and the bonfire ahead extra-blazing and THWOOP, my clothes instantly stick to me like a sponge.

A burst of "Heyheyhey"s and "Whatitbewhatitbe"s claps the air. Hickory smoke billows from the bonfire and the redneck revelers are already in full-on party mode. Dad's instantly swarmed by a few of his new beer-guzzling belchers, with Heather locked on his hip, leaving me standing there like an idiot. At least I'm dressed appropriately.

I drop the six-pack off on a card table and weave through the fast-building crowd of bikini-clad rats and shirtless beasts who all seem to stop mid-cackle or mid-belch to stare at me. Heather's boy races Hot Wheels in the rocks, slamming them into my shoes.

*Keep walking. Don't make eye contact. Navigate the negative. Just go.*

I stop at the edge of the shore, a good few yards from anyone nearby, and watch the crying waterfall gushing in the distance. Man, is she wailing right now. Yeah, I feel ya, sister.

"Hey there."

I whip around. Forgot about rats being sneaky and fast.

"Hello."

She's my age, maybe younger, not sure. Never saw her at school before. She's wearing a hand-knitted bikini top that only covers her nipples and denim strings for shorts. Oh boy.

"Whatchoo doin', cutie pie?" she asks, dangling a bottle of Bud between two fingers and smoking a Virginia Slim. She sounds like a meerkat.

"Oh, I was just looking at the—" Crying Princess Waterfall? Uh. No. "Nothing," I say. Her hair's shagged like Jane Fonda from that movie *Klute* and her face is painted like Jane Fonda from *Barbarella*, so I say, "You look like Jane Fonda."

She blinks. "Huh?"

"Nothing."

"You're weird."

"Yeah. That's what they say."

"Lookin' for someone?"

"What? Oh, yeah . . ." I crane my neck from side to side. Where is that . . . someone . . .

She slops her arms around my neck. "You're cute," she says. Her breath smells like rotted cabbage. "You ain't like them other boys."

"Nope. No I am not."

"You're Jonathan?"

"Yeah?"

"Not what I pictured. So you live in the city."

"Oh. Well not—"

"I live right there. In that trailer."

"Oh. Cool." Okay. It's been a trip; gotta run. But I can't. Her arms squeeze tighter. I giggle, look around for . . . someone . . .

"There's somethin' different about you," she says.

"Oh? Not really, no."

"Yeah, yeah there is." She scrapes her fingers on my cheek. One of her fake nails chips off. "Shit," she says and burps. "You ever kiss a girl before?"

"What? Yeah, of course. Why?"

"You wanna kiss me?"

"Oh, no. But thank you."

"Why the hell not?"

"Oh, well, I have—"

"Think you're too good for me? S'at it?"

"No! No, not at all. I . . . have a girlfriend, so—"

"So what?"

"So I just don't want to hurt her feelings?"

"What the hell your daddy send me over here for, then?"

Bingo. Okay. Got it now. The girl who's going to fix me. At least she could've brushed her teeth.

"I don't know," I say. "To talk maybe?"

"Talk? What the hell we gonna talk about?" She pushes herself away. "How purty the sky is? How del-i-cate the lake looks? How you readin' some big book I ain't ever heard of?"

"No. Sorry. I didn't mean—"

"You and your fancy-boy self. I don't need you. I don't need you . . . Who the hell you think you are anyway, huh? Huh? HUH—"

KA-BLEWIE. Her head explodes in a million pieces of rage and splatters all over me. I try to calm her, but she's lost in a cacophony of obscenities being hurled in every direction. People have turned to see what the ruckus is about. *Nothing to see here, folks. Just keep . . . doing whatever it is you're doing out here.* My body's caught in her cyclone of fury. Dad's definitely going to kill me now.

"Hey hey, Tammy, what's going on here?" Hal pushes through some oafs in bib overalls. He slithers between us, gripping her shoulders.

"This *fancy* boy thinks he's too good for me!"

"Hey, that's not true. This here's a friend of mine," he says, giving me a wink.

"I'm sorry. I didn't mean to upset you," I say.

Hal shakes his head and turns back to Tammy, who grabs some wadded-up tissue from under her bikini top to wipe her nose.

"I'm pretty, too, goddammit!" she yells to Hal.

"Of course you are."

"You ain't no better than me," she screams, looking over his shoulders to me.

"You're right. I'm not."

"Listen, Tammy, why don't you go get yourself cleaned up," Hal says. "Get yourself another beer, and when you come back, the fiddlers will be here again and I'll get to steal you away for a few dances. How's that sound?"

She snorts in her tissue, smears black makeup across her face, and stuffs it back in her bikini.

"You would?" she asks.

"Yeah, for sure. Sound good?"

She flicks his hat off and squishes it on her head. "You're always such a tease, Hal Loomis," she says. "I'll see you on the dance floor." She pecks him on the cheek and stumbles off. I think she's already forgotten about me.

"Sorry," I say. "Thanks." I start to walk past. He steps in front of me.

"Don't mention it," he says. "She's a loose cannon, if you know what I mean." He whistles and twirls his fingers by his ears. His teeth are yellowed and pointy. Without his hat on, he looks like Mr. Clean's brother who did hard time and escaped Alcatraz, roughed-up and *disturbed in the eyes*, as Grandma used to say.

"Yeah."

"Why don't you join me? I was just about to roast a hot dog."

"Oh, I can't, thanks, my dad is—"

"In a trailer with Heather."

"Oh."

"Come on." He leads us to the bonfire, now flocked by the Three Hillbillies and a handful of other extras from *Deliverance*. I barely glance up, deciding it is much better to focus on whatever is currently being twirled on the spit.

"Well, well, well, if it ain't Robert's boy," BillyBob says. Turns out he's one of the oafs in bib overalls. His face is voltage red and dripping with sweat; his long beard shoots off him like fried corn silks. "Get yourself in a little Tammy trouble there?"

"Oh. Yeah . . ."

Hal pulls me down on a log to sit by him, then hands me a stick with a hot dog piercing the end.

"Don't worry, boy," Five-Teeth Terry says, smoking. His head glows as bright as the end of his cigarette. "You ain't nothin' special. Ain't nobody here escaped the wrath of Tammy."

A round of cackles, grunts, and other indecipherable noises.

"What y'all laughin' at?" Porky Joe booms. He stops whittling a piece of wood with that unusually large knife of his. "That's my goddamn daughter you're talking about—"

"Hell, she even tried to get that Injun boy across the lake," Terry spits out.

Joe suddenly thrusts his knife at him. "Say it again! Say it, you got-damned bumpkin! I'll cut you so hard you'll wish those Indians would've scalped you instead. Say it!"

No one in the circle moves.

"Come on, boys," BillyBob says, mopping his head with a handker-chief. "I'm sick a yer shit. We're here to honor our friend, remember?" He gestures to the man sitting across from him, probably not that much older than me. A cigarette with a three-inch-long ash dangles from his fingers. And like me, he hasn't blinked or stopped staring at the fire since I sat down. Probably stuck in his head somewhere in Vietnam, still fighting a never-ending war.

Guess we all are.

"He knows not to bring them up, Billy," Porky Joe yells. "He knows how I feel about them redskins." His knife hovers inches from Terry's neck. "Bring up my daughter again in the same breath as them, and I'll slice you in two. I ain't even kiddin' here, you ugly trailer trash hick. Got it?"

"Got it. Jesus, man, it's a damn joke."

"Goddamn hillbilly." Porky Joe thwacks the side of Terry's head. So hard I'm sure he broke something. He turns back to the fire, huffing and puffing and blowing it ten feet higher in the air.

Everyone's quiet.

I twist my hot dog in the fire.

Only the crackle and sizzle of meat pierce the stillness.

"Let that be a lesson to all you boys," BillyBob says. "You stay away from them Indians. They don't belong in these parts. I don't know what they're doin' over there in the first place, but this here's a white man's town, and that there's our land and they know it. They ain't nothin' but trouble. See what happens?" He gestures to Joe, who's still fuming, then looks at me. I nod. *Does he know? Did he see me?*

"And you need to calm your ass down, Joe," BillyBob yells. "You forget our plan already? They gonna get what's comin' to them— Hey! Joe! You hear me?" Porky Joe snaps back and shrugs. "Yeah, that's right. Hoo boy, we gonna be puttin' a pow in their wow and get rid of them Indians real soon. Ain't that right, Hal?" He turns to Hal, who looks at me, smirking. "And it looks like we got us a couple new friends here to help us out, ain't that right? Hey! Robert's boy! Ain't that right?"

He means me? No. I don't move. I don't breathe. I don't know what to do. I want to scream, *"YOU'RE ALL ROTTEN, NO-GOOD PIECES OF REDNECK TRASH"* so each word stabs their eyes out. I want to yell so loud the bonfire shoots fireballs and disintegrates them all to a pile of ash.

But I don't.

Instead, I glare at the fire, and nod.

*"HeyBOYS!"* a velociraptor screeches through the silence.

"Hey, hey, if it ain't Bernadette," BillyBob yells. "Where you been hidin', girl?" She waves two six-packs over her head and does a weird catcall whistle thing back at them.

"Well, you know me, boys! I gotta keep you waitin' for more!" Thinking she might be the Madam of Trailerville. She looks like a page from a coloring book that's been scribbled all over, crumpled up, and thrown in the corner trash can.

Whatever. She's a welcome distraction from me and wherever that conversation was going. But what the hell are they planning? I need to run. I need to warn—

"How do you like it out here so far?" I jump. Hal. A little too close to my ear. I turn back to my twirling hot dog and scoot a few inches away.

"Fine," I say.

"They mean well, you know."

I shuffle some rocks under my shoes, quick-glance around. Can't run now, too many people: Madam Bernadette has an army of toads hopping around her.

"They're just real protective. You know, of their friends, their land, their secrets . . ." He laughs, shoves his shoulders against mine. "Guess we all are, huh?"

I don't move.

"You're burnin'," he whispers.

"What?"

"Your hot dog. It's on fire."

"Damn!" I blow out the little flame.

Hal scoots the three inches I'd taken away from him and whispers, "Hey, don't worry. Your secret's safe with me."

I swallow.

"You know what I say? Live and let live. Just don't mess with me." His hand squeezes mine. "I mean, come on, man. It's the seventies, right? Sexual liberation and all that jazz?"

The world starts to whoosh; Madam Bernadette gyrates in slow motion. I'm getting dizzy. I need to get out of here. *Think, Collins. Navigate the negative and think.*

"I'm serious, man," Hal says, gripping my wrists tighter. "You don't have to worry. Hey, look at me." I do. His copper eyes glint. He lifts a grin that stretches his scar all the way to his ear. "Trust me, okay?" I nod. "You just gotta be more careful. There's eyes all over this lake."

"I should get another hot dog," I say. "This one's burnt."

"Of course. They're right over there." He points to the card table. "Glad we had this talk. I'll keep your seat warm."

I jump up, zigzag through the dancing blur of bib overalls and bikinis, and fold myself in the crowd, disappearing in the shadows. Hal stands. He starts to walk toward me. I could roll under the trailers and hide, but then—

SWOOSH. Tammy swoops in, wrapping her talons around his neck, and saves the day! Never thought I'd be so happy to see her. He tries to wriggle free, but I know that grip. Like a frigging bear trap. He's not going anywhere.

Without thinking and before anyone notices, I run. I need to warn Web and his family.

No light pours through the door this time as I inch my way up their back stairs. The screen door's kicked open, but otherwise no movement, no laughter, no one. And except for the distant echoes of fiddles and cackles and the pounding bass drum of my heart, no sound—

No. Someone's grunting and—*BOOMCRASHBANG*—broken glass and books and Godknowswhat thud to the floor. My body slaps against the house. Someone's dragging something. Maybe they already got them. Maybe it's a body they're trying to hide, and—

I peek my head in. It's Web. A small desk lamp illuminates his shadow-self dragging a box. What the hell is he doing? I should say something. This is definitely crossing over into stalker territory—

"This will help. It always helps . . ." He's mumbling to someone. Who else is with him? I see no other person in the house, no other lights on.

When he reaches his room, I jump out of sight, scaling the wall. Okay. Now I'm officially stalking. Still, I peek my head back in.

He sits on the floor by his bed. He's wearing his Pink Floyd T-shirt—*the* one!—and a pair of plaid boxer shorts. Is he crying?

He flips the lid up on his record player, the one stashed under the bookshelf. He holds one of my records in his hand, wipes his eyes with his forearms. Oh, he *is* crying.

"Yup, she always helps," he says to no one. He stares at the album. I lean in to see which one it is— He snaps up.

OHMAN.

"Who's there?" he yells.

I inch my head into the screen's frame. Wave.

"Jonathan?"

"Sorry. Yes."

"You came back." He wipes his face again. "How long you been standing there?"

"Not long. I just got here, I—"

"Come in."

"Where is everyone?"

His boxers hang loosely below his waist when he stands, exposing a few perfectly carved ridges on his stomach. I do not notice this.

"They went to town to grab a few things from the market. You okay?" He walks toward me. Slowly.

"Yeah. I mean, no. Listen, I just . . . came over to . . . say . . ." Oh man. I rehearsed a speech on my trek across the lake, but it's all turned to gobbledygook now that I'm standing in front of him again. I close my eyes. *Let's run now and never look back, and we can hide together for the rest of our lives on the moon, staring at the stars where no one can touch us, and no one can hurt us, and*—I open my eyes. He's inches from me now. Shimmering with sweat. I clear my throat. "I'm here because you need to know: Those people across the lake—I know for sure they're planning—to do something—I don't know what—but I think they're planning to hurt you guys . . . maybe . . . so that's why I'm here . . . to . . . tell you that . . ."

He hasn't blinked. He's standing so close there's no more darkness between us and he still smells like he's been playing out in the woods all day: sweet boy-sweat.

"You . . . hear what I said . . ." I whisper.

"Yeah, I heard you," he whispers back.

"Okay . . . well . . . that's . . . good . . ."

"Is that the only reason you came back?"

"Well . . . I mean . . . no . . . I mean . . ."

"Jonathan . . ."

"Web . . . I . . ." And our lips smash together with such force the rest of my words disappear in his mouth. And the rest of my body disappears into his everything. And I scream. For real. Like Dr. Evelyn turned the knobs up to NINETY, which basically eviscerates your nerves in two seconds flat.

He leans back slightly and whispers, "You okay?" The puff of his breath feels like a feather brushing my lips, and I can taste the honey on his lips, and I try to say something, but instead, I pull him right back into me so we will never have to talk again, because I know the minute we do it will be over. I don't care how much it burns. Another scream leaps from my mouth into his. Oh man . . . it hurts. But . . . I don't . . . ever want this . . . to end—OW. I force myself off.

"What is it? What's wrong?" he asks.

"I'm sorry. I shouldn't have—we shouldn't be—we can't—" I rub my wrists together so hard, it only makes them ignite more. "It hurts—"

"What hurts? What's wrong?" He keeps inching into my lips and I keep pushing him away.

"Stop. What if your—family shows up—I need to—get back before Dad knows I'm—I'm serious, Web, STOP." He does. And looks like someone who just got slapped across the face a few times, stumbling and stunned. "Aren't you scared? Didn't you hear what I said?"

"Hell no, man, I ain't scared. I'm staying right here."

"But those assholes are coming over here to do—something—"

"So what, man? Empty threats—"

"And I sure as hell can't be here, because if we get caught I'll end up in jail or the psycho ward or—I don't know what—GOD. I'm so sick of *saying that!*" I punch my thighs to try and stop the stinging. "Fuck, it hurts!" Tears suddenly burst from my eyes like we're back on the cliff. I can't stop them.

"Jonathan, it's okay—"

"No. No it's not okay! Maybe I don't want to go to the moon anymore, Web. Maybe I don't want to pretend, you know. Maybe I want to stay here with you, because these are the realest feelings I've ever felt—but I can't—we can't—you can't stay here. It's not safe and—"

He folds me into his arms. His heart beats against mine like a wild drummer. His breath sears my neck. It scorches, but I never want him to let me go. And I'm so angry and confused I scream in my hands again.

"Hey hey hey, Jonathan, look at me. LOOK at me." I do. "This is exactly what they want."

"Who?"

"Everyone out there. To make you feel crazy. Don't let them."

"I hate this. All of this. I don't want you to get hurt, and—"

"Nobody's going to hurt me."

"But you should hide somewhere . . . or something, I don't know. Just for now—"

"We've been running our whole lives, Jonathan. And they always get away with it. Always." He clasps my cheeks. "We're not people to them. We're frigging animals to them, man. Get it?" Tears leap from his eyes. "At some point you have to stop and say, 'Enough. This is me.' And fight for it as hard as you can. Get it?" His hands tremble, shaking me.

"I hate this so much. So much—"

"I know. Me too . . . Come here." He pulls me toward his bedroom.

"Web, I need to go—" I dry my face with my T-shirt.

"Just hold on a sec . . . it's time I told you . . ."

"Told me what?"

"Come in here."

Hammered-up pieces of wood cover his walls like a patchwork quilt. Besides the bed, and a dresser piled high with books, there's nothing else in his room. So sparse, it could be mine.

He bends over the record player. I do not notice his boxers slowly inching down the small of his back. He slips the vinyl out of the paper covering, places it on the turntable like I would, like it's part of the crown jewels collection, and clicks on the player. Carole King pounds the piano like nobody's business.

"Come on." He closes his eyes, starts swaying to the music.

"What are you doing?"

"Come on, man. It's my turn, remember? Our game? This is how I want to tell you." He waves his hands toward me, doing some funky dance moves that make him look ridiculous. I can't help it; I start giggling. "Why aren't you dancing, Bowie boy?"

Sweet Ziggy. I bounce my knees like an idiot.

"No, no, not like that. Like this." He pulls me into him. A spark rips through us.

"Ow . . ."

"You okay?"

"You . . . wanna slow dance?" I ask.

"I do."

"To this?"

"Why not?"

"It's . . . weird?"

"Is it?"

"I don't know." *Oh, shut up and put your head on his shoulder.* I do. And I melt.

"There," he says. "Much better."

I nuzzle my head into his neck, scalding my scar with his sweat. His arms blanket me and I close my eyes to Carole King's voice.

"Your song," I whisper.

"Yeah, man. The song. This is the one that played when my father—" He stops and I try to lift my head, but he only holds me tighter. "I never forgot that cop's face. Not ever. And then I saw him at this bar in town. Plastered out of his frigging mind. He stumbled out to take a piss. I followed him until we were in the shadows. And I don't know what happened." His breath shudders. "Next thing I know, my fist was in his jaw and he was on the ground. And I jumped on top of him and pounded his face like it was the baton he used on my father, and before I knew it, he was a bloody mess. Just lying there. He started moving, reaching for me. So I ran. Ran all the way back home. And when I told my grandfather, we jumped in Uncle Russell's truck and drove. Because they both knew the minute they found me I'd be dead. We drove all the way here. To hide me."

I pull my head back.

"That's why I was hiding when we met," he says. "That's why I've been hiding, and I'm so fucking sick of hiding. And when I'm with you I don't want to hide anymore, Jonathan. I want to stay right here . . . but . . . that's why we can't go home yet. We're still waiting to hear what happened to the cop, if he's looking for me or—" He pulls me back in. "I don't care about those stupid assholes across the lake, man. Get it now?"

I nod into his chest.

"Good," he says. "Good . . . Your turn . . ."

But I can't answer.

We sway and disappear in each other's arms, and

"So Far Away" starts crooning through the speakers, and

for one moment in time,

two lonely astronauts floating in space

finally find each other.

## -13.

"Two days left, that's all we got," Dad says, wiping a tsunami of sweat from his forehead. Some color's come back to his face, but he still looks like a black-and-white filmstrip. Man, that fever must've really sunk him. The only tint to his frame is the bright-orange polyester shirt he's wearing, with a few buttons bulging in his middle.

"Okay," I say.

We're walking through rows and rows of fireworks in a red-and-yellow circus tent that's been set up outside the lake district. You aren't allowed to shoot them off at the lake, but laws be damned!

"Then you're home free."

"Yeah. Mission accomplished," I say.

"Think we did it?"

"I don't know. You?"

"I don't know." His takes his aviators off, drying his eyes. "Man, it's a doozy today. Ain't you hot?" I shrug. He throws a cardboard cylinder—literally the size of my head—in the basket. "You feel any different since we got here?"

"Oh yeah," I say. Understatement of the seventies, but anyway.

"Well, good, son . . . good . . ." He lifts his Robert Redford beam.

Huh. Been a while since that smile's appeared. Maybe Dr. Evelyn was onto something here . . .

"These are neat," I say. "Personal favorite." I throw in three boxes of those black pellets—the ones you light and they slither out to become styrofoamy snakes.

"Grab some more if you like 'em," he says. So I do. He finds the table with bottle rockets and basically scoops up every last one. "So I heard Tammy wasn't such a good idea . . ."

"Let me think about it . . . No," I say.

He laughs—for real laughs! "Yeah, heard she's kind of a mess." He starts coughing, thumping his chest. "Not like—my Heather—damn, this cough—"

"No, not like your Heather," I say. "You okay?"

He waves me off and throws in twenty packs of Black Cats. Then he thinks about it and throws in a handful more. He picks up a box of sparklers. "You used to . . . love these as a kid . . ."

"Yeah. I loved drawing in the air with them."

"So did your momma . . ." We stand in silence. He twists the box. Are his hands shaking? I don't look in his eyes, still imagining him smiling down on me like we're having a real-life father-son bonding day. He throws the box in the basket and grabs a few more. We keep walking. "You seem happier, son."

I do? So that's what it feels like. I keep thinking about the way we kissed, the way we slow danced. The way he looked at me when he said you have to fight for it as hard as you can—

"Good to be out here, huh?" he asks, launching me back to the tent.

"Oh. Yeah . . ."

"Look, I know I ain't the greatest father in the world. Hell, I ain't even the most pleasant man to be around. But, well . . . you know . . . oh hell, I don't know." His voice quivers. What is happening here?

He throws in some Roman candles and another cylinder the size of Missouri, and pulls a crumpled pack of Camels out of his pocket.

"Uh, Dad, you probably shouldn't do that in here."

"Why not?"

"Because we are literally in a tent full of explosives."

"Right . . . here." He shoves the basket in my hands. "Fill it up." He walks out to the furthest outskirts of the tent and starts pacing, rubbing his hands through his hair. Something is definitely off right now.

I stroll up and down the rows, throwing in whatever looks most sparkly for me and whatever looks most scary for Dad. Two basketfuls later—and lost again in my tangled thoughtstrings about dancing with Web, and how to stop the hillbillies from whatever it is they're planning, or if they really were *just empty threats* like Web said, and how I can sneak back over to see him again—I don't even notice the small crowd that's gathered around Dad until someone yells.

I drop the baskets and run, pushing through elbows and bellies to find him lost in another apocalyptic thunder of coughs.

"Should we call a doctor?" someone else says.

"Is that his kid?" another says.

"Someone should help him," a woman says.

I kneel next to him, but he pushes me away. "I'm fine!" he coughs out. "Let . . . me be!" He slowly stands, wavers over to a net fence, trying to steady himself. It folds in and he smashes to the ground, tangling himself in a web of orange plastic and another quake of coughs. Jesus.

The woman screams.

"Someone call for a doctor!" another man yells.

She starts running toward the tent, but somehow between a convulsing net and chest Dad yells, "STOP."

We do. And watch him lying there like a car wreck as he slowly catches his breath again. He heaves in and out. In and out. The redness in his face and eyes softens to a flushed pink. He reaches toward me. With the help of a big-bellied extra, I lift him up.

"You sure you're okay, mister?" he says, holding Dad's other arm steady.

Dad nods, waves absently in the air. "Fine, fine," he says. He takes in a few deep breaths, lets out a few more deep coughs. "Good god-damn . . . Couldn't catch . . . my breath . . . sorry . . . 'bout that, folks!"

"You need us to call you a doctor or somethin'?"

"No, no . . . I'm fine," he says, undoing the man's arm. "Man, I gotta . . . quit these things." He pats the cigarettes in his pocket and forces a laugh. "Thank you all. Sorry again . . . I'm fine, really. Let's go, son."

We push our way through the crowd. "Dad, seriously, you okay?"

"Yeahyeah. How . . . goddamn embarrassing. Get me to . . . the car."

I plop him in the passenger seat.

"You get the fireworks?" he wheezes.

"Oh. No. We should go—"

"No. Here." He fishes through his pocket, hands me a wadded twenty. "Go get 'em. And tell the guy to . . . keep the rest . . . so he can . . . get the fence fixed." He's leaning over, propping himself up with one hand on the dash, the other on the door, trying to control his breathing again.

I hand him PeterPaulandMary. "Here," I say. "Maybe this'll help."

He shoos me away.

When I return a few minutes later hauling an overstuffed box, Dad's sitting upright, eyes closed. His chest expands like a hot air balloon. "Take me to the market," he says as I climb in.

"Maybe we should go home, get you to—"

"Drive." I do.

Along the way, he recites a list of things he'd promised to get Heather for the big Fourth of July pig roast tomorrow night. Damn. Forgot about that.

I start scheming my way back across the lake . . .

Everyone's gone when we return.

"I need to disappear," Dad says when we climb back in the trailer. "And you're stayin' put, you hear me?"

"Okay."

He guzzles cough syrup like he would a bottle of beer and within minutes he's passed out.

*Yeah, Dad, I feel ya.* I grab the bottle and glug a few gulps to fall asleep, too.

Sometimes disappearing from yourself is the only cure.

## 44.

MY HEAD FEELS LIKE it's stuck in a fishbowl. Like the one I wore with Aunt Luna at the moon landing.

What time is it? No clue. Night-fifteen. I think I must have fallen through a black hole in my sleep: no dreams, it's pitch-black inside and out, and dead silent. Except for the cicadas. Tonight they're extra-loud.

I peek my head through the curtain. No lights in Heather's trailer. Her rusted Bug still sits in the driveway, but the Caddy's gone. Maybe they went to DQ for dinner. Did he ask me if I wanted to go? Did he try and wake me? Not that I would have, obviously, but if he did, I don't remember.

I slap myself a few times, try to snap myself back to reality—

"You should be kinder to yourself."

"SHIT." I throw my body against the side of the trailer.

Hal. Sitting in the shadows on the corner of Dad's bed, like the Grim Reaper.

"You scared me. What are you doing?" I gather the sheets around me. For protection, I guess, I don't know. Every muscle instantly tightens.

"Sorry, sorry," he says. He's smiling. I can hear it, but I can't see it. "Everyone left and I thought we could make some barbecue or something, but you were asleep and I didn't want to bother you. So. I waited."

My scar's twitching. Wires are furiously being rewired within. My body's paralyzed but my mind's racing in some Olympian sprint. Because it knows.

"Oh. Well. You could've maybe waited outside?" I say.

"This is my fucking home." Instant shift. From sugar sweet to serial killer. I can't even begin to navigate whatever the hell this negative is.

He laughs. "But you're right. You are the guest. Just didn't think you'd care on account we're secret buds and all." He's slowly twisting a knife in my gut, pinning me against the trailer like a dead dung beetle. "I mean, you disappeared the other night, and . . . well . . . remember what I said . . . there's eyes all over this lake . . . Anyway, I'll go. If you want."

"That'd be great," I say.

He doesn't move.

Neither do I.

Then he unfolds his hands, places them on Dad's bed like he's about to prop himself up. But instead: "Do I scare you, Jonathan?"

I cannot see his face, masked by the shadows of the trailer, but I can picture it: a pockmarked rat with copper eyes slithering around me, and that crooked scar always smirking on his left cheek.

"I don't mean to if I do," he says. "Just the opposite. I'd hoped we could be friends."

I inch across the trailer wall.

"Or we could be each other's secret-holder. Everyone needs a secret-holder in their life, right?"

A spring creaks on his bed. I freeze.

"Listen. It's tough for us out here. You know what I mean . . . Hard to find others like us . . . and when I saw you that night with that Indian . . ."

I creep to the end of my bed, flattening myself against the curve of the wall.

"I really don't want to have to hurt you. You're so . . . what's the word? Fragile . . . as it is . . . so, it's simple really. We'll help each other out: You do as I say; I don't tell. How's that sound?"

Another spring creaks on his bed. He's moving toward me, ready to pounce.

"You're drunk. I'll tell my dad," I quiver out.

"Awwww, you'll t-t-tell your d-d-d-dad? That's sweet." Bedspring creak, his hands lift and disappear in the darkness. "You think he'll believe his faggot kid over me?" His voice drops a few octaves. "Hey, Robert. I was just gettin' a beer from the fridge, man, and he came at me like some goddamned queer. I don't know what to say, man, but I'm gonna have to call the cops."

He's inches away. "Sound convincing enough?" Puffs of his breath slice through the darkness: soured beer and rotted meat. Finally, his face pierces the shadows and—

NOW.

I spring for the door. His hands clamp around my waist, throwing me back on the bed. My head slams against the steel wall.

"Where you goin'?" His voice slows down like it's a record player set on the wrong speed. His knees lock my legs down.

"GETOFFME!"

He slaps his hand over my face; it smells like fish guts. "You're only making this harder on yourself."

I try to punch him but he grabs my hand with such force I think it's broken now. I scream.

"What the hell did I say?" He smacks me. Hard. Smothers my mouth with his palm. "I know you want it. It's okay. I seen the way you been lookin' at me. I won't tell—"

I can't move. I can't breathe. I try telling him this. Try telling him I need PeterPaulandMary from my pocket. I can't. I can't open my mouth. I cough but it only sends a spasm through my body. Tears push against my eyelids even though I try to hold them back.

Everything tightens: his knees against my legs, his hands against my arms, his breath against my neck.

I float.

*Let go,* I think. *Give in,* I think. *Play dead,* I think.

"There you go. See, it's not so bad, is it? We can help each other . . ."

His grip loosens some.

I don't move. I wait. I breathe. I wait.

His hand reaches for my shorts, and—KA-BAM—I throw my knee into his nuts so hard I swear I hear something shatter. He falls over, wailing some crazy high-pitched scream that disappears in the cicada rattles.

I kick and fumble through the tangled sheets, hurdle over his body, which is wedged between the beds. He's writhing back and forth in a ball of pain. Noises I've never heard. I grab my satchel, throw open the trailer door, and run.

I run so fast I can't feel the earth below me.

I run to the only place I feel safe anymore. Even though I know it's the most unsafe of them all. Web's. I don't care if they catch me. I don't know what else to do.

I cross to the other side of the lake in a matter of minutes, in between a thousand PeterPaulandMary poofs. Just keep going. When I reach the bottom of the steps, I stop.

Breathe. Wipe my face, pat down my hair, tuck my shirt in my shorts, lift up my tube socks. Breathe.

Muffled laughs.

*Knock knock knock* on the closed screen door.

Silence.

A chair scoots; the door creeps open a few inches. His grandfather.

He opens it wider with his growing smile. "Jonathan! To what do we owe this honor?"

"Is Web here?" I say this like we're neighbors and I just came by to see if he can play.

"Of course! Come in!"

Everyone sits at the table. Web jumps up, because he knows. "What's happened? What's wrong?"

I burst into tears.

He runs over, strokes my hair, and whispers, *"Shhhh, shhhhh . . . you're okay now,"* before leading me to his room.

We sit on his bed and he holds me and I'm sure I will be crying in his arms for the rest of my life.

# 45.

WHEN I WAKE, I am wrapped in a sheath of force fields from every superhero ever created since the dawn of man. Invincible from destruction. Safe from enemy peril. Protected from being touched or hurt or shamed ever again.

Web.

We're lying on his bed, glued together.

After I cried a monsoon, I curled up on his floor with a pillow and sheet, and when everyone went to bed, Web pulled me into his. *"What if your family walks in,"* I said. *"They won't,"* he said. I was too tired to argue, and within minutes we fell asleep.

His arms envelop me. His lips press against my neck. His hair sticks to my back. He is my life support. The electric pulses swimming from his body pierce my nerves, but they're the only things keeping me alive right now . . .

The soft glow of the slivered moonlight pricks through the boarded windows and patched walls. Everyone has long been asleep.

I slow my breath to match his. So we become one.

"You awake?" he asks. I swear it's my own voice, so I do not answer.

He kisses my neck, snuggles his nose in my nape.

"Web?" I barely whisper.

He lifts his head. "Yeah?"

"You're awake?"

"I never fell asleep."

"You didn't?"

"No."

"Oh."

Each word follows the next like we're talking for each other. Like I can hear his thoughts in my own brain, speak his words out of my own mouth.

He buries his forehead back in my neck. "You were talking in your sleep," he says.

"I was?"

"Yeah."

My eyes are closed, but I feel like we're looking at each other, like we did on top of the cliff.

"What was I saying?"

He doesn't answer.

I open my eyes, stare at the tie-dyed sheet pulled down over his door.

"Did he hurt you?" he asks.

"Who?"

"Hal."

His face flashes in the darkness: gnarled and maimed and hungry. He must know where I am. I wonder if he's told Dad yet. I wonder if he's on his way. No. He's waiting. Or he would've been here by now. Maybe I really did hurt him. I close my eyes, shake my head to shake it all free.

"No, why would you—"

"You kept saying his name, telling him to stop—"

"He didn't hurt me. Not really. Not like that," I say.

"What did he do to you?"

"Nothing. He's just . . . trying to scare me is all."

"Why?"

"Because . . . he saw us that night."

He's silent. I cannot tell him what almost happened. And I will not. Ever. I'm too ashamed. But also, the Wrath of Web is sure to come torpedoing out and every ending I've thought of in that scenario does not end well.

"So help me, if he so much as lays a finger on you—" See?

I flip over to face him. His eyes spark with comet-fire. This close, they ignite my nerve endings. A shock flares through me. I do not flinch. "He didn't. Okay? And can we not talk about him right now? Please?"

He studies me. Hard. Then he kisses the spot between my eyebrows. "What do you want to talk about?" he asks, nuzzling back on the pillow.

"I shouldn't be in bed with you. What if they walk in? What if we get caught?"

"We won't. They sleep through tornadoes. Besides, they already know about me and they don't—"

I sit up. "They *know*?"

"Yeah—"

"When did you tell them? How'd they find out?"

"Last year. The first guy I ever kissed . . . it didn't end well. I ran home so angry I punched a few holes in the wall."

"Oh . . ."

"That's when I told them. Everything. They've known my whole life, I guess. To them it's a good thing—"

"A *good* thing?"

"Let's just lie here and—"

"How is it a good thing, Web. Tell me. Please."

He sighs, brushes his fingers through my hair. "I don't know, I guess my people revered people like me once. Like forever ago. Because they thought we had some special healing powers or something . . . like, we have these two spirits, male and female, dancing in us—"

"Really?"

"They see it as a gift."

"A gift?"

"Yeah . . . Come here, lie back down with me." He wraps his arms around my waist; I snuggle into him, ignoring the sting.

A gift? It's always been a curse in my world. A curse that can never be broken. The only other time I've seen the words *gay* and *good* together was in that *Interview* magazine Starla gave me, the day she told me she was leaving for the summer. But I never thought it was actually possible. Not in *our* world . . .

Maybe . . . it is . . . I mean, I know I can't be fixed, but maybe . . . that's . . . a good thing . . .

We stare at the ceiling. Our thoughtstrings float skyward, sucked into a water stain that looks like a black hole. I wonder if this is the entrance to elsewhen, a parallel universe . . . Because being with him here, in his arms . . . it feels . . .

"Want me to tell you a story?" he whispers.

"Aren't you tired?"

"Are you kiddin', man? Sleep with you here, like this? Not a chance."

I curl into his chest. We're forehead to forehead, smiling, and for a moment I'm so happy I feel like we just discovered a new planet. "Okay, then. Tell me a story."

"It's a good one," he says. "I think you'll love it." He wipes some sweat from his brow and without thinking I take his hand and wipe it on my cheek. I have no idea why I do this, but he doesn't seem to notice.

"Once there was an angry young boy who had a vision. And in this vision he floated in a lake shaped like a torn heart, looking up at the stars. And the stars started dropping from the sky." He takes his fingers and slowly twiddles them down my cheeks. "And when they fell to earth, they turned into white spiders dancing all around him." His fingers tickle my neck, my arms, my chest. "And as they danced, they spun their threads, until the boy was caught in a cocoon, *trapped*. He yelled for help, but no one came. Until—" With a *poof*, he explodes his hands over my face. "A star fell from the sky and turned into another boy. And this boy was covered in streaks of color and he smiled and said, 'I'm here.'

"And the color-streaked boy took the cocoon-wrapped boy to shore and carefully untied him thread by thread." He's fake-pulling thoughtstrings from my head into the wind. "And as he threw each thread in the water, it began mending the broken lake stitch by stitch, until the last little thread that set the boy free was thrown in the water and sealed the broken heart together. Forever."

His palm lands on my chest.

We do not move.

"Is that the end of the story?" I ask.

"No. It's only the beginning . . ."

"Web?"

"Yeah?"

"Kiss me."

His lips fall into mine, and KABOOM, a flash of brilliant white light explodes out of us, so bright I am permanently blinded. And we tangle ourselves together . . .

He caresses my cheek, pecks my eyelashes, and when he reaches my forehead, he stops. "It's okay," shudders out of me. He kisses my scar. I twitch until he soothes the sting. *Please, let's never go back,* I think. It is my only thought. He smiles, licks a tear that has sprung from my eye, kisses it closed.

"Will you . . . take off your shirt . . ." I whisper in his ear.

He throws the sheet off the bed, squirms out of his tank top. Tears scald my cheeks. I guide my hand along his chest, watch his eyes close, his mouth open. Hear his soft moan.

I stop breathing.

"Can I take yours off?" he whispers.

"Yes."

He carefully lifts my shirt over my head, treating my body like his most prized and perfect vinyl record. He sinks into me . . .

His fingers trace a star-map pattern on my chest, stopping at my waist.

I nod.

He slips his hand underneath my boxers. A volt shoots through me. I scream in his hand.

"Shhh. Are you okay?" he whispers.

I nod again.

"You sure?"

"Yes. Don't stop. Please." Because I want to push through this once and for all.

He kisses my waist. I shiver. Tears spill from my eyes, but at least I can feel them. Not like in my treatments. He slides his shorts down, pressing every high-voltage muscle and nerve into mine, until we stitch ourselves together. I do not flinch. I do not blink. His face starts skipping like on the Slide Projector of Shame, but I keep pushing forward, fighting the fallen power lines snapping and thrashing my nerves, until

I can feel me again.

And I fix what's been broken in me all along . . .

I don't want to imagine hiding on the moon or being on some space adventure in the stars anymore. This is the world I want to live in. Right here. With him.

Because for the first time in my life, being in Web's arms,

I feel free.

## -16.

*Wednesday, July 4, 1973*

I RUB MY EYES, blink back and forth between sleep and wake. My heart is a steady, quiet, pulsing peace. So that's what it feels like . . .

The morning sun pricks through the boards on the window. Dust swims through the lights. We are safe. For now.

Except there is no *we.* I flop my arm over to a Web-less pillow. Where is he?

I close my eyes, strain my ears to listen for . . . anything.

Muffled chatter buzzes from behind the house. Can't tell who it is. Could be Web and Family, could be Hal and the Hillbillies, could be Officer Andrews and the National Guard come to cart me away.

I slide into my shorts and his too-loose-for-me tank top—my shirt's nowhere to be found—and peer through the window's boards. No movement below us or across the lake. Dad's Caddy is back, though the curtains are drawn in the trailers. Everything is still. Even the water.

*Has Dad found out yet? Does he even realize I'm gone?*

I walk to the doorframe. Wooden planks creak under my feet. Oh man, definite horror film giveaway. I peek my head through the tie-dyed sheet. "Hello?"

No one's here.

It's strange being alone in someone else's house. Like being a for-real space invader. I creak toward the screen door. A framed Polaroid on the mantel glistens in the light. Never noticed that before. Web. Standing between two older men, all three in white tank tops and blue jeans. A white wooden church sits on a hillside in the distance. Underneath is written: HOME. He looks charged, angry even. Like when we first met. *A ghost of his own history*, as Starla would say.

Muffled laughter breaks my trance. I glance through the screen.

Web sits motionless, staring into a small fire, wearing my shirt! Which looks ridiculous on him because the sleeves end just below the shoulder and the shirt ends just above his waist. Silly boy. Still. Another couple has joined his family, sitting in a circle around the fire. All sip from steaming mugs.

When I open the door, everyone looks at me. Oh man. I wave and walk down the steps like I just won the Mr. Alien of the Universe Pageant. Here I am: barging into their home last night, flooding their house with a lifetime supply of tears, then disappearing in their boy's room, SLEEPING NAKED WITH THEIR BOY. Do they know? Did they hear us? Web said they *sleep through tornadoes*, but I don't know. Sweet Ziggy. I have nowhere to run, or run I would.

Web pats the log next to him. The crackling fire: the only other sound in the circle.

"Mornin'," he whispers in my ear.

We look in each other's eyes, take a quick caravel ride together in mind-kisses, and I turn back to the fire. The slight morning breeze means one thing: Today will be a blistering hot, too-hard-to-breathe kind of day.

In related news, no one has breathed or moved since I sat down.

"Coffee?" his grandfather asks. He's wearing a thick leather glove and pours me a cup from a percolator that's been bubbling over the fire.

"Thanks," I say, and take a sip.

"Jonathan, are you okay?"

"Yes. I didn't mean to . . . I'm sorry about last night . . . Web's the only one I can talk to sometimes . . ."

"We just want you to be safe," he says.

"I am." I turn to Web, who lifts a smile, the flip side of the picture on the mantel. I hope to Ziggy on the Cross he stays like this forever.

"Well, we'll leave you boys to it, then," his grandfather says, standing and gathering his things. The others follow him.

"What? No. I should go, really. I *will* go—"

"No. You stay here." He's already halfway up the stairs. "Oh, and if you're staying the night again, you're sleeping in the main room. You hear me?"

Web chuckles. My face flushes the color of the fire. "Yessir," I say. And everyone's gone.

I punch Web's arms. "You said they sleep through tornadoes. Oh my God, Web!"

"He's teasing. They didn't hear anything."

"Why did they leave?"

He looks at me and my mind turns to mush and I instantly return to last night, under the sheet of stars—but when I look closer, something's changed. His eyes hide nothing.

"What's wrong?" I ask.

"I have some news," he says. He looks down, brushes his feet back and forth in the rocks. "You know that cop I busted up?"

"Is he—"

"No. He's fine—I mean I guess I messed him up pretty bad . . . but, well, we just found out he was arrested last week. For domestic violence or something. Gonna be locked up for a while, I guess . . . So it's safe again, you know, for me . . ."

"Oh. Well, that's . . . good news, right?"

He shrugs, shakes his head, throws a rock in the fire.

"Then why do you look— Oh . . . right . . ."

"It's a funny thing," he says, leaning back, tilting his face toward the sun. "Ever since I got here, all I could think about was this day, when I'd finally get to go home. And now that it's here . . . I mean, I want to go back, there's so much I miss, but . . . well, you know . . ."

"Yeah . . ."

Web inches his bare feet in the sand and lands on top of mine. Maybe the fire will weld them together so we have no choice but to stay connected for the rest of our lives. Maybe.

We sit in silence for a long while. The sun starts glinting through the oak trees behind us.

"I'm glad you get to go home," I say.

He squeezes my hand. "You have to come. Anytime. Stay with us as long as you want. Forever, even."

"Forever, huh?"

"Oh man, you'd love it. We don't have much, but it's somethin'. And you'll have no choice but to sleep in the same bed as me, because we barely have any room in our house . . ." He winks.

"Oh yeah?"

"Yeah . . . Hey, maybe we could open our own ice-cream truck business—"

"And only serve Push-up Pops and Bomb Pops—"

"And with all the money we make, we can hitch an Airstream—"

"And travel the country in search of the best pies in every city."

He lifts that dimpled smile. "That would be amazing . . ."

"Yeah . . . I'd like that . . ."

He holds my cheeks, and we look into each other's eyes, and his palms feel so soft against my— I don't flinch. His touch doesn't burn

277

or twinge my nerves; it doesn't shock . . . it feels . . . warm. Safe even . . . for the first time in my life . . .

I pull him into me and smell his soap and sweat and still taste him on my tongue from last night, and I bottle this moment up in a jar, so I can live in it

forever.

"Stay for the day," he whispers in my ear.

"Web . . ."

"And tonight we're having some friends over. The family who owns this place always has people over on the Fourth, I guess. You can stay for that, and—"

"Dad's going to start looking for me *eventually*. And who knows who else. And it'd be way better if I find him first."

"Look, I'm just sayin' your dad probably won't even get up till later this afternoon anyway, right? And then he'll start drinking and forget you're not there, and then they'll be too busy with all that Fourth of July stuff, right? So we can have one more day and night together."

I laugh. Because, actually, that sounds just about right. I gaze up at the sun. *This makes no sense. None of it does. But maybe that's the point. Maybe the things that make the least amount of sense are the things you're supposed to do. I don't know.* I look at him, looking back at me. *But one thing I know: I'm not crazy for feeling this way. They're crazy for trying to stop me. And if it's the last time I ever get to feel joy again, I won't let them have it.*

"Web Astronaut?"

"Yeah?"

"What should we do today?"

He cracks the sky open with his smile. "Your turn," he says.

## 47.

WE SPEND THE DAY alone in his room, lost together in our own little galaxy.

No windows can be opened and no air filters through, but with PeterPaulandMary at the ready, neither one of us cares. We throw our shirts off within minutes because of the heat. His grandfather's fine with this as long as we "keep the curtain open." Web protested, but it was "absolutely not up for debate." And I stood there thinking, *Is this real life?*

After listening to Carole King and slow dancing, Web finds the tape recorder stashed in my satchel and wants to record something again.

"So you'll never forget this day," he says.

"I never could," I say.

But we do it anyway.

"Hello. My name's Web Astronaut and I'm here again today with Reporter Jonathan Collins on—what day is it today?"

"The Fourth of July, silly."

"Oh, right. So tell me, Mr. Collins, what do you want to be when you GROW UP?"

"Not so close, remember? It distorts the mic."

"Right. Sorry."

"Well, I used to want to go to California and be a rock-n-roll star—"

"Of course you did, Ziggy—"

"But now, I don't know. If we get an Airstream, we could—"

"Travel together and I could teach—"

"Wait. You want to be a teacher?"

"Yeah. I want to teach the *real* history of this country. *Our* history."

"You'd be a great teacher, Mr. Astronaut."

"And we could drive across the country—"

"Gettin' big and fat from all the pie we eat from every diner along the way—"

"Watching sunsets—"

"Until we're smothered in stars—"

"And live happily ever after."

"Yeah . . ."

"Yeah . . ."

We lie on his bed, silently dreaming and holding hands for the rest of the day . . .


Dad finally discovered I wasn't around hours later, when the sun was setting behind Trailerville. We're watching him through the window boards now: He tapes a note to the trailer door and walks down the path, juggling a bag of groceries and the huge box of fireworks to the barbecue.

"Probably thinks you went for a walk," Web says.

"Maybe, but—" I kiss the back of his neck. He kisses my nape, tickles my ears. "We should stop. Your grandfather might—"

"They're all outside now," he says, slow dancing with me again.

"Yeah, but they're all *awake*, and they could walk by at any second—"

We fall back on the bed.

"Web!"

He laughs and holds my face in his palms. "You're so beautiful, you know that?"

Gone. I close my eyes. He kisses my cheeks . . . my nose . . . my ears . . .

"Web?"

"Mmm?"

"You've been with other boys before?"

He lifts his head. "A couple times, yeah." His hair drapes down. "But it's never felt like this."

"Like what?"

"I don't know, man . . ." He slowly traces my lips. I kiss his finger. "You wanna know somethin' my dad always told me?"

"What?" I tuck his hair behind his ears.

"He always said, '*There's only one superpower worth fighting for that can destroy any enemy. It's also your greatest weakness, so you must use it wisely.*'"

"What is it?"

He shakes his head, smiling. "Your turn," he says, lying on my stomach. "When did you first know that you were gay?"

"Oh . . ."

"It's okay," he whispers. "You can trust me . . ."

I close my eyes. "I guess . . . when I was little . . . and I got my first Ken doll . . . I guess I knew then . . ."

"Really?"

"Yeah. I've never told anyone that before . . ."

"I'm glad you told me . . ."

We lie in silence, lost in the ceiling.

"Web?"

"Mm-hmm?"

"Can you tell me more about how it's a gift for you . . ."

He looks at me, lifting those dimples, then lays his head back down. His hair twirls all around us like Van Gogh's *Starry Night*. "It's like Ziggy, I guess. The guy comes down from the stars, right? And he sparkles and glitters and is like this Androgynous Messiah, singing songs of truth. And no one cares how he looks or who he loves or what he wears. They just care about his special star powers, you know, his special words. I guess that's me . . ."

I stroke his hair.

"It doesn't mean I'm gay, necessarily, just means I'm different, you know, special . . . not everyone sees it that way, of course. There's still some Natives that don't like it at all because it got lost over the years. White people took that away from us, too—tried to take our spirit away, make us Christians and all that, so it was considered evil . . . we still can't even practice our spirituality in public, man."

"Really?"

He props his chin on my chest. "My family remembers the truth, though. 'Give it time,' they say, 'One day all people will see who you are as a gift again.' But I don't know, man . . . I don't know. Anyway, no time like the present, right?" And he sweeps up, kissing me again when—

"Web! Everyone's here now," his grandfather yells. We stop, panting on top of each other. "This is your boys' fifteen-minute warning to unglue yourselves and get down here!"

My eyes bulge out of my head.

Web laughs. "Can't get anything past Grandfather."

"Ohmanohman . . ." I bury my face in his hair.

"Guess we should get ready," he says.

"Guess so," I say.

He starts kissing me all over again, when:

"*TWELVE MINUTES!*" Teasing, but still.

Web throws his head down on my belly in defeat. "Okay. We need to get ready. For real."

"Okay," I say. "Okay . . ."

He doesn't move.

"Soooo?"

"One more kiss." He swoops up and grabs one before I can answer, then leaps off the bed.

"Hey, can I play you an album real quick?" I ask.

"Yeah, man."

Been waiting for the perfect moment. Since that night in my room, I guess . . . This is definitely it. I can feel it . . . I plug in the player, scoot it over by the bed, and pick up Roberta Flack. The *First Take* album. I can almost hear her honey-dripping voice swim through the room as I lift the record from its sleeve.

I click the player on: Microphone static pops through the speakers the second I place the needle on the vinyl and skip to *the* song. "The First Time Ever I Saw Your Face."

The soft strums of bass and guitar . . .

Tiny trembles of her piano . . .

Web throws on a tank top and plops back down on the bed. I sit across from him. And she sings.

*"The first time . . ."* Oh man, I swear. If Ziggy's my Jesus, then she is most definitely my God.

"Whoa," Web says.

"I know."

*"And the moon . . ."*

I watch him listening. He looks at me, brushes the hair away from my scar.

I do not stop him.

He traces my scar like a tiny bird feather.

I whisper, "My Web . . ."

And he whispers, "My Ziggy . . ."

We listen to the song, lost in each other's eyes.

## -18.

THE SECOND WE STEP outside we're swooped up in hugs and kisses and "Heyheyhey"s and "Who's this handsome guy?" and "We've missed you, man, you ready to come home?" Web has a permanent smile on his face, surrounded by friends.

I guess this is what family feels like.

When we reach the bonfire, his grandfather accordions me in a hug and I think my lungs collapse. "Grab some food!" he says, pushing me over to a lime-green VW van parked in the back.

I zigzag through more strangers, holding my chest. I actually do think he collapsed my lungs when I realize the breeze this morning has become a thick layer of fog swamping the air.

I fumble through my satchel. Oh no. PeterPaulandMary is still in his bedroom. I run back to grab it, when someone calls my name.

"Jonathan? Jonathan Collins? Is that really you, daddio?"

That voice. How do I know that—"Mr. Dulick?"

He stands there beaming, wearing a tie-dyed shirt, corduroy cut-offs, and a long peace-symbol chain that's caught in his chest hair. Like he just stepped off the stage performing *Hair*.

And he's definitely stoned.

"Alright alright alright," he says. "It is you!" He hugs me, squeezing me tight. His thick sideburns tickle my cheeks.

"What are you doing here?" I ask, bending over slightly to steady my breath.

"This is my family's place, man—well, was—they're tearing it down. This'll be our last Fourth—"

"This is *your* place? But how do you know Web and—"

"Oh. My man! I met Dennis and Russell a few years back in San Francisco." He tightens his tie-dyed headband, and tucks his curly hair out of his eyes. "Joined up with them when they occupied Alcatraz. Where it all started for me, man. Best time of my freaking life. Been friends ever since. Where's Web?"

"Oh, he's around . . . somewhere . . ."

"Present, sir," Web says, clasping my waist, kissing my neck. I flinch, waiting for the sting.

Nothing happens.

"Well, look at you two! *Fan-freaking-tastic!*" Dulick yells. We both jump. "Oh, this makes sense . . . this makes *perfect* sense . . ." He cocoons the three of us together. "Positively *beautiful*, man. Fate sure has a funny way of doing her thing, doesn't she?"

Please don't cry again. He's this close, I can tell. "Yeah . . ." I say.

He pats our shoulders, our cheeks, our heads . . . Yup, stoned out of his gourd. Web giggles.

"Freaking beautiful, man. Hey, let's boogie later, kiddos," he says. "Gonna grab me some grub." And he dances off.

"Did you . . . know this was his place?" I ask.

Web shrugs. "I wasn't supposed to say anything—"

"Crazy—"

"Yeah. Crazy, crazy, crazy . . ." He kisses me.

Uncle Russell lifts me from the ground. "Enough of that kissy-face stuff. Come on, Jonathan! You need some good Lakota food. Give you a nice belly like mine." He plops me down, slaps his stomach.

"I just need to—"

"Heyhey, fix this man up with a plate, will you, sweet?" He yells this to Sunny, who's standing by the van with a few other women adorned in similar knitted vests spun by the Archangel of Frigging Yarn. Holy shimmering stars.

"What would you like?" she asks.

The van behind her is filled with coolers labeled "Pop" and "Water" and "Burgers" and "Fry Bread and Tacos."

"A taco and a Coke, please."

She smiles and says, "We're so happy you're here."

I smile back and dash through the crowd to get PeterPaulandMary, because oh man, I feel it now: My breath's lodged in my lungs, trying to break free.

First: quick security check across the lake.

The sun's vanished, and in its place a bonfire blazes extra-high between the trailers, rising above the fog so the clouds look like they're burning. Not good. Can't see anything. I need to go. I need to get back before it's—

"All clear?" Web grabs me. My taco flops to the ground. "Oh, whoops, sorry! There's more."

I push away. "I—have to go."

"Now?"

"I can't see over there anymore. Fog's too thick. I don't—like this. And I can't—the smoke and—"

"You okay?"

"I—have to go." *I need PeterPaulandMary!* "Have to—"

"You're safe here," he says.

"No, I—"

And suddenly my breath is all at once extinguished.

Gone.

I see it in Web's face first. His smile disintegrates. His eyes flash from starlight to rage. I follow his gaze and—

The world disappears. Everything blurs. Except for a clump of hate with five men at the helm: BillyBob, Porky Joe, Five-Teeth Terry, Hal. And Dad. Demon red. Glowing extra-bright against the sweltering smoke. Hungry.

"Fifty dollars for your braids!" BillyBob yells.

The clump hollers and whoop-whoop-whoops.

No one moves.

Dad and Hal crane their necks, searching. I bend over, clutching my chest.

"Any Indian givers out there?" BillyBob says.

"Fuck you, man," someone in the crowd yells back. No, oh no no no.

"What'd you say to me?"

"Hey, come on, brothers, just leave us be," Dulick says.

"We aren't doing nothing to hurt you," someone else yells.

"Oh, but you are. You're on *our* land. I'd say that's doing a whole hell of a lotta something. Wouldn't you boys?"

Porky Joe and Terry snarl. I can't tell what's in their hands, maybe guns, maybe axes, knives, I can't see.

"This is OUR land, man." It's Uncle Russell.

The universe goes silent. Then. Billy slowly nods to Joe, and we all watch as he lifts the box of fireworks over his head and plunges it into the fire.

The planet explodes. BOOOOM. Bottle rockets and balls of fire and firecrackers and huge blasts of gunpowder KAZEW BLAST

POPOPOPOPOP and pummel through the smoke, whizzing past my head, into my lungs, circling the fire, twisting around us like an untamed storm. I'm frozen, stuck in time while the world dies around us. Trying to grab a breath, any breath—

I fall to the ground. Fireworks blur with cries for help. I don't know which is which anymore.

Web dives down. His face: shaken, settled, fierce. "Hang on," he yells.

WHAT? I CAN'T—*I can't breathe. Help. It hurts.* A flipbook of images flashes through my mind: Stingraymobile rides, Ziggy's prayers, Mom's fluttering eyes, Starla's freckles, green Martian Aunt Luna kisses, Web.

"Look at me!"

*Try to focus. Try to grab a breath.*

"Follow my breath," he screams. "In and out. In and out and—"

NO.

Hal's face leaps out of the shadows, hovering behind Web. A total eclipse. He grabs Web's hair and yanks his head back. Web's smile mangles, and the shriek shreds my heart. He kicks and flails and grabs at Hal's hands that claw his hair, and in a flash, he's gone. Lost in the shadows.

Dad stands over me. He's screeching, raising demons from the earth, but I cannot hear what he's saying.

He scoops me up.

I'm walking on the sky.

The world dangles like a yo-yo.

That's all I remember.

✴

## **part three.**

## ONE.

*no matter what or who you've been . . .*
*i've had my share,*
*i'll help you with the pain.*
*you're not alone.*

—ZIGGY STARDUST

## 49.

*Wednesday, July 11, 1973*

IT'S BEEN A WEEK. I guess.

I see his face flash in everything. The broken one. Not the one I really want to see. I even see it when my eyes are closed. Which is pretty much all the time now.

I don't know if he's still alive. Can't ask. Can't leave the house. Can't.

Barely made it myself. The Invasion of the Asthma Attacker almost prevailed. I don't remember much. The past week has been a succession of waking dreams.

Six days ago:

My eyes open. I'm in bed. White everything. At first I think I'm in my bedroom. And then I think I'm dead. And then I wonder if dead people can think.

I lift my head, but only slightly, because it feels like someone smashed it on the concrete. I lie back down.

A lady walks in wearing all white. Her lipstick is too red for her face. I don't know. "Well, hello there," she says with a cheerful wink. If I could raise my arm I would punch her.

"Am I dead?" I have to ask it three freaking times because my voice is scratched.

She laughs and says, "Oh no, sweetie. You're very much alive. You gave us all a good scare, though."

I don't know what's so funny. It's a logical question because of the white everything and I don't know. Anyway, I guess I was hoping I was dead.

"Vitals are good," she says. "BP normal, breathing's stabilized, scans are clean."

I thought she was talking to me, but then I see someone else standing by her, scribbling on a clipboard. I think it's Web: the long black hair. I try to leap up, but I can't move.

"Hi, Jonathan. You're going to be just fine." It's Dr. Evelyn. She's wearing a white crocheted jumpsuit thing and looks like a doily.

Then I see Dad slouching on a chair in the corner, heaving. A lump of gray unmolded clay. The only uncheerful one in all of Candyland.

Three days ago:

My eyes open. I'm thirsty. Not thirsty. Parched. Been lost in the desert for days, I guess. For my whole life.

I'm alone in the room. No, I'm not. Someone stands. As he steps closer, my heart stops. Hal. His face: a mutilated Picasso, covered in jagged bruises and a bandage over his left eye. That ugly scar on his cheek lifts into a smile.

The heart monitor pulsates.

"I see I still get you excited," he whispers.

I try to scream, still don't have a voice. Isn't there some button you press for a nurse or—

"Looking for this?" He holds it in his hands. "Don't worry, I won't stay long. Just wanted to say hi and that you're awfully missed at the lake. And to say—" He bends down closer so his tongue brushes my ear.

"See what happens when you mess with me?" He leans back. "I think his last words were, 'Stop please stop!' Tsk tsk tsk. Terrible last words."

I lunge at him, but he jumps back. "*IT'S NOT TRUE. YOU WON'T GET AWAY WITH IT,*" I want to scream. Can't. The heart monitor starts wildly beeping. A nurse runs in, followed by another.

Hal throws his arms up. "I don't know what happened! He tried to hug me and—"

"It's okay, we've got it now. You might want to step out for a minute, sir."

"I'm goin'." He stops at the door, winks. I thrash up; the nurses pin me down; a needle lodges in my vein.

Yesterday:

Mumbles turn to soft chatter. I open my eyes to see Dr. Evelyn and Dad at the end of the bed. She's wearing a scarf around her head, hair pulled back, face recently kissed by the sun. His hair's oil-slicked and his skin looks like a pile of ash in an ashtray. He's hunched over, wheezing. They don't see I'm awake, so I close my eyes and listen.

> **DR. EVELYN**
> He can't endure another round of treatments like that, Mr. Collins. His body's been through so much. Surely you understand?

> **DAD**
> Yes, but what else is there to do? I've done everything I can.

> **DR. EVELYN**
> He needs to be home with you first. To

readjust and settle back into a normal routine. We can discuss options after that.

> ### DAD
> I just want to help him. I want him to be happy.

*(He starts to cry. Can't decide if it's real or an act. Sounds fake.)*

> ### DR. EVELYN
> I know, so do I.

*(Guess she's rubbing his back.)*

> He's a strong kid. One of the strongest I've ever known. I was wrong, Mr. Collins, to—

> ### DAD
> Wrong?

*(Wrong? I peek my eyes open. Knew he was faking it. Not a tear in sight.)*

> ### DR. EVELYN
> About my assessment—I'm sorry, I didn't mean to get into it now—Jonathan's health is the priority, but—there are other . . . options to explore, other . . . treatments. Maybe. I've been doing some research on this for a while now, and I need to talk with my colleagues more, but—Sorry. I don't mean to be vague. I want to discuss this with Jonathan first when he's out of here, okay? To find out what he wants before

moving forward. But he will. Move
forward. Okay?

(*She has real tears streaming down her cheeks.*)

He tries to cry some more. Fake fake faker.

I close my eyes tighter, to make the sounds disappear, to make myself disappear. Back to sleep. *What did she mean wrong? One thing I know for sure: I'm never doing those treatments again, so you can forget it, Dr. Evil-lyn. I'll turn my own damn self in—no, I'll run away to find Web. Yeah. We'll ride our Airstream into the sunset, through the stars, start our new life together on the moon . . . Yeah . . .*

### DR. EVELYN
He's a very special kid, Mr. Collins.

*To the moon . . . Yeah . . .*

This morning: driving home.

In the front seat of the Caddy, there's a rip in the cloth I hadn't noticed before. By the seat belt. I wonder where it came from. Maybe when Dad was crazy drunk that night before we went to the lake . . .

He's silent; I'm silent; the world is silent. Better that way. I think maybe I'll never talk to people again. People use words to hate each other too much. I don't want to be one of those people. I'll just talk to myself like I have been all these years anyway. It's safer that way . . .

I feel like one of Starla's discarded pincushions, pricked so full of holes I'm useless. More than tired. Whatever's beyond tired. I didn't even know that feeling existed. I wonder if there's a word for it. I'm going to invent new words.

Man, I miss Starla. It's been a month since she's left. One whole month. Only one more to go. Never going to make it . . .

We turn the corner to our house. Everything looks the same, but feels so different. How did Starla put it in that postcard? Like I'm a ghost of my own history. Yeah. Like I'm floating back into an old life that doesn't fit me anymore . . . Makes sense, I guess.

The only reason I know what day it is is because of the TV: *Wednesday, July 11, 1973* is stamped at the bottom of the screen. The Watergate thing. Dad's still obsessed, or he's too lazy to move. We sit and stare. Two explorers who lost the one person they care most about.

Once in a while I'll cook him a frozen dinner and bring him a drink. But he never eats. He just lies there, staring at the TV. He even sleeps there, doesn't go to the Blues Note or see Heather anymore. Something's definitely wrong. Guess I messed him up pretty bad. He quit smoking, that's something.

I join him to watch it sometimes—the Watergate thing—when I'm sick of staring at my ceiling. It's weird watching it. It makes me feel like everyone's one big liar sitting in the middle of one big lie.

Guess we all are.

## 50.

*Thursday, July 12, 1973*

THE NEXT DAY, I walk outside to get the mail and some fresh air. First bite of sun, too. Had too much a week ago, now I don't have enough. I'm paler and skinnier and smell like pepper and sick. Guess I should put on some deodorant. Maybe shower.

In other news, I think they stretched my legs in the hospital: I hit my head on the ceiling coming down the stairs. That's never happened before. And my voice: like it fell to the floor. Finally catching up to the Apes, I guess. Not that it matters. Whatever.

The mailbox is stuffed. I'm surprised the postman hasn't called the cops or something, thinking we might be dead. Jesus. Two weeks' worth, I'm guessing. I stuff it in my satchel I carry with me everywhere now, because it still has his smell from the last night we spent together: burnt wood, herbs, Irish Spring, cherries, boy sweat, dimple-dimple smile,
gone.

A postcard from Starla flutters to the ground. Postmarked July 5. It's the one I bought from Vinyl Tap: a picture of Ziggy Stardust praying. On the bottom of this one I'd written: KEEP THE FAITH.
Yeah, right.

The guy on the news said David Bowie retired Ziggy Stardust on July 3; never going to perform him again; killed him once and for all. People were crying in the streets, left in a state of shock and awe, roaming aimlessly like the A-bomb actually went off . . .

Makes perfect sense to me.

Another Polaroid's stapled to the back of her postcard. This time she's standing in front of the White House holding a sign she's made in rainbow colors that says I AM A WOMAN, NOT A TYPEWRITER. Her hair's still clouded on her head. Her other hand's wrapped around the waist of another boy: black, skinny, beautiful, perfect. They both smile. Well, he smiles while she's kissing his cheek. I study the picture for a long time. They belong together. I can feel it.

> *JONNYBOOO!!! Life has been CRAZY here. Like REALLY crazy. And you better believe I'm the most fabulous girl in this town! I met a new friend. His name's Eric. That's him in the picture. SO much to tell you. And OH, Jonny, you would've died! The fireworks last night—with the White House and everything in the background—oh I cried and cried and cried. I know how much you love fireworks. SO beautiful!!! OHOHOHOHOHOH I finished the jeans!!!!! I'm attaching a Polaroid here of just a small part of it so you can see. ☺ I'll try calling soon. We REALLY need to talk. Catch you on the flip, baby.*
>
> > *To be continued,*
> > *Starla xx*

I lift the postcard to my nose. It still smells like her: faded vanilla and incense. There's no other Polaroid. Guess she forgot.

I dig through my satchel. Can't find them anywhere. They're gone. Her cross pieces. Gone for good, I guess.

Perfect.

## 51.

Friday, July 13, 1973

ANOTHER DAY IN BED.

I scream into my pillow again.

Guess this is what my life is now. Some life. I think I'm losing my mind. One minute I want to cry, the next minute I want to yell. So I do both. Into my pillow. Sometimes I want to punch the wall. Not because I'm angry; so I can feel something. Anything. Maybe that's what Web was trying to do all along . . .

Guess *they* won. The ones *out there* Web talked about. The ones who want me to think I'm crazy, to keep me broken. Fine. I surrender. Hoist the white flag, because I can't do it anymore.

I shriek into my pillow.

See, I'm losing my mind.

I stay in bed staring at the ceiling. And thinking about him. It's the one thing that makes me feel sane. My Web Astronaut, floating somewhere. I wonder where. Hal says they killed him, but I don't believe him. No. I can still feel him . . .

My stomach wrenches. Thinking about what Hal did to us . . . how he gets to keep smirking, dancing by a bonfire, while we lie here, torn apart . . .

I close my eyes to see Web's face again. The other one. The one I want to always remember. There. Looking down on me: eyes full of wild desperation and worry . . . and maybe love. I don't know . . .

I can't hold it that long because then his face contorts into that mangled mess from when he was whipped into darkness, and I have to stare at the ceiling again. To forget. God, it hurts. I screech into my pillow so loud, so hard, I think I rip my vocal cords.

I wish I could touch him and smell him and see him and taste him. One more time.

I need to know. Somehow I need to find out if he's okay. Wherever he is . . .

## 52.

I CRAWL INTO MY closet, clutching my satchel.

Haven't been here in a while. It smells stale. Dry almost. I don't know. Words.

I click on the lamp.

Did we have an earthquake? Things look different. Shifted. I know there's some fault line in Missouri . . . *Ziggy's eyes blink back at me: glam-glittery, smiling, and waving,* but some of his eyes paper the floor now, and Mom's portrait is tilted. Because of my screams? My *National Geographic*s are strewn about, and—

The *Interview* magazine peeks out.

The one.

The one I stashed here that day Starla first told me she was leaving; the one she was *dying to give me* . . . I flip it open to the article. Huge muscles and toothy grins look back at me. And that headline punches me in the gut again: *"GAY IS GOOD!"*

A tear shoots from my eye before I can stop it. NO. I slam the magazine closed. Something's in it. I shake the pages; it drops in my lap: Web's pin. The one from his jacket, when he was last here. Oh man.

I flip it through my fingers. Let the sharp needle prick my thumb a few times. I wish I were this pin. Then I could stick myself to his jacket and still be next to his heart . . .

Like when we danced in his room, when he called me his Ziggy, when I felt me for the first time. Me. The real me. What life could really be—not on the moon or in some parallel universe. No. It was right here all along. On this broken little planet, in broken little Missouri, in the broken little city of Creve Coeur. Here.

I twist my Ziggy T-shirt. My face flushes, stings. Like when Web slapped his palms on my cheeks that night he told me he was done hiding, when he looked me square in the eyes and cried and said—

I hurl the pin against the wall and scream.

*"What is it, honey? What's wrong?"* Mom. *She tilts her head toward me, her ocean eyes unblinking.*

"They won't win—I won't let them win. I won't—" I thunder through a sludge of snot and sobs.

*"Let who win, honey?"*

"THEM. Out there. All of them. Dr. Evelyn and Dad and HAL and—I won't—do it anymore, I can't live—like this—" Her face blurs, a river of oil paints. "The treatments—lies—hiding—I won't pretend—I can't act like they work—because they don't. They don't work, Mom. They never worked. They never *will* work—"

*"Then don't pretend anymore, sweetpea. You don't have to."* She tries to reach through the painting, tries to embrace me—

But she can't. And she never will.

"That's the whole point—I don't have a choice—Dr. Evelyn told Dad she's wrong. Probably still thinks I'm the confused crazy one, the high-voltage freak—but no, she *is* wrong, because I'm *not crazy.* I'm not—I'm not gonna be strapped down or thrown into some stupid tiny closet never to be seen again—GOD. Maybe I am crazy—"

*"I don't think you're crazy, sweetheart, or a—"*

"You're a picture! You're a picture that talks and moves and tells me I'm not crazy, that's crazy!"

*She laughs. "Oh, you know better. You're just imagining me. But you also know you don't need to anymore. Because you do have a choice, honey. Remember the game?"*

"What—"

*"Every step you take is a choice. And as long as you get to choose, you always win."*

"Some choice—I'm stuck here—and Web's—Hal says he— No. I don't believe him and I hate him for what he did— No. I think Web's still out there—somewhere—"

*"You have to go find him, then," she says. "It's the only thing worth fighting for . . ."*

I inhale a few shuddered breaths.

*"And you have to do it now."*

I picture Web and me floating, tangled together. Not out there. Here. Where I can choose to lie in bed, and rip my vocal cords screaming into a pillow, and stare at nothing, and let *them* win. Or here. Where I can—

*"It's all a choice, honey," she whispers. "And it's—"*

"Up to me," I say.

I stare at Mom . . .

*"Go to him," she says. "Time's running out."*

"How can I? I can't leave."

*"I'll help you. We'll figure out a way. But you have to go back to the lake. To see Web. To stop Hal from ever hurting anyone again. You'll know when; you'll know what to do. Trust me—"*

"JONATHAN." Dad. Downstairs.

"How will I—?"

But she's already gone. No, she was never there.

It was me.

It was me . . . all along.

## 53.

"WHAT IS IT?"

Dad's head pops through a huddled mess of afghan, rivers of sweat rush down his sunken cheeks.

"Git me a supper, willya." He coughs.

I throw a TV dinner in the oven and wait. Still adjusting to my newly stretched legs and arms: Everything's farther away from me now. Even the oven shrunk to an Easy-Bake. Jesus. I stare and I bounce and I wait. Can't stop buzzing. My mind's been electrocuted. Alive again. I have to figure out a way to get out of here.

The Watergate thing blares through the TV. Dad flutters between sleep and wake, still coughing. I bring him his dinner.

"Who were you talkin' to?" he asks.

"What? No one."

"I heard you. Talking."

Damn, should've closed the bedroom door.

"Nope. No one," I say.

He looks at me. "Why you always carry that satchel around with you?"

"Because."

He nestles his head on Grandma's favorite butterfly pillow. I look up, but Grandma hasn't danced or laughed since we've returned. I know it was all in my head, but still. Can't blame her. No more joy left in this house to come alive to.

"Caught him. Bet that bastard's goin' to prison," Dad grunts through more coughs. Back to Watergate. Some news guy says it's possible they had a recording system in his office, so everything Nixon said has been taped all along. Whoa.

"I'm going outside," I say.

"Why?"

"To the backyard. Get some fresh air." The room's so full of my floating thoughtstrings, I'm surprised he's not swatting through them to see the TV.

I fly down the hallway, flap the screen door open.

Our grass hasn't been mowed since 1922. It's overgrown and weedy and covered with curvy strings of seedless dandelions that look like a world Dr. Seuss lives in. Without the wishes. My old swing set sits rusting in the corner. One plastic seat sways in the breeze; the other dangles off the chain. Even the swing set looks dead.

I flop down in the grass until it consumes me, ruffling my palms through the long blades and crushing dandelion strings. It's scratchy and smells like the earth above the crying waterfall, and I suddenly want to pull up every weed until there's nothing left but worthless dirt that can never grow anything again.

I gaze at the ring around an almost full moon. It's going to rain soon.

My thoughtstrings: *Watergate tapes and secret recordings, Dad always coughing, Mom always helping, Web always floating, Dr. Evelyn always electrifying, Starla always smiling, Hal always smirking, me always lying, me . . . me . . . Web . . . me . . . Web . . . me . . . Web.*

Until my mind's all clear and I can figure out a way to see Web. And to stop Hal from— My tape recorder. Maybe I could sneak over to Hal's and secretly tape him— No. It's too dangerous. How would that even work? He'd probably kill me before I could push Record— First, I need to find Web to make sure he's okay, to see him again one more time. But how? Mom said she'd help, but Jesus, Collins, she's not even real. Get it together. Okay, when Dad's asleep I'll sneak away. But he's always on the couch now. I'll drag him upstairs. Yeah. Tell him he needs a good night's sleep in bed. Okay. Then I'll sneak away and— Will that even work? I don't know. But it's the only way.

A CRASH from inside the house. What was that?

THUDCRASHBANG. Jesus, did Dad fall off the couch?

CLANGBAMPOW. What the hell is he doing?

I run back inside. TV's still blaring. Dad's no longer there. Weird.

I look up the stairs: Dad's bedroom door is open; mine's closed.

Weird again. Don't remember closing it.

I creep up, try to listen for any movement, any noise. Nothing.

I creak my door open.

Dad: leaning over the edge of my bed, trying to catch his breath. He lifts his head. His eyes are red, wild, vibrating.

I look around the room. Closet door's open. No.

Heart pulsates. Breaths. Tight, fast, fiery breaths.

Ziggy pictures. Ripped off the walls. Eyes sprinkling the floor.

NONONO.

I gather the shreds in piles, stuff them in my satchel, try to—

Tears falling, snot dripping. "You—you—you shouldn't have—why did you—these are my—he's my—" I'm muttering like a madman to myself, to the pieces, to the—

"Jesus Christ, son." And he starts laughing, no, howling, no, demonic wailing.

I wipe my face and look up at him, heaving. Mad like a rabid dog. Everything's ablaze. "Stop . . . laughing . . ."

It only makes him laughhowlwail louder. "I'm not—laughing, son—"

"STOP IT, GODDAMMIT!" It explodes out of me. I can't see.

"You've—lost your mind," he spits out between laughs or coughs or demon cries, I don't know. "I have a—crazy person—living in my house."

"Your SON, you mean?! Your crazy SON? Your freak of a SON? Is that what you mean? SAY IT. YOU CAN'T. You can't even say it—" Tears and words spill out of me so fast I can't reel them back in, until—

His laugh, his cough, his wheezing stop. He slowly lifts the picture of Mom. "Where. Did you get this?"

"Give it back!"

He snatches it away. "TELL ME."

"I grabbed her from the pile before you burned her to death!"

"It wasn't yours to—"

"Why'd you have to kill her? If you loved her so much, why'd you have to kill everything about her?"

"Me? ME?!"

"Yes. YOU—"

"I'm done with this." And inch by inch he rips the portrait, slashing her face in half.

The world hopscotches. My body ignites.

"How—could you—"

"I'm trying to help you, Jonathan."

Rip-slash-rip-slash-rip, then POOF: Mom pieces twinkletwinkle down in silence.

I can't move. Can't breathe.

"I hate you," I say.

"What'd you say to me?"

"I HATE YOU."

"How could you—"

"I'M NOT SICK—"

Each word punches his face.

"Jonathan—"

"YOU ARE."

I pounce up, push him off the bed.

"Jesus Ch—"

"FOR MAKING ME THINK I'M BROKEN!"

I scream and pummel his chest, punch his face for real. My fist sinks into his body. He tucks in a ball, coughing, holding himself tight.

"I HATE YOU!" It's all I can say, all I can think.

He clutches his throat, gasping for air through violent coughs, barely scraping my name out. "Jon—a—"

But that's all I hear.

I blaze downstairs, through the screen door. Jump on Stingray-mobile, start pedaling. So fast, my legs and lungs cramp in seconds. I don't care. I pedal faster.

Lightning rips through the clouds, tattering the sky. Thunder booms. Rain pelts my body. I'm crying. Stingraymobile pulls me into an empty bus stop to wait it out.

Every sound high-kicks my spine.

Headlights swerve around the corner. *Is Dad coming after me?*

I leap back on Stingraymobile and GO. I dive into the open fields, follow the trail off the main road, the path I've taken so many times before. To him.

I can't see behind me. Can't see in front of me. Can't pedal fast enough.

I stop at the edge of the clearing. Through the trees, I see the shadow of his house waving in the rain. I strain my eyes. Everything around me disappears; his house zooms into focus. A spark: the teeniest ember of orange flickering through the boards on the corner window.

Stingraymobile flies, soaring through the slapping rain—until I'm at the bottom of his stairs, looking up.

The windows and door are triple-boarded; glass shards still glitter the ground. Faint mumbles drift through the walls. I climb. Now more worried than ever of what I'll find on the other side of that door.

## 54.

I POUND THE DOOR, wipe the hair out of my eyes.

Rain gushes down the white-flecked aluminum awning like I'm standing under a waterfall. Perfect.

A chair scrapes the floor.

Jesus. Could be anyone. Didn't think about that. Could be Hal. Could be—

The door flies open.

"Jonathan." It's his grandfather.

"Oh, I'm so glad—" He's more worn, more lined with worry, but still shimmering. Stitches crisscross his forehead, a deep purple half-moon under his eye. But he's okay.

"Come in, come in," he says. "You're shivering."

"I'm so glad . . . you're okay."

Burnt herbs and peace fill the room. Water sprinkles down from every corner of the ceiling, pinging in metal pans that dot the floor.

"Your voice," he says. "So deep now . . ."

"Yeah. It's like Thor."

"You're becoming a man. Already more of a man than they will ever be," he says, waving across the lake.

I lift my shirt, try to wipe my face of rain and tears and hurt. "I'm sorry for everything, which seems so futile to even say. Words, you know, they seem so—"

"My Ziggy."

I open my mouth, try to say Web's name. Can't. He stands in the doorway, still dimple-smiling. Somehow. The left side of his face is splotched in blue and purple and green and yellow, like an unfinished watercolor. And his hair's torn to bits, ragged and cut just above his shoulders. Shredded like my dead Ziggys.

"Oh—no, Web—"

"You should see that ugly white guy."

"I'll be in the other room," his grandfather says, dropping the sheet-curtain behind him.

"I'm sorry, Web . . . I'm so sorry . . . I'm—" And without a second thought, I kiss him.

And kiss him.

And

kiss

him.

A charge flickers on my lips. Just barely.

"Hey," he says. "It's okay. It's going to be okay—"

"No, it's not. It's my fault. I should've never—"

"Come here." He pulls me into his room.

"I'm going to fix this," I say. "He won't get away with it. I promise you he won't—"

"Hey, no. Stop. Look at me." He lifts my head. "Don't you go back over there, you hear me? We took care of them. Trust me. They're never gonna bother us again, okay? Don't do anything stupid."

Our faces hover like a mirror image. Only he reflects back what I look like inside.

"Let's not talk," I say. "I just want to be here. With you."

He nods, but doesn't smile.

I lay my satchel on the floor and lie on the bed next to him.

"Jonathan?" he whispers.

"Yeah?"

"I'm going home."

I lift my head. "Tonight?"

"We leave in the morning. Early. I've been waiting, you know, hoping you'd—"

"Oh . . . I'm sorry I couldn't get back here sooner. I—"

"It's okay. I know . . ."

I nestle into his chest to become his pin, forever stuck. "I wish I could come."

"Me too," he says. "Maybe one day . . ."

"Yeah. One day. Maybe . . ."

He kisses the top of my head. "There's always the moon," he whispers.

"Yeah . . ."

We hold each other tight. And I am safe again. My force field.

I disappear in the water splotch on his ceiling, the black hole to an elsewhen.

*One day,* I think. *Maybe . . .*

I inhale fresh-cut eucalyptus leaves and a meadow of herbs. My breath slows to match his.

I close my eyes, float away . . .


My eyes flutter open. To the heat, the burnt herbs, my cheek stuck to his.

I hear his grandfather's soft snores in the other room. And a breeze whispering through the window. I do not know how much time has passed. Could be decades. Feels like it. Feels like we've been glued together for lifetimes. Web's chest rises and falls with his steady breaths. A quiet peace we can finally share, together.

I never want to leave this moment. I want to bottle it up in a jar or take a Polaroid and tattoo it to my face so I can always see it . . .

But I have to go.

Web still sleeps. I cannot wake him, or he'd never let me leave, especially if he knew where I was going . . .

So I gently kiss his lips, and slide out from under his arms.

## 55.

---

I CREAK DOWN his stairs and hop on Stingraymobile. The rain has stopped. The clouds have rolled away. The almost full moon shines like a lighthouse, guiding me forward. My stomach churns with each wavering pedal. Man, even Stingraymobile's resistant. Never thought I'd be going back here again. Never.

The world is silent. Even the cicadas. The earth is holding her breath with me.

Maybe I haven't thought this all the way through. Maybe he won't be home. Maybe when he sees me he'll knock me out cold before I can open my mouth. Or worse. Yeah, I definitely haven't thought this all the way through. Whatever. I keep going. There's only one thing that matters anymore.

The trailer's eyes glint in the darkness, springing me back. A shadow zips across the curtains, zips up my spine. Music blasts. Zeppelin, I think. Could be Steppenwolf, I can't tell. I stop just before turning the final corner. My nerves are afire, but it's different this time. Not jangled in a jittery mess. Focused. Never felt so fiercely focused in my life. I am ready.

Stingraymobile pedals to the shadows. Hal's singing. If that's what you want to call it. Squawking, more like. Definitely Steppenwolf. I look up. The moon's brighter than I've ever seen it before, strangely iridescent, like I can see through to the other side. I close my eyes, take a deep breath, walk toward the trailer.

Two shadows now. Definitely didn't plan for that, didn't plan for—Heather's cackle cuts through the trailer. Of course. Perfect. I smell grass. And incense: the woodsy kind that Dad used to light. The curtain by the bed is slightly pulled back and for the first time I can see in.

Heather swishes to the music—her hair's frizzled in that rat's nest ponytail—wearing pink hot pants and a cutoff Dennis the Menace T-shirt. A shirtless Hal lies on his bed in red athletic shorts and that red mesh hat, flipping through a *Playboy,* smoking a joint.

Man, Web wasn't kidding. It's been nine days since that night, but he still looks thrashed: His left eye's bandaged, circled in some crazy color I've never seen that spreads to his ear. His right eye's a red mess. His entire face and chest: swollen. Splattered with bruises and cuts and dried blood like a trashed Pollock painting.

"Where your cigarettes at?" Heather yells, scavenging through drawers. "Bernadette wants me to bring her over some."

"Check under the sink."

She flips him the bird, then looks directly at me. "Someone's outside!"

*Dammit. Duck down, don't move, don't breathe.*

"Who's out there?" Hal says, his voice vibrating the plexiglass.

Heather trips, a few plates crash in the sink. Her hands slap against the window. "Who is it, Hal?"

The trailer bounces. The door swings open. "Who's there?"

Oh man. Okay. Here we go. I fumble through my satchel to find my tape recorder and click Play/Record.

## 56.

"WELL, LOOK WHAT the cat dragged in. Heather, you gotta see this!" Hal wobbles down the steps, holding on to the door for support.

"Who the hell is it?"

"Just come out and see."

Heather steps out, wiping her hands on her shorts. "Jonathan? What the hell you doin' here? You got a gun or somethin'?"

"No. Why?"

"Why's your hand in that bag for?"

"Oh. Just, uh, getting my inhaler . . ."

"Freak." She tries pushing past Hal, who grabs her shirt to stop her.

"We thought we'd never see you again, Jonathan," he says.

"Oh. Yeah."

"Hey, you freak—"

"Heather, quiet—"

"No. Let me go!" She slaps his arms off and charges toward me. "You and your Indian freak girlfriend."

"Leave him, Heather—"

"No, NO, I won't *leave* him." She shoves me against the trailer. My head wallops back, but I don't wince. I won't let her see fear. "We ain't ever told your daddy because Hal made me swear not to. No more. I'm gonna call your daddy—"

"That's enough, Heather—" Hal stumbles over, holding on to the trailer's wall.

"No! It's not enough." Her breath smells like dead animal and it takes everything in me not to hurl in her face. "Fine if your daddy don't wanna never see me again. I don't care. I'm still gonna call him and make him git rid of your sick ass once and for all—"

"Go on down to Bernadette's," Hal says, clutching her forearm. "I'll take care a this—"

"Don't push me! I'm goin'. You faggot freak—" She trips over Stingraymobile, smacks to the ground. "Stupid got-damned BIKE." She kicks it, brushing herself off. "You holler if you need me, Hal. I'm only a few trailers down."

"Yeah, yeah. Just go."

"I said I'm goin'! Damn." She disappears in the shadows singing some Alice Cooper song.

"Sorry 'bout her." He leans against the trailer. This close he looks like he's wearing a sewn-together Halloween mask: Frankensteinish. His unbandaged eye flicks back and forth, swollen and blistered red. "Awfully good to see you out of the hospital, Jonathan. Just couldn't resist me, could ya? . . . Come on in, let's have a beer." His hand grips my elbow, jerking me forward.

My heart pounds. "So, uh, Heather doesn't know about . . . you know . . ."

"What's there to know?"

"That . . . you know . . . you like boys . . ."

"Who said I liked boys?" He clasps my arm, squeezing. So tight, my knees buckle from the pain.

"Ow, I didn't—"

"FUCK YOU, QUEER—"

"Sorry, I just thought—"

The jagged scar on his cheek lifts. "Just teasin'."

"Oh."

"I mean, you know. I don't like *just* boys . . ."

"Oh . . ."

"Yeah . . . come on." He pulls me into the trailer; I fumble up the steps. When he turns, I check to make sure the Record button's still pressed down on my tape recorder, buried deep in my satchel. It is. "And no, she don't know. She don't ever have to know. What kinda beer you like?"

"Oh . . . uh . . . whatever you got . . ." The second I step inside, my mind instantly flashes to the last night I was here. In that bed. With him snarling on top of me. I whip that thoughtstring out fast. "So . . . you don't care . . . that I'm younger—"

"How old are you?"

"Seventeen."

He corners me against the wall, lifts his hand. *Is he going to hit me? Knock me out cold? Do not show fear. Do not show him fear.* Instead, he rubs his fingers through my hair, brushing the swoop out of my eyes. "So blond. Always liked blonds . . ." He clamps his fist around a clump of hair, pulling my head back. "I won't tell if you won't tell—"

"Please get off me, that hurts—"

"I know you want it, like you did the other night—"

"I didn't—"

"Yeah you did—"

"No I didn't. Stop!" I shove him off. He staggers back some, but it only makes his scar lift higher.

"Oh, you like it rough, do ya?" He creeps toward me.

"I saw him, Hal."

"Who?"

"My friend."

"The Indian?"

"Yeah."

"They still here?" He flings the trailer door open.

"NO. They left already. A few days ago." Lying. But if he knew the truth . . .

"Good. 'Bout time," he says, still looking across the lake. "You sure they gone?"

"Yeah, uh, hey—you messed him up pretty bad, Hal."

"Yeah, I know," he says, peeking his head back in.

"So, how'd you get so beat up?"

"Why the hell does that matter?" He pushes past me, cracks open two bottles of Bud. "Drink."

I do. Still tastes like warm piss and almost makes me barf. "Tell me what happened—I wanna know—"

"Why?"

"Because . . . I . . ."

"Oh, you like the dirty talk, do ya? Little fuh-reak-ay like me?"

"Just tell me." I take another swig.

"Well, I grabbed that Indian by his hair like this—" He lurches forward and throws my head back so fast, I think he sprained my neck. "Quit your whimperin', that don't hurt—this why you're here, ain't it? I know you like this shit." He shoves me down on the bed. "I threw him to the ground and he was screamin'. Some Indian crap. And I whacked him across the jaw—BAM!" He punches his fist in his palm; I jump. "He screamed again. So you wanna know what I done?" He bends down, inches from my face. I smell tuna on his breath. My stomach coils. "I grabbed that sissy hair of his, held Joe's knife to his throat—" And he whispers in my ear, "'Don't you fuckin' move,' I said.

'I'm gonna make you into a real man.' And I start sawin' that hair to nothin' . . ."

He slides his clammy palm up and down my face. I feel tears, but push them back with everything I am. I stare him direct in the eye. I will not back down.

"AND WHOA BOY," he yells, leaping up. "You shoulda seen his face, Jonathan. So pathetic—" He laughs. "Jesus, he was pathetic. And so I spit in his face. Like it was my marker, my bull's-eye, you know. And then—"

"He beat the crap out of you?" I whisper.

"What'd you say?" He snaps down, grabbing my cheeks with his hand. "What the hell you say, boy?"

"Nothing. I didn't—I mean—aren't you scared?"

"Of what?"

"They weren't doing anything to—"

"They don't need to be doin' NOTHIN', boy. They shouldn't even *be here*, GIT IT?" He spits. His face flushes the color of the red streaking through his eye. "What the hell you fishin' for anyway, huh? *Huh?*" He slinks down on the bed, pinning me against the wall. My satchel's wedged between us; my tape recorder lodges in my groin. A sharp stab shoots through me, but I don't let him see. One inch closer and he'll know. He'll feel the tape recorder and it'll all be over. "I know you're friends with him," he whispers. "I seen you two that night . . . *kissin'* . . ."

"I'm . . . I'm not . . . I'm . . ."

"You're gonna learn one way or another, boy. You can't be hanging out with them Injuns, you hear? You *hear?*"

"They're . . . gonna tell the cops—"

He gasps, covering his mouth. "The cops? Oh no. The cops? *Ooooooh nooooooo. I'm scared.*" He laughs, thwacks the side of my head.

"You idiot. Cops won't do nothin'. They got their quota to git them Indians in jail. That's what I've been tryin' to tell ya, stupid. You gotta stay away from them Injuns, or you'll be right there in jail with 'em. I'm only tryin' to help . . . We're each other's secret-holders. Remember?" He leans in, burrowing the tape recorder deeper into my groin. A tear leaps out. "Oh. Don't you worry. I'll protect ya. Imma keep beatin' the shit outta them Indians until they all good and gone forever. You hear me?"

"Yeah . . ." I clutch my stomach. "I think I'm gonna be sick."

"Don't be such a pussy—"

"I'm gonna throw up."

He leans back. "You for real?"

"Yeah, the beer or something . . . I don't—"

"Well, go outside." He jumps up, thrusts me toward the door. "I don't want that crap in here."

"I'll go out to the bushes. I'm too embarrassed."

"I'll be right here waitin'."

I run.

Okay. Okay. Okay. I'm in the shadows. I jump on Stingraymobile and pedal for my life. Where is it? There. My tape recorder. Still recording. Hello? Testing? My name's Jonathan Collins. I am seventeen years old. Today is . . . some day in July 1973. And I am okay. Scratch that, I am more than okay. I am . . .

I am . . .

I AM—

## 57.

"Well hey there, Jonathan! Long time no see, son!"

"Hey, Chester."

He stops cleaning a glass, still dressed in his pressed white button-down and black pants. Carole King croons. Alma sits at the same table, lost in nothingness, wrapped around a bottle. There's a couple at the other end of the bar mauling each other, and some guy in an army jacket playing pool in the shadows, alone—not Uncle Russell, but I can't see who it is—And no Dad. Huh.

But man, like life pressed Pause here, while mine went wham-bamthankyouma'am FASTFORWARDSLAM.

"You okay, son?" Chester asks.

"Heya, kid," Alma says, running over to me. "What the hell happened to you?"

Man, I must look a sight.

And I do. I catch myself in the mirror behind the bar. Oh man, do I ever. I don't even recognize me. Aside from the tangle of leaves and twigs and Godknowswhat in my electric-static hair, and my face smudged with mud, my eyes are more vibrant. Clear. Like I unzipped my protective, extra-sanitized shiny space suit, and underneath is a scraggly wild mess of the real me. Finally free.

"I'm fine. Really, I am."

"You run away from home? Your old man hurt you? Where is he?" Chester asks, his face wrinkling, quick-switching to the Godfather. He's all of five feet tall, but I'd hate to be on the receiving end of his fury.

"No no, I don't know where he is. I thought he'd be here by now— But hey, remember when you said you'd help me out?" I ask. "If I ever needed it?"

"Of course. Anytime. What do you need?"

"You said your brother's a cop, right? A good one?"

"The finest in St. Louis."

"Good. Got a pen?"

He hands me one. I pop the cassette out of my recorder.

"What's the date?"

We turn to the Bud girl calendar behind the bar. She's wrapped in an American flag and holds two bottles of Bud in her outstretched hands.

I scratch on the label:

*HAL LOOMIS CONFESSION. JULY 13, 1973*

"Can you make sure your brother gets this?"

"Hal Loomis? That good-for-nothing SOB who lives out by the lake?"

"Yeah."

"Shouldn't be hanging out with lowlifes like him, Jonathan."

"Just please make sure he gets it. And stay there while he plays it. You'll see why, trust me. And you'll know what to do then. That's how you can help me."

He lifts his eyes to meet mine. They're blue, but clouded, so they're hard to read: I can't tell if he's actually going to do it, or if he thinks I'm crazy. He holds the tape against his chest. "I'll guard it with my life."

"Thanks, Chester."

"Glad I can finally help ya."

"Yeah. Me too . . ."

"I'll call my brother right now," he says. "Whatever he done . . . well, believe me, son, we're going to take care of it."

"When Dad shows up, tell him I'll be back for him later," I say, walking toward the door. I smack into the guy playing pool. "Oh, sorry, man—*Scotty*? Scott, I mean? Sorry I—"

"Heya, Jonny—" He fidgets with a pool stick, puffs some shaggy black hair covering his eyes.

"I thought you were at camp—"

"I was. Got kicked out."

"Oh. Okay . . . I gotta—"

"Guess a baseball bat's not for smashing windows or something." He chuckles and looks down, clearing his throat. His Aerosmith T-shirt's too tight.

"Well, I'll catch ya later—" I start to weave past him, but he steps in front of me, wielding the pool stick.

"Wait—how's your summer been?" he asks.

"Oh. Uh. Okay . . . ?"

"Damn, you're like my height now. Weird," he says, still fidgeting.

"Yeah."

"You sound different. And you look different, too. Kinda crazy. I don't know." He laughs.

"Oh. Right." I start to brush my hair down, then stop myself and look at him. "I am . . . I am different."

"Cool . . ." Something's changed. I can't explain it. Like I can see a few cracks in the muscle marble, a few chips in his perfect veneer. And his eyes aren't filled with toothpick-creature-beating rage. No, they're different, too. Sad. Maybe they always have been.

"I should go—"

"Hey. You know . . . all those assholes are still at camp . . ." He shuffles his Pumas on the linoleum. "It's stupid, I know, but I thought maybe, I don't know, if you want to hang—"

"You shouldn't hide," I say.

"What?"

I look in his eyes and see him: the lonely boy I once was, floating through a silent space. "I said I am different, Scotty. I'm happy."

He doesn't move. Then his face slowly lifts to a smile, a tug-of-war smile. I know that look.

"Actually," I say, "I don't think I'm gonna be around for the rest of the summer. I'll see you in school."

"Okay, yeah . . ." He turns back to the pool table, and I walk past.

I can't be sure, but I think I just grew a few more inches.

Oh, I like this new me a lot.

# 58.

It's 10:37. Dad's Cadillac glints in the driveway under the moonlight. My stomach lurches with Stingraymobile. *Come on, girl, we got this.* There's one thing left to do now.

As we pedal closer, I hear our phone ringing.

And ringing. And ringing.

I wait in the shadows for him to answer it, so I can shoot up the stairs and— No. No more hiding. You have to face him. No time like the present.

*Rrrrinnnnggg . . . Rrrriiinnnngggg . . .* Silence.

I park her on the porch and peek my head through the screen door.

Couch is empty. TV's still on: This Week in Watergate. I go inside and switch it off.

"Dad?" No answer.

*RRRINNNGGGGG.* JESUS.

I yell up the stairs, "Dad?" Still no answer. "Dad. It's me. Look. I'm sorry for what I said. I was angry and—" I creep to my room, eyes skipping in every direction. "Dad?" Where I'd left him, cowering and coughing in a ball, he's no longer there. The confetti of dead Ziggys still blankets the floor. "Dad, come on, quit playing games, I said

I was sorry . . ." Nothing. I tiptoe down the hallway, switch on his bedroom light. Peek in. No sign of him. No life anywhere.

The phone still rings.

I bound downstairs. Two of the dining room chairs are flipped over. Huh. Hadn't noticed that walking in.

I pick up the receiver. "Hey, Chester, is Dad there?"

"How you are a spawn of that man, I shall never know."

"Starla?"

"Jonny-boo!"

"Oh man, Starla, I can't believe—"

"Lord, this connection is awful, I can barely hear—"

"It's so crackly—where are you?"

"D.C. Don't tell me you forgot—"

"No, I mean, I just hoped maybe—"

"I've been trying to call for *ages* but your line's been busy all night and—"

"Man, I miss you. There's so much—"

"—so much to tell you."

She laughs. I slink down the wall. "You first," I say.

"Oh, I don't even know where to begin. And I can't talk long or Daddy'll *kill* me—long distance, you know—but anyway, I just love it here, Jonny, absolutely LOVE it here. You would, too. It's glorious. So many people like *us*, you know: Different. *Revolutionaries*— Hey, maybe you can come here. Stay with us for a bit?"

"Wow. Yeah. That would be amazing, actually—"

"Because . . . I don't know. Momma was offered this job teaching at a university here, and . . . she might take it, so . . ."

"You mean like . . . permanently?"

"Maybe. Yeah. I don't know . . ."

"Whoa. Wow. That's so . . . I'm . . . just . . . so . . ." Gone. I start crying into the receiver.

"Jonathan? What is it? What's happened?"

"Nothing . . . sorry . . . nothing . . . just hearing your voice . . . I'm so happy for you and—" I cradle the phone against my ear, like I'm cradling her in my arms. "So much has happened and there's something I need to tell you but I don't know how and it's crazy I know but it's the Ziggy Truth and I'm just—"

"Shhh . . . you can tell me anything, you know that . . . just talk louder and slower because you seriously sound like you're in hyperdrive."

I wipe my eyes and take a breath. "Okay . . . Oh, hey, I got the postcards, you know, and that picture of Eric."

"Right—"

"I'm happy for you, Starla . . ."

"Yeah. I'm happy, too, Jonathan . . ."

"Good . . . good . . ."

"Why are you crying?"

"I don't know. I guess, because, I am, too, you know . . . Happy, I mean. I met someone who—"

"Really? That's . . . wonderful! Who is she?"

"No."

"What?"

"I mean . . . I don't know . . . it's . . . not a she—"

Static crinkles through the receiver.

"Jonathan? Hello?"

"I said the someone who makes me smile is not a she. It's a—"

"Jonathan?"

"He."

"What?"

"IT'S A HE, IT'S WEB."

The galaxy goes silent.

Then, another voice pops through the static: *"DeeDee, get off that phone right now and get back to bed!"* It's her dad.

"Just a sec!" she yells back.

"You hear what I said?" I ask.

"Yeah."

"Oh. Okay . . ."

More silence. She's either praying or scheming her way off the phone. "Never mind, forget it, I'll let you go—"

"Jonny, how could you let me go on like that? I've been waiting for you to tell me since last year when we— Oh, I'm so frigging happy for you I could crawl through the receiver and hug you so hard you'd burst—" Her voice wobbles with the static. She's crying now.

"I wondered . . . if you knew—"

"What do you think I've been praying for all this time?"—*"DEEDEE, NOW!"*—"Ugh. Hold on. *Just one more second, I promise!* Fool still won't call me Starla . . . Jonathan?"

"You have to go."

"I'm sorry, we're taking the train to New York in the morning, and we have to—I didn't expect you to tell me all this and—you have more to tell me, don't you?"

"It's just . . . No. It's okay, Starla. Really."

"Listen, I'll call again. Soon. I promise."

"Okay."

"Now I'm absolutely *convinced* you need to come here . . . Oh, Jonny, I wish I were there so I could . . . I don't even know what . . . Lord, what a summer, right?"

"Yeah, what a summer . . ."

". . . So, so happy—" She blows her nose and starts laughing. "And you lucky boy, he's a damn fox!"

"Oh man . . . Yeah . . ." I push back more tears. *I only hope I get to see him again . . .*

"I told you to keep prayin' to Ziggy on the Cross—"

We laugh. Sort of.

"So. To be continued . . . ?"

"Yeah . . . To be continued . . ."

I hang up. And just as I do, a memory flashes through my mind: When Starla snuck me downtown to the Ziggy concert last year, we met this orange-sparkled-hair boy who blew glitter in our faces and he said we were so bright we were stars to make wishes on. So we did. We wished. Starla said we probably wished for the same thing. Maybe we did . . . I wished for this: to tell her who I really am.

The phone rings again.

I dry my face with my shirt. "Couldn't get enough of me, could you? I was just thinking about—"

"Oh! Oh, hello?" It's another woman's voice.

"Hello?"

"I didn't expect—we've been trying to call all night."

"Who is this?"

"Sorry. Sorry. Is this Jonathan Collins?"

"Yeah?"

"And is your father Robert Collins?"

"Yeah. Who is this?"

"Sorry. I'm new. I just started yesterday and—sorry! My name's Stacey Adkins. I'm a nurse at St. Louis Mercy Medical Center. Your father's here. He was admitted tonight—"

"What? Why? What happened? Is he okay?"

"I'm not supposed to . . . is there a way you can come down to the hospital?"

"I guess?"

"That would be recommended. Oh, are you old enough to drive? I don't know, maybe we can send someone."

"No, I can drive. I'll be right there."

## 59.

HE LIES IN BED asleep, hooked up to ticking machines and tentacled with plastic tubes. The small fluorescent light buzzing over his bed makes his already ashen face more ghostly.

"Jonathan?" A man taps my shoulder. I jump.

"Sorry," he says. "I'm Dr. Tennant." His eyes glow a cheerful green even this late at night.

"What's going on? What's wrong with him?"

"We're not sure exactly yet. He's resting, but we need to keep him here to do some tests. He had a lot of fluid in his lungs, and was in quite a bit of pain. We gave him some codeine, so that should help for now."

"Oh. Okay . . ."

"He asked us to call you after he couldn't reach you, and to get in touch with your—" He flips through pages on his clipboard. "Dr. Evelyn Smith?" I nod. "She should be here soon. She's going to help you. Do you have a change of clothes in there?"

"What?"

"In your satchel."

"Oh, no."

"Do you want us to take you home, or—"

"I'm going to stay," I say. "I'll stay here with him."

"Jonathan?" We look up to see Dr. Evelyn jogging down the hall. Her hair's tousled, pulled back with her blue-tinted glasses, and her face is pinched into that overprotective-mom look again. "Jonathan. It's so good to see you. I'm glad you're alright." She hugs me. "You are alright, aren't you?"

"I'm fine."

Dr. Tennant clutches the clipboard to his chest. "You must be—"

"Sorry. I'm Dr. Evelyn." She shakes his hand. "Mind if I have a moment with Jonathan? I'll come find you after."

"Of course." He pats my shoulder. "You're going to be just fine. And we'll take good care of your dad. Okay?"

"Thank you," I say.

Dr. Evelyn squeezes my hand, leading me down the hall. We find an empty row of orange plastic chairs next to a vending machine, and sit.

We don't speak. There's so much I want to say to her right now, but the words are trapped. She brushes the hair off my face, examining me. I never noticed the color of her eyes before: They're violet. Or maybe it's the dark circles charcoaled under them making them glow. She lifts a smile, revealing that great, wide gap between her teeth.

"Jonathan . . ." She pats my hands. "Jonathan, I know you want to get back to your dad, but I'm glad I caught you before—I've much to tell you. Goodness, I don't even know where to begin, I—"

"I'm not sick," I say.

She stops massaging my hands.

"I don't need to be fixed. I never did. And I'm not doing those treatments ever again." The words fall out of my mouth, along with the tears from my eyes.

"I know," she says softly. "And I'm sorry . . . I was wrong . . ."

I flick my hands out from under hers. "What?"

"I was wrong." She looks up at the ceiling, shaking her head like she's talking to herself. "I was only doing what I was trained to do, what we were taught in school. But I knew something wasn't—I should've trusted my—" She grabs a tissue from her trench coat pocket, blows her nose, and clears her throat. She untangles the glasses from her hair and puts them on. Back to Analytical Doctor.

"You know I went to that psychiatry conference in Hawaii, right?" I nod. "Well . . . there was a lot of . . . commotion this time. People from the Gay Liberation Front stormed in, demanding to be heard, including one of our own doctors, and . . . well, the things they said, Jonathan, sharing their sincerity and passion and pain . . . it changed me. There's been so much research done lately rebutting everything we were taught in school about . . . homosexuality . . . and whether or not it can be cured and, well . . ." She's shredding the tissue in her hands, not looking at me as Analytical Doctor, no, more like Five-Year-Old Lost Schoolgirl. "I was wrong. And I'm sorry. The treatments—I hated giving them to you, but I thought that's what was best for your—what you wanted, I mean—what I was taught to do—but they won't work. Not ever. Because you're right, Jonathan. You're not sick. You never were . . ." She dabs her cheeks with her tissue, wipes underneath her glasses, still crying. "And I'm sorry I—"

"But . . . you . . ."

"I should've said something earlier, but I didn't."

"You . . . made me think I was . . ."

"And I will always live with that regret—"

I spring up. "You were making me feel crazy this whole time."

"I'm so sorry—"

"But I knew. I *knew* you were wrong and—" I pace the hall. So fast, I feel like I may actually fly right through the ceiling tiles. "You and

Dad convinced me I was sick, that I'd be broken for the rest of my life, but I knew I wasn't and—"

"You have every right to be angry, Jonathan—"

"I'm not—I don't know what to feel, but I'm not angry, I'm . . . I'm . . . I don't even know—it's weird to hear something said back to you that you've always known—especially from *you*, but—it's also . . . I don't know . . . it's not a surprise, it's—like everything just clicked and—I have to go. I need to talk to Dad. I need to be with him now." I start walking away.

"Of course you do. We can talk more—"

I turn back. She's curled up, holding herself. Oh, I know that feeling. "No, Dr. Evelyn. There's nothing more to say." And I leave her, to finally tell Dad the truth.

Beeps and whooshes and Dad's scratchy inhales swim through his room. The light buzzes over his head. It smells like dried puke and piss covered up with bleach. He sleeps, so I curl up on the recliner and watch him lying there, more peaceful than I've seen him my entire life.

Maybe he's finally found it . . .

Like me.

## 60.

*Sunday, July 15, 1973*

LIKE DAD, I'VE COME in and out of consciousness the past two days.

More tired than I thought, I guess.

I shot up from my own dreamless state when he screamed, from pain or nightmares or both. His eyes fluttered, his mouth twitched. So ashen-gray and slick he looked like a phantom. Nurses flew in, fiddled with this box and that tube, cleaned up pools of sweat and sick. Then he was lost again in Codeineland.

When I wake this morning, it is silent. The light outside sears my retinas. So sharp and bright, I can't see clouds or trees or hills or any semblance of life: The world is one big blank white canvas. Guess the nurses threw the curtains open—

"Hey, bud."

"JESUS."

"Sorry."

He's sitting up, hands folded in his lap, smiling—for real smiling—like he's been waiting up for hours. Some color's come back to his face, but his eyes are blackened and sunken in.

"Hey," I say. "You're awake."

"Yeah, didn't want to wake you. I liked watching you sleep. You looked so peaceful."

"Oh." Great, he's been visited by the Three Ghosts. Not sure I'm ready for this.

"Man, your voice," he says.

"Yeah."

"Wow."

"I know."

"Huh . . ."

I'm not sure what to do. I'm not sure what exactly is going on. He hasn't looked at me this way since the moon landing. He turns to the window and shakes his head. I don't move.

"Pour me a cup of ice, willya, son?"

"Sure. You want some water? I could get—"

"No, I only like the shaved ice."

"Oh." I grab a Styrofoam cup from the sink, scoop out little shards of ice from the plastic jug. I scoot the recliner over and sit next to him.

"My mouth's so damned dry," he says, crunching ice bits in his mouth.

We sit in silence.

"Nurses said you've been here ever since," he says after a while.

"Yeah."

"Thanks."

I mumble a *youknowwhatever* and shuffle my Chucks on the tiles. Whoa, first time I've really noticed them. Holy scuffed to hell.

More silence.

A rumble of ice hitting Styrofoam.

A *sq-squeak* from my Chucks.

"You in pain?" I ask, still looking down.

"No, I'm feeling better. Still got this damn cough, but better . . ."

I nod.

"Been walkin' around with pneumonia for weeks, I guess. You believe that? Then I got that fever thing and—damn near died. Thought I was a goner, bud."

I quit shuffling, eyes locked on the floor.

"It's strange. You know it's going to come one day. But you never really think about it. Then something happens and, I don't know, the whole world looks completely different. Upside down. So strange . . ."

I look up. His eyes aren't lost or clouded over with a thick haze of anger. No, they actually twinkle. I see him. For the first time I see him again: my dad.

"I saw your mother," he says.

"You did?"

"Oh yeah. She gave me a damned good scolding. Always knew how to put me in place." He laughs and turns to the window, drying his eyes. "I miss her . . . Man, do I miss her . . . Anyway, they still gotta do more tests on me—but I'm going to be fine, son. When I'm better and outta here, things'll be different. Not gonna drink or smoke, gonna get a job—I'm a changed man." Huh. Not sure I'm convinced about that— He grabs my hands. I flinch because, well, he's *holding my hands*, but he grips them tighter. "And so are you."

"What?"

"I'm sorry if I ever—" He starts crying. For real crying. "I don't know. I guess a part of me died with your mother that day. Never really let myself love again. I guess . . . I never let myself love you."

Whoa. Okay. Whoa.

"Thank you," I say.

"For what?"

"The truth . . ."

"But it's never too late to start, is it?"

"No, I guess it's—"

"Dr. Evelyn came back yesterday."

"She did? I didn't hear—"

"You were dead asleep. Didn't want to wake you."

"What did she say?"

"She told me you're fixed now, you know, cured."

"Did she . . . tell you why?"

"Huh? No. What do you mean, why? She wants to talk to you more about it, but that's all she told me."

"Oh, well—"

"You did it, bud. I'm really proud of ya. I knew you'd get rid of that sickness inside you. Like I'm gonna do with myself. And now that you're cured, we can maybe have some *real* father-son bonding time. Not at the lake. And without worrying about all that crap, you know?"

"Oh . . . yeah . . . right . . ."

"We can be a family again," he says. "You and me. And go to the Arch and a Cardinals game and maybe even take a road trip to Branson and . . ."

"Uh-huh . . ." He's still talking, but I no longer hear. Something's happening: The linoleum's melting; my body's twitching. In fact, I can't be sure, but I think the feral creature I saw in the mirror at the bar is rapping his fists against my rib cage, screaming to get out. I have to tell him the truth. No. I *need* to tell him.

"Dad, no—"

"What?"

"I mean—I don't know—" I look at him. So happy I'm fixed, so proud I'm his son again. I don't know. It's like this weed was planted inside me when he first sent me to Dr. Evelyn. And no matter how hard I try to ignore it, it lingers and grows. Maybe I can never kill it . . . or maybe I can only tame it for a bit . . . or . . . maybe it will stop growing altogether if I—

"Dad." I squeeze his hand. "I am changed, just not how you think . . ."

"What?"

"I'm not fixed, because there was nothing to fix in the first—"

"Jesus Christ, Jonathan." He shakes his hand free. "Don't start that up again. Not now, not after I—"

"Just listen to me. Please—" I stand.

"You were sick, son, and you're fixed now, you hear me—"

"No. Stop. Jesus. Please stop saying that. Stop looking at me like I'm the Crazy Son here, because I'm not, I'm *not*—"

"You're tired. You aren't talkin' sense—"

"NO. This is the most sense I've ever made. Listen to me! I don't need to be cured by Electric Boxes of Shame or hide in a moldy closet or be saved by Jesus or Ziggy or whoever else is out there. I don't need to pretend anymore that I'm anything other than who I AM. Because . . . Because . . ." I stop at the end of his bed, panting. "Because, I don't know . . . I think maybe I love him, Dad. *Him*. Web. And that is who I AM. And I'm sorry you never let me in or let me be me, because it feels fantastic and I almost missed out on it and—" I'm sweating, no—crying, no, I don't know what, my protective skin melting into oblivion. "You almost missed it, too, Dad. Me. The real me. But you don't have to anymore. You don't have to, if you don't want to. Maybe, like you said, we can have that time together now, the time we missed— you're right, it's never too late . . ."

He looks back at me, chest heaving, eyes burning. It's possible he may detonate right in front of me. I have no idea what's coming next.

Then: He shakes his head and turns away from me. "No," he says. "I will never understand that part of you." And he closes his eyes. Gone again.

"Oh . . . oh . . . I . . ." I stand there, unable to move, unsure what to do . . .

I look out the window. Swipe a tear. I see the oak trees. And the hills. And the clouds. And a few birds flitting across the clear sky. And people scurrying in the parking lot. Life. Going on. As it does.

And us. Two people. Existing in the same room, on the same planet, living in two very different worlds . . .

I don't know.

Maybe one day, he'll understand.

Or maybe when he comes home, I'll pick him up from the Blues Note and we'll watch *All in the Family* eating TV dinners in silence, and he'll still believe in his version of me, and I'll believe in mine.

But at least I know which one is real. And for now, that's enough for me.

I look at him one more time. "I love you, Dad," I say.

Then I walk out the door.

## 61.

WHEN I PULL INTO our driveway, I see a package on the front stoop. Wrapped in Web's faded-sheet curtain! I fling open the car door and dash over.

A scrawled note lying on top reads:

> *To Ziggy. Open later tonight. Outside. No sooner. You'll see why. 2TM4VR, Web.*

Oh man . . .

Our phone starts ringing. I run inside.

"Web?" I yell into the receiver.

"It's Chester, son. You okay?"

"Oh. Yeah. Fine. How are you?"

"Good, kiddo. Was just callin' to check in on you two. Haven't seen you and your pops here in a couple days and—"

"Yeah, he's been in the hospital. But he'll be okay." I lift the package to my nose. It smells like him: Irish Spring and burnt herbs.

"Oh. Well . . . that's good . . . I hope he . . . Well, anyway, kid, we listened to that tape of yours, me and my brother, and—"

"Oh. That's right. Almost forgot about—"

"Did Hal hurt you, son?"

"No . . . not really. He tried—"

"Yeah, thought as much. That sick bastard's in jail."

"He is?"

"Think he's gonna be in there for a long time. What he done to you—you're just a kid and—makes me boil up just thinkin'—and all that stuff he said about them cops and Native peoples. Man, oh man. You thought I could get angry? You shoulda seen my brother. Nearly flung that damned trailer door off its hinges and into the lake. I ain't ever seen him like that."

"Oh man . . ."

"You did a brave thing, kid. You shouldn't have done that alone. Wish you had called me or somethin' sooner. You coulda been hurt. Real bad."

"I had to," I say. "For Web and me."

"Yeah . . . well . . . I just wanted you to know . . ."

"Thanks, Chester. For everything."

"So . . . maybe I'll see ya in here again soon?"

"Yeah . . . maybe . . . See ya, Chester . . ."

"Oh, and hey, Jonathan?"

"Yeah?"

"You're just . . . well . . . you're a good kid, you hear me? Don't you let no one tell you any different, no more . . . you got that?"

"Okay . . ."

"Okay. Well . . . I'll be seein' ya."

We hang up. And I spend the rest of the afternoon outside on my swing, swaying back and forth, reading his note over and over and over again . . .


Now, six of the *LONGEST HOURS OF MY LIFE* later, here I am.

I gently place the record on the player and walk back outside. *Dark*

*Side of the Moon* whispers through the speakers. Like the breeze. I lie down and—

KAPOW.

The great big, beautiful full moon.

Whoa.

I circle it with my thoughtstrings: Remembering the Martian-moon-landing like it was yesterday. Remembering the night in my room with him like it was today. And remembering a quote President Kennedy once said: *"We choose to go to the moon not because it's easy, but because it's hard."*

I think I finally get it now. It's a lot like love, isn't it? It's hard work, but if you don't give up and keep pushing forward, the rewards are infinite . . .

I slowly untie the string wrapped around the package.

It's the framed Polaroid from his mantel: the one he labeled "HOME."

I flip it over.

And smile.

On the back, he's written two words:

*Your Turn.*

# Author's Note

ON DECEMBER 15, 1973, the American Psychiatric Association changed history.

After a long and rigorous, seemingly insurmountable battle fought by the Gay Liberation Movement, the APA officially removed homosexuality from the *Diagnostic and Statistical Manual of Mental Disorders*. Simply put: If you identified as queer, for the first time in recorded history, you were considered "normal."

I first learned of this pioneering moment in time when a friend passed along an episode of *This American Life*, titled "81 Words," which beautifully documents this fight, struggle, and ultimate life-changing decision that some consider to be the birth of the modern LGBTQ2+ movement. And the initial seed for Jonathan's story was planted.

This was in 2014, when I was nearing the end of a decade-long international tour playing the central role of "Gay Jesus" in Terrence McNally's *Corpus Christi*. To give you a quick backstory, the play, told in a divine, respectful and heartfelt way, is a retelling of the story of Jesus with Jesus as a gay man living in 1950s Corpus Christi, Texas. Although "controversy" followed the production, it was easily overshadowed by the audience's love and support: For the first time, LGBTQ2+ peoples were witnessing the story they grew up learning through *their* lens.

Being gay and raised in St. Louis in a Catholic home, I was told by the church that I did not belong, and therefore never felt a deep connection to spirituality. But as we traveled the world performing this play, I saw my story mirrored back to me through every person we'd meet along our journey, and it was here I began to understand the deep pain LGBTQ2+ peoples felt on an innate level. For the first time in my life, I didn't feel alone.

During this tour I met LGBTQ2+ peoples from every walk of life and outlet of faith, including those from the Two-Spirit community. I'm embarrassed to say, even as an openly gay man, how little I knew about Two-Spirit peoples and, for that matter, every other letter our queer rainbow represents. And it dawned on me how although we claim inclusion, the individual communities within the queer identity can feel so separate. I wanted to change that for myself.

I attended my first Two-Spirit Powwow with Bay Area American Indian Two-Spirits (BAAITS) in 2015, and my life changed. I laughed, I cried, and I humbly witnessed Native peoples and their allies coming together in harmony, peace, and love. As a non-Native I cannot be Two-Spirit, but being welcomed into their community I felt a re-ignition of my own spiritual connection to being a gay man for one of the first times in my life.

Although the layers to this are much more complicated, to put it simply here: "Two-Spirit" is used by some American Indian/First Nation peoples as an umbrella term for gender and sexual orientation variance. It was coined in the early nineties by a group of Indigenous community leaders as a counterpoint to colonial terminology, created as an addition, not a replacement, for Indigenous languages that already have a word for non-binary Native peoples.

Being Two-Spirit is exclusive to Indigenous peoples who are in touch with their traditions, and although they commonly identify as LGBTQ2+, not all do. Pre-colonization, Two-Spirit peoples held a special role in their communities as healers, balancing the masculine and feminine sides. Christianity helped to chip away at these roles in the 500-plus nations, and the movement today is focused on reclaiming their voice from pre-colonial society.

In 2015, the play ended and my journey as an author began. I was reminded of the historic moment in 1973, the APA's decision to remove homosexuality as a mental illness. And when I started researching the world events of 1973, and the months leading up to that December day, I read about the Occupation of Wounded Knee—another moment in time I knew nothing about that dramatically changed the lives of Native peoples. I've always believed we have the most potential to learn by compassionately listening to and observing others; to try and untangle our own stories and struggles with someone and something outside of our own experience. This is how the two stories organically merged for me to become *Ziggy, Stardust and Me.*

Although this novel is a fictionalized account of that time, and I've tried to be as historically accurate as possible, I've taken a few liberties in creating the narrative. One very real moment in Jonathan's journey remains: Not only was he considered mentally ill, the treatment he endured was a validated form of aversion therapy. You might think that after forty years we would have learned from history. But here we are. Again.

Even as I write this in 2019, and even though we have made some incredible strides since that time, the LGBTQ2+ community still struggles for full equality, and conversion therapy is still legal in thirty-four US states, not to mention numerous countries around the world. Any number of states and countries is too many, and it must change.

Jonathan's story is one of thousands. And the damage one suffers after such treatment leaves everlasting, sometimes irreparable scars. If you are currently experiencing a piece of Jonathan's story, or know someone who is, first and foremost seek help. The Trevor Project is a great place to start. You need to know you are not alone. There is a community for you. We are here.

History may continue to repeat itself, but it has also taught us that when communities come together in one voice, change is not only possible, it is imminent. For my part, I believe Two-Spirit peoples are the bedrock of the LGBTQ2+ community: their innate power to balance the masculine and feminine, and their healing roles as mediators, can ultimately bring us all together, whether you identify as queer or an ally. I hope you'll one day join a BAAITS (or other regional Two-Spirit) Powwow to experience it for yourself.

Either way, remember: It's your choice. You can be part of the change, not only through mobilization and protest, but by listening and learning from others' unique perspectives, and by simply being You. Please don't waste another breath being anything else. There's just no time.

# Acknowledgments

TO TRY AND THANK everyone for making this moment in time possible would require another 120,000-word novel that I'd have to figure out how to edit down. But there are an extraordinary few who made this book manifest, without whom these words would still be floating in the cosmos.

My Patronus Agent Gemini Twin, Barbara Poelle: For never giving up on me. For always believing in me, especially when I didn't. For somehow knowing me better than me. For dancing with me to Christmas music in July, and laughing with me till we crack ribs, and crying with me till we start laughing all over again. For encouraging and supporting me (in all my messy forms) and loving me since that day we met many moons ago: *"Do you wear Lever 2000?"* she asked. (I did.) Without your everlasting patience, pushing, and unconditional love, I would undoubtedly still be flapping my wings, stuck in the same spot on Chester Ave. BJW2-4VR.

My Goddess Editor, Stacey Barney: For somehow, someway finding the story I really wanted to tell in the glorious mess I gave you. I may have breathed some life into the story, but you found its soul. I am forever grateful for your brilliance and genius, your thoughtful and careful notes, your wisdom and enthusiastic love for these two boys, and especially for pushing me to not only be a better writer, but to be a better human.

And to the incredible Penguin Team for bringing all the beautiful elements together: Jennifer Klonsky for always championing, Lizzie Goodell for being the publicist extraordinaire, Caitlin Tutterow for her sweet kindness keeping me organized and calm, Robert Farren for his careful copyediting, Dave Kopka for his typesetting wonderment, Jacqueline Hornberger and Cindy Howle for their proofreading mastery, Kristie Radwilowicz for designing this gorgeous cover, and to Tomasz Mro for his most stunning artwork that I still sometimes stare at in utter awe.

To my friends of Bay Area American Indian Two Spirits (BAAITS): For providing a sacred and safe space for all, for helping me find my joy again in a time I felt so lost, and for all you give to the LGBTQ2+ community and the world at large. It's been an honor and privilege to serve by your side. And in particular to Derek Smith and Roger Kuhn for your Two-Spirit sensitivity reads and notes, and for your encouragement and support, I thank you. Proceeds from the sale of this book will benefit the BAAITS Annual Powwow, helping to further their mission of inclusive love for all peoples.

To my early readers, my gratitude and apologies (for asking you to thwack through a jungle of words, oh boy): Stephanie Dees and Steve Susoyev. Stephanie for being the second part of my Holy Trinity, the third chamber of my heart, for putting up with my endless neuroses and helping lift the words off the page (and my soul) to soaring new heights. (And for the hours of talks that kept me grounded and sane through it all. Coco, Sugahbee!) And Steve, an editorial genius who also happens to be one of my guardian angels: Your notes and encouragement helped me make sense of my rambles and allowed me the confidence to keep going when I was sure I couldn't. And they still do.

To my later readers Elizabeth Cava and Jennifer Matthews for providing me sustenance in the form of loving notes and a belief in me to help me cross the finish line. To my dear friend and teacher Sara Eaglewoman for sharing your words, wisdom, and guidance every step of the way. And special gratitude to Alex Villasante for being my Fairy Bookmother!

To Cathy Renna for the awe-inspiring work you do for the LGBTQ2+ community, for devoting your life to making lasting change, and for helping me tell my story for the past decade.

To my uncle Greg Venneman, a prolific storyteller and writer in his own right, for sharing his teenage stories of bike-riding and hijinks on the St. Louis streets in the seventies. (I promise never to tell Mom what you told me.)

And speaking of: To my mom and stepdad for never once giving up on me (even though I swear you had so many chances to do so), and for always believing in me no matter where I chose to go and what new wild endeavor I decided to pursue. You always said yes to me, and that is why I am who I am today.

To my dad, who will always and forever be my greatest teacher.

And most of all, to my Ernie: For taking me to the moon since the moment I passed around a tray of Toll House cookies and said, *"I need to know you in my life,"* to nine years later as you help manage my insecurities, encourage my flights of imagination, and continue to be my light in the darkness. I love you.

Finally, I'd like to thank you. I am immeasurably grateful you have chosen to hold these pages in your hands, because without you, none of this would be possible. I dedicated this book to all the Misfit Mapmakers in the world, those humans who've had to forge their own path in this wild and wonderful world because they've been told they don't belong. If that's you, you are my hero.